"Forsyth writes all this with a quick, dialogue-driven tempo that will keep readers turning the pages. The snappy pacing and the sly undercurrent of humor (including a running gag about Chadwick's behemoth old Bentley) keep the whole tale moving along briskly. A rousing, detailed RAF thriller that delivers an effective climax."

- Kirkus Reviews

"Forsyth's deep knowledge of his subject matter, combined with his enthusiasm for flying, is evident throughout the novel. Historical war fiction fans will be pleased, especially those fascinated by the high-flying lives of pilots."

- Publishers Weekly BookLife Review

"A grand tale well told. Solid historical fiction. Provides an excellent feel for time, place and dialect, and character development is very well done. I read it straight through during every free moment I had."

- Jack Doyle,
U.S. Naval Flight Officer who flew
F-4 Phantoms and F-14 Tomcats

I0784817

WINGS OVER THE CHANNEL

Other Works by Eric B. Forsyth

Wings Over Iraq (2020)

Historical novel set in Iraq in the turbulent 1920s between the wars. Introduces the main character featured in the current novel (*Wings Over the Channel*), Allan Chadwick, a newly qualified RAF pilot posted to a bomber squadron near Baghdad. His story plays out against the background of Middle Eastern conflict, the rise of fascism in Europe and the slow build-up to another world war.

An Inexplicable Attraction: My Fifty Years of Ocean Cruising (2018)

Memoir in which Captain Forsyth recounts his many years sailing the oceans and exploring remote corners of the world on his Westsail 42, *Fiona,* including two circumnavigations of the globe, cruises through the Northwest Passage, the Panama Canal, and to the Baltic, and several excursions to both the Artic and Antarctic. Included on Kirkus's 100 Best Memoirs of 2018.

WINGS OVER THE CHANNEL

A NOVEL

ERIC B. FORSYTH

This novel is a work of historic fiction. It is loosely based on actual events which occurred in the 1930s during the development of a radar defense system in Britain. Although several well-known historic figures are mentioned to give the story some credibility—King Edward VIII, Stanley Baldwin, Hermann Göring—all incidents and characters are products of the author's imagination. Dialogues concerning those persons are entirely fictional and not intended to portray actual events. Any resemblance to any other actual person, living or dead, is entirely coincidental.

Copyright ©2022
Eric B. Forsyth

Published by:
Yacht Fiona Books
www.YachtFiona.com

Edited by:
Margaret Daisley
Blue Horizon Books
www.bluehorizonbooks.com

Cover and design by:
Jay R. Pizer
Imax Productions
www.imaxproductions.com

Publisher's Cataloging-in-Publication data:
Forsyth, Eric
Wings Over the Channel
ISBN 979-8-9853220-1-9

Table of Contents

LOSSIEMOUTH
SCOTLAND
N
LEUCHARS
EDINBURGH
NORTH SEA
IRELAND
CHURCH FENTON
THORNABY
DUBLIN
LIVERPOOL
THE WASH
CROMER
NORWICH
HONILEY
MILDENHALL
WOODBRIDGE
OXFORD
BAWDSEY
ST. DAVID'S HEAD
MARLOW
LONDON
PANGBOURNE
MANSTON
BATH
CHIVENOR
FARNBOROUGH
BIGGIN HILL
ST. EVAL
ENGLISH CHANNEL
0   100 MILES
160 KM
THE BRITISH ISLES, WITH AIRFIELDS AS
THEY MIGHT HAVE BEEN IN THE 1930S
(NOT TO SCALE - SHADED AREAS INDICATE HIGH ELEVATIONS)
FRANCE

Preface

When I was posted to an RAF fighter squadron in the 1950s, much of our flying was devoted to Ground Controlled Interceptions (GCI), which were intended to train neophyte radar controllers in secret underground bunkers. Flights of two or four aircraft from two squadrons were vectored onto each other to within range of their guns, typically a few hundred yards. Although I did not realize at the time, this was the twilight of the interception techniques developed in the late 1930s, fictionalized in this novel. Although the Spitfires and Hurricanes had given way to the first jets, Meteors and Vampires, not much else had changed. The advent of accurate air-to-air missiles with a range of many miles, way beyond the possibility of a visual sighting, changed everything. Looking back nearly seventy years to those exciting times in my early life, I was lucky enough to witness the end of an era.

I believe historians of World War II do not emphasize enough the strategic importance of the Battle of Britain, which occurred in the summer of 1940. The emphasis is more often on the tactical situation. The Germans had invaded much of Europe, with only Great Britain remaining free to oppose them. In order to execute a successful seaborne invasion of the British Isles, the Germans needed air superiority over the English Channel. The Luftwaffe attempted to achieve this by eliminating RAF Fighter Command, either by destroying airfields and planes on the ground or by air-to-air duels. Fighter Command was outnumbered but historians credit radar with making one British fighter equal to two by removing the need for standing patrols. In the end, the Germans did not achieve air superiority over the Channel and as summer faded the plans for an invasion were canceled. Thus, tactically it could be considered a draw, but if the RAF had faltered, it is very likely the British Isles would have been invaded, or the British government forced to strike an armistice with Germany, like the French. With either of those two outcomes consider the possibilities:

- The U.S. would have been deprived of a base in Britain.

- There would have been no mass bombing of Germany.

- German resources would not have been occupied with building the Atlantic Wall or with significant air defense preparations.

- Without support from Britain and the U.S., parts of the Soviet Union may have been occupied permanently.

- Without supplies and intelligence from Britain, the army in Egypt may have succumbed to Rommel and permitted occupation of the Suez Canal, providing Germany with oil from Iraq and Persia (Iran).

- Without North Africa, an invasion of Italy and southern France would have been impossible.

- The U.S. could have been threatened by a German alliance with Mexico, promising the return of California and Texas.

- The Holocaust would have continued for many years after 1945.

The strategic "what ifs" of a successful German victory in the Battle of Britain are endless, which is why the Battle must be considered one of the most crucial turning points in World War II, and why, in the end, the Battle was a strategic victory for the British.

The 1930s was a period of astonishing change. Aircraft developed from wood and canvas biplanes to swift all-metal monoplanes. Bombers of increasing load and range meant that Britain was no longer an island. It could be attacked from the air. It was firmly believed by many politicians in Britain in the early '30s that "the bombers will always get through," and the rise of Fascism in Italy and Germany made war likely.

The British put an immense effort into the development of a comprehensive radar defense which could warn of the approach of enemy planes anywhere along the coast. In this fictionalized story we see the development of radar during the late 30s through the eyes of Allan Chadwick, whom we first met as a young pilot flying Vimy bombers in my first novel, *Wings over Iraq*. The Royal Air Force in which Chadwick was serving before the start of the second world war was largely the creation of one man, Air Chief Marshal Hugh Trenchard, who was head of the Royal Flying Corps in the Great War and realized that the technology and tactics of an air force were completely different than the army and justified a separate military arm, the Royal Air Force, which was created in 1918.

As the second world war grew closer, Trenchard formed large reserve units manned mostly by personnel who had served in the RAF so that their skills would not be lost—the Royal Auxiliary Air Force. These squadrons, manned by trained pilots and ground crews, were vital when the Battle of Britain began less than a year after the outbreak of the Second World War. Although his name is almost unknown today, the world we live in, which escaped domination by the Third Reich, owes a great deal to Viscount Hugh Trenchard.

Eric B. Forsyth
Brookhaven, New York
September 2021

Wings over the Channel

Chapter One

The Luftwaffe High Command held a meeting at the Reich Air Ministry on Leipziger Strasse in Berlin in October 1938. It was for senior officers only, presided over by the chief, Reichmarshall Hermann Göring. When the auditorium was full, an officer at the door called for attention. As Göring entered, the men rose to their feet and snapped a stiff-arm salute, shouting, "Heil Hitler!"

"Ach, enough of that. We're all pilots here. Sit down."

Göring, in an immaculate white uniform, strode to the front and sat down in a wide chair specially placed there for his corpulent body. A colonel made the introductory remarks.

"For two years, Luftwaffe intelligence has been following the development of a radio detection system by the British, which they term RDR. We obtained a confidential report on the performance during 1937 exercises. The performance was relatively poor and in line with our own trials in the Baltic. We found that, although the equipment can detect aircraft over one hundred and fifty kilometers away, it is difficult to get fighters in the air in time to intercept them.

"This year the British RAF organized a massive trial simulating attacks by bombers on the British Islands. Over thirty-nine mock attacks were made. Only fifteen per cent were intercepted by fighters. The bombers were detected at a range of about one hundred and sixty kilometers. From that point, it took an average of twenty-five minutes to get fighters airborne. They would, of course, require another ten to fifteen minutes to reach the altitude of the attacking force.

"Doing the arithmetic, our current bombers, Heinkel 111 and Dornier 17, would travel about two hundred kilometers during the period, from detection to fighters at an intercepting position. Clearly, interception would not be possible. When our most modern bomber, the Junkers 88, is in full service it would travel two hundred and fifty kilometers in the same time and would be about a hundred kilometers ahead of the fighters by the time they reached altitude.

"The purpose of this meeting is to discuss the tactical implication of the intelligence reports and also the strategic moves in terms of future bomber development. Any questions?"

A general stood up, "How reliable are the intelligence reports?"

In response the head of the Abwehr* rose to his feet. "The '37 report was checked several ways and deemed accurate. The '38 report was obtained from the same source. We have no reason to doubt its authenticity, but I have asked the head of the London desk to burrow for any other reports he could find on the '38 exercise."

The colonel rose again. "I have here a report from our technical people. Photographs of the RDR aerials were examined closely. They are using a very low frequency for this type of work and the results quoted in the report are probably the best that can be achieved with such technically inferior equipment. The chain of stations, which covers most of the east and south coasts of Britain, needs an enormous manpower to operate on a continuous basis. So much so, the stations are mostly manned by women—"

There was a general snigger from the audience,

"—and I have had intelligence that the women lack the ability to be trained to the same level one might expect of a male crew."

At this point the Reichmarshall lumbered to his feet. "The need for four-engined heavy bombers has been a debatable

* A definition of "Abwehr" and other unfamiliar terms can be found in the Glossary, starting on page 349.

subject for some time in the Luftwaffe. Naturally, in considering such strategic matters, the manufacturing capacity of this country enters the equation. We could build two medium bombers for every heavy bomber produced. However, this intelligence analysis disposes of the issue. Our Heinkel, Junker, and Dornier medium bombers are quite sufficient for a war involving such ill-prepared foes as the British."

The debate continued, but everyone knew the matter was finished. The Reichmarshall had spoken. It was a profound decision, with ramifications that plagued the Third Reich until its tumultuous, catastrophic finale. The question "Was the intelligence reliable?" went to the heart of the matter. There was no simple answer. Instead, a chain of events had led to that fateful meeting, which began with the posting of a junior officer to an RAF research establishment a few years earlier.

Chapter Two

Flying Officer Allan Chadwick sat at a desk in a sparse office at the Royal Air Force aircraft research center, Farnborough. He had been posted there several months earlier after spending nearly four years flying Vimy bombers in Iraq. His face was tanned by the many hours in an open-cockpit plane. Chadwick had been sent to Farnborough after an operational tour because he had entered the Air Force via Cranwell College, where permanent officers were trained in flying and engineering.

He stared at a blank writing pad, attempting to compose a report of the results of three weeks of flying a new prototype bomber. His wiry frame shifted on the uncomfortable, government-issue chair. In his opinion the plane was a dog—underpowered and stiff on the controls. But that wasn't his responsibility. The aerodynamic characteristics had already been evaluated by pilots with far more experience than he had. His was the more mundane task of ascertaining range and ceiling with various bomb loads.

In that regard, the plane didn't meet the requirements specified when the construction order was placed by the Air Ministry back in 1933. Now, more than a year later, he had to summarize the results of his tests so that higher authority could decide if the plane should be scrapped or possibly modified to improve the performance.

Along with several crew he had droned over the English countryside in fair weather and foul with different combinations of bombload and fuel. With a load of 2,000 pounds, he could scarcely persuade the plane to leave the ground and he had a few sweaty moments landing with that load.

His thoughts were interrupted by a knock on the door and his immediate superior, Squadron Leader Codrington, popped his head around the door jamb. "Meeting in my office in half an hour. Can you make it?"

"Oh, yes sir. No problem."

Thirty minutes later he knocked on Codrington's door. As he entered, he saw a squadron leader and two flight sergeants sitting at a table.

Codrington rose from his desk, "Ah, Flying Officer Chadwick, meet Squadron Leader Elliot and Flight Sergeants McBride and Stewart."

Chadwick saluted the officer and nodded to the sergeants. All three men showed wartime campaign ribbons on their tunics. The squadron leader was a tall man sporting a mustache. On his chest with the campaign ribbons was the insignia of the Distinguished Flying Cross with bar.

"Sit down. I want to bring you up to date on a new order just received by the commanding officer from the Air Ministry. Farnborough has been directed to create an investigative team to formally report on all aircraft accidents in Great Britain, both civilian and service incidents. Until now the gentlemen here have looked at service accidents, mainly to decide on a cause, which would allow senior officers to determine if a court martial was appropriate for the aircraft pilot or commander."

Chadwick was not sure how this information tied in with the trials he was flying with the new bomber. But he said nothing.

"Civilian passenger flights are increasing every year, particularly with the introduction of tri-motor aircraft," Codrington went on. "The powers that be feel that an independent assessment of accidents is essential for those involving civilian aircraft. Up to now most accidents were investigated by the aircraft manufacturer, who usually found ways to blame everything except their own plane. The gentlemen here have as much experience as anyone in the country when it comes to examining the wreckage of a crash—fortunately, that's still a pretty rare occurrence."

Elliot broke in, "Sergeants McBride and Stewart are very experienced in engine and airframe technology. I look at the bigger picture—pilot training, weather, flight orders, navigation, things like that. For some time now I haven't been on flying status due to medical problems I must attribute to old age," he chuckled. "As a young man I flew over the Middle East, the Far East, and Europe during the war, and, of course, the British Islands. I have, in fact, walked away from a few crashes myself and been carried from a few, which probably hastened my non-flying status."

He lifted his left arm which Chadwick now noticed was sheathed in a leather sleeve under his uniform which also covered his hand.

"Burns," Elliot explained casually. "Now that we're gaining some kind of official standing our team must be enlarged. I believe we need an active pilot on the team, familiar with modern aircraft and procedures. Squadron Leader Codrington has suggested you might fit the bill, mainly because you write decent reports."

Codrington broke in. "I was joking. Your engineering training at Cranwell will also be valuable. The job is not full-time. You would still continue the evaluation of the planes here but would be on call should an accident occur. What do you think?"

"I'm very flattered, sir. I was once in a Vimy in Iraq that fell out of the sky rather precipitously, if that qualifies me."

One of the flight sergeants lifted his hand and Codrington nodded to him. "Have ye got a strong stomach, sirr?" the sergeant asked in a Scottish accent.

The question hung in the air like a black cloud. Nobody spoke until Elliot coughed. "Ahem, I think Flight Sergeant Mc-Bride may be concerned that occasionally our investigations can be a little messy. Normally the wreckage at a site has been cleaned up by the emergency crews before we get there. But with extensive damage, that takes time. We sometimes arrive in the middle of the clean-up."

Chadwick hesitated and then looked squarely at Elliot, "I'd very much like to join your team."

"Good! I'll let you have a few of our recent reports to browse over."

Chadwick returned to his office feeling elated. He loved variety and he tackled the report he had been writing with new enthusiasm.

The next morning an orderly dropped off a half dozen buff folders, each containing a report on an RAF flying accident, typically two pages long. Two had occurred at a Flying Training School. The first described an accident in which the instructor and pupil had both been killed. The plane was subjected to intense vibration and had plummeted to earth because the propeller had disintegrated. Pieces of the propeller were found in a field a mile from the crash. Examination of the maintenance logbook for earlier flights on the same day gave no explanation as to why the propeller had failed.

He returned the report to the folder, feeling a burden of sadness. He realized he'd let himself in for an emotional load that may be hard to deal with. The sadness prompted a reverie as he stared through the window. His mind was a thousand miles away as he thought of the simple funeral service when his beloved commanding officer was buried just before he left Iraq. The C.O. had been brought down by machine gun fire from the ground. He had encouraged Chadwick's desire to improve bombing accuracy and to fly using instruments in bad weather. He had been a true mentor.

He opened the second report, and a quick glance lifted his spirits. A student pilot, flying solo, had been beating up his girlfriend's house when his lower wing encountered a tree, which brought the plane down. The student walked away from the wreck, which must have really impressed his girlfriend, Chadwick thought with a smile. A note at the end of the report showed the student had been court martialed and punished by a loss of six month's seniority. Chadwick decided the young man had been lucky, in more ways than one.

Chadwick lifted a report from another folder. It revealed a much more somber story. A Boulton Paul Sidestrand had crashed into the moors of Yorkshire, killing everyone on board. The accident had been witnessed by a farmer plowing a field. He reported the aircraft emerged from low cloud and almost immediately collided with a hill and burst into flames. The report estimated the cloud base was only about three hundred feet above the ground, which was eight hundred feet above sea level. Close examination of the cockpit wreckage showed the plane was equipped with gyroscopic flight instruments. Squadron Leader Elliot was of the opinion the pilot had been practicing "blind" flying in cloud and had lost track of the plane's position.

At the end of the report was a strongly worded recommendation that instrument flying practice should only be attempted in clear weather using an aircraft carrying a safety pilot. A second recommendation was that a system of instrument flying ratings be adopted, based on written and flying tests that would permit a pilot to take off and land under given weather conditions. A pilot without a rating would not be permitted to fly except in clear weather.

That seemed sensible to Chadwick. He wondered if the suggestion was making its way through the RAF bureaucracy. He let the report slide through his fingers onto the desk. Looking out of the window again, his view of the landing field was now obscured by rain lashing against the panes. His mind wandered to the panic the unlucky pilot must have felt as the ground suddenly appeared through the murky cloud, and the involuntary, futile jerk to the stick before oblivion consumed them all. He shook his head. Too much imagination was not a good thing, he realized.

Chapter Three

A case officer at the Abwehr Headquarters in Hamburg, four hundred miles away from Farnborough, wearily picked up a stack of dockets forwarded by the Sicherheist Dienst, or SD, the branch of the SS concerned with security in the Middle and Far East. When they encountered incidents or personnel connected with Britain or the Americas the matter was referred to the Abwehr, which had responsibility for those parts of the world.

One case caught his eye—a British officer had been arrested by the Gestapo on suspicion of spying but was released within a few hours. He was an RAF pilot, Allan Chadwick, on leave traveling back to Great Britain from Iraq where he had been stationed. He initialed it and routinely forwarded it to Luftwaffe security. Anything to get it off his desk.

But the docket didn't disappear for long. Within a week it came back with a request for information on the subject officer's current posting and duties. The case officer filled out a slip and forwarded the paperwork to the British desk. Several days later another bored civil servant forwarded the request in the diplomatic bag to the Luftwaffe liaison officer, Hauptmann Carl Loeffler, attached to the German Embassy in London.

The German Embassy was in a prestigious part of London, Belgravia, and strove to maintain the trappings of a first-class world power. They had meticulous records of the British armed forces, updating their records of personnel postings, promotions, and retirements from official British publications. The function of hundreds of British bases was not generally publicized, but for many, the purpose of an establishment could be gleaned from newspapers, magazines, and the old-fashioned way, a visit on foot to the perimeter and, perhaps, a cocked ear at the local pub. Spying was not a dare-devil mission in the middle of the night but rather a slow, tedious, steady drip, drip accumulation of facts.

The Luftwaffe attaché became intrigued when it emerged that Chadwick was now stationed at Farnborough. An entrée into that establishment opened the possibility of learning the most recent advances in British aviation. He decided to discuss the matter with the station chief, who was responsible for all tactical espionage in Britain.

The chief was Dr. Gerhard Kegel, officially listed as the Cultural Affairs Attaché, although his true function was known to everybody on the embassy staff and to MI5, the British counter espionage agency. Dr. Kegel was a coldly rational man initially trained in mathematics. His family had been ruined by the horrendous inflation that gripped Germany in the 1920s. He believed only the Nazis could restore the standing of Germany in world affairs.

The other branch of German spying activity in Britain was termed "strategic" and operated at a much higher level of security. It was whispered that the head of the strategic branch was actually English. His identity was top secret. The purpose of strategic espionage was to place pro-German politicians and power brokers in positions that guaranteed Britain would never come to war with Germany. The rise of communism and the Soviet Union frightened many upper-class Britons, which facilitated the goals of the strategic espionage branch.

When Hauptmann Loeffler broached the subject of approaching Chadwick, the chief was skeptical, "Why should he betray secrets? Has he shown any sympathy toward Germany?"

Loeffler persisted, "Young officer, not rich, may be open to bribery or possibly a little blackmail."

The chief turned it over in his mind. "I know the Luftwaffe could use this kind of information—what the British specify for defense, a fighter, influences how we specify our bombers. Let me think about it."

Later in the day he started to organize a reception for some visiting German singers who were going to present lieders. At the reception they would sing a well-known piece by Schubert,

"Der Erikönig." The presentation was to be followed by cocktails. Dr. Kegel had the happy thought that he should invite several British aficionados of Schubert to the reception who he knew sympathized with the appeasement wing of the Tory Party.

With no clear plan of action, Dr. Kegel had launched the stalking of Allan Chadwick. He had a dilemma. It was a steadfast rule that people considered sympathetic to the aims of the strategic branch were never involved in tactical branch operations. The reasons were obvious—the opinions of anyone remotely connected with covert German plans would be discounted. And yet he felt that any attempt to contact Chadwick would have to be done through social channels.

He began formulating a guest list for the reception. He knew a couple of people who might have a few ideas.

Chapter Four

At Farnborough, Flying Officer Chadwick finished gathering data of the loading curves for the plane under normal operating conditions. Squadron Leader Codrington now suggested investigating flight under abnormal conditions—for example, when flying on one engine. This would simulate battle damage that caused the loss of an engine.

The plane was equipped with an early version of adjustable pitch propellers. All the pilots flying the plane at Farnborough had been briefed by the manufacturer on the advantages of variable pitch, which allowed a better match of engine settings to the aircraft speed. In addition, the blades could be feathered—turned so that the leading edge was pointing directly into the air flow to produce minimum drag. Codrington suggested the single-engine tests should be done with an engine feathered, not shut down completely. There was no intention of executing a single-engine landing, which was a maneuver only to be evaluated by the most experienced test pilots. When the load tests were completed, Chadwick was told to unfeather and open up the engine so that a normal landing could be made.

One morning Chadwick took off with a flight engineer and one other crew. They carried a load of one thousand pounds, consisting of four 250-pound bombs. The bombs were not armed; concrete inside the casing was used to simulate the weight of a real bomb. At an altitude of three thousand feet, Chadwick throttled back the left engine, feathered the propeller, and adjusted the rudder to maintain a constant heading. He then began a series of runs at different engine and pitch settings to maintain a fixed altitude. The test conditions were noted by the crew and Chadwick kept track of the stick and rudder bar forces.

The tests would have to be repeated at different heights, but Chadwick thought they had done enough for one day, and he judged the weather was deteriorating. He asked the flight engineer to unfeather the left propeller. The engineer pushed the red button, but nothing happened. He pushed the button again and jiggled the pitch control lever. The propeller blade angle did not change.

"Won't unfeather, boss," he yelled into the pilot's ear.

"Bloody hell," said Chadwick to no one in particular. He turned the plane on a compass course for Farnborough, which lay about thirty miles to the north. His right leg was beginning to ache from the force he had to exert on the rudder bar. The wind was gusting to twenty knots from the south, pushing up the ground speed.

Chadwick signaled the flight engineer and shouted in his ear, "I'm planning a single-engine landing. Open the bomb bay doors. When we cross the southern airfield boundary, jettison the bombs. As soon as they're gone, shut the doors. The plane cannot land with the doors open. I'll make a left turn and land into wind."

Chadwick knew the situation was dangerous. As the plane slowed to landing speed the rudder would become less and less effective. He would not be able to increase power on the right engine. They would inexorably continue to descend. If Chadwick judged it right, they would be over the field when the wheels touched ground. A blast of cold air into the cockpit told him the flight engineer had got the doors open.

He waved to the remaining crew. "Help flight get the doors up and then brace yourselves against the bulkhead."

Familiar landmarks appeared and he knew he was approaching the perimeter fence. He eased the plane down a hundred feet, a height he could never reclaim if things went wrong. The plane gave a sudden lift as the bombs hurtled down, the airspeed fell, and the plane started to turn left. Chadwick fought the controls to bring the plane onto a southern heading and to ease off the height. Quickly pushing down the undercarriage lever, he glanced over the left wing and saw some small huts appear. He was already over the northern perimeter.

The undercarriage panel glowed with two green lights, but he had misjudged his ground speed; events were moving out of his control. He pushed the stick forward to maintain airspeed, and the ground rushed toward him. The plane flared as Chadwick pulled back on the stick and chopped the throttle of the right engine. They hit the ground with a crash, bounced into the air and settled back. To his amazement the plane continued to roll. He had not smashed the landing gear, after all.

He had landed in some gorse on the very edge of the field. When the plane stopped, he shut down both engines, as he could not taxi with one engine. He felt the adrenaline coursing through his veins and then he felt suddenly drained,

The flight sergeant climbed into the cockpit, "Damn good show, sir."

"See if you can arrange a tow, flight."

Chadwick waited in the plane until a tractor showed up. The flight sergeant also returned with a Crossley and gave him a ride to the hangar. He signed the logbook and noted the propeller fault. At his office he started to organize his notes on the just-completed flight but found he was still too excited to concentrate, and so he walked over to the officer's mess for some lunch. He was sorely tempted to pop into the bar for a lunchtime drink, but pilots who might fly in the afternoon prudently avoided alcohol until the evening.

After lunch he settled into an easy chair in the lounge and glanced at some photographs of the Prince of Wales in the *Illustrated London News*. In a few seconds his eyes closed, and he nodded off.

Chadwick awoke with start thirty minutes later. He felt wonderfully refreshed and walked briskly back to the office. The wind had picked up and he glanced instinctively at the weather cock on a roof. The wind was still from the south, but gusting. He started to write a summary of the trip results in longhand but was interrupted by an orderly who told him he was required at Squadron Leader Codrington's office. He straightened his tie, put on a hat and walked down the corridor to the squadron leader's office. He knocked, marched inside and saluted.

"Ah, Chadwick, heard you had a little trouble this morning." Codrington waved his arm at a chair. "Sit."

"Yes, sir, the trials went off fairly well, but when I came to power up the idling left engine, the prop would not unfeather."

Codrington scratched his chin. "Hmmm, how did you handle that?"

"I jettisoned the bomb load on the south side of the field, made a single-engine approach and landing. Misjudged the ground speed a bit and just made a touchdown inside the north boundary."

"Good show. You didn't bend anything. Well done. I'll be interested to hear what the squadron engineer makes of the propeller."

"So will I, sir."

Just then the telephone on Codrington's desk rang stridently. Codrington picked it up and answered. "Squadron Leader Codrington." He listened to the voice on the other end and his face became serious. "Sounds bad. Yes, of course. Right away."

He replaced the phone. "That was Squadron Leader Elliot. An Imperial Airways Avro 6-18 has crashed at Croydon. Sounds bad. He'd like you to report to him at Croydon as soon as possible."

Chadwick stood up as Codrington said, "I'll authorize a car. Take a coat—you'll be outside, and it looks like rain."

A blue RAF car driven by a leading aircraftsman was waiting for him at the entrance to the officer's mess. He climbed in and the airman passed him a note and put the car in gear. The note was from Squadron Leader Codrington. It was clearly scribbled in a hurry and gave some details of the crash. The plane had come down in a built-up area and hit a house. Elliot had commandeered a room in the control tower as a temporary office.

Chadwick spoke to the driver, "Do you know the way to the Croydon Airport?"

"Yes, sir."

"Good, make the best time you can. We should report to the control tower."

The drive from Farnborough took them through several small villages. The countryside was pastoral, and dotted by magnificent houses, briefly seen through stands of trees.

Codrington had placed on the back seat a 1930 edition of *Jane's All the World's Aircraft*. Chadwick absorbed the details of the Avro 6-18. It was built under license from Fokker. The plane carried a passenger load of eight, with one or two pilots. It was a high-wing monoplane powered by three engines. The range was about four hundred miles, and it cruised at ninety knots.

It took them nearly an hour before they pulled up to the control tower. Chadwick told the driver to wait, and he dashed inside. He soon located Squadron Leader Elliot, who was engaged in a rancorous discussion with two civilians in his office. As soon as Chadwick appeared, he introduced them.

"Mr. Jenkins, Airport Manager, and Mr. Drummond of Imperial Airways."

They nodded to Chadwick. Both were frowning and looked upset at the unexpected arrival of the Air Force officer.

Elliot continued, talking smoothly. "I've tried to explain that the Royal Air Force has been directed to investigate all aviation accidents in the United Kingdom. This will be promulgated soon as an Order in Council from Whitehall. I'm sure they'll cooperate with us fully in looking into this sad affair. Flying Officer Chadwick is an experienced pilot with many hours of flying multi-engine aircraft. He also has an engineering degree from Cranwell. Hopefully, he can give us the view from the cockpit, so to speak."

Both civilians looked daggers at Chadwick, and one mumbled that Imperial Airways was quite capable of investigating any accidents.

Elliot turned to face Chadwick. "I understand the accident was witnessed by several people. Perhaps you could organize taking some statements, which I understand the police have in hand."

Chadwick saluted and went back to the car. He was glad to leave the heated atmosphere behind him. He found the inspector in charge of the police detachment at the main gate. The witnesses had already been interviewed and their statements were summarized by the policeman, who told Chadwick that the plane was apparently making a normal approach when it suddenly turned right, that is to the west, and dove steeply into the ground. It hit a house and came to rest a few hundred yards outside the airfield boundary. It immediately caught fire and apparently everyone on board was killed. They were not sure if anyone was in the house when the plane crashed into it.

Chadwick decided to visit the crash site, and the inspector told a police sergeant to go with him and clear it with the police there. The site was still crowded with fire engines and several ambulances. Chadwick told his driver to stay with the car.

He soon spotted Flight Sergeants McBride and Stewart, who were grimy and covered with ash. They were both Scotsmen and had served their apprenticeship at RAF Halton, then years of squadron service. Chadwick greeted them warmly.

"There's nothing to be done for the poor souls," Stewart told him. "The ambulance men are taking out the bodies, as best they can."

Chadwick asked McBride for a description of the wreck, which was still shrouded in smoke.

"The right wing hit the ground first—outer ten feet broke off. You can see it down there." He nodded down the trail of plane and house wreckage. "The main fuel tank is in the wing over the cabin. The cockpit and cabin were doused in petrol and went up like an incinerator. There's nothing left except a bit of the fuselage, the tail end. The nose hit the house and set it on fire."

"Did the piece of wing that broke off burn?" Chadwick asked Stewart, who was an aircraft rigger.

"No, sirr, there's no fuel in that part of the wing."

"Let's go and take a look at it." They walked over the churned-up ground to the wing fragment, which was guarded by a policeman. Chadwick paid special attention to the aileron which was poking up on the end of the trailing edge of the wing. He shook it and found that it was rigidly held in place. Ducking down to look at the underside of the wing, he tried to see the hinge that held the aileron, but the area was covered by an inspection panel.

"Can you get that off?" Chadwick asked Stewart. The sergeant produced a screwdriver and unfastened several screws. The panel fell away. Chadwick reached inside the wing. He could feel the stranded steel wire that operated the aileron. It was stretched as tight as a violin string.

"Flight, see if you can find out why that control cable is so tight."

Leaving the two technicians to work on the wing, he walked back to the site of the burnt fuselage. Standing downwind he caught the stench of scorched metal, wood, and flesh. There was virtually nothing left of the center of the plane. Even the aluminum struts had melted.

An ambulance man came over and introduced himself. "I've been ordered by the coroner to take the bodies directly to the morgue. There's really nothing left, just bones jumbled up in the nose. Not even sure how many were aboard."

"We'll have to depend on the manifest to find out," replied Chadwick. "Sorry you had to deal with this."

"Part of the job," the man replied. "Nowadays I'm seeing just the same thing in more and more car accidents."

Chadwick walked back to the two sergeants. They had removed another panel from the wrecked wing.

"Look at this, sirr," said Stewart. He pointed to a space inside the wing where the outer hinge of the right flap could be seen. It was attached to a substantial-looking bracket which had been wrenched from the structural part of a rib. The wire to the aileron was trapped between the bracket and the underside of the wing covering. "The bracket broke and moved up, pulling the aileron control." Stewart explained.

"That could explain the accident," exclaimed Chadwick. "If the bracket broke loose when the flaps were lowered, the ailerons would move to make a hard right turn. The stick would be jammed over. Nothing the pilot could do!"

"Aye," said McBride slowly. "But this damage could have been caused by the impact when the wing hit the ground. Then it is a result of the accident, not the cause."

"A very important difference," mused Chadwick. He walked to the wing tip and felt the lower surface. The aluminum had been deeply gorged by the impact, and soil was forced into the cracks. "Look here," he showed the sergeants. "The wing tip is deeply scored, but the aileron is unblemished. It was up when the wing hit." He paused for a minute, thinking. "Furthermore, the normal reaction of the pilot if the ailerons were functioning normally would be to make a hard left bank to counter the right turn. The right aileron would have been pointing down and would have hit the ground first."

Chadwick thought of the terrible moment the pilot must have endured when the plane suddenly banked right and he saw the ground rapidly growing in the windshield, with stick jammed irrevocably on the right side of the cockpit.

"Aye," said Stewart again. "You're a reet Sherlock Holmes, sir. It all makes sense."

"I'm going back to talk to Squadron Leader Elliot. Tell the police the wing must not be touched."

He went back to the car and was driven to the control tower. Elliot was alone. Chadwick explained their findings and said it implied the crash was caused by a structural failure of the flap mechanism.

"I'm not sure Avro will buy that," said Elliot. "However, we must get the pieces back to Farnborough for a complete formal inspection. I'll set that up now and have a lorry and crane here in the morning. Well done, Chadwick."

Chapter Five

The reception at the German Embassy started as twilight cast the London streets into shadow. Taxis and ponderous Rolls Royces dropped off their passengers at the door of the imposing building on Belgrave Square. Inside, a butler took their capes and coats and passed them to flunkeys dressed in Tyrolean outfits, dark jackets with knee-length shorts and white stockings.

The ballroom literally glittered as dozens of heavy chandeliers spilled a thousand points of light on the walls and ceiling. The air was rich with the smell of perfume and cigarette smoke. A low hubbub of conversation almost drowned out the music from a grand piano, played by a man in tails. More flunkeys circulated with glasses of sherry. It was all very civilized.

A compere asked everyone to take a seat—chairs were ranged along the walls—and he then introduced Dr. Kegel, the cultural affairs attaché, who welcomed them to the embassy and began describing the enormous repertoire of songs composed by Schubert in the nineteenth century. He explained the subtle counterpoint of the piano and the singers. And then introduced the baritone singer and the piano accompanist who walked into the center of the ballroom and bowed. He gave a brief list of the compositions they would hear that night, starting with "The Elf King" and concluding with a famous piece, "Gretchen and the Spinning Wheel."

After the recital began, Kegel carefully searched the faces of the guests. He was looking for a particular woman, Honoria Pomeroy. She was married to a British diplomat, Thomas Pomeroy, who had held the position of Second Secretary at the British Embassy in Berlin before the war. When he first met Honoria, she was a young bride who had joined her husband in Germany after the birth of her first child in 1912, her daughter Penelope. Honoria was very fond of German culture and spoke the language well. Kegel was a rising star in the German Diplomatic Corp and was immediately attracted to her. He contrived to form a growing friendship, which was rudely interrupted by the start of the war

Mrs. Pomeroy was evacuated with all the diplomatic staff to Switzerland and spent the first two years of the war in Basel, where her husband had a temporary, confidential position at the consulate. After two years, the family returned to London. Like many upper-class Britons, she was devastated by the carnage inflicted on both her British and German social circles. A whole generation of young men, the cream of both countries, had been wiped out. After the war she renewed her friendship with Gerhard Kegel by letter, and when he was posted to the German embassy in London, they met occasionally for high tea at Simpsons on the Strand.

Kegel nodded to one of his underlings, who moved to his side. He whispered, "See the couple across the room, just to the right of the German Eagle. The woman in blue. I want you to keep the man busy while I talk to his wife after the singing is over."

When the recital concluded, and the applause died down, servants moved tables piled with hors d'oeuvres to the center and began to serve cocktails. Kegel kept his eye on Honoria and when she was not occupied, he moved casually next to her. "Hello, my dear. *Wie gehts*."

She replied in English, "Hello, Gerhard! The singing was wonderful. Thank you for the invitation."

"Honoria, I especially invited you because I need your advice about a delicate matter."

"Ow, sounds exciting! What is it?"

"It's a little too public here to discuss it now. When are you planning to come to town?"

"We're staying at our apartment at the moment. I've been in town for a day or two, but I'm headed back to the country soon."

"Could you meet me tomorrow afternoon?"

"I think so. Simpsons for tea?"

"I think not. Do you know the restaurant at the National Gallery?"

"Yes."

"Tomorrow at four, then."

"I'll be there, Gerhard, dear." Honoria was puzzled. She had no knowledge of Kegel's true function at the embassy.

Dr. Kegel marshaled his thoughts carefully before the meeting with Honoria Pomeroy. He knew her country house was only a dozen miles from Farnborough, and she had an active social life. It was his hope that maybe Chadwick could become embroiled in her orbit. He knew she was sympathetic to the dilemma of Germany's fate after the war. On the other hand, she was British to the core and would never scheme against her country. She was simply the entre and he would play his cards as they lay.

When he arrived at the restaurant, she was already seated, staring moodily at a piece of Swiss roll and a cup of tea. "Greetings, Gerhard," she said when she spotted him. "This place is a touch plebian for your taste, is it not?"

"Just a precaution, dear. I don't want our friendship to be widely known. The security people at the embassy say the British secret service take an interest in our comings and goings."

She laughed. "I hardly think a man who organizes Schubert Lieders is a threat to the British Empire!"

Kegel laughed with her. A waitress approached and asked if he would care to order.

"I'll have the same as my friend—cake and a pot of tea, please."

Honoria chattered away about the reception the night before and how much she and her husband had enjoyed it. "Gretchen especially. The piano accompaniment was simply breathtaking."

"Honoria, there is something we must talk about very seriously. It is sixteen years since the dreadful war ended. A new generation is maturing. They must never experience the horror we have known. Every day young men and women from Germany come to my office wanting guidance on how to gain appreciation of British culture, British history. We represent the two most civilized nations in Europe, if not the world. I want to take the opportunity to cement friendship and trust between the new generations."

"And what can I do to help, Gerhard?"

"You live in a historic region of England. Stone age people built Stonehenge. The Romans occupied London for centuries. The Saxons crowned their kings at Kingston-on-Thames. The royal family live at Windsor Castle. I would like to organize tours, for selected German visitors, students, accompanied by young Englishmen and women of similar class. You can help me find those English hosts."

"How?"

"Well, are there any military camps nearby? Young officers are often away from home, perhaps lonely. They may be interested. Possibly the Anglo-German Alliance could help."

"Oh! Don't mention the AGA. Tom thinks they are a bunch of clowns. But yes, there are military bases near my house. Aldershot is a large army base. Farnborough is RAF."

Kegel's ears picked up at the mention of Farnborough. That was the target he was homing in on. "They must have public affairs officers. I could write in my official capacity, but I would like to suggest a local person for liaison. That is what I want to discuss. Possibly, too, you might know a couple of local young ladies willing to help. How old is your daughter now?"

"Penelope—she's twenty-two but she's rather giddy."

"Twenty-two! Amazing how the time flies. She was a baby when I last saw her, and so much has happened in between."

"Let me think about it. I'll mention it to Tom. He's very sensible." Honoria glanced at a small watch on her wrist. "My goodness, I must fly. There's a good train in twenty minutes. I can just catch it if I leave now. I'm going back to the country tonight. Goodbye, Gerhard. I'll be in touch."

Kegel watched her weave her way between the tables. For a woman in her mid-forties, she was still very attractive. But an affair was the last thing a German station chief could afford. He was fairly sure the SD kept an eye on him.

He reviewed the conversation with Honoria. She was hardly enthusiastic, which was not surprising. He was casting a rather a wide net to catch one fish. Success looked problematical, but the next day the chances suddenly brightened. A memorandum arrived on his desk informing senior staff that a foreign affairs bigwig was visiting from Germany in a few days, Plenipotentiary Ambassador Frederick Emsden.

Chapter Six

For a couple of weeks after the accident investigation, Flying Officer Chadwick continued routine flying assignments. Then he got a call from Squadron Leader Elliot to attend a briefing on the Avro accident. The wreckage had been carted to Farnborough and examined by experts. Elliot introduced a civilian, Dr. Robert Hampshire of London University.

"Dr. Hampshire is a metallurgist—he's made a specialty of metal fatigue."

Hampshire took over. "There is no question that the plane made a fatal turn to the right as it approached Croydon airfield. Engineers and riggers have concluded the outer hinge of the landing flaps broke away from the supporting member. The aerodynamic force on the flap caused the hinge to move upward, into the wing. There it encountered the control cable of the right aileron, causing that element to move upward, producing an involuntary bank to the right. Loss of lift steepened the descent rate and the plane crashed into the ground. The question I attempted to solve was why the hinge failed. Fatigue is a progressive failure of a material as atomic bonds are broken by repetitive stress. It's usually exponential in character."

Chadwick was enjoying the scientific nature of the presentation and wondered how many of the audience really knew what "exponential" meant. Some of them were becoming restless and fidgety.

Hampshire went on to describe the design of the hinge and show some slides. The hinge was part of a steel bracket bolted to a specially reinforced wing rib. The slides clearly showed the bracket had torn away from the rib due to failure of the aluminum. The doctor explained that the failure rate is often exponential because progressive breaking of the bonds puts more and more stress on those remaining, which then fail faster.

A hand shot up, "Dr. Hampshire, how can you be sure the breakage you showed on the slides was not caused by the crash itself?"

"I believe the pilots who investigated the crash have already stated that, if the aileron controls had been working normally, the right aileron would have been down as the pilot fought to correct the right bank. However, I can substantiate that conclusion. Fresh aluminum oxidizes when exposed to the atmosphere. By examining the crack in the rib under a microscope it's possible to see the progressive nature of the oxidation. Older portions of the crack were more corroded, although the effect is minute. That bracket had been breaking in slow motion until the final disaster."

Another hand was raised. "How can fatigue be minimized?"

"There are many answers to that question. Anything that reduces the number or severity of repetitive cycles is good. The initial design of load-bearing parts should be robust. The maximum stress at any point should be reduced. For example, square corners are more prone to fatigue than rounded ones. Avoid any resonant structure."

Elliot thanked Dr. Hampshire and told the audience that he had recommended grounding all Avro 6-18s until the brackets on both wings could be examined by staining with them with a dye and examining them with a powerful magnifying lens. A repair was up to the manufacturer, which would have to be approved by Farnborough.

Most of the participants went for lunch at the officer's mess. A crowd gathered in the lounge for a glass of sherry. Allan Chadwick knew he was scheduled to fly in the afternoon and settled for a cup of coffee. He asked Dr. Hampshire how much flying he had done. To his surprise, the metallurgist said he had never flown in a plane.

Chadwick glanced at Squadron Leader Codrington, who was standing next to Hampshire. "Perhaps Dr. Hampshire would like a trip this afternoon? I'm going to air test a bomber that's had a new propeller fitted. It's been extensively ground-tested, so the flight is routine. If you're going to diagnose aviation mishaps, I'm sure you want to experience flight. What do you think, sir?"

Hampshire looked far from happy at the suggestion. "The analysis I presented today was an academic exercise. I think I'll leave the practical side to you flying chaps, thank you."

When Chadwick spoke to Codrington before he took off that afternoon, he mentioned Hampshire's reaction to the offer of a flight. They both laughed. "Better safe than sorry," was the squadron leader's slightly bitter quip.

Chapter Seven

When Dr. Kegel received the notice of a visit to the embassy by Ambassador Emsden, it rang a bell, but he could not place the connection. A few days later, he suddenly recalled the name and asked his secretary to bring him the Chadwick file. The first paper in the file was an SD report of the arrest of Allan Chadwick in Berlin on suspicion of being a British spy. He had claimed to be a commissioned officer in the Royal Air Force traveling home from a posting in Iraq. His identity was confirmed by Ambassador Frederick Emsden, who had boarded the same train from Rome as the suspect. Ambassador Emsden was a plenipotentiary diplomat of the Foreign Affairs Office and Chadwick was released to the British Consulate.

Kegel digested this interesting piece of information and realized here was a chance to establish a personal contact with Chadwick. He went to the head office to request a few minutes alone with Herr Emsden when he was in London. The resident ambassador was a diplomat of the old school. He detested the Nazis and knew his days as ambassador were numbered. He looked at Kegel distastefully and said, "I don't like the nature of your secret work and I don't particularly like you, Kegel. I hope you don't plan to burden Herr Emsden with tittle-tattle concerning this embassy."

"Far from it, your excellency. A few months ago in Berlin, Ambassador Emsden was instrumental in securing the release of a suspected British spy from the Gestapo. That person is now resident in England, and I would like Ambassador Emsden's help in establishing contact with him. He probably feels a debt of gratitude that I may be able to exploit."

"Very well, see the secretary drawing up the itinerary for his visit and insert fifteen minutes for your discussion."

When Emsden checked in at the embassy in London, the first order of business was to present an up-to-date picture of the situation in Berlin. The meeting was attended only by senior staff, which included Kegel by virtue of his position as head of tactical espionage, not as cultural affairs attaché. Emsden stated that the armed militia of the Nazi party, the Sturmabteilung, or SA, had been effectively dissolved and many of its members incorporated into the Schutzstaffel, or SS. The rest were drafted into the army, which greatly exceeded its maximum manpower strength permitted under the Versailles peace treaty. Germany had been secretly rearming the army anyway and training a new Luftwaffe, in violation of the peace treaty. Thus, it was pointless to keep these violations secret anymore. Emsden adroitly fielded the questions thrown at him after his talk.

Later that day he sat down with Kegel, who reminded him of his encounter with Allan Chadwick in Berlin. Emsden remembered it clearly. Kegel explained that he believed Chadwick was now involved in the development of advanced British aircraft and he was trying to establish a connection with him on the social side. He suggested that Chadwick may appreciate the chance to thank him for his intervention in Berlin, and in that way meet himself as Cultural Affairs Attaché. He would take it from there.

Emsden was willing to help but pointed out he would only be in London for a few days. Kegel had already considered the next step. He suggested they have a private dinner party, not at the embassy but in a neutral restaurant or even a pub. Emsden glanced at his diary, "I see I have an evening free in two days, see what you can do."

Kegel had wondered how to contact Flying Officer Chadwick in a plausible way. He knew his father owned some butcher's shops in Liverpool. It was relatively simple to track down the elder Mr. Chadwick by phone. When he came on the line, Kegel adopted his best British accent and introduced himself as Gerry Geoghan, claiming to be a friend in Iraq and now home on leave hoping to catch up with Allan. He asked Allan's whereabouts and his father said he was stationed in the south, at RAF Farnborough.

That was all Kegel needed, it gave him the cover to call Chadwick in the early evening at the officer's mess after he had talked to Emsden. When Chadwick picked up the phone, he introduced himself. "Good evening, Flying Officer Chadwick, this Gerhard Kegel. I am a cultural affairs officer at the German embassy in London. I believe we have a mutual acquaintance, Herr Emsden, who is visiting for a few days. He mentioned meeting you a few months ago and wondered how things worked out for you. I suggested that we meet if possible and that's why I'm calling."

Chadwick was taken aback, but stammered, "Yes, Herr Emsden was a great help in Berlin."

Kegel continued smoothly, "Would it be possible for you to come up to town the day after tomorrow for dinner? Nothing formal."

"Yes, I could make that."

"Wonderful, I suggest the Cheshire Cheese Pub on Fleet Street at half past seven, if that is convenient."

Chadwick said he would be there, and Kegel gave him his number to call should things change. It was a private line and did not go through the embassy switchboard. He mentioned he would reserve a table in the name of Kegel.

Chadwick was still a little confused, but his social life was meager, and the thought of a London dinner seemed attractive.

Chapter Eight

The plane Chadwick had been testing had been fitted with an experimental short-wave transmitter and receiver by Telecommunications Research, and he was told to try it out for some boffins from that establishment. He had two passengers from Telecommunications Research, a young technician and a rather elderly engineer. They explained that many trials had been carried out using aerials like the one that had been mounted on a plane. Now they would conduct a trial similar to those done previously, but with the aircraft banking and turning, thus introducing a new factor in the performance. Chadwick showed them how to use a parachute and then took off on a slightly misty, humid day with a cloud base of five thousand feet. He stayed just below the clouds, and at the direction of the boffins, began a series of three-hundred-sixty-degree turns while they contacted a base station.

For a while the engineer came and stood by his shoulder while the technician fiddled with the equipment. Pitching his voice above the noise of the engines, Chadwick asked him if the unit would also provide intercommunication between crew, which he suggested would be useful. The engineer said it did not, as finances were strained for the work and it was therefore kept simple. In addition, he said, it wasn't wise to have too many eggs in one basket, as battle damage could remove two functions at once. Chadwick conceded that was a good point.

The engineer went back to his equipment, and then Chadwick suddenly realized he could not see the ground anymore. The plane was flying in clear air, but a ground fog had developed. Chadwick twisted in his seat and yelled to the rear, "Is that thing in contact with anyone on the ground?"

The engineer made his way forward. "Yes, that's what we're working on, voice telephony."

"Good, ask them what the horizontal visibility is. I think it's got foggy,"

The engineer returned in a few minutes. "The people at our ground station telephoned the tower. Visibility is a quarter-mile, wind southwest, five knots. Is that bad?"

Chadwick groaned inwardly and cracked a wan smile. "It's not good. I think we must suspend your experiments and try to find our way home. Before you shut down ask the tower for the barometric pressure. Go!"

Something in Chadwick's voice alerted the engineer to the danger they were in. He was soon back. "Ten twelve point seven millibars, captain. Is that satisfactory?"

Chadwick explained he needed the pressure so that the altimeter could be adjusted for maximum accuracy. He knew the countryside near the airfield quite well, but with the very low visibility he planned to use an old pilot's trick—fly Bradshaw. Bradshaw was a comprehensive railway timetable used throughout the British Isles. Chadwick would follow the steel rails to Farnborough. He knew his general position, somewhere to the southwest of Farnborough. He spiraled down and as the plane entered fog at nine hundred feet, he set one-third flap, fine pitch on the propellers, and turned on the navigation lights. Chadwick flew carefully at five hundred feet above sea level. He knew the airfield elevation was two hundred and forty feet and the ground was fairly flat.

He brought the two boffins into the cockpit with an admonition to look ahead for anything that seemed to be higher than they were. Water droplets were whisked off the windshield by the air flow. He flew on a northerly course at eighty-five knots, straining his eyes for a glimpse of the twin railway tracks. He was looking for the main line to Southampton, which he knew passed a few miles north of the airfield. Houses and trees flashed by two hundred feet beneath their belly. Soon he spotted the line and turned smoothly to the northeast to follow it.

As dimly discerned obstructions in the murk flashed under the nose for a few seconds, the two boffins suddenly realized the extreme peril they were in. Chadwick pulled back the stick as a building appeared with a tall brick chimney. They missed it by feet. But Chadwick recognized it with relief. He knew the turn onto the field was only a few miles ahead. When his next landmark showed up, a bridge over a river, he turned quickly to the right and began searching for the airfield perimeter. He warned the passengers to brace for landing, dropped the under-carriage, selected full flap, and began a slow descent by easing back the throttles, at the same time banking a little to the right to counter the crosswind. The fence slid by the window and within seconds the plane touched down with a bump. Even as they taxied, he could not see the buildings until their lights materialized out of the gloom. An airman met the plane by signaling with batons, and Chadwick turned into wind and shut down the engines.

The senior boffin came into the cockpit and seized Chadwick's hand. "That was rather frightening! You're a very skilled pilot. Thank you!"

Chapter Nine

The next day the fog persisted, and so flying was out. Chadwick spent the morning instead reading King's Regulations, the legal basis for discipline in the Royal Air Force. A good knowledge of it was needed to pass the examination for promotion to Flight Lieutenant. He knew he would also have to swot up Administration and Equipment Procurement among other things. He got permission from the squadron leader to take the afternoon off, and after lunch changed into a suit and caught a bus to Farnborough center. At the station he bought a third-class return ticket to London, Waterloo. He took the Tube to Tottenham Court Road and decided to walk to the British Museum.

When he emerged onto the street for the five-minute walk, the acrid smell of the fog hit him like a blow. It was wet, miserable, and chilly. Huge double-decker buses loomed out of the yellow murk with blazing headlights that were diffused in the thick mist. Pedestrians were muffled up and breathed through their scarves. He was more than happy to step through the heavy portal into the warm, dry atmosphere of the museum.

Chadwick headed for the Egyptology exhibit. During his stays in Cairo, he had found the museum there to be fascinating. To his disappointment, the British Museum could not compare. *I guess they kept the best stuff in Egypt*, he thought to himself.

After a couple of hours, he walked back to Tottenham Court Road and took the Tube to Blackfriars, on the Thames. It was a short walk to Ye Cheshire Cheese on Fleet Street. Inside the ambiance was dark wood, subdued lights, and roaring fires. He felt right at home. He was early for the meeting with the Germans. The maître d' suggested he wait in the bar. Chadwick gave him the name of the reserving party and was told he would be alerted when the party arrived. The maître d' guided

Chadwick to the bar, indicated a vacant stool and smoothly pocketed a shilling that Chadwick passed over.

Chadwick ordered a pint of Guinness, took a sip, and looked around the ancient room. A sign pointed to a chair near the fireplace which stated it was the favorite spot of Charles Dickens. Several well-dressed men wreathed in cigar and cigarette smoke stood near the fire talking quietly. There was a sprinkling of women seated with companions at side tables. On his immediate right was a thirty-ish, attractively dressed woman. When she caught him eyeing her, she said, "Ghastly weather."

"I can't agree more."

She was a buxom, well-built woman wearing a form-fitting dress with a boa. Her hair was peroxided and fashioned into tight curls.

"You remind me of someone—um, Mae West."

"I'll take that as a compliment. Have you traveled far?"

"No, just twenty miles."

"You sound northern, Manchester?"

"Close. Liverpool. But I'm stationed near here."

"Ah, a military man."

"Sort of." Chadwick didn't correct her.

"Do you know the story of the French military cadets at the St. Cyr Academy?"

"No, I don't think so."

"During the war they were suddenly told they were all going to be sent to the front. One of them said it's certain death, and they all agreed. Another said plaintively he would just like to spend one night with Colette before he dies, the most famous Parisian courtesan. But she was rumored to be inordinately expensive, five thousand francs a night. Then one of the cadets spoke up, there are a thousand cadets at the Academy, we can chip in five francs each, have a lottery and one lucky cadet will get his wish. So that is what they did, and one young man had the most wonderful night of his life.

"After breakfast he paid her, and she said he was a lucky young man to be so rich at his age. He looked at her and he confessed he was just a cadet, but before they went to the front, the cadets at the Academy had all chipped in five francs so that one of them could spend a night with most beautiful courtesan in Paris. She was very touched and said, 'That's the most marvelous thing I've ever heard. I'm a patriot. At this dire time in our history, you cadets shouldn't have to pay. I'll give you your money back.' And she handed him five francs!"

Chadwick laughed. "That's good. You tell a good story. What's your name?"

"Joyce. What's yours?"

"Allan." And then, surprised at his own boldness, Chadwick added, "And what do you charge, Joyce?"

"It depends. No discount for the army."

Just then a waiter stepped up and said, "Your party has arrived, sir."

"Ah," he said. "Bad timing." He finished his drink and set down the tankard. "Perhaps we'll meet again, Joyce. Excuse me."

"It's up to you," she said and slipped her card along the bar.

Chadwick followed the waiter to a table hidden in a secluded corner. Two men stood up as he approached, and he recognized Emsden, who grasped Chadwick's hand and said, "This is a pleasure. Let me introduce Dr. Gerhard Kegel, our cultural affairs man at the embassy."

"Pleased to meet you." Chadwick shook hands. They all sat down, and the waiter hovered nearby. Emsden and Kegel both had drinks in front of them. Chadwick ordered a glass of Amontillado sherry.

Kegel started, "Ambassador Emsden is here on the perpetual diplomatic round, but he mentioned he had met a young British Air Force officer in Germany a few months back that he felt he owed an apology to. I was intrigued and thought it seemed to fall into the bailiwick of cultural affairs. So, I decided I should try to track you down."

Chadwick said nothing.

Emsden spoke in hesitant English. "That contretemps in Berlin, the police official was over zealous. Is that the right word?"

Kegel broke in, "Our government is quite new, following a tumultuous period. Sometimes junior officials are too ambitious."

The waiter passed out menus. Kegel said he had eaten at the Cheshire Cheese on several occasions and recommended staying with traditional pub food. Emsden and Kegel both ordered toad-in-the-hole and Chadwick ordered fish and chips.

When the waiter left, Emsden said, "I apologize on behalf of the government for any inconvenience."

Chadwick assured him there was no harm done and to forget the whole thing.

Kegel then launched his master stroke. "I must confess I had an ulterior motive in asking you to dine tonight, Mr. Chadwick. Quite frequently, I have young German students visiting England who are very interested in British history and the culture. It is my hope that by ensuring knowledge and trust between educated British and German young men and women that any war like the last one becomes inconceivable. I have some very old friends, British diplomats I knew before the war, who live quite close to Farnborough. The husband was Second Secretary at the Berlin embassy until 1914. His wife is fluent in German and sometime acts as host for the visiting students. I was hoping you would agree to being introduced to my friends and perhaps join them when they entertain some German visitors. You are much closer to their age than my friends."

Chadwick was extremely flattered to be considered on the same social status as British diplomats and had no difficulty in agreeing to Kegel's suggestion.

The waiter cleared away their plates and asked if anyone would care for a sweet. Nobody did. They asked for coffee and Kegel suggested a final Schnapps. When the drinks came, Kegel raised his glass in a toast. "To new friends."

After drinking their coffee and exchanging small talk, Kegel said he would call for a taxi. "We can drop you off at the station," he said to Chadwick.

Chadwick demurred. "In this fog it will be quicker for me to walk to Blackfriars and take the Tube to Waterloo."

Kegel paid the bill with a crisp five-pound note. "What's the best way to reach you, Mr. Chadwick, if a suitable cultural opportunity arises?"

"Just write to me care of the Officer's Mess, RAF Farnborough, Hampshire. Thank you very much for dinner, Dr. Kegel, and nice to meet you again, Ambassador Emsden, under more cheerful circumstances."

They struggled into their heavy coats and on the way out Chadwick glanced into the bar, and saw that Joyce was gone.

Chapter Ten

In early 1935, Allan Chadwick spent several weeks flying with a group developing a bombsight. His commanding officer felt that his bomber experience in Iraq could be of value to the team. However, when Chadwick explained to the team leader that the bombers in Iraq usually flew at one thousand feet or less, he was told they were designing for an altitude of ten to twenty thousand feet. When Chadwick asked for the accuracy they hoped to achieve with the bombing targets, he was skeptical when the figure of a five-hundred-foot diameter circle was mentioned. "That's an accuracy of about one and a half degrees," he pointed out in a dubious voice.

He frequently flew the team to a bombing range in Suffolk, where specially marked dummy bombs were unloaded at varying heights. He then landed at a nearby airfield and the team went by car to examine the target area. He usually drove with the team to the target area but withheld comment when the error was often over half a mile. The team tried to correlate errors with wind speed, atmospheric pressure, air speed, altitude, and any other factor they could think of.

He had almost forgotten about his part-time job with the accident investigation group when he found a message waiting for him at Farnborough. A Luft Hansa Ju 52 had gone down near Ipswich, killing all on board.

He was flown to the field closest to the crash, RAF Martlesham, where Squadron Leader Elliot had set up his headquarters. Elliot described the crash. "Went down in fairly open country. Was seen from the ground plunging earthwards trailing flames and smoke. The plane was en route to Croydon from Amsterdam, originating at Hamburg. Two pilots, ten passengers, the plane wasn't full. Tail section broke off at the crash and burned. The front part, including the wings, did not burn, but all the crew and passengers remains were found in the front half. A morgue has been set up here at the base. The coroner's pathologists are working on identifying all the bodies. When that's completed, I assume the coroner will release the bodies to their relatives.

"Luft Hansa is flying in tomorrow with the first relatives and an investigator from the company. They're also bringing the passenger manifest. Do you wish to visit the crash site before it gets too dark, while McBride and Stewart are still there?"

There were still a few hours with daylight. Chadwick told Elliot he would like to visit the crash and was soon talking to the two flight sergeants near the wreckage. He asked if they had any theory of what brought the plane down. They both shook their heads,

"Funny business," McBride offered. "Fire in the rear but no fuel was stored there. The front section didn't catch fire even though the wing tanks had fuel remaining in them. In fact, the port tank sprung a wee leak. You can still smell the petrol."

Chadwick went with the two NCOs into the wrecked cabin. He had brought along a pair of overalls for that eventuality. All the bodies had been removed, but the forward bulkhead was covered with blood and bits of flesh and clothing. The distinctive smell of death lingered. He made his way with difficulty into the remains of the cockpit. The Ju 52 had three engines, and the middle one had been forced into the cockpit by the impact, leaving most of the instrument panel shattered and unrecognizable. The engine ignition switches on the left were hanging by wires.

Chadwick picked up the panel. All the switches were in the off position. He brought it to Sergeant Stewart's attention. Stewart raised his eyebrows.

"Aye, that's a wee bit mysterious," the sergeant said.

"I wonder what the throttle and mixture controls were doing," Chadwick said.

"The control console was smashed to pieces, sirr," McBride answered. "No one will ever know."

Treading carefully. Chadwick led his little team back into the cabin. The seats were twisted and warped. Some had pieces of fleshy tissue caught on sharp corners. Bending down, Chadwick picked up the two halves of a leather strap. One had a buckle on the end. "See how many more straps you can find," he told the sergeants.

They pushed and grunted as they moved and bent tubular seat frames. Eventually, they found several intact belt halves and some pieces of broken leather straps.

Let's go see what's left in the tail," Chadwick announced, and the group walked across the black soil to the tail section, which was burned but not destroyed.

The group stepped inside the burnt shell of the plane tail section. The seat upholstery and part of lining of the cabin side had melted. The bare seat frames stood like park railings. Each still had the leather seat strap with a buckle on the end. The leather was charred but not destroyed. At the extreme rear was a jumbled pile of passenger baggage behind some netting. The cloth ones were badly burned, but the leather suitcases seemed intact.

"It's not as damaged as I thought it would be," Chadwick commented.

"There was no fuel here, sir," Stewart explained. "In fact, I'm nae so sure why it burrned. Possibly an electrical short circuit."

"The fuses should have blown and prevented any large-scale conflagration," countered McBride.

"Well, it's getting dark," said Chadwick. "Let's make our way back to the station and bring the squadron leader up to date."

Elliot greeted them in his temporary office. "What do you make of it, chaps?"

"It's a strange accident," Chadwick began. "Not clear why it crashed. The fire in the rear section was not much more than superficial. Curiously, the ignition switches were off. The pilot must have done that just before impact, perhaps to prevent a fire. The seat belts in the rear were not snapped and apparently were unbuckled. The passengers must have been in the forward part of the plane. That wouldn't account for the crash. The pilot could have compensated for the change in balance."

Then he had a thought, "Do you know I've flown on one of those things."

"What, in Iraq?" Elliot asked.

"No, in Berlin. They were giving tourist rides in a Ju 52. I just hopped on for fifteen minutes."

"By Jove, Chadwick, you've led an interesting life," Elliot said.

Both sergeants looked impressed.

"The Germans will be here tomorrow morning," Elliot told them. "I've arranged a meeting with the chief investigator and a Luft Hansa official at nine. We'll meet here."

In the morning they met with the two Germans, who both spoke English. The squadron leader offered his sincerest condolences for the families and for the company, and he introduced Chadwick and the sergeants. The German investigator introduced himself as Karl Spiegel, and the Luft Hansa official as Horst Hefner.

The investigator was a tall man of almost saturnine appearance; Hefner was a man of average height, balding. He glanced at Spiegel before opening his mouth. "I have the passenger manifest here and copies of the files on the pilots." He opened a briefcase. "I assume this data will be needed for the British accident report. Ten passengers left from Hamburg, and one joined the flight in Amsterdam."

Elliot held up his hand. "Wait a minute. That makes thirteen on board, including the two pilots. The coroner's office told me they had autopsied twelve bodies."

Spiegel spoke up. "Were the bodies badly mutilated?"

"I believe so," Elliot replied.

Spiegel pressed on. "Very often it is difficult to account for every piece, particularly in a severe crash that burned the passengers. I have seen many accidents that made it almost impossible to reconstruct all the victims."

Chadwick spoke up. "It's true the plane went down trailing smoke, but it broke into two major pieces on impact. The passenger bodies were all in the forward section that didn't burn."

"Curious," Spiegel mused. "Perhaps the Dutch authorities in Amsterdam have made a mistake about the lone passenger joining the flight."

"I have the names of all the passengers here," said Hefner, waving a piece of paper. "Have the pathologists identified each body?"

"I'm not sure," said Elliot. "I think most of the passengers had identification documents that weren't lost. For those we're uncertain about, I assume the relatives can recognize personal effects."

Spiegel turned to Hefner, saying, "This is your department. You sort it out." To Elliot he said, rather peremptorily, "Now I would like an escort to the crash site."

Squadron Leader Elliot said he would stay with Herr Hefner to sort out the administrative details of getting the bodies back to Germany or Holland, and to talk to the coroner about the missing person.

Flying Officer Chadwick and Flight Sergeants McBride and Stewart drove with Herr Spiegel to the crash site. A guard of

RAF airmen had been on duty all night. Chadwick spoke to the sergeant in charge and dismissed the guard until later in the day. The British team stayed back while Herr Spiegel poked through the wreckage. He carefully examined the wings and tail section. Chadwick told the German that the fuel in the wings had been removed for obvious safety reasons—and the RAF recovered eighty-five gallons, so lack of fuel was not a cause of the accident, though some fuel had leaked out before the rest was recovered.

When Spiegel seemed ready, Chadwick mentioned his concern over the seat belts, the fact that some in the forward part of the fuselage had apparently broken as the occupant was flung forward by the impetus of the impact. The belts in the rear were all intact, as far as could be ascertained. He also mentioned the fact that the ignition on all three engines had been turned off. Spiegel grunted but advanced no ideas on the cause of the accident.

A flight sergeant from Martlesham appeared and said he had been ordered to take photographs. Chadwick told him to work that out with Stewart and McBride. While the photographer was busy, Chadwick stood with Spiegel about twenty yards from the wreckage and quietly asked him if he had any notion of what had brought the plane down. Spiegel was reluctant to discuss any details and asked Chadwick to take him to the morgue, saying that sometimes the nature of the injuries can be a clue.

When they got to the morgue at Martlesham, the station doctor told them that some of the bodies had been transferred to the morgue in Ipswich, where it was more convenient for the pathologists to complete their report. While Spiegel examined the bodies remaining at the base, Chadwick found Squadron Leader Elliot and asked permission to take Spiegel to the coroner in Ipswich. Elliot suggested he also take Herr Hefner.

An airman drove them to Ipswich, where the coroner's office was in the same building as the morgue. Chadwick introduced Herren Spiegel and Hefner and said the German investigator wished to view the remains brought to Ipswich from the crash. The coroner raised no objections and phoned the pathologist at the morgue to warn him to expect a visitor. Chadwick and Hefner stayed in the coroner's office.

The coroner mentioned that a new body had been brought in by the police that morning. The corpse looked as if it had fallen off a cliff, but there were no cliffs in the area it was found. Chadwick asked where the body had been found and was interested when he was told the place was about five miles from the crash site. There was a local map on the wall of the office and Chadwick became more than interested when he noticed the body had been found on a direct line from the coast to the Luft Hansa crash site. He asked the coroner to speak to the pathologist to see if the new body carried identification.

Five minutes later there was a call back with a name. Herr Hefner rapidly checked it against the Luft Hansa passenger manifest. It tallied—the missing passenger had fallen or jumped from the Ju 52 before it crashed.

Herr Spiegel entered the office. "I was in the morgue when the pathologist sent you the name of the new corpse. Well?"

Hefner said, "The name is on the manifest, Herr Spiegel, he is, or was, a doctor, Max Stein. A German from Hanover."

Chadwick put a finger on the wall map. "This is where the body was found. I estimate he fell from the plane two to three minutes before the crash."

Spiegel's lips curled as he snarled, "The man panicked. He was a coward." In a German sotto voce he added, "*Er war Jude.*"

Chadwick said, "Foolish, rather than cowardly, jumping without a parachute. This whole accident is crazy. Nothing adds up."

Chadwick and the Germans drove back to the RAF station, and after lunch Chadwick sought out Squadron Leader Elliot. He described the events at the morgue and again expressed his feeling that something was wrong. He was interrupted by the jangling of the telephone on Elliot's desk.

"Excuse me. Yes, Squadron Leader Elliot here." He listened intently for a few minutes, and then suddenly exclaimed, "My God!" He put the phone down with a "thank you" and turned to Chadwick. "If you thought the accident was all wrong before, how about this—that was the coroner's office. The autopsy has revealed a 9mm bullet in the pilot's chest, obviously fresh but not immediately fatal."

"Where was the entry wound?" Chadwick asked.

"Didn't ask. Hold on." Elliot picked up the telephone and, after some delay, had a long conversation with the pathologist at the morgue. "The bullet entered his body through the back— he gave the rib number, if that means anything to you. The bullet lodged in a lung. He would have been coughing blood. He guesses the bullet was traveling on a slightly downward trajectory if the pilot was sitting straight up. The pathologist also mentioned that Doctor Stein was carrying a lot of money—one hundred and seventy-six pounds in notes, and ten shillings and five pence in change. Please bring the Germans to my office."

Chadwick came back with the two Germans and Elliot informed them of the message from the coroner's office. "That discovery complicates your investigation because the coroner has informed the local police, a move required under British law."

Chadwick escorted the Germans back to the officer's mess and then returned to Elliot's office. "With your permission, sir, I'd like to talk to the policeman now in charge of the case."

"All right, you have a car. Get the driver to take you to Ipswich and let me know if he has anything useful to add."

When Chadwick arrived at the police headquarters in Ipswich, he discovered no officer had been assigned. He asked to see the chief detective inspector, and on the way to his office, the smell in the building seemed familiar. He suddenly realized it reminded him of the Gestapo building in Berlin.

He introduced himself to the chief inspector and quickly described the role of the RAF in the investigation of the Luft Hansa crash. He mentioned the unusual facts of the case—a passenger who had apparently jumped to his death just before the crash, and the fact that the pilot was found to have a fresh bullet wound. The whole thing was mystifying.

The chief inspector, a very worldly-wise copper, opined human behavior was often mystifying and rarely straightforward.

Chadwick asked if there was an officer skilled in detecting arson, as he would like him to visit the crash site.

The chief said, "Ipswich is too small for that kind of expertise, but there's a very good man in that field attached to the Norwich police. I'm sure he could be borrowed for a day."

After several telephone calls, Chadwick arranged to meet the arson expert, Inspector Clark, at the RAF base in the morning. When he returned to Martlesham, he asked Spiegel and Hefner if they would like to re-visit the crash the following day. Both declined. Spiegel was preparing a report for the German Air Ministry and Hefner had to touch base with the German Embassy to arrange numerous administrative matters—transporting the bodies back to Europe, paying the undertakers, arranging for the wreckage to be scrapped, and a hundred minor details.

The next morning Chadwick met the police inspector at the entrance to the base. He was a small, bright button of a man with a large black, drooping mustache. As Stewart and McBride came out of the guardhouse, they caught sight of Inspector Clark.

"Nobby," cried McBride, and they enthusiastically shook hands.

"Obviously, you don't need an introduction," said Chadwick. "You've met before?"

"Och, aye, there are lots of airfields in East Anglia, and lots of crrashes. We've climbed over a few together when the RAF is careless enough to land on someone's house."

They drove to the crash site. As they approached the wreckage, Chadwick asked Inspector Clark to pay attention to the tail section, which lay alone several hundred yards from the main cabin and wings. They all donned overalls and rubber overshoes, as the ground where the tail had come to rest was marshy. Small rills and ponds dappled the soil.

Clark climbed in through the gaping cavern formed when the tail tore free from the rest of the fuselage. It was not pointing directly at the rest of the wreckage. As its motion slowed, the structure had spun round. Chadwick asked the NCOs to search the ground for loose objects that might have been ejected from the tail section, and then he joined Inspector Clark in the tail.

The inspector asked Chadwick to help him move some of the baggage behind the netting. When they could see the aluminum floor panels, he bent down and sniffed. "Plain as a pikestaff," he announced. "Arson without a doubt."

"How do you know?" asked Chadwick.

"Smell those bags near the floor."

Chadwick bent down. "There's a faint smell—aniseed, I think."

"Just so," cried Clark triumphantly. "An accelerant, diethyl ether, if I'm not mistaken. Look at the burn marks on the cabin side. That triangular shape, we call that 'Shark's fin.' The arsonist flung a stream of ether against the wall, where it burned fiercely."

"Let's go and see what the men have found."

They stepped out of the wreck and saw the NCOs roaming in the distance. When they noticed Chadwick and Clark standing outside the tail section, they returned, their shoes covered in mud.

"Guid farming country, this," said Stewart, who grew up on a farm. "Wonderful soil, though it would need draining."

McBride held something behind his back. "I know Nobby will love this," he said as he produced a large jar made of brown glass.

Inspector Clark held his nose over the mouth of the jar and inhaled delicately as if savoring a fine wine.

"Ah, yes, ether for sure. I don't think there's any point, but protocol requires that we check the jar for fingerprints. I'll take charge of it."

Chadwick said, "We have the name of a suspect, Doctor Max Stein. He fell from the plane and his body is in the morgue at Ipswich. Perhaps an attendant could get his prints from the corpse."

"Thanks for the tip, sir. I'll look into it," Stewart said. "I found a wee treasure, too." From under his rain cape, he produced a small brass hand-held fire extinguisher. It was empty.

"While we're here, I want to take a look again at the main cabin," Chadwick announced. "Would you like to come along, Inspector?"

They walked to the other wreck site and climbed into the tangled metal. "What are we looking for, sir?" asked McBride.

"I'm not sure, to be honest. The pilot was shot. Maybe more than one bullet was used. I want to look around the first pilot's seat, on the left side."

"It's a mess, sir. The middle engine came reet into the cockpit," Stewart reminded Chadwick.

They maneuvered around the shattered metal until Chadwick could stand immediately next to the pilot's seat. The engine had forced a panel that normally attached to the center console to break and fold over the space for the pilot's right leg. Chadwick couldn't explain his motive. He simply asked the three other men to try to push the engine remains back.

With a determined push, the ruined engine moved a little, freeing the panel. Chadwick lifted it up and saw that it was covered in dried blood. Stewart produced a torch. In the yellow beam, the blood traced out in shaky letters: "PISTC."

Chadwick said, "The pilot was coughing up blood. His last act was to write that with his finger." He asked one of the NCOs to recall the photographer to make a record of the bloody message. The men left the wreckage and Chadwick spoke to the sergeant in charge of guarding the site.

Chadwick bid farewell to Inspector Clark at the main gate of RAF Martlesham. The inspector turned to get into the police car he had left parked, and then turned back. "Tell me, Flying Officer Chadwick, why you were so keen to get to that panel in the cockpit?"

"Inspector, it sounds a little silly, but I just had a strong compulsion without knowing exactly why."

"Interesting. There's more to our existence here on earth than we know about. I have examined many fires. Some resulted in the death of a brave person trying to save someone else. Sometimes, if there is a question unanswered, the dead leave a compulsive aura if they have been under extreme stress. That pilot wanted you to see the panel. But don't tell the chief inspector I said so."

Chadwick went in search of Herr Hefner, who told him he was leaving on an afternoon train to London.

"Before you go, Herr Hefner, please answer two questions for me. First, when the passengers entered the plane at Hamburg, who handled their luggage? Secondly, what is the German word for gun?"

"On the flight in question, the passengers carried their own bag and placed it behind the netting before taking a seat," Hefner said. "You can look up German words in an English-German dictionary for more choices than I can give you. But the word '*kanon*' comes to my mind, also 'gewehr,' '*pistole*,' '*revolver*' — many words are the same as English."

"Many thanks, Herr Hefner. Have a pleasant trip to London."

Chadwick saw Squadron Leader Elliot in the mess and told him they were just about done with the investigation. Elliot said he would lay on a flight back to Farnborough later. On arrival at Farnborough, Elliot said there would be a meeting in the morning to agree on the bones of the report they had to deliver.

Squadron Leader Codrington dropped into the morning meeting, along with the two NCOs. Squadron Leader Elliot kicked off the meeting. "We have to prepare a report summarizing our conclusions about the crash of a Luft Hansa Ju 52 near Ipswich, and we have to tread carefully. The German Air Ministry is involved and there appears to have been some criminal activity which has come to the attention of the British police. Our responsibility is to stick to the aeronautical facts which I can summarize."

Codrington listed the time, date, trip number and location and weather at the time of the crash. "There was criminal activity in the plane, which resulted in a fire in the rear section, and the first pilot being shot with a wound that was not immediately fatal. There is no reason to think there was engine failure or a structural problem. At the time of impact, the ignition switches for all three engines were in the off position. Just before the crash a passenger fell from the aircraft to his death. As all the witnesses to the events in the air are dead, a cause for the crash cannot be determined. That is our official position."

Chadwick spoke up. "Squadron Leader Elliot has stated the official verdict of our investigation. No lawyer can dispute it. However, I'd like to propose a fairy tale which conforms to the facts, but which can't be proved. When Dr. Stein boarded the plane, he had a plan. Maybe the police in Germany will find the motive for his plan. He carried a large suitcase containing a parachute, a gun, and a jar of ether. He placed it behind the netting at the rear so it could be easily reached. When the flight crossed the English coast, Dr. Stein opened the suitcase, pocketed the gun, splashed ether over the cabin sides and the baggage, attempted to strap on the 'chute and set fire to the ether.

"Either the passengers grabbed him, or he panicked, and in the melee, he shot the pilot and jumped or was thrown through the door. He wasn't strapped to the 'chute properly and fell out of the harness. One motive may be that he was hoping to 'disappear,' and it would be assumed he was one of the dead when the crash was investigated. Skeptics may discount the idea of him having a parachute, but then no man except a lunatic would set fire to a plane while he was still in it, unless he had a way of leaving. The pilot wrote 'PISTC' in his own blood on a panel next to his seat. I believe he was trying to write 'PISTOL' but was killed by the crash before he finished. Probably the second pilot was fighting the fire and did not realize the first pilot was badly wounded, so he did not return to the cockpit. All the passengers were in the front, some seated. When the plane crashed, the momentum caused the bodies to hurtle forward, breaking the seat belts.

"Ether would be relatively easy for a doctor to obtain, but the police have not been able to get fingerprints from the container we found. If a search was started near the spot were Dr. Stein fell to earth, we might find an unopened parachute, perhaps also an empty suitcase and a gun. The German police may discover a reason why Dr. Stein wanted to 'disappear.' It's a mystery worthy of Sherlock Holmes."

There was a long silence after Chadwick spoke. Finally, Squadron Leader Elliot said, "You have a vivid imagination, Chadwick, but I think you'll agree the official position is the one I outlined."

Chapter Eleven

Chadwick returned to the routine of flying for the bombsight development group. The results continued to be disappointing. The civilian in charge of the team, Dr. Thorpe, was a career civil servant who had spent years since the war refining artillery ballistic tables. He had little sense of humor, disliked amateur scientists, and treated Flying Officer Chadwick as simply an aeroplane driver. He rarely took part in the flight trial, confining himself to statistical analysis.

One day, discussing problems with Squadron Leader Codrington, Thorpe learned that Chadwick had made worthwhile improvements to bombing accuracy in Iraq. He also found out that Chadwick had an engineering degree from Cranwell, which greatly improved his estimation of the team pilot. Drinking tea in the group office after a day of bombing trials, Thorpe made an attempt to mend fences with Chadwick.

"I know you've been a little skeptical of our bombsight so far, Chadwick, but I appreciate the fact that you've had actual experience in Iraq. Would you like to give a talk to the group about some of the things on your mind?"

Chadwick was surprised. "Well, of course, I'll be happy to put a talk together, but it will take me a few days to prepare."

"Jolly good. Next week, perhaps, when the weather precludes flying?"

A few days later, Chadwick stepped into the squadron office to check the day's flying schedule and was greeted by the sergeant in charge. "Good morning, Flight Lieutenant Chadwick."

"Flight Looie?"

"The Air Ministry has just promulgated the latest promotion list, and you're on it, sir. Congratulations." He handed Chadwick a few feet of braid. "Your batman can probably manage to sew these extra stripes on your uniforms."

"Thank you, sergeant. It's a bit of a shock. Now I'll have to start behaving responsibly."

Dr. Thorpe asked Chadwick to give a talk to the whole group one day when the weather was atrocious. They gathered in a conference room with the wind howling outside and rain battering the casements. Chadwick started in a contrite manner. "I'm sure I'm not going to bring up anything that will be a surprise to you fellows who've been working on the problem of aerial bombardment for years. But I do have the experience of bombing in the field, and sometimes I think the practical realities of life on the frontline tend to overwhelm the subtleties of carefully developed, complicated equipment.

"I'll divide the problem bit by bit so it is clearly defined. To start with, bombing can have strategic or tactical aims, according to Air Publications on the subject. Strategic engagement intends to take an enemy out of the fight by denying supplies, destroying manufacturing ability or by breaking morale. Tactical bombing aims to win an immediate battlefield situation. By looking at our trials from ten to twenty thousand feet, I assume we're furthering strategic bombing. The planners of this type of bombing must have a specific goal, which affects the type of plane, the size of the attacking force, the type of bomb, and the expected outcome. For example, if the destruction of a target is not achieved then they'll plan more raids, with concomitantly more aircrew losses. Thus, the probability of a given raid to inflict the expected damage must be known accurately. The analysis of our bombing trials may yield this probability. As I'll emphasize later, there are many factors that affect probability *not* covered in our tests."

A flurry of hands went up and Chadwick dealt with a few questions, including why he thought a few years in Iraq was equal to the combined brain power of the experts in the room. Even Dr. Thorpe smiled when that question arose.

Chadwick conceded the validity of the argument but plowed on. "I will further subdivide, so far as I can tell we are investigating the errors inherent in using the new bombsight. The mechanism attempts to calculate the factors which will affect the trajectory of a bomb once it leaves the aircraft. Mathematical analysis has been covered in many books, using a standard atmosphere in which the air density and pressure vary in a known way with height. Real atmospheres deviate from the model, causing errors, which we're nailing down. Despite what we learned in school about Galileo dropping weights from the Leaning Tower of Pisa, bombs drop at different speeds, depending on their design. Galileo's theory is only true in a vacuum. Real objects are affected by air resistance, again modeled with assumptions prone to error in the mechanics of the bombsight. So far as I can see, the errors just mentioned by me will lead to a five hundred feet circle bombing from twenty thousand feet, accumulating solely due to the combined tolerances of the bombsight calculation."

Somebody shouted, "So we're doing fine."

"Not really," Chadwick answered. "We're rather like the Captain of the Titanic, worried about the ashtrays being full in the first-class lounge when there is a huge iceberg directly on the bow. Sources of much larger errors are looming, which make five hundred feet irrelevant. We can further subdivide those—navigation, weather, enemy action."

Chadwick glanced through the window where rain beat steadily on the panes. "Considering what it's like outside, perhaps I'll start with the weather." There was a ripple of laughter from the listeners.

"That is, the weather over the target, probably several hundred miles from home, thus difficult to predict. Weather often obscures visibility, clouds, fog, mist, rain. Snow may cover the target. Ice may hide important landmarks, such as rivers and shorelines. With visual bombing what you can't see you certainly can't hit.

"The navigator has several vital duties to ensure the bombs are on target. First, he must get the bomber close enough to the target that the bombardier has the target in the bombsight. The field of view in the sight is limited, so that with magnification the bombardier can make out the target. For example, say the field of view from twenty thousand feet is ten miles wide. The bombardier must identify the target ahead and maneuver the aircraft in time to get the crosshairs over the aiming point before the bomber has overflown the target. Most navigators would have difficulty putting a bomber inside a ten-mile-wide square after a trip of several hundred miles with indifferent weather and lack of landmarks.

"Secondly, the bombardier needs an accurate figure for the wind at altitude. The value is cranked into the bombsight for two reasons. One, the bomb leaves the aircraft at the speed and direction of the bomber. If the plane is crabbing sideways due to crosswind, so is the bomb. This is compensated for in the bombsight calculation, but the value fed in must be accurate, or it is another source of random errors. Two, the wind affects the bomb during its descent. This is an average wind, again, provided by the navigator. Chalk up another source of random errors.

"Finally, and perhaps the most disturbing, is the fact that the enemy is not going to sit quietly while you drop bombs on him. You can expect fighters and anti-aircraft gunfire. The pilot will swerve and jink the plane to avoid these dangers. That compromises accuracy, but a plane shot down achieves nothing. In Iraq, my commanding officer, a man I greatly admired, was shot down by machine gun fire from the ground while on a bombing run.

"To put it in a nutshell, in my opinion what we're doing here is providing the planners with the accuracy that might be expected under the most favorable conditions. The probability of achieving that accuracy under real life conditions is close to zero."

There was a shocked silence from the audience with Chadwick's closing words. Then the hands shot up. Chadwick pointed to one man. "Yes?"

"What can be done to improve accuracy?"

"I assume other scientists, engineers, and pilots are working on this problem, probably in several countries. Radio waves are unaffected by weather and can be directional. Maybe a system employing them can be devised to define a target."

Several members of the audience started to argue, and finally Dr. Thorpe brought the meeting to a close. "I'd like to thank Flying Officer Chadwick for a stimulating discussion. I also applaud the wisdom of the RAF in putting an experienced pilot in our group."

Chadwick said, "Thank you! And, by the way," he added with a grin, "I've just been promoted to Flight Lieutenant."

Chapter Twelve

At Abwehr Headquarters in Hamburg, the head of the British section, Conrad Nordemann, studied a request from Kegel in London asking for a temporary assignment of two agents, for perhaps as long as six months. The agents, one male and one female, were to pass as German students in their early to mid-twenties. Good English was essential, but it was not necessary to be completely fluent.

Nordemann reached for the files of agents nearing the end of the one-year Abwehr training cycle. He rationalized that a few months in England would be a good experience for an agent by exposing them to everyday English living. If they ever had to go undercover at a later stage, familiarity with normal English habits may save them from making a tell-tale slip, such as eating with the fork in the right hand.

He selected a photograph and studied the face of Gerd Stiller, a young man being trained primarily for work in Britain. Prior to joining the Abwehr, Stiller had attended courses in English and history at the University of Munich, without completing a degree. He had labored on the construction of the autobahn in the Organization Todt and joined the Nazi party.

Nordemann asked his secretary for Stiller's current assignment, and within minutes she told him he was in Dresden, completing a one-week posting to SD headquarters. He was there to study interrogation techniques.

"Have him report to me when he returns," Nordemann told her.

Two days later the secretary knocked on Nordemann's door, entered, and introduced Herr Stiller.

"Sit down, Stiller. I have a request from the London station for the temporary transfer of a young man to pose as a student visiting Britain. The assigned will gain the friendship of a man we feel holds information that could be useful to the Fatherland. Does that sound interesting? Perhaps the training you just received in Dresden would be useful?"

"I will be happy to serve in any capacity for which you think I am qualified. Most of the methods explained to me by the SD would not be applicable."

Nordemann laughed, "I didn't think so. Too fond of violence, were they?"

"Actually no, sir. They didn't trust violent methods to obtain information except in the most specific circumstances. In actual combat under battlefield conditions, violence may be necessary to get an immediate answer—for example, finding out from prisoners the location of the nearby enemy."

"How so?"

"If more than one prisoner is captured, question them together. One may be induced to talk by the sharp application of a rifle butt to the knee-cap. If that doesn't work, shoot him. The next prisoner is almost certain to cooperate."

"And in non-battlefield situations?"

"Most people talk when subjected to pain, but the information is often not reliable. With training, an interrogator can extract much more reliable, truthful information using psychological techniques, but it may take time. Sometimes two interrogators work best, one hostile and one apparently friendly. We had daily lectures from psychologists and working policemen. One subject that will be useful to me as an agent is how to detect if a person is lying. However, we had some amusement with that."

"How so?"

"They introduced the students to an American card game called poker. In order to win it's necessary to lie or bluff. But there must be a serious payoff to make the game work. We were each given a thousand marks and told we could keep anything we won."

"And?"

"We all lost the money. Those fellows were experts. I was up five hundred marks at one stage but finally lost everything."

"Well, training is over. For the next few days, you will be briefed on the persona you are going to adopt, and we will prepare the appropriate paperwork. Ask my secretary to take you to operations. Thank you, Herr Stiller, and good luck. And by the way, the intent of sending you to Dresden was to prepare you for the day you may face an interrogator, so that you know a few of their tricks."

Nordemann turned his attention to the second request from London—a female agent, fairly young. There had been a long debate in the higher levels of the Abwehr about whether it was necessary to train women in the arts of being a secret agent. In the end it was decided to train a few to function as communications experts in the field.

He picked up the files of the only two graduates not currently assigned. One was a dowdy-looking woman in her early thirties. Not the student type he decided. He opened the other file. This one looked more promising. The picture of a plain young woman fell out of the file, and it triggered his memory. She had been strongly recommended for admission to the training course by a prominent Nazi, the Gauleiter of Schleswig-Holstein.

Fraulein Inge Fischer had the fair hair and Nordic look so beloved by the Nazis. Nordemann strongly suspected a romantic liaison had developed between the Gauleiter and Fraulein Fischer, which had become a liability and prompted the politician to put her out of circulation by enrolling her in the Abwehr course for a lengthy period. He asked his secretary to call her to his office.

When she was comfortably seated, they exchanged a few pleasantries and then Nordemann said, "Miss Fischer, I am assigning you to a mission in London for a few months. You will oversee all mission communications between Abwehr HQ and London. You will also be a part of the mission. The head of the London station has asked for a young woman who can play the role of a German student visiting England. The mission is code-named Amalgam. The other agent you will be working with is code-named Bronze. You will meet him tomorrow. Your code is Pewter, and the head of the London Station is Silver. The code name for the target is Nickel. Only code names shall be used in all secret communications.

"You may also write to your 'mother,' whom we shall create at an address in Lubeck. Letters should be typically innocuous of a girl visiting abroad, using the four-letter code system. I believe you have practiced this method? The four letters form the first letters of selected sentences and have an associated message, which can be quite long."

"Yes, Herr Nordemann. I've spent many hours mastering this system. I know most of the four-letter messages by heart."

"I am not quite sure where the mission will go. We have as a target a young Englishman who gains information in the course of his work that would be on interest to this country. It is possible you may be in a position to seduce him, although that is not why we train female agents. Famous spies, like Mata Hari, happened by chance and most of the stories one reads are concocted by the authors of those Penny Dreadfuls. But there is a possibility of an intimate relationship and I want you to spend some time with a lady who is familiar with the dangers—the Madam of a very exclusive house here in Hamburg. She has some practical advice on avoiding pregnancy and venereal diseases, either of which diminishes your usefulness to the Party."

His last remark was an attempt at gallows humor, but it fell completely flat.

The next day Nordemann had a meeting with Gerd Stiller and Inge Fischer to brief them on the Amalgam mission and give them papers confirming the identities they would adopt for the mission. Each got a new passport. Stiller was traveling as Olaf Runge. He was already signed up to attend lectures at the British Museum. Fischer was assigned the pseudonym Julia Fassbender. She was signed up as a student at a secretarial school. Her cover was that she was planning to become a translator.

Stiller would be staying at a boarding house in Lambeth. It was a German front, although operating openly. Only boarders sent by the Abwehr were accepted by the landlady, Doris Blackwood, who was born in London of German parents at the turn of the century. She maintained a surreptitious link with Dr. Kegel. Miss Fischer was staying in a hostel for women. They would travel separately, and first contact would be made by Dr. Kegel via the boarding house landlady.

Nordemann answered their questions and then dismissed Stiller and asked Miss Fischer to stay for a minute. "I've arranged for you to meet Madam Lisette tonight. She is aware of my position here. Our usual practice is to have her give a frank mother-to-daughter talk to young ladies like yourself going into the field for the first time."

A taxi dropped off Miss Fischer at a magnificent dwelling hidden behind trees about two miles from the center of Hamburg. A woman dressed in a full-length evening gown with an ample décolleté greeted her in the entrance hall. She looked at Fischer curiously—Fischer was wearing a sweater and a nondescript pleated skirt.

Madam Lisette was expecting her. Fischer was escorted up a wide staircase, and as she ascended, she caught a glimpse of an opulent reception room crowded with well-dressed men and women. Inside the madam's office, the thick door shut off the noise from downstairs. The room was quite dark, illuminated by a solitary lamp on an ornate French desk. A woman in a cream-colored suit rose to meet her. She was slightly on the plump side; her brown hair was cut short.

"Good evening, my dear. I am Lisette. And you are?"

"Inge Fischer."

"Herr Nordemann told me you are about to embark on your first mission for the Abwehr. To which country are you traveling?"

"I am leaving for England in a few days."

"That doesn't sound too bad. The English are relatively civilized. Not that they won't hesitate to hang you if you're caught. Are you scared?"

"A little. My duty consists mainly of maintaining communication with headquarters."

"Oh, really. Is that what Herr Nordemann told you?"

"Well, I understand we are tracking some Englishman with a sensitive job. He has information that could be useful to us. Herr Nordemann mentioned that there is a small chance I might meet him and there is a slight possibility he might try to seduce me."

A wintry smile crossed Lisette's face. "And that is why you are here?"

"Yes."

"Well, my dear, in my experience of your situation, the 'small possibility' is quite a large one. A woman in your position is in no man's land. Men on both sides will regard you as fair game. If you are caught, the guards will abuse you, which is true of any country. I take it you are familiar with the sins of the flesh?"

"If you mean to ask if I am a virgin, I should mention that I was the mistress of a damned politician who dumped me a year ago. He committed quite a few sins of the flesh."

"Good, then we can deal with practicalities. In this place the always-present threats of pregnancy and disease pose economic risk. The workers here are highly trained, and a loss is hard to fill. One of our clients, when he is not screwing his brains out, is a highly regarded medical research scientist He has concocted an ointment which is applied internally by an applicator and kills small live things like sperm and nasty germs. It is also a good lubricant. I will give you a supply. Are you familiar with condoms? They are effective but most men will not use them. You might be able to slip one on, but it is a bit like trying to put a collar on a puppy."

Fischer laughed. "You certainly see the seamy side of life here."

"Actually, it's not too bad. The women who work for me, and a few men, lead a more comfortable, a safer life—if they are careful—than thousands of workers in factories, mines, sweatshops, and farms."

"You're tempting me. Maybe I should apply for the training."

Lisette looked at her contemplatively. "Undress for me."

Inge slipped off her outer clothes.

"Take the rest off." There was a pause. "You're nicely put together, Inge. Do you know women make the best lovers?"

"I've heard it said. Do you want to show me?"

Chapter Thirteen

The arrival of two agents in London caused a flurry of activity for Dr. Kegel. First, he telephoned Honoria Pomeroy. "Good morning, Honoria, Gerhard Kegel here. *Wie gehts?*" Without waiting for a reply, he pressed on, "You may recall our conversation about providing some British culture to visiting German students. Well, two students have recently checked into my office. One of them is taking courses at the British Museum. I wonder if I could be bold enough to ask you to invite them to your place in the country to meet a few Britishers one evening? Normally I would arrange a tour to a historic site, but the weather is problematical this time of the year."

"Oh, yes, Gerhard, I remember. I don't see why not. Let me talk to Tom. I'll call you back."

Later, when her husband returned home from work, she mentioned Kegel's call. He was a little put out. "Bit of a damned nuisance. Gerhard is sticking us with doing his work for him. Still, Gerhard is an old friend. You know, I invited a few chaps from the Foreign Office for drinks and munchies next Saturday. How about inviting them to that shindig?"

"Well, I'm not so sure. Would it be a little undiplomatic to talk shop with a couple of Germans?"

"Nothing serious is going to be discussed. There's been some concern that the Germans are violating the terms of the Peace Treaty by expanding the army, but the general feeling is to let it ride, no point in kicking up a fuss. These chaps are not anti-German and may even find it interesting to meet a contemporary German citizen."

Mrs. Pomeroy called Kegel the next day and finalized the rendezvous. He said he would drive them out to the Pomeroy residence, which was not far from Farnborough. Then he said, "I recently met a fine young Englishman who is an officer stationed at Farnborough. Would it be too much to ask him along as well? I'll do all the driving."

"Of course, if he's your friend, ask him along."

Next, Kegel wrote a letter to Allan Chadwick—

Dear Flying Officer Chadwick,

I still recall with pleasure the dinner I enjoyed with you and Ambassador Emsden at the Cheshire Cheese. You may remember I mentioned the possibility of strengthening cultural ties by meeting visiting German students? Two students are currently staying in London, Olaf Runge and Julia Fassbender. Olaf is attending lectures at the British Museum and Julia is studying to be a translator. The students and I have been invited to a soiree at the house of my friends Honoria and Tom Pomeroy, a week from Saturday. They live in Birchwood, just a few miles from Farnborough. I have Mrs. Pomeroy's permission to invite you if you would like to attend. I knew the Pomeroys before the war when Tom was Second Secretary at the British Embassy in Berlin. I can arrange to pick you up at the officer's mess. Please give me a call at the telephone number above.

Yours Sincerely,
Dr. Gerhard Kegel
Cultural Attaché

The letter was typed by Kegel's secretary on the letterhead of the "Embassy of the German Reich, Cultural Affairs." The telephone number was a direct line, not going through the switchboard. Kegel surmised, correctly, that Chadwick would be impressed by social ranking. It still remained to brief the two agents.

Kegel set up a meeting via the boarding house landlady, Miss Blackwood, at an inconspicuous tea shop. The three Germans sat at a corner table and conversed in low voices, speaking

English. Kegel confessed from this point on they would play it by ear. Chadwick's reaction to the meeting was an unknown quantity. He briefed Stiller and Fischer on the way Chadwick first fell into the attention of the Abwehr.

Stiller was surprised when he heard that Chadwick had been questioned by the Gestapo. "He is going to hate everybody German. Those gentlemen are rough customers," he said, thinking of his briefings in Dresden.

Kegel said, "He wasn't harmed in any way and was released within hours. His arrest was a small mistake due to an over-zealous official at the airport. A very high-ranking officer has apologized to him for the incident. I don't think he holds any animosity."

They went on to discuss how the two agents should play their cards. Kegel suggested setting up a meeting in London some evening with either one or both of them, depending on Chadwick's desire. He mentioned it was fairly easy for Chadwick to get into London by train in less than an hour.

He then described his friendship with the Pomeroys. "I have known them for many years. They are sympathetic to Germany's problems and would probably be in favor of any diplomatic way to avoid a future war. Under no circumstances must you promote German ambitions or brag about progress under Herr Hitler. You are just simple students, with little knowledge of world affairs."

Kegel promised to tell them when Chadwick confirmed the invitation to the Pomeroy house. Using code names, Inge Fischer sent a message of Amalgam's progress to the Abwehr in Hamburg via the diplomatic bag.

Flight Lieutenant Chadwick telephoned Dr. Kegel to discuss the invitation to the Pomeroy party. "They'll serve sherry, cock-tails about half past five," Kegel told Chadwick. "Suppose I pick you up at the officer's mess about five? Will I need a pass from you to enter the station?"

Chadwick was still a little doubtful. "I'm not sure I'll fit in. The Pomeroys sound a bit out of my league."

"You'll enjoy it," Kegel reassured him. "The students are young and eager to have some fun while learning about England."

"All right then, five o'clock on Saturday. You don't need a pass, just follow the signs to the officer's mess."

The next morning, on the way to a meeting of the bomb-sight group, Chadwick ran into Squadron Leader Elliot. "By the way, Chadwick, I had a message from the Norfolk police. The German criminal police, the Kripo, had been in touch. Dr. Stein was under suspicion of selling drugs. He would have been arrested if he had stayed in Germany, so he fled just in time. They also discovered he had purchased a parachute which has never been found. Maybe your fairy tale was close to the truth!

"We in Accidents Investigation have been quite busy," he continued. "The RAF is averaging a crash a week at the moment. I don't know why the rate has suddenly increased. Perhaps it's the weather. The investigations have mostly been straightforward. Stewart and McBride are on top of things, so I haven't bothered to include you. Squadron Leader Codrington tells me you're having some positive influence on the bomb-sight people."

"Thank you, Squadron Leader. I'm just off to a meeting with the group now, and the weather looks fair for a few more trials."

Dr. Thorpe addressed the group. "In order to remove some randomness from the observations, I'm going to suggest we drop four bombs in a quick sequence so that atmospheric conditions do not change, and we use the same navigational landmarks. We'll drop four unarmed practice bombs, two hundred and fifty pounds, from ten thousand feet, always heading into wind. Naturally, Allan, I know you'll try to repeat airspeed and height as closely as possible for each run. Do you have any other suggestions to hold the initial conditions for each drop constant?"

"I've been giving the problem a lot of thought. Your suggestions make sense. There's one other thing—air turbulence increases dramatically when the bomb bay doors are opened. Maybe the bombs aren't tightly held by the release mechanism and tend to wobble immediately before release. At the moment they leave, they may possess an angular error with respect to the aircraft heading."

"Good point, Allan. How can we deal with that?"

"I'll speak to the chief rigger this afternoon and ask him to make sure the bomb release clamps are as tight as possible. Also, we can open the hatch over the bomb bay and watch as the bombs are released. It's going to be a bit chilly."

"Sounds like a good plan. Tomorrow we'll fly with you as captain, Dick Jewel as bombardier, Frank Nesbit as navigator, and I will fly as observer."

All the personnel except Chadwick were civilians, but all except Dr. Thorpe had served previously as RAF aircrew. After a hearty breakfast in the mess, Chadwick joined the group at the airfield. It was a sunny day with a temperature in the fifties, Fahrenheit, at ground level. The wind over the range in Suffolk was forecast to be northerly, twenty knots. It took them an hour to reach the bombing range. They crossed over the northern outskirts of London, which were shrouded in a smoky smog.

Nesbit set up an initial navigational landmark for the run to the target. It allowed the bombardier about two minutes to focus on the crosshairs. Each time the 250-pound bombs left the plane, they felt a small jump in height. Three runs passed quickly. Dr. Thorpe, peering through the access hatch, shouted that he saw no signs of excessive vibration in the bomb racks before release. The air at ten thousand feet was cold. Everyone was shivering despite thick flying suits, and praying to get the last run over with.

Chadwick swung the plane onto the northerly heading and Nesbit shouted to Jewel to start the timed run to the target. After two minutes Jewel cried out, "Bomb gone." Instead of the usual vertical lift there was a loud, jarring crash and the plane dove steeply. Dr. Thorpe was flung forward and came to rest on the floor next to Chadwick.

"What happened?" the pilot shouted.

Thorpe replied, "The rear clamp did not release immediately, and the bomb pivoted backward. Then it tore loose and hit the tail, I think."

"Christ!" Chadwick struggled to get the plane level by throttling back and trimming the elevators. The rate of descent was about a thousand feet per minute. He tried every trick he knew to reduce the rate of descent—flaps, engine speed, and trim. Nothing worked. Jewel and Nesbit climbed into the cockpit.

"Get your 'chutes buckled on. We're going to have to jump."

Chadwick knew he couldn't bail out. In an uncontrollable dive, the plane tended strongly to bank left and only remained level with a hefty sideways pressure on the stick. He knew he couldn't leave the cockpit for the exit door without being pinned by centrifugal force. The three crew jettisoned the door.

"Go," shouted Chadwick at the top of his voice and the three men pushed themselves into space, one after the other. Chadwick eased the stick. As the plane turned, he saw three parachutes blossom, then he leveled the turn and started to look ahead for a good crash-landing site. Suffolk is fairly flat, and the area ahead was devoid of trees and houses. He turned off the fuel valves, switched off the ignition on both engines, and pulled his shoulder straps tight with one hand. The ground was coming fast. The stick was already hauled back into his stomach, but with a last spasm of adrenaline-fueled strength, he pulled it a few inches more and the nose lifted, converting speed into height. The plane skimmed over the ground for a few hundred yards and then hit. The nose section broke off immediately on impact and Chadwick, still strapped to the seat, was thrown clear. The seat burrowed into the soft earth and the left wing flew over him, missing him by inches as the plane disintegrated. A thought flashed through Chadwick's mind— *Another job for Stewart and McBride*—and then the world went black.

Chadwick awoke three hours later in the sick bay of RAF Mildenhall. A doctor was peering into one eye with a light. The ground crew had been standing by at RAF Mildenhall to drive the team back to the range to tabulate the results. They quickly scooped up Chadwick and the rest of the team after the crash. After rushing Chadwick to the sick bay, Dr. Thorpe insisted on being driven to the bombing range to check on the accuracy of the run they had nearly completed. When they were told that Chadwick suffered only from a mild concussion, they returned to Farnborough on a plane which was sent for them.

The doctor at Mildenhall insisted that Chadwick get plenty of sleep, told him he had been very lucky, and instructed he should stay the night. A plane picked up Chadwick and took him back to Farnborough by mid-morning the next day. There, another doctor examined him, told him he been lucky and said he should sleep it off for the day.

Chadwick stopped at Squadron Leader Codrington's office on the way to the mess. Squadron Leader Elliot and Flight Sergeants Stewart and McBride were waiting for him.

"Good morning," said Chadwick and saluted.

"Good morning, Flight Lieutenant Chadwick. Sounds like you've been very lucky."

Stewart piped up, "Och, sir, I dinna ken why ye had to crrrash a kite just to keep us busy."

Everybody laughed, but Chadwick was getting a little tired of people telling him he was "lucky."

He ate lunch at the mess and settled into an easy chair with the newspaper. He noticed the heading, "Friday." Suddenly the light dawned. Tomorrow was Saturday. *Christ*, he thought, *the Germans are coming for me. Oh, what the hell, a few drinks and a bit of company will probably do me good.*

Chapter Fourteen

Inge Fischer sat in the back seat of an elegant Rover automobile. Her stomach churned. Dr. Kegel sat in front with Gerd Stiller They were heading for a rendezvous with Allan Chadwick. She was finally on a mission, and she was scared stiff.

The days she had spent in London had passed pleasantly, almost as if she were on a vacation, but now she would soon enter the lion's den. She would meet the enemy. Madam Lisette's words echoed in her mind—*They won't hesitate to hang you if you are caught.* The year of training, and the events at Abwehr Headquarters in Hamburg, seemed like a game, so long ago. Now the stark reality hit, and she felt sick.

Dr. Kegel said, "This looks like the place. Chadwick was right—there is no entrance gate. Smarten up and keep your wits about you. Wait in the car. I'll look for our subject."

Kegel soon reappeared with Allan Chadwick. "Climb in the back, Allan, next to Julia. And this is Olaf."

Chadwick nodded to both. "How do you do."

Kegel sat behind the wheel and twisted round. "How can you have an RAF base without the guardhouse?"

"Well, this is joint RAF and civilian. There are different government branches here. Many organizations come to do experiments on the wind tunnel, for example. And we have an investigation team looking at all aviation accidents in Britain."

Kegel started the engine and drove off, thinking furiously, *We don't need Chadwick. This place is wide open, just a simple burglary.* Within a short time he pulled up to the Pomeroy residence, a sturdy brick house built at the turn of the century for an affluent family. Originally the house had accommodation for three servants, but now that lifestyle was beyond the reach of even upper middle-class people. Mrs. Pomeroy had help cooking and cleaning by women who came up from the village for the day.

Several cars were parked in the circular driveway. Kegel led the way in and introduced Chadwick, Stiller, and Fischer—alias Runge and Fassbender—to Mrs. Pomeroy as they hung up their coats in a small cloakroom off the entrance hall. Inside, two fires were burning cheerfully at either end of a large room. A dozen men and women sat or stood near the fires.

Mrs. Pomeroy took the Germans to her husband and introduced them. He started to talk to the two would-be students and Mrs. Pomeroy led Chadwick away and introduced him to a tall, slim young woman. She looked as fresh as a daisy in a floral frock, especially when compared to the somber clothing of the other women in the room.

"This is my daughter Penelope. Penny, this is Allan. He's in the RAF, stationed just down the road."

Penny looked at him and asked, "Do you fly?"

"As a matter of fact, I do." Allan forbore to mention that two days earlier he had been lucky to get way with his life in the crash of a bomber near Mildenhall.

"How exciting! I would love to fly. It must be better than driving fast."

"Well, it's different. You really have no sensation of speed unless you're close to the ground."

"I love to drive, but my parent's car is such a pokey old thing. I bet you drive a Jaguar."

"Actually, I don't have a car, but I'm seriously thinking of getting one. I just got a little promotion, and I might be able to manage it."

"I'll help you get one. You need a car to get a car. Mummy lets me borrow their old wreck during the day. Of course, when Daddy's home he needs it."

Chadwick was surprised at her enthusiastic offer, but on a moment's reflection he thought it made a lot of sense. "Maybe one afternoon we could work something out. Do you work during the day?"

"Oh, no. Fancy free, that's me. Here, let me give you our telephone number."

Chadwick jotted it down on the back of one of his visiting cards, and he gave Penelope another card. She waltzed off, shouting to him, "It's a date. That's what Americans say!"

Chadwick moved to join Tom Pomeroy. Gerd Stiller, as Runge, was telling him that he was studying history with hopes of becoming a teacher. Tom called over to a friend standing near a fireplace. "Freddy, I want you to meet someone who wants to be a history teacher. This is—what was it?"

"Olaf Runge, sir"

"Olaf Runge, visiting from Germany He's taking in lectures at the British Museum."

Chadwick could see that Freddy was a portly figure in his forties.

"Any particular period of English history you're interested in?"

"No, sir," the young German replied. "I'm not familiar with it well enough to pick a period."

Then Tom Pomeroy said, "My goodness, we shouldn't stand here stone cold sober." Putting his arms out he guided Stiller and Fischer to a table in the center of the room loaded with bottles of spirits and beer. "Help yourself. The servants are taking a night off." The slurred remark showed that Tom had clearly been following his own advice.

Freddy had followed them to the table. "I might suggest —"

Tom Pomeroy interrupted, "Do listen to Freddy. His family has been cozying to kings and dodging beheadings for centuries. Miracle most of 'em lived long enough to propagate."

Freddy was unperturbed. "As I was saying, you might consider the Tudors. England really became a world power—or should I say European power—in that time, and it is fairly well documented. Go to the National Portrait Gallery and see what they all looked like."

Turning to Fischer, he said, "And you, young lady, are you a student too?"

"I am learning speed typewriting, sir. I plan to make a living as a translator."

"Ah, very laudable. Your English is very good. Are you actually German?"

"Yes, sir. I grew up near the Danish border, in Schleswig-Holstein."

"I suppose ladies have to work these days. Sad, really. Consequence of the war, I suppose."

Allan Chadwick moved to join them. Noticing Stiller and Penelope in animated conversation, he turned to Freddy and said, "Good evening, sir. Allan Chadwick."

"Good evening, Allan, Tom calls me Freddy, Frederick Rutledge. At your service. Are you a friend of these charming German students?"

"I just met them a short while ago. We have a mutual friend who has known the Pomeroys since before the war, Gerhard Kegel over there." Chadwick nodded toward Kegel.

"Oh yes, Tom was stationed in Germany then. He knows so many interesting people. What do you do Mr. Chadwick? Do you work in the Foreign Office?"

"No, sir. I'm a member of the Royal Air Force. I'm stationed nearby at Farnborough."

"Fascinating. Have you traveled much in service of the King?"

"I spent nearly four years in Iraq, sir. While I was there, I got to visit Syria and Egypt."

"Fascinating. Traveling broadens the mind, I always say. I don't want to talk shop and spoil this delightful party, but I would be interested in your appreciation of the situation in the Middle East, from the point of view of a young serving officer. Tell you what, I'm usually in my office most days. Next time you're in town, stop by the Foreign Office and ask to see me. Here's my card."

He passed his card to Chadwick, who put it in a breast pocket without looking at it. "I'll certainly do that, sir, although I should mention that I was at the bottom of the totem pole."

Kegel joined them. "Excuse us, there's someone I want to introduce to Olaf."

They wandered off, and Chadwick turned to Fischer. "What do you do in London for entertainment, Julia?"

"Well, I haven't been there very long. I'm still finding my way around."

"Perhaps we could meet one evening, I can get into London quite conveniently on the train from Farnborough. How can I get in touch with you?"

"I am staying at a hostel for women. There is a telephone in the reception area. Just ask for Julia Fassbender, and someone will find me. Any time after five would be fine. Here's the number."

Chadwick added it to Penelope's number. "I'll do that. And now, if you'll excuse me, I think I need another drink."

His head was starting to ache, probably because of the recent concussion, and he found the cigarette smoke irritating his eyes. He went to find Kegel, and quietly said, "I'm not feeling too well, Gerhard. Would you mind awfully if I drop out? And could you please run me back to the base?"

Chadwick thanked Honoria for the invitation, and Kegel explained to her that he was acting as chauffeur to drop Allan off at his base.

Once inside the officer's mess Chadwick pulled out the card Freddy had given him. His eyes opened wide as he read: *Lord Lowestoft, KCMG, VC.*

My God, he thought. *I'm mixing with high society—Freddy's an aristocrat and was awarded a VC into the bargain!*

On the way back to London, Dr. Kegel was feeling pleased to know that Chadwick had arranged to meet Fischer later. But the visit to Farnborough had convinced him that there may be easier ways to get the information they wanted—a simple burglary. But he also thought that Fischer should stay in touch with Chadwick, nevertheless.

When she got to the hostel, Fischer wrote a coded message which she dropped off at the Lambeth boarding house the next day—

To Zimmer 121. Amalgam. Pewter+Bronze+Silver met Nickel

On the way to the typing lesson, she felt more confident; she had successfully pulled off her first assignment as a secret agent.

Chapter Fifteen

When Chadwick reported to Squadron Leader Elliot after the weekend, he was told he was medically unfit to fly and would need clearance from a doctor at the RAF central medical headquarters in London before he could get airborne again. In the meanwhile, he was to take a few days on sick leave. He decided to travel to London and take up Freddy's offer to visit him at the Foreign Office.

Upon arriving at Freddy's address, Chadwick noticed that the commissionaire, a retired sergeant manning the entrance desk, seemed impressed when he asked to see Lord Lowestoft. He assigned an orderly to escort Chadwick to the inner recesses of the magnificent building. Lord Lowestoft was surprised to see Chadwick but greeted him enthusiastically. His office was luxurious, with bookshelves lining two walls. A fire burned under a mantlepiece loaded with framed photographs of seemingly important people.

Freddy rang a small handbell, and within seconds a woman's head appeared round the doorway,

"Tea for two, Agnes, please."

Freddy turned to Chadwick. "Take a pew." He waved at two armchairs grouped on either side of a small table in front of the fire.

Freddy made small talk about the weather, and when Agnes reappeared, she set a tray on the table between them bearing a teapot, cups and saucers, milk, sugar, and a plate carrying four biscuits. When she retired, Freddy turned suddenly serious.

"I am really interested in your perception of the situation in the Middle East."

Chadwick was a bit taken aback at the turn of conversation but assumed a big wheel like Lord Lowestoft had a higher security clearance and could be told anything.

"I was just a lowly flying officer when I was stationed in Iraq. My concern was the tactical situation. We dealt with lawless Arabs, Turkish incursions, and air fights with Germans flying from the Turkish side. Sad to say, my C.O. was shot down and killed after the Arabs got many more machine guns after a rebellion in the north involving the Turks."

"Sorry to hear that, Allan. I know only too well what it is like to lose a comrade in battle."

"You must have seen far worse than I encountered, sir. You were awarded a VC."

"Believe me, many a man better than I deserved it. But I happened to survive."

"Would you tell me a little about it, sir? I'm intrigued by the last war."

Lord Lowestoft hated talking about the war, but Chadwick seemed very earnest. He rose and stared through a window.

"Well, we were attacking near Ypres when the French on our right collapsed, and the regiment found itself outflanked. We started to retreat over a bridge that spanned a tributary of the River Meuse. It was a choke point—the Boche threw everything they had to get the bridge or destroy it with us on the east side. I was part of a company sent to defend the east approaches. About a hundred men under a captain."

Freddy stopped talking and a faraway look crossed his face.

"It's still a bit painful to think of. By nightfall, the captain and a lieutenant were dead. I was the senior officer, but I was just a sprog. The sergeants were magnificent. Most of the regiment crossed over in the dark but by dawn we were down to twenty men. We were out of ammunition and then I was wounded by a shell landing close. I woke up in a trench, a prisoner of the Boche."

He paused, then drank some tea, pointing to his cup he said, "I would have killed for tea like this when I was a prisoner of war." Anyway, first, I was reported missing in action, then killed in action, and then as a prisoner of war. The colonel believed our action had saved most of the regiment from annihilation and recommended the bumf for a gong when he discovered I had survived. I was still recovering in a Boche hospital. I must say they treated me fairly decently. I spent the rest of the war learning German. But an experience of the trenches and the sheer bloody carnage changes one."

Lord Lowestoft returned to his chair at the fireplace looking forlorn and finished his story. "It is impossible to convey the horror of that war to anyone who was not there. It must never happen again. I sincerely think another war would cost us the empire, not to say wiping out some of the finest families in the land who were nearly decimated by the last one."

Lord Lowestoft—Freddy—proceeded to question Chadwick closely about his experiences in Iraq and became extremely interested when Chadwick recounted his adventures in Egypt.

"I'd like to hear more, but what say we adjourn to my club for lunch?" Lowestoft suggested.

Chadwick was more than willing to continue the conversation. He felt flattered by Freddy's interest.

As they sauntered through St. James's Park to Freddy's club, they chatted about Chadwick's current assignment. Trees were beginning to show green, and it felt like spring.

Over lunch, Lowestoft mentioned to Chadwick that an influential group of friends met occasionally at an old Tudor house south of London to discuss the international situation. If Chadwick was interested, he would arrange an invitation to meet them.

"The war in Iraq was kept so quiet," he explained. "Nobody realized how hot it was getting. Most of the men in this group would love to talk to a member of the forces who served there."

Chadwick agreed to meet them sometime.

Chadwick parted from Lord Lowestoft at the door of his club and walked through winding streets to an old bookshop near Leicester Square, pleased with how the meeting had gone. After browsing the bookshop for a while, he found a pleasant coffee shop and read the paper. Then he phoned Miss Fischer, who was delighted to be invited to dinner.

Chadwick discovered that her hostel was in Clapham, so he arranged to meet her at a station on the Northern Line which she could board near the hostel. They met an hour later at Trafalgar Square. Fischer looked like a typical student with a worn raincoat and wearing a beret. Chadwick showed her the famous lions and Nelson's column, then took her for a meal at Yates Wine Lodge.

"This chain, Yates, is really a northern company. I was surprised to find one in London. Gerhard Kegel said you were interested in English culture, so there's a bit for you."

Chadwick told her that English pubs sometimes served wholesome meals, but he warned her not to go into a pub unescorted. He ordered a mixed grill with a glass of red wine. Fischer, still unfamiliar with British meals, followed suit.

Back in the street they passed a cinema that was showing a new picture, *Captain Blood*, starring Errol Flynn, an Australian actor who was becoming very popular. Chadwick bought two tickets for one shilling and three pence each, and they were shown to their seats by an usher with a torch.

When the show was over, which also included a short film about tennis, another film about a Los Angeles detective, and a newsreel, they talked about the film on the way to the Underground. Both felt it was a typical Hollywood movie— a romanticized version of reality. At the station, they parted. Chadwick took the Tube to Waterloo station and a train to Farnborough. They promised to meet again, although Chadwick thought she was rather a cold fish.

In fact, Fischer had been scared to meet Chadwick alone, in the event she made a slip that revealed her true identity.

Squadron Leader Codrington asked Chadwick to stop by his office. "Dr. Thorpe dropped by yesterday. He was enormously impressed by your actions when the bomb struck the tail during the bombing trial. He felt you could easily have sacrificed your life to save the bombsight."

"What? I stayed with plane because I couldn't let go of the stick without it making a steep turn. I couldn't get to the door. I didn't give a damn about the sight."

"Well, that's what he thinks, and he has a lot of influence. He wants me to put you up for an award. I'm recommending the Air Force Cross, quote, *awarded for an act of gallantry in the air when not opposing enemy forces*, unquote. It will not do your career in the Air Force any harm to have a gong."

"That's very kind of you, sir. Thank you very much."

Two days later Chadwick went up to London for a medical check-up. He endured a series of tests given by junior doctors and finally sat with a very imposing-looking consultant, who had his file on the desk.

"You had quite a serious head injury, Chadwick. You were unconscious for several hours."

"Yes, sir, but I'm feeling good now. I'd like to get back to flying."

"That's understandable, but the brain is a very delicate organ and you've abused it. There are distinct signs of internal bleeding. You're very lucky that the pressure did not build up. The results could have been very serious. To put it in layman's terms, you have bruised brains, Chadwick. I'm recommending that you stay grounded for another month, then come to see us again."

Chadwick took the train back to Farnborough feeling somewhat despondent about being forced out of action temporarily. Then he cheered up when he realized this was a good time to look for a car. Mentally, he went over his bank account as the train click-clacked through the English countryside. He'd spent a good deal of his savings on the trip back to England from Egypt the year before. He decided he could raise about ninety pounds, and he resolved to call Penelope Pomeroy to find out if she had been serious about helping him to find a car.

Chapter Sixteen

Dr. Kegel left a message for Stiller with Doris Blackwood, to set up a meeting at the tea shop. When he arrived, Kegel was already sitting, and he gestured him over.

"I have decided to commit a small burglary at RAF Farnborough, but first we need some reconnaissance."

Stiller leaned in, immediately interested in what Kegel had to say.

"I want you to get out there as soon as possible. Take the train and then a bus to the base. I suggest mid-afternoon. Dress inconspicuously with a hat and scarf. Take a walking tour of the buildings, noting designations posted outside. Look for a parking space for a small van. If you're stopped, your cover is that you met Flying Officer Chadwick a while ago and you thought of looking him up while you are in the area."

Stiller nodded his head, and took a slow look around the tea shop to make sure no one was able to overhear their discussion.

"Write nothing down," Kegel continued. "You can complete a sketch of the area when you're back in London. You'll take part in the burglary with a professional I know who can open any safe. You were trained to use a Minox, so the plan is to photograph any documents you think may be of interest to the Luftwaffe. The documents will be returned to the safe and no one will be any wiser. Any questions?"

"No, sir." Stiller sat back in his chair and nodded assuredly to Kegel. "I'll get onto it the next suitable day, sir."

"What does that mean?"

"No snow and not too much rain. By the way, I had a date in London last week with Penelope Pomeroy."

Kegel digested this information. "Just be careful. In more ways than one."

Stiller traveled to Farnborough from Waterloo and caught a bus, using the handy route guide posted in the station entrance hall. He was dressed smartly with a trilby hat and a rolled up umbrella. He walked down the main street into the complex of buildings in a purposeful manner, like a man who knew exactly where he was going.

The buildings were grouped in a higgledy-piggledy fashion that betrayed the way they had been added to the site over the years. He was soon at the control tower. He walked in and spotted what he was looking for, the men's toilet. Ducking into a stall, he waited ten minutes, washed his hands, and walked back to the entrance road. He spotted some decrepit vehicles parked behind a building made of corrugated steel sheet, designated "Ministry of Works." He believed he had found what Kegel wanted— "Administration, RAF Farnborough"—just a hundred meters from the corrugated hut.

On the main road he waited twenty minutes for a bus, and then had some tea and a scone at the station café before returning to Waterloo. He passed the word to Miss Blackwood that he needed to meet with Kegel. When they met a day later, he had a site plan sketch ready with as much detail as he could remember.

Kegel was dubious that the administration building was the right target. He felt they needed the building that Chadwick was using, finally settling for the one that had been marked "Flight Test," located nearer the control tower.

Two days later, Kegel and Stiller met with a slightly mysterious man that Kegel referred to as "Nev." Nev was middle-aged, a little rotund, mostly bald, and had a bushy mustache that grew beneath a blotchy red nose. He listened without comment to Stiller's account of the "reccy" before giving his opinion.

"We'll need a fake Ministry of Works van. All maintenance at RAF fields is done by Works and Bricks, as they call it. They're all civilians. We'll be one of 'em. Clothing is dungarees, flat cap, boots. No firearms. I'll bring a cosh. How much light do you need for your photos?"

"Not much. A desk light would do."

"We're going to get in after everyone has gone home for the day and get out while there's some activity, so we don't stand out. Say seven to nine o'clock. We'll act as carpenters—I'll take care of the tools."

Nev looked at Stiller, "You're my helper. Try not to say much if we are stopped. I'll arrange the van."

A few nights later, an hour after sunset, Nev parked the van near a single-story building at Farnborough, and Stiller carried a weighty bag of tools to the main door. Nev pulled a paper bag from a commodious pocket and sprinkled some wood shavings on the ground. Near them he place a large metal plane. Stiller held a large electric lantern while Nev fiddled with the door.

"Working a bit late, aren't you, mate?" Coming up to them silently out of the darkness, the night watchman surprised them.

"Door's jammed. Emergency call. Some bigwig is coming tomorrer. Everything 'as to be shipshape and Bristol fashion."

Fortunately, the key that Nev had worked into the lock clicked and he made a show of pushing the door open. "Should be done soon."

The watchman stood by for a minute, then said, "I'll be on my rounds then, mates. Night."

Nev gestured for Stiller to get inside with the tool bag, "Turn off the lantern." Using a small torch, they moved slowly down a corridor examining the names on the doors.

"That man showing up gave me a shock," Stiller whispered.

"Norrer a problem, just so long as he stays away from now on. Your boss wants no trace of this little do, otherwise I woulda put him to sleep for an hour or two." He swung his cosh against the palm of one hand with a meaty *thwap*.

"Here's a Squadron Leader Elliot. He must be in charge of something." Nev opened the door and glanced around, using the torch so that its rays did not hit the window. "No safe."

Stiller riffled though the files in a cabinet. "Accidents reports. Not what we're looking for."

They moved on down the corridor. "'Ere's another squadron leader, Codrington. Let's 'ave look in his office." Nev's torch picked up the outline of an old-fashioned safe. "Pay dirt, I think. Chubb. Shouldn't be no trouble opening that little gem."

Stiller watched, fascinated, as Nev fished out a stethoscope from the tool bag and delicately rotated the dial while he listened. After a couple of minutes, he sat back, removed the earpieces, and confidently set the dial, first clockwise and then counter-clockwise. With a final rotation to the right, he grasped the handle, saying, "Open sesame." He twisted it once more and opened the door.

"Congratulations, Nev," Stiller said, clearly impressed. There were a number of cardboard boxes inside, each holding file folders. He quickly sifted through the headings on the boxes and emptied one marked "Ministry Specs." "This looks good. It's stamped 'Secret.' Bomber specs and flight tests."

They set up a desk lamp on the floor and drew the curtains. As Nev passed him files, Stiller snapped them with the Minox. After an hour they were finished. They tidied up Codrington's office, crept down the corridor, and let themselves out. An hour later, Nev drove the van into the yard at the back of the boarding house and Stiller climbed down.

"Thank you, Nev. You certainly earned the money tonight."

"Nofink to it. Watch out for yourself, mate." Nev let out the clutch and drove noisily into the night.

Miss Blackwood had been listening at the back door as Stiller entered. She gave him a hug, saying, "Looks like everything turned out right. You look tired."

"It was stressful, but you must get these to Dr. Kegel." He put three film spools from the camera on the kitchen table.

"Would you like a little something a bit stronger than tea?"

Stiller nodded.

"Come into my parlor." She led the way out of the kitchen down a short hallway into her suite. She waved an arm at an easy chair. "Brandy?"

"Fine."

"This a good German brandy, Asbach Uralt. Better than that French piss." She poured two glasses and perched on the arm of Stiller's chair.

"*Prosit*." Their glasses clinked.

After two more glasses, he felt completely relaxed. "That was a wonderful idea, Miss Blackwood."

"Oh, please call me Doris." She slid onto his lap and gave him a passionate, wet kiss. "You should take off those ugly overalls."

He did not need another invitation, and quickly slipped out of the one-piece outfit. Doris grabbed him by his underwear and led him into her bedroom.

Chapter Seventeen

Squadron Leader Codrington was notified that Flight Lieutenant Chadwick was grounded pending another medical examination. He called Chadwick into his office. "You're grounded for at least another month, Allan. What are we going to do with you? I've assigned other pilots to the bombsight and accident investigation groups.

"I have a suggestion—I recall you were very much into instrument flying in Iraq. The development of flight instruments is run by a civilian, based here at Farnborough, George Pemberton. Would you like to meet him? There may be something for you to contribute."

"Yes, please set that up, sir." Chadwick was relieved to have an assignment that promised to be interesting.

They met a day later in Codrington's office. Codrington did the introductions. "George, this is Allan Chadwick. He was flying with Dr. Thorpe's group when they contrived to launch a bomb into their own plane. Allan managed to keep everyone alive, but the plane was a write-off and now Allan's grounded for medical reasons for a month or so.

"However, while he was flying in Iraq last year, Allan happened to put in a lot of instrument flying. Is there some way he could help you?"

"Iraq, eh? I remember sending a full panel to 314 Squadron—Squadron Leader Welch."

"That was my unit, sir. I flew a lot with Squadron Leader Welch—until he was killed."

"I was very sorry to learn of his death," Pemberton commiserated. "It must have been very difficult for you chaps."

"It was sir. He was a wonderful man. He firmly believed the future of flying depended on fully instrumented aircraft. I would love to be part of that effort if I could."

"Well, the situation is a bit complicated. The powers that be in the Air Ministry feel that development has reached a certain stage, and the major problem is building up a capability in this country to produce reliable instruments in sufficient volume. Naturally, we're still improving the designs we have— those will form the basis of the next generation. But our focus has moved—we're now looking at autopilots. We think these will be a key part of flight sensing instruments."

Pemberton paused, and Codrington interjected, "Chadwick is a graduate of Cranwell. He has a degree in engineering. That and his flying experience could be valuable to your effort."

Chadwick sensed it would be pointless to push himself on Pemberton. "It sounds like a tricky problem. How are you getting on, sir?"

"We're making strides. We have several aerodynamicists working on the problem from a theoretical standpoint. Basically, a plane must be controlled in three dimensions to follow a flight path set externally by the pilot. Airspeed is coupled into the three dimensions, which means that changes in one dimension produces changes in another. The autopilot can easily become unstable. We're trying to design a system so that the required flight parameters affect the operation of the control surfaces and the throttles without a man in the middle."

"It sounds fascinating," Chadwick said. "What kind of planes need an autopilot?"

"Not fighters. Bombers with long legs to cover to get to the target. Civilian passenger planes."

"I have another question, sir, if you don't mind."

"Yes?" Pemberton replied patiently.

"How do you remotely operate the control surfaces?"

"That's one of the major lines of work. There are at least three ways—pneumatic control, hydraulic control, and electrical motors. All three are being investigated."

Impressed with the types of questions Chadwick was asking, Pemberton made up his mind. "Drop into our laboratory tomorrow morning," he told Allan. "I'll introduce you to some of the engineers."

Chapter Eighteen

After lunch, Chadwick took a bus into Farnborough center, where he went to the main office of his bank and asked to see the manager. After a short wait, he was shown into an old-fashioned office with heavy mahogany furniture. A thin, elderly man with silver hair brushed straight back and a silver mustache rose to greet him.

"How do you do? I am Mr. Flanagan, deputy manager. How can I be of service?"

"My name is Allan Chadwick, and I have had an account with your bank, at several different branches, for over eight years. I'd like to arrange a loan."

"Very good. What is the purpose of the loan?"

"I want to buy a car."

"Are you currently employed, Mr. Chadwick?"

"Yes, I hold a permanent commission in the Royal Air Force. My present rank is Flight Lieutenant. At the moment, I'm stationed at RAF Farnborough."

Mr. Flanagan looked slightly dubious. "What are your current duties?"

"I'm a general duties officer." This was strictly true. All flying crew were classified as "general duties" officers, with an appendage giving their airborne responsibility.

"What sum are we looking at?"

"I have about ninety pounds in savings, and I'd like to buy a car in the two hundred pound range."

Flanagan pushed a button on his desk. When a young man opened his door, Flanagan asked for details of Mr. Chadwick's account. While they waited, Flanagan put a few more questions to Chadwick. "Are you married, Mr. Chadwick?"

"No."

"Then you have no children."

"No." Chadwick smiled ruefully to himself. He thought of his brief affair with Lisa Scharf in Iraq. He was quite sure her son Kurt was his, although she had obviously convinced her husband that he was the father. But in dealing with the bank, the plan was to project respectability, not describe the real world. He wondered if Mr. Flanagan, a desiccated thin stick of a man, had ever known passion.

The young man appeared with a thick ledger book. Flanagan thumbed through it. "You have a savings balance of eight-eighty pounds, twelve shillings and two pence. Do you agree?"

"Yes, sounds about right."

Flanagan's eyebrows contracted in a slight frown. Bankers did not use the word "about." "Your salary from the Air Force is paid directly into your account—four pounds, seven shillings and tenpence per calendar month."

"You must bear in mind, Mr. Flanagan, that the service provides my room, board and clothing. My personal monthly expenses are quite minimal."

"I'm aware of the difference between military and civilian living expenses. Do you carry any life insurance, Mr. Chadwick? That would be required if we make a personal loan. Also, any machine you might purchase would also have to be insured. These things add to the apparent cost."

"I don't have any life insurance at the moment. I'm sure it could be easily arranged. If a loan is approved, what interest would be charged?"

"We would regard this as an unsecured loan, as it is our experience that motor vehicles do not retain their initial value. Our rate is two percent of the unpaid balance, per annum."

"That sounds satisfactory to me. When can I hear from you?"

"First you must complete an application. An assistant will take care of that outside. Good day, Mr. Chadwick."

Chadwick hurriedly filled out the form, asking for one hundred pounds, to be repaid over five years. He was glad to leave the bank; he found the atmosphere suffocating, and the prospect of taking on the debt for the auto loan made him feel a bit uneasy.

As he walked back to the bus stop, he did a quick calculation, and realized the loan payments would take nearly a third of his salary.

Still, he thought, *you only live once*.

Chapter Nineteen

The Luftwaffe attaché at the German embassy in London, Carl Loeffler, reported to the Abwehr station head, Dr. Gerhard Kegel, that the secret British documents photographed during a break-in at RAF Farnborough were of great interest. They indicated that the British expected to field several medium bombers in the next few years. The knowledge provided guidance for the location of important factories.

What was especially interesting was that the prototype tested did not meet the requirements of the specification. Would the British re-design it or try again? Kegel decided to keep in contact with Chadwick and reminded himself to ask Inge Fischer— "Julia Fassbender"— if Chadwick had asked her out again. He idly wondered if Stiller—Runge—was seeing the Pomeroy girl.

Chadwick received a note from the bank to inform him that the loan had been approved. All he had to do was stop by and sign some papers and the money was his. He called Penelope Pomeroy to take her up on her offer to take him car-shopping.

Penelope was very keen to help him find a car. "But it has to be fast!" she said.

There was only a small motor pool at RAF Farnborough, and it was run by a grizzled old warrant officer, Sydney Halstead. Chadwick stopped by his office and asked his advice, pointing out he had about two hundred pounds for the purchase, including incidental expenses such as insurance.

The old man told him he could play it safe and buy a new Austin Seven, which would cost about one hundred and thirty pounds. But it had an anemic performance, he said. Fifty miles per hour tops, if the wind was with you. Also, in his opinion the transverse springing was positively dangerous on wet or slippery roads. He asked Chadwick to leave it with him for a day or two, and he would make a few phone calls.

Chadwick checked in at the laboratory of the group developing an autopilot, and after a couple of visits he found concentrating on the work gave him headaches. He stopped by the sick bay for some medication. The doctor examined him and said that recovering from the concussion would take time. He prescribed aspirin and told him to get some rest.

Chadwick got a message from the motor pool and went to see the old warrant officer, Halstead.

"You, know, in some ways the 1920s were the golden years of motor car design," the warrant officer told him. "Very skilled mechanics and machinists were available for assembly. Engineers had refined the early models. Have you thought of a second-hand quality car? Because of the Crash, many of the manufacturers went broke, but their cars are still around, often with low mileages."

Chadwick laughed at his earnest pitch. "All right, what you have got in mind for me?"

"A Bentley. They're a wonderful car. Built to last. Their models won the Le Mans twenty-four-hour endurance race three years in a row. The three-liter engine is a bit light for today's traffic, but the four-and-half liter engine can beat anything on the road today. The company went bust in 1931, but there are plenty around and spares are easy."

"I think a Bentley is a bit rich for me. I imagine they're very heavy on petrol."

"A little, but if you are traveling a lot faster, you'll get to your destination quicker. Every Bentley will do a ton."

The argument seemed a bit specious to Chadwick, who couldn't quite put his finger on the fallacy. And then he smiled to himself.

"I'm guessing you know where there's one for sale, Mr. Halstead?"

"Yes, sir. A fellow I know runs a second-hand car business in Kensington in one of the old mews. He has a 1928 four-and-half, in excellent condition, only 34,000 miles since new. He could let you have it within your budget as a favor to me. He owes me for a few things."

Chadwick was somewhat dubious and wondered if the old man was, perhaps, getting a cut of the transaction, should he purchase the Bentley. But it was as good place as any to start his search for a car.

"Please let me have the address. I have a friend who will run me over. I'll take a look."

Chadwick lined up Penelope one afternoon and they drove into London to the address Halstead had given them. Queen's Gate Mews was originally a back street where stables and carriage houses were located for the imposing mansions on the main road. After the war, the stables were converted into commercial businesses, often selling old cars.

On the way in, Chadwick did not tell Penelope that they were going to look at an old Bentley. He wanted to see the surprise on her face when the car was revealed. They found the place without too much difficulty, not far from the Science Museum. A large sliding door covered the front of the building. A small door in the main door carried a sign, "Solly's Motor Cars."

They knocked, and a short man in overalls answered. When Chadwick introduced himself, the man said, "Yass, Syd's friend, come in."

It was fairly dark inside the building. A large, green automobile took up most of the space. Penelope stared at it in astonishment, fingering the large, chrome-plated winged "B" on the radiator cap,

"It's a Bentley," she whispered.

"Yass," Solly said. "Vanden Plas tourer, four-and-a-half liter, 1928."

With the canvas top and uncompromisingly erect windshield, the car looked old-fashioned, but the long bonnet and pugnacious, rounded radiator breathed power. Solly walked round the car extolling is virtues, but Chadwick was hardly listening.

"Are you going to get it?" Penelope asked, "It's fantastic."

Solly heard her, "Oh, yass, the ladies love this car," he said, giving Chadwick a licentious leer.

"Can you start it?" Chadwick said to Solly.

"Of course, 'ave to open the doors first or we'll get gassed." He fiddled with chains at the side of the door and slowly drew them back. Daylight flooded into the confined space. The Bentley gleamed in the light.

Solly climbed in the car and adjusted controls on the steering wheel. "Timing, mixture, throttle settings, they're all manual on this car. More reliable, in some ways, than the automatic junk they have on modern cars. 'Ere we go."

The starter motor ground into action and with a roar, the engine fired. Solly adjusted the hand controls again and the engine settled into a slow rumbling cadence. With a loud clunk, Solly put the car into gear and slowly moved it into the mews. He pulled on the handbrake outside the car and climbed out. He nodded to the cockpit. "Climb in, Mr. Chadwick."

Without any prompting, Penelope climbed into the passenger side. Solly stood on the running board as Allan wiggled into the seat.

"Now a funny thing you have to get used to in this car, compared to modern ones, is that the throttle is in the middle. Put your right foot down. See the brass ball in the middle? Just push it gently."

The engine responded enthusiastically, and the rpm shot up.

"Steady, the clutch is under your left foot. The pedal right of the throttle is the brake. Gear shift is 'H.' One, two, three, four. Push it down and left for reverse. No synchromesh. You need to adjust the lay shaft speed in neutral as you go through the gears. Soon becomes automatic. You don't think about it."

Solly reached in and turned off the ignition switches. "Just like a plane—two magnetos, plugs either side of each cylinder." He winked at Penelope. "I was an aircraft mechanic during the war."

Chadwick went with Solly into a tiny, cramped office. The desk and shelves were crowded with papers and catalogs. Solly fished out the registration document. "You gonna take it? I'll fill out your name. Syd mentioned what you can afford. We 'ave to support the forces. One seventy-five. Tell you what, for another ten quid I'll throw in a year's insurance and registration. One eighty-five and you can drive it away."

Events were moving too quickly for Chadwick to fully comprehend. He said nothing, and Solly seized on his silence as a bargaining chip. "Tell you what, one eighty-five and I'll change the oil and fill the tank as well. Sixteen gallons, for free."

"Solly, slow down. I need time to think." But Chadwick had already made up his mind. "Yes, I'll take it. I'll give you a check for one eighty-five and pick up the car this weekend. Give you time to clear the check."

"Lord luvva duck, Mr. Chadwick. I trust you. You're a commissioned orficer. Saturday morning, it'll be orl ready for you, spic and span."

Chadwick completed details for the paperwork and then walked into the mews. Penelope was sitting in the car,

"Did you buy it?" She seemed to be as excited as if she was getting the car for herself.

"Yes, Penny. Come Saturday morning, it's mine. I'll take the train into town and drive it back to Farnborough."

"I'll come in with you if you like. You'll need a co-driver."

"All right, meet me at the station. We'll take the eight-forty train."

Penelope's mother dropped her off with the family car at the station on Saturday morning. Chadwick bought two single tickets to Waterloo. From there they took the Tube to South Kensington station and walked to Queen's Gate Mews. The car was parked outside, Solly had clearly been busy with polish—the two huge, chrome-plated headlamps sparkled in the morning sunshine.

Solly was in the office. "It's all ready to go, boss. Engine warmed up. You 'ave to get used to its little ways. It 'as a cone clutch, a bit fierce till you get used to it. It's a lot better at goin' than stopping. Keep a bit back from the job in front of you." He noticed Penelope standing at the door. "You takin' a bird wiv you?"

"Yes, Penny is going to navigate. We're driving to Farnborough."

"She'll be done to a turn, then, when you get 'ome."

Chadwick frowned. "What do you mean?"

Solly looked at him slyly for a moment, then said, "You don't know about the four-and-a-half liter?"

"Know what?"

"Well, it's something to do with way the engine vibrates. Around about sixty, there's this low frequency resonance, more of a sensation than a movement you can put your finger on."

"So?"

"Drives the ladies crazy."

Chadwick looked at him in disbelief and laughed. He gathered up the ownership papers and put them in a side pocket on the door, shook Solly's hand, and left.

As he climbed into his new Bentley, he said to Penny, "Let's see if we can get this beast back to Farnborough."

He retarded the ignition timing, adjusted the mixture control, turned on the ignition switches, and pushed the starter button. The engine fired immediately. It wasn't too different than starting an aero engine. Bearing in mind Solly's warning about the clutch, Chadwick selected first gear and slowly eased out the clutch pedal. The car suddenly reared forward like a racing stallion and careened down the mews, which was fortunately quiet. Pulling into the road at the end of the mews Chadwick parked by the curb. "Takes a bit of getting used to," he explained to Penny.

"I'm going to take us back the scenic way," Penny said. "Main road to Portsmouth. At Guildford we'll take the Hog's Back to Farnham. That's a nice stretch of road. You can let her go. Then it's just a few miles to Farnborough."

Chadwick let the clutch in and drove circumspectly; his gear changes were noisy. Penny shrieked with laughter, and he found he had forgotten to advance the ignition timing after he had started the engine. When he did that, the engine came to life. With his pilot training he automatically kept his eye on the engine instruments, particularly oil pressure. Water temperature settled at eighty centigrade. The ammeter showed a slight charge. All seemed well.

Driving through the quaint center of Guildford, Penny spotted the turnoff for the A31, the Hog's Back to Farnham. For six or seven miles, the road lay along the top of a ridge with beautiful views of either side. There was a slight down gradient and Chadwick slowly accelerated in fourth gear. The square-cut gears whined as the engine speed crept past twenty-eight hundred rpm. Then the canvas top began to flap wildly. He glanced at the speed—eighty mph. He throttled back and shouted to Penny over the wind noise, "We'll have to drop the top to go any faster. But we'll do that another day."

He drove sedately through Farnham and took the small back road to Birchwood, eventually pulling into the driveway of Penny's house with the exhaust burbling away. Penny leaned over and pushed the horn button, which let out a deep bellow. While she was leaning over, she gave Chadwick a resounding kiss. "Thank you, eighty, that was wonderful." Her mother came out of the front door and threw up her hands in mock horror at the sight of the Bentley.

Chadwick drove back to Farnborough and was just in time to catch Syd Halstead at the Motor Pool, who looked at the great machine admiringly. "You've got a lot of motor car there, Mr. Chadwick. Look after it and you can leave it to your grandson."

Chapter Twenty

Chadwick spent most mornings in the next month with the autopilot development team. The days were getting longer, and on many afternoons, he took Penny for a ride. He folded up the top and clipped on the tonneau cover and slowly pushed the maximum speed.

He decided the wheels needed to be balanced to eliminate an annoying vibration that started at about seventy. The wheel rims carried threaded studs that held small lead washers. By jacking up the car, he was able to balance the wheels by spinning them and moving the lead disks until the wheels stopped at a random position each time, a tedious, dirty job.

The afternoon he completed that task he picked up Penny and drove back to Farnham. Then he swung onto the Hog's Back again, this time going uphill. Snicking the car into fourth gear at about fifty miles per hour, he accelerated without difficulty, the car lunging forward. At three-thousand, three-hundred rpm, Penny glanced at the speedometer. "We're doing a hundred," she cried. "A Ton and uphill too!"

It was very exhilarating. Allan shared the moment with Penny and then eased back and before he knew it, he was in the Guildford traffic. He pulled into a quiet side street and stopped. He put the car in neutral. The engine burbled in its characteristic way at about five hundred rpm. He scanned the gauges, and they were all normal.

"Allan, that was spiffing." Penny, her face flushed, flung herself against him, pressing his hands against her breasts. He left large black finger marks on her white angora wool sweater.

Back at Farnborough, a clerk found Chadwick buried under his new car, and told him a medical examination had been arranged for the following Monday morning in London. This time he drove to the station and left his car with the other commuters. After the usual tests, the consultant was most solicitous and asked him if he had suffered from headaches, dizziness, blurred vision, or blackouts. Chadwick answered in the negative and said he felt fine. The doctor asked him if he felt fully competent to fly. Chadwick was positive that he never felt better. The doctor told Chadwick that some indications made him suspect that he was not fully recovered from the concussion, but he was going to sign Allan off as "Fit to Fly."

Chadwick was overjoyed, he decided another visit to Lord Lowestoft at the Foreign Office would be a good way to use up the rest of the morning. Lowestoft was pleased to see him, and again insisted on lunch at his club. He had arranged to meet another guest for lunch, a man he introduced as Tommy Carstairs, who had something to do with the Palace.

Carstairs proved to be a quiet sort of person but over the course of the meal asked Chadwick some very penetrating questions about his experiences in Egypt the year before. Chadwick got the impression his interest was German espionage. He was sorry Doug Larson wasn't with him, his friend he'd met in Cairo who was with the British Military Police.

Lord Lowestoft remarked that the RAF underplayed the activities in the Middle East and a good deal was going on that people in London would be very interested to hear about. As they parted, he mentioned that a few friends were getting together on Saturday at an old Tudor mansion called Isbell's, built by Henry VIII for one of his mistresses, a few miles outside Reigate.

"We call ourselves the 'Isbell's Insiders'," he told Chadwick. "It's on the main road to Brighton. Shouldn't be too hard to find. Do you have a car?"

"Oh, yes," Chadwick replied, feeling a touch smug. "I can drive to Reigate from Farnborough without any difficulty."

"Good, consider yourself invited. Cocktails at five."

A day later, back at the base, Squadron Leader Codrington told Chadwick that they had been notified that he was considered fit and that a check flight must be arranged, "Just to see if you've forgotten how to fly," Codrington joked.

Chapter Twenty-One

They took off the next day in a twin-engine bomber. Codrington gestured to the pilot's seat. "You fly the thing," he told Chadwick. "I'll just stand back and watch. Let's do a few touch-and-goes."

Chadwick flew downwind, completed the downwind vital actions, and then turned crosswind. On the approach, he needed to add considerable power to cross the boundary fence. He put down full flap just before the main wheels landed on the grass. Chadwick found that his coordination was not up to his usual standard.

Once rolling, he raised the flaps, pushed the throttles to the limit, and took off again. Turning cross wind, he raised the undercarriage, adjusted the pitch, and started the downwind vital actions. This time he turned a little earlier than before and made a smoother approach, throttling back as the plane swept over the fence.

Codrington seemed satisfied. They taxied to dispersal, weathercocked into wind, and shut down the engines.

"You're a little rusty, Allan, but I don't think you're going to kill anyone. Please see me in the office when you get rid of the flying gear."

When Chadwick rejoined him in his office the squadron leader said, "I hear you've bought a car, a Bentley."

"Yes, sir, Syd Halstead helped me find one in London. It's very old. But in good shape."

"It's a slippery slope, Allan. You've heard of the dangerous three Ms for young officers—Motors, Money, and Matrimony, the pitfalls to a service career? Watch out, you've just taken the first step."

"I'm not planning on getting married, sir," Chadwick said, laughing.

Codrington looked skeptical. "Let's see where we can fit you into the autopilot development group. As you know we have two pilots assisting the engineers, Healey and Norton. Their job is to fly experimental equipment. I'm going to press the team to produce an autopilot that is as close to a prototype as possible. It will be your job to evaluate it, from the standpoint of the average service pilot.

"We will fit this prototype into the third aircraft of our little flight. You can get used to its characteristics so that differences on auto flight will become obvious. I've talked about this to Mr. Pemberton—he's all in favor. He'll give some priority to the construction and fitting of a complete unit, which will take about two weeks. Please talk to him about a trial program."

"Yes, sir!" Chadwick thanked Codrington, saluting him before leaving the office.

Chadwick discovered to his delight that the aircraft assigned for the autopilot trial was a brand-new Avro Anson, a metal monoplane with two radial engines. It had just been delivered by the manufacturer. He asked one of the other pilots flying for the group, Healey, to fly with him as second pilot to take the plane up for an inaugural trip. When he climbed aboard, he savored the smell of the new plane.

In the air, it handled very well and cruised at one hundred and fifty knots. They both took turns at the controls, and after two hours they returned to Farnborough, well satisfied with the Avro.

When Chadwick signed Form 700 in the hangar, the flight sergeant rigger mentioned the plane was to be taken out of service in order to install the controls for the new autopilot, which he referred to as the "robot pilot."

Chadwick spent the afternoon with Mr. Pemberton collecting drawings of the "robot." He was determined to be completely familiar with the system when he took to the air.

In the following days he also spent time with the design engineers, ferreting out the reasons for the engineering choices. He was particularly intrigued that the decision had been made to operate the aircraft controls using compressed air. He was told this allowed the smoothest transition from manual flight to auto flight and vice versa, though they had tried both hydraulic and electrical controls before choosing a pneumatic system.

When Saturday rolled around, he refueled the old Bentley, checked the oil and water levels, and dressed carefully in a good suit for his meeting at Isbell's. The day was overcast. It was cold in the open car, and he donned an overcoat and thick scarf, and drove with gloves. He took a familiar route—Farnham, the Hog's Back to Guildford, and then a new road for him, to Dorking and then Reigate. Chadwick recognized the gate house for Isbell's two miles outside Reigate on Cockshot Hill.

After parking in the long driveway, he walked past several other large cars to the typical Tudor doorway. When he rang the bell, the door was opened almost immediately by a butler, who took his coat and directed him into a crowded room.

Lord Lowestoft spotted him and introduced him to a tall aristocratic woman. "Dot, may I introduce Allan Chadwick. Allan, your hostess, Lady Dorothy Addenbury."

They shook hands. "You're very young, Allan, to be mixed up with this gang."

Lowestoft quickly interceded. "He's had a lot of interesting experiences, including adventures in Iraq, Egypt, and Germany."

"Well, I hope we can learn something from you. Please, help yourself to a drink."

Allan took a glass of sherry from a waiter. He had noticed that the hostess spoke with an accent that was distinctly not British. "Are you American, Lady Addenbury?" he asked.

"I grew up in the United States, I guess that makes me American, but I married a Brit, Viscount Addenbury, so you can say I'm mid-Atlantic." She looked at Allan appraisingly. "And speaking of accents, you're not a southerner?"

"No, I grew up in Lancashire, but it's fairly civilized there."

She laughed. "Oh, the English and their class strata."

Lowestoft drew him away. "Excuse us. There's someone I want you to meet." He took Chadwick to a small group, all men on the older side, two smoking pipes. He waited for a lull in the conversation before interjecting, "Allan, these chaps are mostly newspaper men, so be careful of what you say. It might be reported as what the man in the street thinks!"

They smiled, and one of them said, "Allan, it's a pleasure. Freddy tells us you lead an exciting life."

"Sometimes it's exciting, but only when things go wrong," Chadwick said, with a smile. He wasn't sure where the conversation was going, and so decided it was better not to elaborate.

Freddy said, "Allan has served in the Middle East and traveled in Germany last year."

One of the newspaper men asked him if there were signs of German interest in the Middle East. Chadwick replied that it had been his impression that the Germans were very active in the region. He mentioned the German pilot of a fighter plane that was shot down near the Turkish border after it attacked a British bomber. He also mentioned the German archaeological expeditions that were thought to be covers for German intelligence in Iraq.

The dinner gong sounded, and the crowd slowly moved into the dining room. Walking with Lowestoft, Chadwick expressed some concern that his remarks may be misconstrued and result in an article in a paper.

"Don't worry, Allan, they'll write nothing. Those gentlemen don't write for the newspapers—they own them." They parted as Freddy went to find his assigned place.

Chadwick looked round the table. The guests were dressed extremely well, but the men wore business suits, not evening clothes. He judged he was the youngest there. Seating was marked by a small card on the table. Allan looked for his name, and found he was sitting between two elegant women, one in black satin with a large choker of pearls. She was engaged in an animated conversation with her neighbor. The other, to his left, had a well cantilevered bosom on which rested an ornate diamond necklace. She appeared to be in her late thirties, and the smell of perfume was very apparent. Her attention was also distracted by her neighbor, a talkative elderly man on her left.

Chadwick looked at the menu on the table in front of him. The meal started with a choice of appetizers. He decided on prawn cocktail. A waiter quietly asked if he would like some white wine. When the small plate was whisked away, he glanced round the table. Most of the ladies had settled for melon cantaloupe.

While Chadwick was waiting for the main course, Filet de Boeuf Americane, the lady with the ripe figure turned toward him. "My name's Melanie." She glanced down at the seating card. "You must be single, Allan. Dot usually tries to take care of me."

"It's a pleasure to meet you, Melanie. Yes, you guessed right, and I thought I had been invited for my intellectual qualities."

"Very good, I've nothing against handsome men who are also smart."

A waiter came between them for a moment with a dish of Pommes Pont Neuf. He helped himself. This dish was followed by Sauce Chateau Briana and Choix Fleur aux Gratin.

"What do you do, Allan?"

"Well, I could say I work for the government." He felt suddenly reluctant to say he was a member of the Royal Air Force.

"So do half the men in this room. So did my husband until he ran into people that worked for someone else's government. But that's another story. Do you live locally?"

"Farnborough."

Silence enveloped them as they chewed through the main course. Chadwick ate about half the food on his plate and put down his knife and fork. A waiter removed his plate and, without speaking, Chadwick put his finger on one of the dessert choices, Fromage Divers. Some assorted cheeses, with small crackers, appeared before him.

"Farnborough. Do you get about much?"

"Yes, I have a car. I like to drive."

"Splendid, I have a nice place on the Thames, near Pangbourne. You must come out to visit some nice summer day. Bring a friend. Here's my card."

Melanie rummaged in a small purse and passed him a card. He glanced at it, noticing that it said, "Lady Melanie Fitzgibbon, Clair Court Hall, Pangbourne." She whispered to him, "My husband came from a long line descended from a mistress of Charles II. Poor fellow didn't survive the war. Left me a widow, but I have a wonderful son, now up at Cambridge."

Chadwick murmured the conventional commiserations.

"Life goes on. I'm serious. Do drive over some time. My telephone number is on the card. I like younger people around the place."

The desultory conversation faded as the Viscount tapped a glass. "Ladies, please take your coffee in the drawing room." As the women left, the men rose to their feet and then settled back for liqueur and cigars. Chadwick had never acquired a taste for cigars, and so he passed the box to his neighbor when it was handed to him.

The Viscount rose again, "I think we have time for a little business. Last week I had lunch with David. He is very firm that he intends to marry Wallis. I told him how pleased I was to hear the news."

There were murmurs of "Here, here" in the room.

"Stanley Baldwin is proving to be a problem and may have to go. He suggests Chamberlain may be a suitable replacement, as he is known to be sympathetic to our view."

This news also produced a round of murmurs and nodding, knowing heads.

"In about a year David is planning a visit to Germany. He's been in touch with one of his German cousins who is well-placed in the current government over there. The Fuehrer is very taken with the idea and would lay on a state visit. He has implied that Wallis would be treated as a royal."

Several questions were lobbed at the Viscount and Chadwick tried to sort out what he had just heard. When they moved toward the drawing room afterwards, he tagged alongside Lowestoft. "David? Wallis? I don't quite understand."

"Allan, he was talking about the Prince of Wales and his, uh—paramour. This matter has been kept out of the papers here. So, please be discreet."

Chadwick's head was in a whirl. He was just a relatively junior officer and suddenly he was at the nexus of power in Britain. Had he heard right? Were these the people who were running the country?

The party was breaking up. He thanked Lady Addenbury and collected his coat. As he walked to his car, he noticed liveried chauffeurs starting the vehicles parked near the Bentley. Feeling for the controls in the dark, he kicked himself for not bringing a small torch.

With the engine running, he let it warm up for a few minutes, and then swung into the driveway. Cars were picking up guests at the door, but there was room for him to squeeze slowly by. The light blazing from the open door of Isbell's illuminated the great car, and he noticed appreciative glances from the men waiting in the large entrance doorway.

He was soon in Reigate and as he searched for the road to Dorking, it seemed like the headlights were getting dimmer. He glanced at the ammeter. *Christ!* It was showing a ten amp discharge, and the battery was running down. The dynamo was clearly not up to the task of supplying current to the huge headlamps. He knew the car would run even if the twelve-volt battery became completely discharged. The magnetos would keep the ignition firing and petrol was transferred into a small header tank by the vacuum of the inlet manifold. But he needed the lights to see the road ahead.

He had an idea, and he shifted into third gear. The higher engine rpm brought the discharge shown on the ammeter to five amps. When he finally parked behind the officer's mess at RAF Farnborough after a somewhat scary ride, the headlights glowed a dim yellow, and he was sweating.

In the morning he tried to start the engine, but the motor would not turn over. The battery was completely flat. The humor in the situation was not lost on him. *It's ironic*, he thought. *Last night I was partying with the bigwigs who seemed to be running the whole country, and this morning I can't even start my car.*

Chapter Twenty-Two

Chadwick stopped by Syd Halstead's desk first thing Monday. Halstead laughed at his story of driving home in the dark with fading headlamps. He made a few sensible suggestions, including replacing the two six-volt batteries, which were probably as old as the car. Chadwick agreed but argued that was a financial impossibility at that stage. New, they cost about thirty shillings each, an amount that was more than his monthly repayment to the bank.

Instead, Halstead told him how to safely start the car using the hand crank. It was essential to make sure the ignition timing was fully retarded, otherwise a backfire could cause the crank handle to whiz round and strike his hand. This could result in a fractured wrist, a condition that was fairly common at the time, and referred by doctors as the "chauffeur's fracture." Halstead's most useful advice was to get the car into Farnborough and have a garage where he had some "pull" remove the batteries and charge them from a wall socket. Chadwick could drive the car in daylight without batteries, but of course, it was inconvenient to start the engine with the hand crank.

Chadwick followed this advice. When he returned to the garage to have the batteries re-installed, the manager told him they had reconditioned the batteries by cleaning the cells, and short journeys at night should not be a problem. The cost was modest, and Chadwick suspected that Syd had had some influence.

Chadwick was told that good progress had been made on the installment of the prototype autopilot in the Avro Anson. He stopped by George Pemberton's office and asked for a thorough briefing on the new equipment. This was set up for the next day, when Pemberton and two development engineers would sit with him and answer questions until he was sure he thoroughly understood the functioning of the autopilot.

When they met, Pemberton started by telling him that this was known as control or feedback engineering, although some examples were more than a hundred years old. The modern systems were only just becoming amenable to mathematical analysis. As an example, he described the speed control devised by James Watt for the first practical steam engines. Two steel balls suspended in a frame were spun by the engine. Centrifugal force caused them to fly out. As they did so, a valve lowered the steam supply and thus regulated the speed of the engine, irrespective of wide variations in the steam pressure.

"Aviation autopilots have been around for twenty years," he went on, "but they were tailored for a particular plane. We're designing a universal control unit that will function for any plane. Aircraft move in three dimensions. In practice, a change in one dimension produces an effect in another. For example, a roll causes a plane to lose altitude. We term this coupling, which varies from one type of plane to another."

Pemberton then placed a cylinder on the table. It was about the size of a tin of beans. A row of thin tubes protruded from one side. "This is the heart of the autopilot. It's nothing more than an artificial horizon, with the display replaced by a set of small valves. Basically, this unit keeps the plane flying straight and level, regardless of gravity, air turbulence, and changes in loading."

He then fished out another piece of equipment. "This is the control panel that the pilot supervises. The system on or off switch is on this panel. Desired altitude, heading, and airspeed can be set on the dials. The autopilot will maintain them. The final component is here."

One of his assistants placed a cumbersome piece of equipment on the table. It was comprised of several pneumatic cylinders with connecting rods.

"This is mounted under the cockpit floor and connects to the control column and rudder pedals. In response to signals from the control panel, the pistons operate the elevators, ailerons, rudders, and throttles. On both engines there are air compressors which maintain an air pressure of four hundred pounds per square inch in a reservoir."

Chadwick was impressed. "I must say, it looks very good. One question, though. When the autopilot is flying the plane, can the pilot grab the stick and overcome the autopilot if he wants to change the situation. For example, he suddenly has to avoid a collision with another aircraft?"

Pemberton looked dubious and the other engineers shook their heads. "The short answer is no. The pistons can exert a force of up to four hundred pounds. In the situation you suggest, the pilot would have to turn off the autopilot at the control panel."

The group dealt with many other points of interest—rate of response, sudden changes, emergency shut down if the autopilot goes wild, effect of battle damage. Mr. Pemberton felt that the Anson would be ready for flight trials in a week.

Chadwick went down to the hangar and watched the riggers installing some of the equipment in the Anson. Then he called Penelope Pomeroy to arrange a late afternoon run in the Bentley.

They parked at a pub on the River Thames and carried their drinks to a table overlooking the water. It was very peaceful. Two swans floated near the bank. They sat in silence for a few minutes, then Penny suddenly said, "You don't like me very much, do you, Allan?"

Chadwick was startled, "Why on earth do you say that? We've had some fun with the old car."

"Fun! You have never once attempted to make love to me. And I gave you enough hints."

Chadwick tried to make a joke out of her remark. "The old thing is a bit narrow for that." He gave a nervous laugh.

"I don't mean in the car. You've known me for a couple of months, but you've never gone beyond talking about cars, or sometimes, planes."

Chadwick didn't know what to say. He liked driving with Penelope, though perhaps subconsciously he thought a Bentley looked better with an attractive woman in the passenger seat. But he was not romantically attracted to her. Also, deep down, he didn't care for her southern accent, which offended his northern ears. All he could stammer was, "I've behaved like a gentleman. What else did you expect?"

"I expected a lot more from a young man who's been trapped in the desert for four years. Did you ever think about the position I'm in? Twenty-two and not married. You're so lucky to be born a male. You've been able to do more or less what you want—fly, buy a fancy car. What can I do? A mediocre education, too posh to work. I'm supposed to flutter in the sunshine and wait for some male to marry me."

Chadwick was silent.

"Allan, you may be damn clever at some things, but in some ways, you're as naïve as a newborn baby."

Chadwick was embarrassed by her raw emotion. His cheeks flushed. "God, Penny, I'm sorry. I never thought about those things. I didn't give our friendship serious thought, I guess. It was you who said you liked driving in fast cars. To be serious, I'm a career Air Force officer. It's been pointed out to me, not long ago actually, that marriage is a handicap for a successful career in the Royal Air Force. You must be ready for a posting anywhere, for as long as the government feels it is necessary. And to be even more serious, military flying often results in a lot of widows."

They sat quietly for a minute. Then Chadwick asked, "Would you like to eat here?"

"Perhaps you'd better take me home. I'm sorry for spoiling what was supposed to be a fun outing."

The headlamps behaved perfectly on the way to Penelope's house. After she climbed out of the car, Allan let out the clutch with a shower of gravel from the rear tires. On the way to the mess, Codrington's remarks about the three Ms rang through his mind.

Chapter Twenty-Three

Codrington called Chadwick into his office. "Just had a word with Pemberton. Flight trials of the Anson are delayed by about a week."

"Sorry to hear that. What's the problem?"

"Apparently the contraption they made to actuate the controls required more room. Some surgery is needed on the lower part of the fuselage. However, coincidentally, I got a call from the Telecommunications Research people. Do you remember flying a bunch of them around a few weeks ago? The plane with the radios is still here at Farnborough. They want to use it to do some test involving the BBC transmitter at Droitwich. They need to fly around in a pattern while communicating with their mates on the ground. There is quite a panic to get this data. Tests should only take a few days. Do you think you could handle it? When it's over, Pemberton should be close to being ready."

"Where would we be based, sir?"

"I think RAF Honiley is suitable, about eight miles southeast of Coventry."

"How many will be going?"

"I think you as captain and Geoff Healey as second pilot should fit the bill. The T.R. people will supply technicians. We're basically bus drivers."

Chadwick thought about it. Putting some distance between himself and Penelope seemed a good thing, but he would be sorry to leave the Bentley. He had an idea. "Would it be all right if I drive up to Honiley, sir? Flying Officer Healy can fly the plane up."

"Ah, you're in love with that car. All right, do that. Drive up the day after tomorrow. I'll contact Honiley for accommodations and first-line plane maintenance. Let Flying Officer Healey know the drill. Perhaps you'd better go over the plane with him this afternoon."

Chadwick stopped by the office to look at a road map. It was about ninety-five miles to Honiley as the crow flies, about a five-hour trip by car, six hours allowing for lunch. In the afternoon, Codrington authorized an air worthiness flight for the radio-equipped plane, which had not flown for several weeks. Chadwick carefully checked the plane and flew with Flying Officer Healey, who was quite happy to fly it to RAF Honiley the following day.

Chadwick left soon after breakfast. The traffic near Windsor and Ascot kept the Bentley in third and sometimes second gear, but as he cleared the London outlying towns, the road opened up and he was able to tool along nicely in fourth. He stopped for lunch in Banbury, parking the old car near the Banbury Cross, made famous by the nursery rhyme.

He pulled into Honiley in time for afternoon tea in the mess. Codrington had made arrangements for the team from Telecommunications to meet Chadwick. They were staying at a hotel in Coventry. The technicians climbed into the plane to check the radio and install some new equipment.

Chadwick and Healey sat down with the team leader, Dr. Kenneth Bostock, who explained the reason for the tests. "The possibility of building a 'Death Ray' was brought to the attention of the Prime Minister—the idea that a radio wave could kill or injure a combatant is nonsense, of course. But the Telecommunications Research group had been asked to look into it. We did a few tests and concluded that it would be impossible to build such a device using radio waves. But using much lower power radio waves may allow an aircraft to be detected by sensing a signal reflected from the plane.

"The highest power transmitter in England is the BBC transmitter, with aerials at Droitwich. The plane you're going to fly will confirm that such a system could work. There will be two teams, one on the ground near Droitwich with receivers that could sense a reflected wave, and one in the plane to measure the incident wave and communicate with the team on the ground."

Chadwick listened to Dr. Bostock. "I see no problem with tests if the weather cooperates. The aerials are seven hundred feet high. I won't fly lower then twelve hundred feet above the ground. Will that be satisfactory?"

This was agreed, and the team planned the first flight for the next day if the weather was clear. They took off by nine and were soon in communication with the team on the ground. After two hours of flying precisely over landmarks shown on Ordnance Survey maps, they landed back at Honiley. The ground team drove back to the base for lunch and went into a huddle with the men who had flown. After lunch Dr. Bostock asked for some more air time and said he would fly in the plane.

Chadwick took off thirty minutes after the car had left with the ground team. The drill was the same as the morning flight. Chadwick unbuckled and told Healey to move into the pilot's seat. He moved down the fuselage to see what the technical people were up to. Bostock was staring at a flat glass disk which had strange green shadows on it. Chadwick stood beside him, tapped on the glass, and asked, "What's that?"

Bostock shouted back over the noise of the engines, "It's a cathode ray tube, part of this instrument called an oscilloscope. Here, let me explain a little. An oscilloscope enables us to turn electrical currents into a visual pattern." He twisted a few knobs, and the green pattern stabilized on the screen into a sine wave. "This is the carrier wave of the BBC transmitter." He clicked more knobs, and the wave began to dance furiously on the screen, "It's jumping around because the carrier is now being modulated. If we tuned a wireless set to the carrier, we would hear what the BBC is transmitting, probably some music."

Chadwick was fascinated to learn a wireless signal could be transformed into something visual.

Bostock went on. "The chaps on the ground can also see the same signal. But in addition, they can see a wave reflected back from the plane. Because it has traveled further, it's slightly delayed. The delay time corresponds exactly to the distance from the plane to the ground receiver. With this set up, the phase of the reflected wave is changed and can be measured."

Chadwick grasped the idea right away, "I see. This would give you warning of approaching aircraft. Can you calculate the direction as well?"

"Not with this set up. This test just gives distance. We would need specially designed aerials to yield direction. That's what we'll be looking at in the future. We call it Radio, Detection and Range—RDR for short."

After landing, the technical experts returned to their hotel to analyze the results. Healey had relatives who lived near Coventry and arranged to meet Chadwick in the morning.

Chadwick had a hot bath and changed into a sports jacket. After dinner in the mess, he decided to take the Bentley for a tour of the local countryside. There was still a little daylight left.

He drove generally south, taking shaded lanes. Eventually he happened on a wide village green with a charming inn on the west side, topped by a thatched roof. He drove around the green and then parked at the inn, the White Hart. He ducked under the low lintel and entered the public bar. It was almost empty. An old man sat against a wall, smoking, with a nearly full glass in front of him. The barmaid sat on a tall stool, her chin resting on her elbows. Her full breasts were propped up on the countertop, bursting from the frilly blouse she was wearing.

"Good evening, sir, and what can I do for you?" Chadwick was sorely tempted to tell her what lecherous thoughts had crossed his mind when he first saw her, but, gentlemanly as always, he replied, "Pint of bitter, please."

"Watneys? Or the local brew, Donnington?"

"Donnington please." He always made it a point to try local ales, rather than the national brands. She drew a pint and set it on a cardboard mat. He lifted the glass and said, "Cheers," and took a sip. "Very quiet here tonight."

"Too quiet. This is the dullest village in the kingdom. It's busier on the weekend when people have been paid."

Chadwick put his hand across the bar. "I'm Allan. What's your name?"

"Esmeralda," she said. "It's Spanish. It means emerald."

"Unusual."

"My dad was always saying he suspected those Dagos that come around selling Spanish onions were having it off with my mum. But I *think* he was joking."

There was silence for a few minutes, Chadwick was surprised at her coarse language. *They live too close to their bloody animals in the country*, he thought.

"Are you traveling?" Esmeralda asked.

"RAF, just spending a couple of days at Honiley, down the road."

"Oh, it's getting dark," Esmeralda said. She went to some switches and put on the outside lights.

Through the windows Chadwick could see the Bentley gleaming in the spotlights.

"Is that your gorgeous car, Allan?"

"Yes, though it's very old." He drank some more beer. "What's closing time?"

"Ten, twenty minutes. Do you want any more?"

"No, thanks. One was just right."

Esmeralda came out from behind the bar. Chadwick admired her shapely figure as she crossed over to the old man against the wall, who was still staring at his drink.

"Come on, Charley, stir your stumps. Closing time." The old man grumbled, drank up and made his way to the door.

Esmeralda turned and faced Chadwick. "Are you going to give me a ride home in your fancy car? It's just a mile down the road." She smiled, sure that he would take her up on the offer.

"Of course."

"I'll just tidy up and turn off the lights."

Chadwick went to the men's W.C., which consisted of a sloping trough that disappeared through a hole in the wall. It smelled awful. He buttoned his trousers and returned to the bar, Esmeralda tied a cotton headscarf under her chin, "I'm ready." After climbing in the car, she waved a hand to the south. "A mile down there."

Esmeralda lived in a small cottage that soon came into view. Chadwick asked, "Do you live alone?"

"No, it's my mum's cottage." She caught the drift of Allan's question.

"Oh, don't worry, Mum always goes to bed when it gets dark. Saves paraffin."

"Paraffin?"

"Yes, electric only goes as far as the village. We'll get it one day, but we're used to candles and lanterns."

Inside, Allan put his arm around Esmeralda's waist. "Do you want a kiss?"

"If you want to. I don't go for that Hollywood romantic nonsense. I just need a good stuffing, so don't rush it. I hope you're not shy."

She began to undo his belt and shirt buttons.

On his way back to the base, Chadwick realized he didn't even know the name of the village. It was past one when he arrived at the gate of RAF Honiley. The sleepy guard waved him through without looking at his 1250 identification card.

In the morning, Dr. Bostock told Chadwick that the analysis they had done the previous night was very encouraging. They needed to confirm some position data and then they would be finished for the time being. Chadwick and Healey climbed into the plane, checked to see if the technical people were ready, and then took off into a light morning haze that was forecast to burn off. The drill was much the same as before and they landed before noon.

Dr. Bostock came to pick up the team that had flown and turned to thank Chadwick and Healey. "As I mentioned the results are very good. We were able to fix the range to your plane to within half a mile. We're very confident a chain of detectors could be set up to protect the south and east coasts. Of course, we'll design special transmitters, but the BBC was perfect to prove the principle. The Air Ministry chaps would like it operational by the time of the 1937 RAF Summer Exercises, which is a tall order. Please stay in touch, Allan. The more RAF pilots understand it, the better. And perhaps I'll get a ride in your magnificent car."

Chadwick told Healey they would return to Farnborough the next day, weather permitting. He debated about another visit to the anonymous village but decided instead to write a report for Dr. Thorpe, the team leader of the bombsight development group. He described the tests he had just participated in to determine the feasibility of radio detection and ranging. He suggested it could also work in reverse—a signal to a bomber could yield bearing and distance to a target. This would be more accurate than astronomical calculations and it would be immune to clouds and bad weather.

When Dr. Thorpe received Chadwick's suggestion, he called a friend at the Telecommunications Research laboratory. His friend was shocked. The work on "Death Ray" was super-secret and not to be discussed with anyone outside the group. Nevertheless, he conceded the suggestion seemed like a good idea and should be followed up.

When the Anson was ready, Chadwick and Healey prepared for the first flight with the prototype autopilot. They checked the controls on the ground, first manually and then using the control panel of the autopilot. They flew with two engineers from the development team. Several problems came to light and Chadwick found he was spending more and more time in the laboratory with the engineers as they tried to cure each fault. In the long evenings, he often took the Bentley for a spin. But he was never as lucky at the odd pubs he dropped into as he had been at Honiley.

He had been stung by Penelope's outburst and gave her a wide berth. But the lovemaking with Esmeralda had awakened a lust he had not felt since he stayed with Deborah in Rome, more than two years earlier.

Chapter Twenty-Four

Late one Friday afternoon, Chadwick called Inge Fischer and asked if she would like a run in the countryside in his new car. After she accepted for the following Sunday, he called Melanie Fitzgibbon. When she came to the phone, he introduced himself. "Hello, Melanie, this is Allan Chadwick."

She picked up on his name right away. "Allan, I remember you. We sat next to each at that dreary affair at Isbell's."

"Yes, that's right. You invited me to stop by some time. I was thinking of driving out your way on Sunday with a friend."

"Wonderful! Why don't you come in time for lunch? Ask anybody in Pangbourne for the way to Clair Court Hall."

Chadwick told Inge how to catch a train to Farnborough and he met her at the station with the Bentley just after nine on Sunday morning. She was visibly impressed.

Chadwick had pored over the road map, and he told her they were going first to Stonehenge. The roads were quiet, free of lorries, and he drove as fast as he could to Basingstoke, Andover, and Amesbury. He slowed down in the built-up towns and villages to thirty miles per hour, but on the open road the great machine was touching eighty and overtook the small amount of Sunday morning traffic effortlessly.

Just west of Amesbury, he saw the signs for public parking and pulled in next to a sprinkling of small cars. There was a makeshift stall selling soft drinks and he bought two glasses of sarsaparilla. The stall also had a leaflet about the history of Stonehenge. They sat in the car reading and sipping their drinks. Several men came to look at the Bentley and ask questions.

Then they walked through the stone arches that had been hauled from Wales more than four thousand years before. Inge told Allan how much she appreciated his effort to show her some English culture. She wondered furiously how she could get him to tell her what he was doing at Farnborough.

They climbed back in the Bentley and Allan pushed the RAC road map into Inge's hands. "Here, you navigate us to Pangbourne. Head for Marlborough first." As Melanie had predicted, they had no trouble getting directions to her house once they arrived in Pangbourne. They rumbled up the long driveway to the Georgian mansion in third gear. When Allan turned off the ignition there was a loud backfire.

Melanie came out to investigate, wearing a smock and a floppy hat. When she saw the Bentley, she put her hands on her hips and laughed uproariously. "What on earth have you brought, Allan? Is it the first horseless carriage?"

Allan chose to ignore her remark and introduced his companion, "This Julia, Melanie." They chattered as they walked around the side of the house.

"Where are you from, Julia?"

"Germany, the north part."

"Really, I would never have guessed it from your accent." They walked onto a lawn that sloped down to the river. "There are some bottled drinks in the basket," Melanie said, pointing to a table with deck chairs arranged alongside.

"First, I must powder my nose," Inge said, "You, see? I've been learning that English is an idiomatic language."

Allan helped himself to an IPA and walked down to the bank. A small wooden dock protruded into the river. When Inge returned, they all sat and contemplated the river.

Inge said, "It's beautiful here."

"Nice, this time of the year," Melanie conceded. "But come winter we can get flooding up to where we're sitting now. What are you doing in England, Julia?"

Inge gave her the well-worn fabrication, "I hope to become a professional translator. I'm picking up some English culture also. We drove to Stonehenge this morning on the way here."

"Quite a long diversion. Did you like it?"

"It was very interesting. And driving in Allan's old car is fun."

"Whenever you're hungry, there are cold cuts on the sideboard in the dining room," Melanie announced. After a few minutes, she led them into the house. "I'll give you a quick tour before we eat."

They walked through the library, drawing room, and living room. Each was furnished in an austere style, with mostly watercolors hanging on the walls. The living room had a large fireplace and cozy-looking easy chairs. Melanie waved her arm. "There's a solarium down there, and down this corridor are the kitchen and servant's quarters, though I don't have proper servants anymore."

"Then you live alone, Melanie?" Allan asked.

"Not quite. I have a housekeeper and a chauffeur-gardener. My son is back from Cambridge at the moment, but he'll be going back in a couple of weeks. He's leaving early—some work before term begins, he claims. I suspect a girl is involved."

"How old is he?" Allan asked.

"Nineteen. He was just a baby when his father was killed in the war. He'll inherit the title when he reaches his majority."

They carried their food to a large table and helped themselves to wine. When they finished, Inge asked to examine some paintings that had caught her eye.

"Help yourself, Julia," Melanie told her, "I'm going to have another glass."

Inge wandered into the drawing room.

"Is she your current girlfriend?" Melanie asked.

"Heavens, no. I met her a few months ago at a party at Honoria Pomeroy's house. A German chap who has something to do with their embassy introduced us. He said she was interested in English culture, hence the trip to Stonehenge."

"Come again, Allan—by yourself, perhaps." She put her hand on his and squeezed.

He looked at her face and she lifted her eyebrows.

"That dress you're wearing doesn't do much for your figure, Melanie."

"I know it's rather plain, but it's comfy and comes off easily." She smiled.

Chadwick dropped Miss Fischer at the railway station. On parting, she told him she loved the old car, she loved Stonehenge, and she loved Clair Court. She didn't say she loved Chadwick. He still thought she was a rather cold fish.

In fact, Julia/Inge had still been a little scared she might inadvertently make a slip and reveal her true identity. When she returned to London, she wrote another coded message for the Abwehr in Hamburg and a more detailed report for Dr. Kegel. He followed up with a verbal report a few days later. He was disappointed to learn that Chadwick had not made any overt pass and began to think perhaps it was time to return Fischer and Stiller to Germany.

Chapter Twenty-Five

Chadwick realized one evening it had been nearly three weeks since he had driven to Pangbourne. Melanie's coy invitation was still fresh on his mind when he called and arranged to see her the following weekend.

"Come about four, Allan. That gives us time for a cocktail and then we can have dinner at one of the local restaurants. You are welcome to spend the night—save you driving in the dark. By the way, please park your fire-breathing machine in the stables. Just keep going past the main house. Looking forward to seeing you. Ciao."

After lunch on Saturday, he packed a few overnight items in a small bag and threw them on the back seat. It was raining. The Bentley had the top down, and he wore a heavy Macintosh and leather gloves. As he drove past the front door of Clair Court Hall, he sounded a brief blip on the horn. He parked next to an impressive Rolls Royce and a modest Vauxhall saloon. He grabbed his bag and made a dash for the front door.

Melanie was waiting in the hall; she was dressed in a tweed skirt and a pullover. "Welcome, Allan! What a pig of an afternoon it's turned into. You must have got soaked in your old car. Dump your coat in here."

"Hello, Melanie. Thanks for the invite. Actually, it's dry so long as you keep moving, but when you stop the rain comes in."

"You must want something to warm up the insides." She led the way into the living room, where a cheerful fire burned in the grate. Several decanters stood on a side table. She waved at them. "Help yourself. I've already started."

Allan poured a Scotch with a splash from the soda water bottle.

"Cheers." They touched their glasses.

"I see you have a couple of cars—do you drive the Rolls?"

"Goodness, no. The Vauxhall's just my size. The family has always had connections with the county, so I get invited to dreary official palavers. Cedric, the gardener, drives me in the Rolls. So, tell me a bit about yourself, Allan."

Chadwick described his career in modest terms. "I had a scholarship to Cranwell College. Finished there and flew in Iraq for a few years. Now I'm a bus driver at Farnborough."

"I know there's a lot more to it than that. If you're a Cranwell man, the Air Force is a permanent career, right?"

"Yes, I have a permanent commission. But prospects are dim, unless—" he joked" —unless there is a war." Then he realized what a gaffe he had made. "Oh, I'm awfully sorry Melanie. I forgot for a moment you'd told me your late husband was killed in the last shindig."

"You're forgiven. It was a long time ago. I married John when I was seventeen, in 1916. You can't imagine what it was like. The obit columns ran into pages. John had an army commission, and we knew he would be going to France, so we got married, and copulated like rabbits. His son, John, was born in 1917, when his father was at the front. John came home for a few weeks in 1918, so he got to meet his son and heir. When he went back to France, he had left another bun in the oven. But after three months I had a miscarriage. I got the dreaded telegram from the War Office just the week before."

Chadwick's cheeks reddened with embarrassment. "God, Melanie, I am terribly, terribly sorry. I didn't mean to trigger such awful memories. Please forgive me."

"Don't worry, Allan. Perhaps you may be able to help me when you know me better. There is just one thing I worry about, however. My son will be just the right age to fight in the next war." There was a long silence. "But we mustn't sit here getting glum. Let's see what's on the wireless."

Melanie rose and went to a large, polished wooden radiogram. She lifted the lid and fiddled with knobs, and after a delay the sound of light classical music filled the room. "Ah, the good old BBC can always cheer us up. Pour yourself another, Allan."

Suiting her actions to her words she poured one for herself. A Strauss waltz started. Allan stood. "Care to dance?" He put his arm around her, and they shuffled on the carpet which did not lend itself to elegant dance steps.

After a minute Melanie pressed herself against him, and he bent his head and gave her a kiss. "I am an oaf," he said.

"No, you're not, Allan. I think we're going to be good friends."

They sat by the fire for a while and then Melanie stood up and announced she would change before dinner. "Come with me, Allan. I'll show you to your room."

They climbed some stairs and moved down a wide landing. Melanie opened a door. "Bring your things in here." They walked into a pleasant bedroom. Rain beat against the windowpanes. Melanie crossed over and drew the curtains. "My father-in-law spent a fortune adding bathrooms to a couple of the upstairs rooms. Of course, when the place was built, a hundred and fifty years ago, it simply had little closets with a chamber pot they called privies. Meet me downstairs."

After unpacking his few things Chadwick went back to the living room. He picked up his half-finished drink and sat by the fire. He reached out for a newspaper that was lying nearby, the *Daily Mail*, and saw that the headlines read, "Tension on Italian Somalia Border."

Melanie reappeared. She had changed into a woolen suit, saying, "I think it might get chilly later."

Allan was just about to make a derogatory remark about Italian warmongering when he realized that topic was not welcome. Instead, he quickly said, "What are the plans for dinner?"

"I know a cozy place just a few miles down the road, The Blue Bell. It's a pub with a nice dining room. Would you mind driving the Vauxhall?"

"No, of course not. When should we leave?"

"Anytime."

"Give me the key, I'll pick you up at the door. No sense in getting wet."

They walked to the entrance hall, Melanie got a key from a drawer in the clothes stand and gave it to Allan.

"I'll be back in a jiffy." He sprinted to the stable and started the Vauxhall. Compared to the mighty rumble that came from his Bentley, the Vauxhall engine sounded almost tinny. He drove to the front of the house, but before he could open the car door, Melanie darted out and flung herself into the car.

"Turn left at the end of the drive."

Allan followed her directions and in about twenty minutes, they pulled up outside a solid brick building. Melanie climbed out and he parked the car a few yards away. Inside she had already been shown to a table by a waiter who clearly knew her. They ordered drinks and Allan studied the menu. It was high-class pub food.

As they ate their dinner in a leisurely manner, Melanie began to talk. "I mentioned earlier that I'm very worried about my son, John, becoming trapped by another war. In a way, that's how we met. All the people at the Isbell's dinner party are, in one way or another, determined to prevent another war. I made my concern known to some of my political friends and that's why I was there. I'm not sure why you were there. You are, after all, a soldier."

"I'm not sure myself, Melanie. I was invited by Lord Lowestoft. He and a friend of his I met were interested in my experiences in Iraq and Egypt."

"A talk given by a friend of the Viscount emphasized how difficult international relations are, how subtle. He said that nations must be well-matched, that if one nation becomes more powerful than another, hot heads may force a war to gain territory. And this part is hard to swallow—that the duty of intelligence agents is to ensure that a potential enemy knows your strengths as well as your weaknesses, so that it can be matched and avoid an imbalance. It sounds almost like treason. In other words, secrets are dangerous. I think I have that correct. I didn't know that you were Air Force until this afternoon, but you must know a lot of secrets. Is that why you went to Isbell's?"

Allan laughed so loudly that other diners turned to look. "Melanie, I don't know many secrets, and if I did, I wouldn't tell a potential enemy, imbalance or not. That chap sounds a little crazy."

"Well, things are so complicated these days. As I said, my son is nineteen. I can't bear the thought of him dying in some pointless war. Sometimes I have nightmares."

"I'm so sorry, Melanie. It must be terrible sometimes to be a mother. But you know, not all wars are pointless. There are, unfortunately, evil people. History books are full of 'em. They will conquer and enslave people who aren't strong enough to stop them. Don't ask me how you draw the line, but today, it's better for Great Britain to be as strong as possible, not weak. Come on, this is too serious. Tell me why you invited me to Clair Court, Melanie."

"I'm hoping you will take me to bed, Allan, if you want an older woman."

"Melanie, at Isbell's you looked absolutely gorgeous."

"Ha." Melanie gave a short chuckle. "I was wearing an old bustier. I wanted to give the codgers that attend those affairs something to look at. It was rather uncomfortable."

"Well, I enjoyed looking too. You're not old—you said your son was nineteen, so you must be about thirty-six. That's only a few years older than me."

"How few exactly?"

"Eight." There was silence for a few minutes. "Would you like to finish with a liqueur, Melanie?"

"Yes, Allan, I'll have a Drambuie."

He signaled a waiter and ordered two Drambuie. They sipped the fiery spirit very slowly. "Are John's parents still alive?"

"His mother died of the flu, in 1920. His father was very active until about four years ago. Then his mind began to go. He's in a nursing home now. I run the estate, with some help. I have a manager who's part of a partnership with a solicitor. My two servants, Cedric and Myrtle, can't possibly look after the Hall, so now and then I have a professional cleaning company come in and give the place a thorough blast. Same with the outside maintenance. The estate produces a reasonable income to keep things shipshape until my son inherits."

"You sound astonishingly competent." They finished their drinks. Allan paid the waiter, and they made their way to the car. It was still raining. He dropped off Melanie at the door of the Hall and parked the Vauxhall, then dashed back inside, where Melanie was waiting in the hall.

"Do you want to go directly upstairs?"

"You bet. Don't keep me waiting." Allan gave Melanie a sensuous kiss. They undressed quickly in her bedroom and climbed into bed beneath a heavy Eiderdown. He ran his hands gently along her body,

"That's nice, don't stop. I'm not too fond of experimental positions. I like a long, steady grind."

They were both experienced lovers and satisfied each other until sleep overtook them. Allan awoke in the small hours. Melanie was twisting and turning, and her fists were clenched.

God, he thought, *she's having a nightmare. Was I that bad?*

He soon fell asleep again. Melanie was bright and cheerful as she came out of the bathroom in the morning,"Good morning, love. That was a wonderful night, and I think the sun has come out." She drew back the curtain, and sunlight flooded in. Their clothes were still lying on the carpet. She picked up her jacket with her toe.

"We're terrible, but you have to have some fun, now and again." She climbed back into bed,Allan embraced her, and they made love again.

After they dressed, Allan retired to his bathroom for a shave. Melanie ran downstairs and came back to announce breakfast would be ready in five minutes. Fried sausage, eggs, toast, and coffee were laid out on the sideboard. Over the breakfast table they looked at each other.

Allan waved a sausage on the end of his fork."Your housekeeper—was she here last night?"

"Yes, she knows her position. Servants in the great houses are very discreet if they want a reference, but it does raise a point. Your visits to Clair Court Hall will have to be sporadic. I can't afford a scandal. The family is a fixture in this part of the county."

Allan looked a little despondent. "I fully understand your position."

"Don't look so down in the mouth. I feel sure we will be good for each other, and there are plenty of nice places to meet—London, Brighton, Paris. Are you on?"

"Melanie, you make it sound exciting. When I think about it, a mistress may be a good idea. I get a little stressed sometimes. How was I as a gigolo?"

"With practice I might be able to whip you into shape." She laughed,"I think I'm in love."

"The weather has turned nice. How about a ride in the Bentley this morning?"

"All right, I'll get a warm coat. Let's have lunch in Oxford."

The run into Oxford took less than an hour with the light Sunday traffic. They parked without difficulty and walked toward the Thames River. On a small dock they noticed a placard, "River Tour Leaving in Ten Minutes." They looked at each other, and both said at the same time, "Why not?" and laughed. Allan bought tickets and they boarded a steam-operated launch.

When they returned, Melanie looked at her watch. "Lunch time, my love." She knew just where to go. The place wasn't crowded, and Allan found a secluded nook. They ordered two beers. The service was slow, but it didn't matter. They felt on air—they had all the time in the world. There was nobody within earshot. Melanie leaned close to Allan, "There's something on my mind. It's rather delicate. I hope you understand when I explain."

"You're pregnant?" He laughed and rubbed her tummy.

"No, not that, although that's something else we have to talk about. No, this is serious. John was an officer, so I know what the pay scale is. It's designed for men with a private income. If we're going to spend weekends away in yummy surroundings, you couldn't afford it. The estate has a good income, so it's going to pay for our trysts. I want us to have a lovely affair, without scrimping. I know it can be misinterpreted, but I would like you to open a new bank account. The estate will make deposits to cover our expenses, but convention requires that you pay the bills."

"You're a hard woman, Melanie, but logical. But how long will this last?"

"Till we both feel it has run its course. Hopefully, a long time. There is one thing, however. I don't like triangles. We must be faithful to each other."

"I agree, though it sounds a bit like marriage."

"We'll make it the fun part of marriage without the domestic tedium."

"And the other thing?"

"When I had the miscarriage, it required surgical intervention. Afterwards the doctors told me I could not conceive another baby."

Allan put his hand on Melanie's. "It must have been very difficult for you. I'm sorry." But to himself he thought, *Good. That disposes of the Lisa Scharf problem.*

They walked back to the car, Allan told Melanie the myth about the effect of Bentley vibration on females, and she was intrigued, "I'll investigate that on the way home." When they arrived at Clair Court, she said it really worked—he'd better stay an hour, or she would go mad.

When he flopped beside her, exhausted, she confessed, "I don't think the Bentley was responsible. I was pulling your leg. I must be an addict. The more I get the more I want. Go, love, before I chain you down."

Chadwick packed his things and left for the trip back to Farnborough. He was exhilarated and drove with a foot hard on the throttle when the road was open. But there was a black cloud. He was worried by the politics she had mentioned, the so-called "Insiders" appeasement attempts. He desperately wished there was someone he could trust for good advice, as he was out of his depth. And then it came to him in a flash of inspiration; he would write to Doug Larson in Egypt.

Larson was a captain in the Military Police. He had moved into counterespionage in Egypt. He and Chadwick had a brief adventure involving an agent working for the other side. Larson was just the man to offer advice on dealing with the appeasers.

Chapter Twenty-Six

Squadron Leader Codrington invited Chadwick into his office for a review of progress with the autopilot development. Chadwick was very positive—the thing worked.

"But will it work with all aircraft?" Codrington asked.

"I can't say for sure. We've done all the testing with the Anson. Pemberton has designed some adjustments for critical parameters—rate of response and damping. These have enough range to cover all expected aerodynamic characteristics."

"There's a lot of skepticism coming from manufacturers. To compound the problem, I'm told the RAF will procure all new bomber types with autopilots installed. This means more work for you. The manufacturers have agreed to install a Farnborough autopilot in prototypes. Pemberton has contracted to have enough units made by an instrument supplier. When a plane is deemed airworthy, you will brief the company pilots and fly with first autopilot testing flight. There's a lot of money involved here, Allan. We have to be very careful. Related to this, there's a rumor the bigwigs plan a very high-level meeting to discuss current research and development and how it will affect operational readiness."

Four days later Chadwick was told a prototype Handley Page Hampden bomber would be ready for flight trials in a couple of weeks. The plane was assembled at Cricklewood, near London. Technicians from Pemberton's group were installing an autopilot. The pneumatic system was installed by Handley Page, using Farnborough blueprints.

Chadwick called Melanie Fitzgibbon and they arranged to meet in London on the next Saturday afternoon. She would make all the arrangements. He stopped in at a new bank in Farnborough and opened an account with five pounds transferred from his old bank. He took a bus from the base, as he didn't want to leave his Bentley parked overnight at the Farnborough station. Melanie was also traveling by rail. Allan took the Underground to Paddington to meet her train.

In a taxi she told him she had booked a double room at a modest hotel in Chelsea in the name of Mr. and Mrs. Chadwick. She had asked the hotel concierge to book two tickets to see a musical at the Shaftesbury Theatre that evening. When he signed the register, it reminded Melanie to get the details of his new bank account, and she said her bank would transfer fifty pounds.

In the lift, Allan started to tell Melanie about his planned visit to the Handley Page factory in Cricklewood, but he had not got far before they arrived at their room. He unlocked the door and she flung herself on the double bed.

Much later they unpacked their things and walked into the street. An Italian restaurant caught their eye, and after sharing bagna cauda, spaghetti Bolognese and a bottle of Chianti, they hailed a cab and drove to the theatre. The show was cheerful and there was a comedian who told slightly risqué jokes. In the interval, Allan managed to squeeze up to the bar and get two glasses of wine. In the second half he dozed off. Melanie gave him a jab when the show was over, and they picked up their coats and took a taxi back to the hotel.

To Melanie's disappointment, Chadwick fell fast asleep when they got back to the room. "Fine lover you are," she whispered in his ear, with a smile.

He made up for it before breakfast, which they eventually ate in the hotel dining room. It was traditional—kippers, sausage, stewed tomatoes and baked beans, toast, and marmalade featured large on the menu. In the taxi back to Paddington, Melanie told Allan next weekend was out, and she had an obligatory attendance at some civic function in Reading. They kissed in the taxi and Allan stayed in it as far as Waterloo station.

Chapter Twenty-Seven

To Chadwick's surprise he was called to the telephone in the mess one evening after dinner. It was Honoria Pomeroy, who wanted to see him. They met at a tea shop in Farnborough one afternoon. Mrs. Pomeroy got straight to the point,

"When Penelope came back from a ride in the Bentley with you about three months ago, she was distraught. It was nothing you did. In fact, it was apparently something you did not do. She raved at me and my husband, saying she felt her life was wasted, that she was achieving nothing. She had been impressed by news stories of women aviators like Amy Johnson and Amelia Earhart. Well, the upshot was she wanted to learn how to fly."

Chadwick interrupted, "This is really a surprise to me. Nothing I said could be interpreted as a wish for her to fly."

Mrs. Pomeroy snapped back impatiently, "I know that. Wait until I've finished. I'm not blaming you in any shape or form. Tom and I agreed for her to get flying lessons at Marlow Aero Club, just outside High Wycombe. They have a licensed instructor. After ten flights in a Tiger Moth, he said she was ready for solo. In fact, he said she had a natural flair for flying. She now has about forty-five hours of air time, more than half of that flying solo, although she has sometimes taken friends for a ride."

Honoria did not mention that Penelope had become friendly with Gerd Stiller and had twice flown with him as a passenger. "Tom and I simply don't know where this is leading. For one thing, renting a Tiger Moth is expensive. For another we're nervous she might do something crazy."

Chadwick remained silent.

"Well, the reason I asked to meet you is to request a real favor—would you fly with Penelope and give us your opinion about her abilities in this new venture?"

"Mrs. Pomeroy, I have to say immediately I'm not a licensed instructor. In fact, although I fly for the government, I don't even have a civilian pilot's license. Have you mentioned this idea to Penelope?"

"Yes, Tom and I had a heart-to-heart talk with her last night. It's difficult to express our concern without making it sound like we're acting as examiners, which puts you on the spot. Penelope wasn't keen on the idea, but truth be told, we control the purse strings. We'll continue to pay for lessons if she wants to pursue a commercial license. Only a handful of women in Great Britain have reached that level."

"It sounds like you're being very generous. If I fly with Penelope, I will have to go as a passenger, with her as the authorized pilot. A Tiger Moth has full dual controls, so the distinction is academic. I'm free on Saturday afternoon. You can pick me up at the mess and take me to Marlow if there's a plane for us."

Mrs. Pomeroy was overwhelmingly grateful and promised to leave a message for him if all the arrangements were made successfully. When she left a message confirming a flight on Saturday afternoon, he called her back and asked her not to mention the arrangement to anyone at the club. On the surface Penelope was simply taking a friend for a flying experience.

Mrs. Pomeroy and Penelope duly picked him up after lunch. Penelope gave Chadwick a distant, rather cold greeting. The day had started out sunny but high overcast clouds were moving in. Chadwick wore a warm overcoat, as he assumed the club would provide what flying gear was needed.

At Marlow he was introduced to the flying instructor and shown how to operate a parachute. The instructor took his overcoat and lent him a Sidcot flying suit and canvas helmet with an aural intercom called a Gosport tube. While Penelope was checking the plane exterior, Chadwick took a quick glance in the cockpit.

The flight instruments consisted only of an altimeter, magnetic compass, and slip indicator. Engine rpm, oil pressure, and temperature were mounted on the right of the dash. Air speed was read off a pointer mounted on a wing strut; air pressure forced a calibrated plate against a spring. He climbed into the forward cockpit. The pilot sat in the rear cockpit. Penelope asked if he was securely belted in, and he picked up the rubber mouthpiece and confirmed he was. His own voice in the rubber earpiece sounded eerie.

She competently went through the preflight checks, started the engine, did an engine run-up test, and waved away the chocks. Club members pushed on the wing tips to align the plane into wind. The Tiger Moth had no wheel brakes and steered on the ground with the rudder and a tail skid. Penelope smoothly increased the engine rpm, held the stick forward until the plane gained enough speed to get the tail up.. She climbed away holding fifty knots on the primitive airspeed indicator.

"I suggest you head west and climb to three thousand feet, Penny," Chadwick yelled into the Gosport mouthpiece.

She did not acknowledge, which was a breach of RAF flying discipline, but the heading changed to two hundred and eighty-five degrees and the plane slowly gained height. She leveled off at three thousand feet and adjusted engine speed and mixture.

"Try a few turns, Penny, left and then right, and watch your height." Chadwick glanced to the side to make sure the air was clear.

The height jogged up and down a hundred feet as Penelope turned south and then north. Chadwick thought she did quite well for a beginner. "Have you been taught any aerobatic maneuvers, Penny?"

"I've done a couple of loops."

"Fine. Run through the checks and try a loop, heading west."

The wings dipped as Penelope checked clearance under the plane. Then she put the nose down and increased the engine speed. The plane was diving at about ninety knots when she pulled up the nose and started a steep climb. The speed fell off as the plane arched upwards. As it went through the inverted horizontal position, Chadwick noted with satisfaction the wings were parallel with horizon. Penelope pulled back the throttle and pulled a couple of G's at the bottom of the loop. As the plane climbed, she added power and leveled off at two thousand five hundred feet.

"Well done, Penny, that was good. You only lost a few hundred feet. Climb back to three thousand and we'll try something else."

Penelope initiated a climb but held the airspeed low.

"Have you performed a spin?"

At three thousand feet she suddenly pulled the stick back and kicked on hard left rudder. Chadwick said, "You're trying a spin? Please recover after two turns."

The Tiger Moth shuddered and fell into a left-hand spin. After a turn and a half, the spin began to tighten, and the centrifugal force increased.

"That's enough, Penny, recover now." Chadwick tried to push the stick forward, but it was immovable. He pushed hard on the rudder bar. Penelope still maintained left rudder pressure. The plane was now turned faster, and the nose began to pitch up and down.

Chadwick pressed with all his might on the rudder bar. He began to over-power Penelope's force and gradually move the stick. "Penny, what are you up to? Let go the stick immediately. With the stick hard back, the elevators blanket the rudder and reduce its effectiveness. Let go the stick. I have control."

The thought flashed through his mind that he had survived several serious crashes, but it looked like he would cash in his chips in an elementary trainer.

The ride was getting rough, with both occupants thrown wildly against their straps. Suddenly Penelope let go of the stick and Chadwick was able to push it fully forward. The plane stopped turning in an inverted dive. He glanced at the altimeter thinking, *God, nine hundred feet, less than eight hundred feet above the ground.*

Hanging in the straps, Chadwick did a quick assessment and decided there was no air space to complete an inverted loop. He quickly rolled the Tiger Moth and began to pull up. He had to judge the "G" force versus the vertical clearance, too much "G" would pull the wings off the plane. The nose began to rise, and he found he was looking at the horizon, not green earth.

When the altimeter stopped unwinding it indicated two hundred feet. The ground was perilously close. Thankfully, the engine responded instantly to the throttle and he climbed to a thousand feet. He could hear Penelope sobbing over the Gosport tube.

Chadwick wasn't sure what was wrong with her, but he decided to play it calmly. His pulse was returning to normal. "You need some more practice with spin recovery. Do you want to fly back or should I?"

"I'll take it." They landed without any additional incidents, and when the plane rolled to a stop, Chadwick loosened his straps and turned around to look at Penelope.

"What was that all about?"

Tears streaked her face and she looked flushed.

"Better clean yourself up before we taxi in."

There was silence between them. The engine ticked over smoothly.

"Why should you control my future? I am nothing to you. Men rule this god-damned world."

"I'm not trying to control you, and I will say nothing to your parents. You'd better mention to the instructor that the plane should be checked for possible overstressing."

Penelope taxied back to the clubhouse and shut down the engine. When she went to sign in, Chadwick climbed down and began to shake himself out of the Sidcot suit.

Mrs. Pomeroy came up to him, "Well?"

"Wait till Penny gets back."

When she returned Chadwick spoke to them both. "I think Penny is very competent considering her level of experience. But if she wants a commercial ticket, she must get time on much heavier aircraft. Maybe she could get a job with one of the local ferry companies that fly from Marlow or a nearby airfield."

Penny shot him a look of amazed gratitude.

"Also, there's a lot of study needed for the written exam, and she needs to learn navigation if she truly wants to fly as a commercial pilot."

Looking at Penny he said, "It's a long path to learn a new profession, but worth it. Bonne chance!"

Chapter Twenty-Eight

Chadwick returned to the mess with Honoria Pomeroy, while Penelope stayed at Marlow to get another flight before the end of the afternoon. Mrs. Pomeroy told him that she and her husband had decided to lease a Tiger Moth for Penny if Chadwick's assessment was favorable, so that Penny could accumulate the flying hours needed for a commercial license. Several weeks later, he got a letter from Penny with a photograph showing her standing proudly by her own plane.

When Mrs. Pomeroy dropped him off, Chadwick went straight to the bar and downed a stiff Scotch. Then he took the Bentley into the town to get some special tools for work he planned to do on the engine the next day. When he checked into the office, he found a mass of material describing the Handley Page Hampden bomber, which he was expected to absorb before flying it in the following week.

When he telephoned Melanie, they agreed to meet in London on the weekend. As he drove to Cricklewood in the Bentley, he felt a certain irony, as that was where the car was made, though the Bentley factory was long gone. The Handley Page Company found him accommodation in Cricklewood near the airfield and he met the test pilots. They had already flown the first prototype and pronounced it a pleasant plane to fly but very cramped. Chadwick was surprised to learn the fuselage was as narrow as a fighter, even though the plane was rated a bomber. The company pilots were very eager to try the autopilot, and Chadwick spent a couple of hours with them going over the salient technical details.

They flew the next day. Chadwick had to stand behind the pilot, as there was no room to fit in beside him. He showed them how to test the performance by flying manually on a fixed heading, selecting a heading on the autopilot, which was different by ninety degrees, and then switching to auto control. With a well-adjusted system, the plane swung smoothly to the new heading without over-shooting or losing height. The company pilots were impressed, and after a several hours in the air, Chadwick felt he had done all that was expected of him.

One of the younger pilots, Neil Bishop, suggested dinner together. They met at a restaurant in Cricklewood and exchanged stories over drinks. Chadwick was interested to hear the young man had joined the company as an apprentice and learned to fly with company pilots. When Bishop found out that Chadwick had served in Iraq, he was agog for details and bemoaned the tedious flying the company required for production aircraft. Chadwick had had just enough to drink that he told the young man to wait, prophesying that there would be a war within six years, and then he would get all the excitement he craved.

Chadwick walked back to the hotel and slept soundly. In the morning he put a few things in a small bag. He did not check out when he left to catch the Underground into central London; the company had paid for his room through Sunday. The hotel had parking behind the building, and he felt he could leave his car there safely for the night.

Melanie had booked a room at a hotel near Euston Station. They had agreed to meet in the bar at lunch time. After he signed the register for both of them, he went to bar and waited. He was toying with a bottle of Heineken lager when it reminded him of waiting for the Germans, Emsden and Kegel, at the Cheshire Cheese on Fleet Street. He wondered what Joyce was up to. If he had not planned to meet Melanie that evening, he might have been tempted, while he was in London, to look her up again. *My God*, he thought, *I am turning into real satyr.* But his libidinous thoughts were interrupted by Melanie's arrival.

"Darling," she exclaimed and gave him a chaste hug. She was wearing a smart purple hat with a cockade. The color of the fur trim on her jacket matched her dark hair.

"Melanie, how nice to see you! Good trip?"

"Lots of shoppers coming into town but first class was not crowded."

"Lunch?"

"Yes, we can eat here. Saves time."

They moved to the dining room, where Allan ordered another Heineken and Melanie opted for shandy. He had just read a newspaper article about fishing in the North Sea, so he ordered Dover sole. Melanie had a pork chop. He stared at his fish when the plate was put before him. According to the article he'd read, this fish had been thrashing in the well of a trawler less than twelve hours earlier. Amazingly, it had been entrained to London, whisked through Billingsgate, and delivered to the hotel kitchen while he was traveling to eat it. *What an astonishing world we live in*, he thought, *and yet so fragile*.

"Darling, you look so philosophical. What's the matter?"

"Oh nothing, really. What entertainment have you laid on for our visit, apart from the unmentionable?"

"We have seats at the Savoy. I think they're doing *The Mikado*."

Both were silent while they ate. There was an unspoken desire to get upstairs without wasting time. Chadwick signed the bill, and they went to their room.

"I've been dreaming of this moment for days, love," Melanie whispered.

"So have I, dear," Allan murmured in her ear. He felt it would be unromantic to mention that Bentley engines and tricky autopilots had mostly been in his thoughts.

Melanie began to get passionate. Allan paced himself, and she moaned loudly.

"My love, it's the middle of the afternoon. You mustn't make so much noise."

"Shush!" she cried as a violent paroxysm shook her body. It lasted for half a minute, then she pushed him away. "God, that was fantastic. I can't believe it. The sensation is like standing in front of a furnace door."

Allan let her lie for a while, recovering, and then he reentered and had an orgasm of his own. They clutched each other in a sweaty embrace. Afterwards, they shared a hot bath, and later walked into the lounge in time for afternoon tea.

The weather was dry, and they decided to stroll to the Savoy Theatre, as they had plenty of time before the show began. On Tottenham Court Road they enjoyed leisurely window shopping. When they got to the theatre district, they crossed the busy road and walked on Garrick to a cozy pub with flowers outside. In a shady room, they ordered drinks and tried a few small sausage rolls which had silently appeared. It was only a short walk to the Savoy on the Strand.

Allan had never seen *The Mikado* before, and he was taken by the bright costumes and sets. The libretto was clever and the tunes catching, and they thoroughly enjoyed it. They took a taxi back to the hotel and fell asleep after rather restrained lovemaking, though they were less restrained in the morning before breakfast.

Allan paid the bill, but they left their bags with the concierge and took a cab to Petticoat Lane Market. It was packed. "Keep a close eye on your pockets, dear," Melanie warned Allan. "They can pick you clean and then sell the stuff back to you twenty minutes later."

She mulled over the bric-a-brac but in the end bought nothing. They shared a small paper bag of cockles, which they sprinkled with vinegar and pepper, and ate with toothpicks. After a walk to Aldgate, they found an empty cab for the ride back to the hotel and Paddington station. Allan kissed Melanie warmly as they parted and told her it had been a lovely weekend. He then caught the Underground to Cricklewood, checked out of the hotel, fired up the Bentley, and drove west.

On the way back he pondered carefully about his work with Mr. Pemberton. He decided it was probably important, but the conviction had been growing that the urgent development of radio detection by Dr. Bostock was of supreme importance for the RAF and the country. He was back at the mess in good time for a drink before dinner.

In the morning he briefed Squadron Leader Codrington on the visit to the Handley Page factory, saying that the autopilot performed flawlessly, and the test pilots had no difficulty learning how to handle it. He suggested to Codrington that the Telecommunications Research team developing radio detection could benefit from an RAF officer organizing their flying activities, namely him. He pointed out that familiarizing companies with new bomber prototypes to the new autopilot could easily be fitted in.

Codrington told him he had it on good authority that a high-level decision would be made shortly, one that would give priority to research and development projects. He advised Allan to just wait and see.

Deciding a little politics could do no harm, Chadwick called Dr. Bostock and mentioned his idea of an RAF liaison officer attached to his team to facilitate airborne trials. His idea was received enthusiastically.

Chapter Twenty-Nine

The meeting of high-level officers took place at RAF headquarters in High Wycombe. The purpose of the meeting was to give the operational commanders an overview of what to expect from current research and development, and to urge them to set some priorities. Naval and army leaders were also invited. It emerged that developments of more powerful engines and new alloys were the death knell of biplanes and fabric-covered aerofoil surfaces. The new aircraft would be all metal, and fighters, at least, would have desirable top speeds of about three hundred knots. Bombers would be capable of operating at a minimum of twenty thousand feet and possess a range of at least one thousand, five hundred nautical miles.

Due to concerns of bombing accuracy, specifications were being prepared for four-engine heavy bombers capable of carrying a load of over ten thousand pounds. The defense of the British Isles fell to a newly formed Fighter Command and Army anti-aircraft batteries. Early warning of an attack was essential, together with as much information as possible about the strength, location, and speed of the attacker. Very early detection could be provided by wireless direction finders monitoring wireless traffic as bombers assembled. Early warning and tracking could be provided by several techniques—acoustic, infra-red, and radio signals.

After some trials, the priority was given to reflection of radio waves, a project they called Chain Home. It was planned to have at least twenty stations in operation on the southeast coast within two years, some of which would be ready for the 1937 summer exercises. It was emphasized that the design of the Radio Detection and Range (RDR) system was far from optimized. It was being assembled quickly using mostly commercial components already available and when in operation would be heavy on manpower requirements.

Range depended on many factors, including sunspot activity. It was estimated that a minimum accurate detection range of fifty to seventy-five miles could be depended on, perhaps half an hour or less at expected bomber speeds. The next generation of RDR would use much higher frequencies, and components were being devised. Chain Home would not work once attackers crossed the coast. Defense then would depend mainly on barrage balloons and anti-aircraft guns. Detection would be provided by the Observer Corps and possibly acoustic means. Estimation of height was not very accurate and took time. It was believed RDR range accuracy would be better than several miles. Measurement of the direction of attacking forces was the most urgent development under way at the present. A very wide telephone network would be required.

Questions, answers, and opinions were voiced well into the night. Summaries of this important meeting filtered down to more junior officers and even eventually to the Isbell's Insiders, although original transcripts were not available. Security had been good.

When he heard the gist of the meeting, Viscount Addenbury spoke to some of the men he regarded as his most senior advisers. "This RDR system seems potentially to have great promise and great drawbacks. We must keep abreast of development. We must consider a very fine line in our attempts to prevent another devastating war by passing what we think is important information to a possible antagonist to maintain a balance of power. But we shouldn't tip the scale to give the same antagonist an advantage that may lead to a conflagration— and the possible subjugation of our country. Some of my colleagues in the House have expressed an admiration for events in Europe to counter the rise of the Soviet Union which may threaten our liberty.

"Enough said," he concluded. "Let us turn again to the RDR system, which is under development mainly for the RAF, though clearly there are naval implications. Who is running this work?"

Lord Lowestoft spoke up. "Technical development of this nature is carried out by experts, typically at the Telecommunications Research establishment. But coordination with RAF requirements will almost certainly be controlled by Fighter Command and the Research Center at Farnborough. Curiously enough, I became acquainted with an officer who serves at Farnborough because of my interest in German intelligence activity in the Middle East where he spent four years. Quite by chance his next posting was Farnborough. He's a single man, and I've encouraged Melanie Fitzgibbon to become close. You may recall she lost her husband in '18. The family estate is in Bucks, and she lives only an hour from Farnborough. I've authorized our Insider's treasury to provide some small funds to assist the friendship. The Fitzgibbon estate itself is in parlous shape."

"My God, Freddy, you are a devious soul," said the Viscount. "So, fortuitously, we have a possible line into developments we must track."

Squadron Leader Codrington spoke to Chadwick a few weeks after the high-level strategy meeting. "Allan, there's been a lot of planning activity to further and accelerate the implementation of RDR, ever since our wise leaders were briefed and set some priorities. Coordination of trials requiring aircraft to act as targets will be the responsibility of Farnborough. Two bomber squadrons have been chosen to provide aircraft when we need them—328 Squadron under Squadron Leader Michael Pomfret-Jones, and 452 Squadron under Squadron Leader Jimmy Collins. The 328 Squadron has the new Blenheim bombers, and 452 has the old Fairey Hendon, though those will be retired soon. All the planes will be equipped with wireless telegraphy.

"Here's the good news. Because of your experience working with Dr. Bostock, you'll be in charge of the coordination effort. To give you clout with Mike Pomfret-Jones and Jimmy

Collins, you've been promoted to Squadron Leader, brackets, acting. Congratulations."

"Thank you very much, sir. I'm overwhelmed!"

"I'm going to assign the plane used by the telecommunications people for your liaison. When you're ready, I'll assign a second pilot, engineer, and wireless op on a permanent basis."

"I have to think hard about this, sir. I'll have to talk to Dr. Bostock and, of course, Mike and Jim. Do you know where their squadrons are based?

"The 328 is based at Binbrook and 452 has a home at Bassingbourn. I suggest a visit to Bostock first. This work is top, top secret. If wireless communication is needed, you'll have to encode any messages that may be intercepted by unfriendly ears."

Chadwick headed to the mess feeling like he was walking on air. At the same time, he felt bowed by an immense responsibility. In his pigeonhole in the mess, he spotted a letter. He noticed immediately that the air mail envelope carried Egyptian stamps and several postmarks. He flopped into an easy chair and tore it open.

Dear Allan,

Nice to hear from you. You seem to be mixing with high society. I am not familiar with the appeasement movement you mention. It takes two to tango for that to work. It needs appeasers on both sides. I see no signs of that. Here, almost daily I see German attempts to kick out the British and take their place. My time in Egypt is running out. Early in the new year I'll be returning to England. I have approached MI5, which dovetails nicely with what I've been doing here. Maybe appeasement will buy time, I'm sure war is coming, I hope the government is rearming as fast as possible. I'll contact you when I arrive

in Blighty, we can chat over a pint of draught bitter, which
I am looking forward to.

Your old friend,
Doug

Chadwick felt an immense relief when he read Larson's letter. He had an ominous feeling that something bigger and more dangerous than he could comprehend was hovering over him and he needed help to understand the situation. In the meanwhile, he was bursting with excitement to tell the news of his promotion. Squadron Leader before age thirty, that was something.

He dashed off a letter to his parents. On impulse, he went to the public phone in the lobby of the mess and called Melanie. When she answered, the news spilled out. "Melanie, dear, I want you to be the first to know. I've just been promoted to Squadron Leader. That's the equivalent of major in army talk."

"Oh, how marvelous, darling! What did you do to deserve that?"

"Well, actually, it's not what I did, it's what I am going to do. I hope. It's rather hush-hush, and it will involve a lot of flying. I suspect I won't have many weekends free."

"Love, we will find a way, I'm sure."

They chatted for a while, exchanging endearments. When he returned to the Flight Test building, he called Dr. Bostock and arranged to meet him at his research laboratory in Suffolk.

Lady Melanie Fitzgibbon called Lord Lowestoft. When he came on the line she said, "Freddy, this Melanie,"

"Hello, my dear. How goes it?"

"The game's afoot, as Sherlock would say."

"Yes, that corresponds to other reports I've received. I know you're in a difficult position but stay with it. You're doing it for England, and for your son."

"I hope Allan will understand that, if he ever finds out."

Chapter Thirty

Chadwick called Dr. Bostock and arranged to meet him at his laboratory. Two days later he made the long trip in the Bentley. Comfortably seated in his office, the scientist gave Chadwick a general briefing. "Detection of things by reflected wireless waves is old hat. A patent was granted in Germany in 1904 to sense the movement of vessels in harbor. I completed my doctorate more than ten years ago measuring the height of ionized layers in the atmosphere using reflected wireless signals.

"But the problem we face now is quite new—we need to detect an on-coming bomber fleet in sufficient time to get fighters in position to bring them down. Under the most advantageous circumstances we can't expect to detect an enemy more than a hundred miles away. Wireless signals are erratic. They're affected by the sun, so that performance is quite different by day or by night. To put some numbers together, a round trip of two hundred miles—that is, the initial wave and the reflection—will take about a thousandth of a second, called a millisecond. We must gain information on the incoming fleet's azimuth, speed and height. To do that we need to receive many reflections. Correlating data from several sites yields position. The transmitters operate in the range of twenty million cycles per second. They're pulsed on for a few millionths of a second about twenty-five times per second."

"Kenneth," Chadwick interrupted, "all these numbers are confusing me. I'm sure they'll become as familiar as the national anthem at some point. But for now, what do they mean?"

"The upshot is that we'll know where and when the enemy will arrive only half an hour before they get there. Somehow, we must get fighters in place in that half hour. Not only that, height-finding is technically difficult. We're working on it, although I suspect entirely different transmitters will be needed for heights below a thousand feet."

"So, what is my major job?"

"I can divide it into two parts," Bostock said. "First of all, solving the technical difficulties with the prototype equipment. We need to verify the accuracy of azimuthal predictions, and how to get height information quickly enough to be useful to a defending fighter. Secondly, the plan is to have perhaps as many as a dozen stations up and running in a little over a year. They'll cover the coast from Dover to Northumberland. Another year should see complete coverage from Cornwall to the Hebrides. Each must be calibrated. In the next few months, we must clear up the major technical issues so that the equipment can be copied for an initial twenty stations. It will be a crude design but available quickly. It can always be refined later."

Bostock paused, and then said, "There are other problems of a non-technical nature. Not everyone is convinced this is a wise expenditure of the enormous funds needed. There are political opponents in the government. The intelligence people believe the Germans will strive to learn as much as they can of this work. Communication between your aircraft and the ground will be essential, but it is thought the German listening stations know the RAF operating short-wave frequencies. Therefore, all communication must be encoded without delaying the interchange too much."

"For the purposes of refining your equipment to the level they can be put into production—how much flying time and how many aircraft will be required?"

"Tomorrow I shall give you a tour of the laboratories and then we'll sit down with some senior people and see if we can come up with some estimates."

Chadwick drove back to the small seaside hotel he was staying at, his head swimming with unfamiliar numbers and terms. The next day he met several scientists and engineers working on the first "Chain Home" equipment. Wherever possible it was adapted from commercial gear so that parts were readily available.

After lunch they sat down in a conference room. Bostock opened the meeting by stating they were there to plan the involvement of the RAF. The first question to be solved was how to determine the accurate position of a target aircraft during initial calibration so that RDR accuracy could be ascertained. Astronomical sightings were not accurate enough on a moving plane. It was decided to use radio direction finding based on the known location of short-wave aerials in Britain and on the continent, since the target aircraft would be most times over the sea where landmarks were not available.

An engineer with a passion for navigation was assigned to develop the system within two weeks, and he was assigned an aircraft for this purpose. Chadwick made a note.

Next, they discussed refinement of the prototype transmitter and receiver. Aerials would be erected near several sites on the south coast. A goal of operating four sites within two months was adopted. This was to solve the problem of synchronization—two transmitters could not be powered at the same time without causing interference. A ring of timing pulses across the British Islands was proposed, and personnel assigned to build it.

Chadwick raised the problem of trials at night, as not all crews were trained to fly at night, and not all airfields were equipped to handle night landings. The list of problems seemed endless.

That evening he called Melanie. As phone calls were expensive, he kept it short. When he apologized for skipping the weekend, she wanted to know where he was. He told her he was near Felixstowe, and she offered to drive over or come out on the train. He reluctantly dissuaded her and promised to make it up.

The next day, Chadwick drove back to Farnborough and briefed Squadron Leader Codrington. "Sir, I'll spare you the details, but this is going to balloon into a huge effort. The squadrons assigned, 328 and 452, will do for a start. They'll cover the southeast and south coast a far as Dover. I suspect the Hendons of 452 Squadron will have to be replaced. In a few months, another squadron will be needed for calibration of RDR from Dover to Cornwall. All the crews must be capable of operating in any weather, day or night. They'll need additional equipment on board for encoded or encrypted wireless communication and radio direction finding.

"No attempt has been made yet to set up centers to handle the RDR information as it is gathered. This must be done extremely efficiently—there will only be about thirty minutes to get fighters into the right position to attack raiders coming from Europe. This probably requires centers at Ten, Eleven, Twelve and Thirteen Groups. An overall tactical control center may be needed in the new Fighter Command.

"I'll fly to Bassingbourn tomorrow to brief Squadron Leaders Collins and Pomfret-Jones. When I return, I'll summarize what I've just told you and include their comments. When I get back from Bassingbourn I'll need an office with a telephone, a sergeant, and a clerk."

"Very good, Allan. As I expected, you've excelled. You're building an empire. Please keep me informed."

Chadwick felt exhausted, but he summoned up the energy to arrange a flight to Bassingbourn in the morning and let the two squadron commanders know he was coming. After a meal, he had a hot bath and fell into bed. But before he fell asleep, he fantasized how nice it would be if Melanie was lying next to him.

Chadwick's discussion with the two squadron commanders was slightly rancorous. The two men felt that his demand for the best pilots and navigators in their squadrons to man the target planes cast some shadow on the others. In their opinion, all their crews were good. He didn't argue and pointed out that within a few months every plane in their squadrons would be in use full time. Those not involved with the early phase should hone their instrument flying and navigational skills to the highest possible level.

Chadwick stressed the extreme secrecy of the flights, as emphasized by the need for encrypted wireless transmissions. He endeared himself to Squadron Leader Pomfret-Jones by assuring him he would push for replacement planes as soon as possible. He was beginning to realize that dealing with people could be as stressful as dealing with the vagaries of flight.

Chadwick flew back to Farnborough in deteriorating weather and spent a few hours summarizing his meetings with Dr. Bostock and the squadron commanders on paper. For the next several weeks he flew the exploratory missions demanded by the Telecommunication Research engineers and scientists himself. He firmly believed he could only properly direct the missions to be flown by 328 and 452 squadrons if he experienced them firsthand.

His social life suffered. As the nights lengthened into winter he managed to find a few hours to see Melanie on only three occasions. And then came the startling news of the death of the King. He called Melanie from the mess the next time he was there. "This means the favorite of the Viscount is going to ascend to the throne, doesn't it?"

"Yes, the Insiders will be pleased. They believe he has the right instincts."

"But he doesn't run the government, Parliament does that. How can he influence events?"

"He has powerful friends and relatives in the governments of Europe, especially Germany. I believe he'll visit Germany at some stage. I think there will be a meeting at Isbell's soon. Do you want an invitation?"

"Yes, that would be interesting. I hope we can get together soon, anyway. I've just been so busy with this new job."

After a few endearments they both hung up. Walking back from the lobby, Chadwick checked his pigeonhole and found a letter from Doug Larson.

Dear Allan,

As you can see from the stamp I'm back home. I'm fitting in to MI5. I have some temporary digs in Chelsea, but I hope to rent a flat soon. If you drop me a line with an account of how you got to be involved with the Isbell's crowd, I will look at some files here. Perhaps after that we can get together for a noggin.

Your old friend,
Doug

Suiting action to the thought, Chadwick picked up a sheet of writing paper in the lounge and outlined the way he'd wound up at Isbell's. He mentioned the first curious meeting with Ambassador Emsden, organized by Dr. Kegel, and the party he had been invited to by Honoria and Tom Pomeroy to meet the two German students. He described the two meetings with Lord Lowestoft and the lunch at which he met Tom Carstairs. Then he described as much as he could remember about the meeting of the Isbell's Insiders and the talk by Viscount Addenbury. He added that he had met Lady Melanie Fitzgibbon at the dinner and later visited her place in Pangbourne, though he didn't elaborate on their ensuing relationship. Finally, he mentioned that there would probably be another meeting of the Insiders soon, triggered by the death of the King. He asked Larson if he thought he should go. He popped his letter into an envelope and dropped it in the letter box in the lobby.

Chapter Thirty-One

The next day Chadwick was up early and by nine was flying over the English Channel working in cooperation with Dr. Bostock to iron out some remaining problems with RDR development. He was warned by radio that there was a strange signal coming from an object several miles east of his position. He turned and almost immediately was surprised to see something he had never seen in the sky before, a Zeppelin. The huge machine carried German markings and was almost stationary. Hanging down from several gondolas were thin cables. He realized that the cables were wireless aerials and that the crew of the airship were probably monitoring British RDR emissions. He instructed his wireless operator to contact Bostock and shut down all RDR transmissions at once.

When Chadwick returned to Farnborough, he called Dr. Bostock by telephone. Bostock had no idea how much material the Zeppelin had gathered but said that shutting down had been a good idea. While the Germans would probably not work out how RDR was designed, they could calculate how to jam it. He also mentioned that they planned to test two prototypical stations in the next few days.

Bostock asked to borrow two trained RAF navigators to assist with the first tests, and Chadwick passed that onto Squadron Leader Collins. Chadwick was intrigued to see an actual trial of the first working operational RDR. He arranged for a Blenheim to fly as target aircraft, and then asked his clerk to book him into the mess at RAF Biggin Hill, and drove the Bentley to the south coast.

Early the next day he met Bostock at the RDR station—four huge vertical towers about three hundred feet high made it easy to find. The target established communication and flew from the French coast heading north. Two operators stared at small cathode ray tubes to get range. There was considerable interference which blurred the display. Bostock attributed this to air traffic in France, which was well within the distance scanned, adding that height information was not yet available.

Two RAF officers with "Navigator" brevets on their tunics stood by drafting tables with parallel rulers and protractors. They were using the techniques developed to plot the position of aircraft in flight. The azimuth of the target was plotted on a chart with the bearings from the adjacent station and a position calculated by penciling lines on a paper chart.. Chadwick couldn't believe his eyes—the system was archaic and far too slow.

He sat down with Kenneth Bostock for a cup of tea. "Ken, I can see the bare bones work, but it will be no good for Fighter Command unless some things are greatly speeded up. Take the performance of a Hurricane. Flat out it climbs about twenty-five hundred feet a minute. It also has to travel about forty miles horizontally, at a climbing speed of two hundred and fifty knots, say ten to twelve minutes. Ideally, he would then be up sun and above the attackers. At the moment of takeoff, an interception vector must be calculated and passed to the pilot. If calculating the RDR information takes four minutes and calculating the interception vector takes four minutes, then eight minutes have elapsed from the first sighting. A scramble and takeoff would take two minutes, and the climb to altitude ten minutes, a total of twenty minutes since the first RDR sighting. By then the attacker has traveled about seventy miles, maybe more, and it's already passed the interception point.

"One can conclude the derivation of RDR information and calculation of an intercept must only take seconds, at most a minute. They must be done mechanically using calculating machines. For it all to work boils down to seconds if the fighters are above the attackers and up sun. All this information must be combined with the state of readiness of fighters and presented for a tactical controller."

Bostock smiled, somewhat ruefully, and shook his head. "Allan, my job is to produce an RDR which works reasonably well and to have most of the south and southeast coast protected in a year. Besides the erection of dozens of massive aerials, we must manufacture scores of transmitters and receivers and devise a timing system to make sure the transmitters do not cause mutual interference. Then we must train thousands of operators. Assuming the system is on seven days a week, twenty-four hours a day, each warm seat requires five personnel to fill it, not to mention maintenance. What you just described are the layers to be provided by the RAF above and beyond my little effort."

"My God," exclaimed Chadwick, "I hope somebody at RAF Fighter Command Headquarters at Bentley Priory understands this. The layers above the RDR will take more work than the RDR itself."

Realizing his concerns were falling on deaf ears, Chadwick quickly changed the subject. "Speaking of Bentleys, how about a ride in the green machine for lunch at Biggin Hill?"

Chadwick drove to Farnborough the next day, feeling full of misgivings about the operational effectiveness of RDR. He drafted a report of his visit, which was typed up by his clerk. He emphasized the need for considerable processing after an attack was detected if fighters were to make a successful interception. He sent the report to Squadron Leader Codrington and hoped it would be passed up the chain of command. He decided to start his own file of the RDR system. A copy of his report of the trial he had witnessed was the first entry.

The weekend was coming up and he felt a lusty yearning for Melanie's embrace. When he called Pangbourne, her first words were, "Well, hello stranger, did you lose my telephone number?"

He apologized abjectly and pleaded that he had been so busy he was not even able to get back to Farnborough very often. She told him that there was a meeting of the Isbell's Insiders the next evening and asked if he would still like an invitation. Chadwick turned over the idea, deciding, *why not?* Melanie was delighted. She told him she had booked a room at a charming inn in Reigate to save the tedious drive back to Clair Court in the dark, explaining that her chauffeur was unavailable on that day.

The dinner started at six, business suits. Guests were gathered in the drawing room, as waiters passed among them with sherry. Chadwick edged his way toward Lord Lowestoft.

"Good evening, sir."

Lowestoft swung around, "Well, good evening to you, Allan. I'm a little surprised to see you here tonight,"

"Thought I'd catch up on the latest scandal on our new King."

Lowestoft frowned and was obviously bothered by this flippant remark. Chadwick realized he had overstepped his position as a very junior guest in such august company. He nodded and kept moving, finding himself near Lady Addenbury. He thanked her for the invitation.

"Oh, you must thank Melanie. I must say she's looking a lot more cheerful these days." Was it his imagination or did she give him a slight wink?

The gong sounded and Chadwick found he was again seated next to Melanie, but on his right was a taciturn older man who introduced himself as "Leacock." Leacock, after the introduction, stared straight ahead. Chadwick gave Melanie's thigh a surreptitious squeeze. She passed him the seating card. On the back she had written, *The Four Feathers, rm 245*.

As soon as the dessert was cleared away, the Viscount shooed the ladies into the drawing room and addressed the men as brandy circulated around the table. "A good deal has happened since our last gathering. I know we all felt the deepest sympathy for the royal family as George Five sickened and passed away. David, of course, has ascended to the throne as Edward the Eighth. I have had the privilege of a brief audience with him, and he feels the greatest responsibility at this time as tensions rise across the globe. British politicians are driving madly for rearmament and, of course, Germany is following. An arms race like this can only lead to a holocaust none of us want. The King is determined to act as a peacemaker. He is uniquely qualified for this role. He feels inspired by his love for Wallis, and feels love is sadly missing in this world."

"Damned fool," Leacock muttered under his breath, Chadwick turned to look at him more carefully. Leacock had a small, sandy mustache and conveyed a military bearing.

Addenbury carried on. "He feels that people like us—rational, caring people—can greatly influence public opinion. He recently gave an audience to a famous American, Charles Lindbergh, who was returning from a visit to Germany. He was greatly encouraged to learn that Herr Hitler had no territorial ambitions except to reunite German-speaking groups who had unfairly been separated from the father country by unscrupulous politicians after the war. The famous pilot told him the vast majority of Americans are in favor of peace and pray that Europe will find amicable solutions to whatever problems now exist. David was very impressed by Colonel Lindbergh, who is trying in his own way to achieve what we are aiming for."

Viscount Addenbury answered a few questions and then suggested they join the ladies. Chadwick drank a little coffee and glanced at his watch. It was nearly nine. He sidled up to Melanie and whispered, "Half an hour. I won't stay the night."

He drove into Reigate, found the Four Feathers, and parked on a side street some distance away. Parking on the street meant he had to leave the side lights illuminated on the car. He walked to the inn and ordered a drink in the public bar. He knew the clock in the bar would be set a few minutes fast, and when it showed twenty minutes to the hour, he climbed the staircase to the second floor and quietly knocked on the door of Room 245.

Melanie opened it immediately. She was dressed in a black negligee. She pulled him inside and gave him a lingering kiss, and then started tugging at his jacket and tie. "Oh, God, Allan, I need this."

They were stripped in seconds and fell on the old-fashioned four poster bed. "Push, Allan, I'm lusty tonight."

After a few minutes, she moaned loudly. Allan tried to muffle the noise by kissing her. An orgasm started and they both laughed. "Oh, oh, I'm so happy."

Allan buried his face in her breasts. When she had calmed down a little, he lay on his back and said, "Dorothy said tonight that you were looking better."

"She knows what's going on. Probably jealous. Her husband is too high and mighty to let himself go, I bet."

Allan snoozed lightly in the exhausted languor that follows violent lovemaking. Suddenly he awoke with a start. "Mustn't stay too long. I had to park on the street and leave the lights on. First chance I get I'll call you. Another weekend in town would be wonderful. But I have been so damn busy."

"Are you involved with those towers that are going up all over the place?"

"Why do you ask?"

"The girls were talking while you men were discussing David's love life."

"We weren't discussing the King's love life—at least not much. Apparently, he's very impressed by the American aviator, Charles Lindbergh. So, what did the girls say about the towers?"

"One of the ladies said that her husband had told her they emitted death rays and could stop the engines of planes approaching England."

Allan laughed. "Well, I fly over the Channel frequently, and the engines haven't stopped yet. They're just wireless aerials, to my knowledge."

"Yes, but what do they do? Why do they need so many?"

"It's secret, dear. Flooding the countryside with wireless waves reduces the unseemly lust of lonely widows."

"Oh, you!" She thumped his chest with her fists, and they kissed again. He put his arms around her and felt passion rising.

An hour later when she was asleep, he reluctantly crawled out of the warm bed, quietly left the room, and walked into the chilly street. The sidelights were still burning brightly as he approached the Bentley, so the battery was holding up. Within a few miles the heat from the engine made the cockpit cozy and he drove to the mess feeling all was right with world, at least for the moment.

A few days later Chadwick received a call from Squadron Leader Collins, who complained bitterly that the demand from the telecommunications people were robbing him almost full time of two bombers. He was having difficulty matching the squadron monthly training commitment. Chadwick had never really given much thought to just how flying time would be needed for the calibration of RDR aerials. He had assumed a few flights would provide all the data needed.

He called Dr. Bostock and outlined the problem. The scientist suggested a face-to-face meeting and Chadwick arranged to fly to RAF Biggin Hill the next day. He took the twin-engine liaison plane to the airfield and left the second pilot, Flying Officer Healey, to look after a small maintenance problem while he met Dr. Bostock.

Bostock said that Chadwick would have to understand a little of the physics of electromagnetic radiation to appreciate what they were trying to do. He described typical aerials which were designed to enhance the transmitted or received energy of a wave at a specific frequency. On a piece of paper, he drew a diagram that looked like the petals of a flower, except that one petal was larger than the rest.

"This is the response of an aerial. It shows the signal strength as the horizontal azimuth is varied; the large petal is the preferred direction. You can see the aerial would also work at azimuths off the preferred direction but with less gain. These lesser responses are called lobes. They complicate the job of the operator. The same thing is also true in the vertical direction. In fact, we have incorporated three aerials between the towers—the vertical lobes of each have been designed so that by switching from one aerial to another, we can estimate the height of a target by judging the strength of a received signal. This requires considerable operator training, for which we require a target aircraft."

"Once erected, are all the aerials the same?" Chadwick asked.

"Good question, but unfortunately no. The lobes depend strongly on nearby objects, such as power lines, metal buildings, and the ground contours. This effect will be diminished with the next generation of RDR, which will operate at a much higher frequency. But for the time being, this is what we must deal with."

"What happens with aircraft at low altitude, say a thousand feet?"

"The range at which they can be detected is reduced, perhaps by a factor of two. No attempt will be made to measure the height of low-flying aircraft. That will be the job of the Observer Corp."

"So, all this calibration and operator training has to be done for each of the first twenty stations now being built?"

"Yes, I'm afraid so. It has to be accomplished within a few months if the system is to be ready for the '37 tests."

Chadwick ran a hand through his hair. "Christ, there has been some serious under-estimation of the problem, I think. For one thing, each station will require operators trained to the specific characteristics of that particular RDR. For another, for the next few months each station coming online almost requires a calibration squadron for itself."

The scientist looked apologetic, "Yes, you're right. We've been concentrating on just the technical problems, rather than the overall picture, including manpower needs."

After lunch Chadwick returned to his aircraft and told Flying Officer Healey to fly him back to Farnborough. During the flight he sat at the navigator's table, composing a report on the visit. In summary, he pointed out that technical short-cuts had been made to get a workable system up and running as soon as possible. The price to be paid was that RDR required a huge manpower pool of highly skilled, trained operators.

There were also two major short-comings that he felt should be dealt with as soon as possible—a new RDR should be designed to supplement Chain Home, in order to detect attackers flying at five hundred feet, and fast calculators must be designed to solve the trigonometry of an interception. He handed the draft to his clerk to be typed and went to find Codrington for a verbal discussion. He put the written report in his RDR folder including Bostock's sketch.

Chadwick's talk with the squadron leader was much more pessimistic than the written version. He thought that the actual equipment could be in place for a majority of the planned Chain Home stations, but it was highly unlikely that operators would be trained to the necessary level. Basically, the structure of an organization to direct an actual interception after the RDR data was available seemed nebulous. Two essential elements were missing—RDR designed to detect low-level intruders, and a calculator to produce the three-dimensional track for a defending aircraft.

The squadron leader was sympathetic and supportive, but pointed out that Chadwick's role was to provide the aircraft as required by the telecommunications people for target tracking and aerial calibration.

Chadwick picked up on that, noting to Codrington that the construction of Chain Home stations located on the southwest coast would begin soon, and more aircraft would be needed for target tracking. He suggested two more aircraft and crews be assigned, based at RAF Chivenor in Devon.

Chapter Thirty-Two

Back in the mess, Chadwick found a letter from Doug Larson, who suggested a quiet drink in London sometime soon. One evening not long after that, he took a train and met Larson at a pub near Paddington. Larson told him his recent letter describing the meetings with Dr. Kegel, Ambassador Emsden, and the two German students had aroused considerable interest at MI5.

"Why is that?" Chadwick asked. "The meetings seemed innocuous."

Larson faced a dilemma. Kegel's role in German espionage in Britain was known to MI5, but such information was not only highly confidential but could be dangerous. As Larson's experience in Egypt had shown him, the German Secret Service was prepared to kill if their activities were threatened. He decided on a middle road in his conversation with Chadwick.

"We find it very curious that a very high-level diplomat met with you to apologize for a fairly trivial incident in Berlin several months before."

Chadwick conceded that phrased that way, it was curious.

"So, what did the Germans achieve?" Larson asked. "You met Dr. Kegel, and through him you met the two students, Runge and Fassbender. Have you met either of them again since the party at the Pomeroy house?"

"I have not met Runge again, but I have met Julia Fassbender on two occasions."

"What were they?"

"A couple of weeks after meeting Julia, I went to the pictures with her in town. A month later I took her to Stonehenge in my car, as Dr. Kegel had stressed her interest in British culture. We had lunch at the country house of Lady Melanie Fitzgibbon, someone I met at a meeting of the Isbell's Insiders. I haven't seen her since. Frankly, she's not really my type."

"Ah, yes, the Insiders. We should talk about them, too. You seem to have become involved with some very interesting people, Allan. Look, I've signed the Official Secrets Act. Tell me as much as you can about your work at Farnborough. What is the jam that's attracting the wasps?"

"Farnborough is a development establishment. They like aircraft pilots with a technical background, so my engineering training at Cranwell fits the bill. At first, I simply checked that the performance of prototypes met the specifications. I've been involved with investigating aircraft accidents and the development of autopilots. Recently, I've been given much more administrative authority in order to organize aircraft for the testing and calibration of a new wireless system called RDR. There's a big push and it's very hush-hush."

"What does it do?"

"It will detect aircraft intruders approaching the coast at sufficient range for an interception."

"Really? Sounds very important."

"I wasn't working on RDR when I met Kegel and Emsden, however. This all pretty new."

"Let me think about it. In the meanwhile, I'll tell you a bit about my job. Several foreign powers have agents working in Great Britain. The Germans are very busy. One way and another, MI5 tries to keep an eye on them."

"Why don't you just arrest them?"

"It's not that simple. Put one out of circulation and they're just replaced. Then we have to identify them and start over. If a spy behaves egregiously, commits a murder perhaps, we try them in a secret military court. They can be sentenced to death, but we usually try to turn them. Then their masters think they are still working normally, but in fact, they're working for the

British. This is a very powerful way of passing misleading information to the enemy.

"That bunch that meets at Isbell's are a funny lot. Some hold very high positions in government, some own newspapers and can greatly influence public opinion. Some are just idealists. If you're invited to any more of their meetings try to remember as many names as possible. The borderline between wanting peace at any price and actively assisting an enemy can be very narrow."

Chadwick gave a short laugh. "Sounds like you're recruiting me for part-time MI5 service."

"That's not as funny as it sounds. I'm still a new boy at MI5, so I'm not aware of a lot of their penetrations. But I'll discreetly sound out RDR concerns and the Isbell's Insiders. I will also recommend that we look at those two students. Can you please let me know if there is any further contact? And how about another natter in a couple of weeks?"

Chadwick agreed. In fact, he was very happy he had Doug Larson to talk to.

Back at Farnborough, he became interested in the problem he had discussed with Dr. Bostock, namely the calculation of an interception course for defending fighters. In his spare moments he began to look at the mathematics. The RDR operators would provide a position, direction, and speed for the intruder once they had sorted out azimuthal errors and lobing of the RDR equipment. After that, a controller had to pass a heading and target height for the defenders.

He had always liked coordinate geometry when he was a student at Cranwell. But he was sadly out of practice when it became clear to him that the solution depended on solving a differential equation. What he hoped the solution would provide was the acceptable error for height estimation, speed, and direction of the target so that an interception was possible. Even without any mathematics, it was clear that if the defenders climbed too slowly or left too late an interception was impossible.

Chadwick wanted numbers that would set tolerances for the time a defender had to leave the ground after target data had been acquired. He sounded out Squadron Leader Codrington, who suggested an informal visit to the Navigational School at Calshot. He made an introductory telephone call to a friend stationed there.

RAF Calshot was an RAF base primarily concerned with seaplanes and flying boats. It was located on Southampton Water and in the late 1920s had become the center for the development of high-speed seaplanes. Their creations won the Schneider Trophy on three occasions, thus retaining the prize permanently. Navigation had been promoted when the Royal Navy first acquired aircraft, but the study of aerial navigation was somewhat sporadic and ad hoc.

Chadwick was warmly received—they rarely met a squadron leader who had an active interest in navigational problems. The most significant progress was due to the USA, especially the work of Lieutenant Commander Weems. RDR was so secret that Chadwick could not mention it directly. Instead, he framed the problem in general navigational terms, simply stating that if an incoming aircraft trajectory was determined, how long would it take, working under pressure, to calculate an interception track for a defender. The navigation experts agreed it was in interesting thing to think about and said they would get back to him.

They called after a few days and Chadwick made the two-hour drive to Southampton and then to Calshot in the Bentley. The experts were very pleased with themselves—they had modified a calculator used to find dead reckoning position when allowing for wind. It used a roller blind that a navigator could mark with a wax crayon. Normally it could handle drift angles of up to twenty degrees.

The navigators enthusiastically demonstrated several solutions, but when Chadwick gave them numbers to try involving distances of a hundred miles and interception angles of ninety degrees, the accuracy was hopeless. It was obvious that kind of calculator would not work. They pointed out that for the accuracy he needed, a device had to mechanically integrate the intruder's velocity to generate an accurate position for the target. Such machines existed and they suggested a word with the National Tabulator Company.

Chadwick realized the organization of the actual fighter interception after an intruder was detected by RDR was far beyond his limited responsibility. He wrote an outline of the various steps needed, from processing the RDR signal, to making the tactical decisions to choose a target and an intercepting squadron, to supplement his earlier report. He pointed out several calculations were needed and the fact that decisions based on these calculations had to be performed at lightning speed. This was imperative, he noted, if the fighters were to stand a chance of intercepting the intruder before it penetrated inland, and defense then depended on anti-aircraft guns, which were notoriously inaccurate. He added his estimate that the time from recognizing an enemy RDR signal to fighters getting airborne should not exceed fifteen minutes.

Chadwick sent copies of his outline to Dr. Bostock and Squadron Leader Codrington. He added it to the growing files in his own RDR folder. At first, little attention was paid to it. Then a job came up that jerked Chadwick back in time—the first Vickers Wellington bomber prototype had been flown and the company was waiting for guidance on using the autopilot. He made arrangements to meet the company test pilots at Brooklands, an airfield only twenty miles from Farnborough.

He was able to park the Bentley at the flight office right next to the dispersal area. The Vickers crew were so interested in the car that it was only with great difficulty that Chadwick got them to listen to a description of the equipment and then climb aboard for a test flight.

The Wellington was a very successful, albeit expensive, medium bomber. It was built in an unusual style to minimize the effect of damage from flak and enemy fighters. The loads in flight were distributed over a complicated geodesic frame. No guns were mounted on the prototype, these would be added by the RAF when the plane was delivered.

Chadwick discovered it was a pleasant plane to fly. When he demonstrated the autopilot, he found no problems and the crew loved it. It was christened "George," from a popular phrase of the time, "Let George do it," meaning someone else could do the work.

Brooklands also contained a private banked racing track over two miles long, Chadwick could not get away until he drove the chief test pilot round for a few circuits in the Bentley. The Vickers pilot was a former Royal Flying Corp ace in the war, Stewart Piggot, who had an infectious grin and a cheerful demeanor. "Just call me Stew," he said to Chadwick.

Under Stew's urging, Chadwick pushed the old car to a hundred and fifteen mph, and the engine was roaring at 3800 rpm, flat out. The pilot was so enamored with the car he struck a deal with Chadwick, strictly between the two of them, that he would swap the Bentley for a couple of hours on a quiet afternoon for the loan of a Wellington. Chadwick was dubious that this was legal, or even possible. Stew explained that the plane was still privately owned by Vickers. The company often took wives and girlfriends for rides until a plane became the property of the Government.

Chadwick knew that Penelope Pomeroy would give her right arm for a flight in a Wellington, and probably a lot more. When he mentioned the possibility to Melanie, it turned out that she, too, was eager to take to the skies. It took a couple of weeks before Chadwick was able to find a time convenient for himself, Stewart, and the women to make the flight in a Wellington. Stew explained to Chadwick that they would be accompanied by a young company pilot, Norman Jones, just to keep things square with Vickers, but that Allan could take the plane where he wanted for two hours. It would be logged as a company test flight.

When they were all gathered by the plane, Allan introduced the two women to Stew and Jones. They climbed aboard, and Jones strapped himself into the single pilot's seat for the take-off. The weather was clear with upper level cirrus clouds. Allan, Melanie, and Penny sat on a canvas bench in the fuselage, which had been rigged from green canvas between two aluminum poles.

There were no safety harnesses. Allan noticed a number of parachutes hanging in the rear of the fuselage, but Jones made no attempt to show his passengers how to use them. They took off smoothly and climbed slowly on a southerly heading. Jones unstrapped himself and walked down the fuselage. "You can take over now," he said to Allan. "George is in command."

"Who's George?" Melanie cried. "I don't see anybody at the front."

Allan laughed, "George is the name for the automatic pilot. Still, somebody should keep a look-out. Melanie, why don't you climb into the front turret? You'll get a lovely view from there."

Allan adjusted the automatic pilot to fly at five thousand feet. "We'll fly over Brighton and then take a look at France," he announced. He was interested in how many RDR aerials had been erected, although he said nothing to the others.

He helped Melanie squeeze past the pilot position and into the forward gun turret. "Oh, Allan," she shouted over the engine noise, "what a great view!"

By this time, the plane had reached the coast and Allan adjusted George to fly parallel to the shore. "Keep your eyes open for the White Cliffs," he told Melanie.

"This is wonderful," she shouted, "I can see Eastbourne and I think I can make out Hastings. What are all those ugly towers?"

The towers were made of steel lattice and grouped in sets of four. They reached skywards three hundred feet.

"They seem to be all over the place. I think they're the things we talked about earlier. Can't they stop the engines?"

A little sarcastically, Allan replied, "Ours appear to be still running."

Jones held Penny's arm to steady her, as the plane was shaking slightly in the thermals coming off the coast. "Move back to the rear turret, Penny. Without guns there's plenty of room and you get another great view."

Penny supported herself by pushing her arms against the walls of the fuselage and climbed through a narrow door into the turret.

Jones squeezed in beside her. "We're at five thousand feet, Penny. A mile high. Have you ever heard of the mile high club?"

She shook her head.

"It's very exclusive. Not many people get a chance for jig-a-jig this high. It's quite different." He put his hand on her knee and slid it up, pushing her frock away. She didn't object. The plane droned on.

Eventually, Penny and Norman Jones walked back into the cockpit. Penny's cheeks were flushed, and Jones looked rather smug. "Do I get to fly it?" Penny asked.

Allan moved out of the way and Penny sat in the pilot's seat. "Hold the stick lightly," Jones said. Then he turned off George.

Penny gently moved the stick to give a slight climb, and then turned left. "It's much easier than flying a Tiger Moth."

Up forward, Melanie cried out that she had Dover and the White Cliffs in sight. Allan leaned over and re-engaged George, adjusting the course to the southeast. "How about a tour of France?"

Calais soon came into sight, and he flew northeast along the coast to the intricate sandy shoals of the Netherlands. As the Friesen Islands emerged out of the slight haze, he adjusted George for a westerly course and made a landfall near the Wash. This was country he knew well, and the visibility was good. He stood behind Melanie and gave running commentary on the towns and villages as they came up.

Keeping the great sprawl of London on the left, Allan slowly adjusted the course. And as Windsor Castle appeared, Jones slid into the pilot's seat. "I'll make the approach and landing."

Melanie and Allan sat on the uncomfortable bench. Penny had decided to sit in the front turret for the landing. Jones taxied to the dispersal area and shut down the engines. As they climbed out onto the tarmac Stew drove up in the Bentley. "I saw the plane land, Allan. That's the most amazin' motor. If you ever want to get rid of it, please let me know."

Allan thanked him for the chance to take the ladies for a spin. Jones and Penny walked to her car, had an animated conversation, and agreed to meet again.

Melanie suggested to Allan that he drive home via Pangbourne. It seemed like a good idea to him.

The next day at Farnborough, Chadwick dropped into Codrington's office. He pointed out the commissioning of the RDR stations was taking a good deal more time than originally planned, and that he would need more aircraft to be assigned for the job. He also suggested that Mr. Pemberton's autopilot development group could take care of training the crew on the last prototype plane to be outfitted with "George" when the makers were ready. He really was getting too busy.

Chapter Thirty-Three

Chadwick decided he could help solve the problem of more aircraft needed for RDR calibration. He button-holed Codrington and suggested that the twin-engine plane assigned to his group could be used for RDR calibration and operator training. He could get by with a single-engine plane for liaison visits to other airfields. He mentioned that Flying Officer Healey was quite capable of carrying out RDR calibration flights.

Codrington grunted and said he would look into it. Later the same day he was told Supermarine was flying in a prototype Spitfire Mark I which had been modified to incorporate changes suggested by Farnborough test pilots. They didn't want the original prototype returned. Codrington knew exactly how to use the original Mark I prototype—he told Chadwick to talk to some of the pilots who had flown it and then take it up for familiarization. In other words, it was Chadwick's for the RDR liaison flights.

Chadwick knew the other test pilots well. In the informal hierarchy, he was near the bottom. He had primarily assisted with the development of ancillary equipment, such as bombsights and autopilots. The real stars were the pilots who had flown the early prototypes of new aircraft. They had an extensive education founded on thousands of flying hours. Chadwick talked to Squadron Leader Chris Bligh, who had done much of the flying with the first Spitfire prototype at Farnborough.

"So, you are going to fly a real plane, Allan, and not some lumbering bomber?"

"Chris, Codrington has just lent it to me for liaison with some of the chaps involved in the RDR calibration, which is turning into a huge effort."

"Well, don't kill yourself, Allan. The Spit is a lovely crate, but she can bite. That thin wing is perfect for the bod chasing a bomber, but if you get caught by a similar opponent, perhaps the new Messerschmitt, and stall in a tight turn, you'll spin like a roulette wheel and drop like a stone. If you're landing with plenty of fuel on board, keep the speed up and add a few knots for the wife and kids. Even wheel her in but watch the ground clearance to the prop tips. That crate needs a new prop anyway. At present it's fitted with a two-bladed wooden job.

"It'll be fine for what you want to do, though. You'll have some fun zipping round the countryside at two hundred and eighty knots. But that brings up another point—that Merlin engine gobbles petrol. I wouldn't count on flying further than three hundred and fifty miles on a full tank, leaving a few quarts in reserve. And you'll get wanker's cramp from pumping the undercart up and down. But I'm told the fifth prototype will have an engine-driven hydraulic pump. What else?"

He stopped and thought for a minute. "You don't intend to pull negative G, I imagine. If, for some reason you get the urge to fly inverted, the engine may stop, at least for a few seconds. What else again? Swing on takeoff. If you bring the tail up too quickly, she'll swing left. You need some rudder. Be careful with the brakes. You can tip the nose and possibly damage the prop if you're too rough. Keep an eye on engine temp when taxiing. She overheats quickly. If you see a hundred centigrade, just take off. She doesn't like to kiss the ground. On landing, wants to stay airborne. Be very careful with a crosswind. Just treat the lady gently, Allan."

"Many thanks Chris. I'll try not to bend it. You called her a lady?"

"Yes, she's wonderful if you treat her right, and pretty vicious if you don't. Don't you have girl friends like that?"

Chadwick made a close acquaintance with the lady that afternoon and decided they would get on well with each other. He selected gear down and pumped until the green lights appeared. Approaching the field, he made a curving approach so that he could keep it in sight until the touchdown. He slid the canopy to the locked half-open position and used full flap as he crossed the fence at sixty knots. She settled down nicely for a three-pointer as the speed dropped to fifty knots.

Partly as an excuse to fly his new toy, Chadwick arranged to meet Dr. Bostock for a briefing on RDR progress the next day. The scientist was back at the laboratory. Chadwick arranged to fly to RAF Woodbridge and get picked up by a driver from Bawdsey, about ten miles away. The meteorological forecast predicted no violent weather, though the visibility downwind of London was poor for many miles. He crossed the coast, let down over the North Sea and flew west until he picked up the big lighthouse at Harwich. He pumped down the undercarriage as he flew north to Woodbridge. When he gave the tower a call on the Spitfire's H.F. radio, he was slightly surprised to get a reply giving him landing clearance. He taxied to dispersal, swung into wind, and shut down the big Merlin before it overheated.

Several officers and airmen came out to examine the Spitfire. Someone excitedly welcomed him to Woodbridge. He walked to the tower and thanked the duty controller, asking him for a forecast for Farnborough later in the day. He then called Dr. Bostock. The flight from Farnborough had taken forty-five minutes. In his Bentley it was an all-day trip.

He was soon closeted with the scientist, who told him the construction of RDR was going well, and that a dozen stations should be operational by early in the new year. Whether they would be properly manned was another story. Bostock was somewhat chagrined to confess the training was taking much longer than first anticipated, because one team of experts was needed to calibrate each new station and then a second team of neophyte operators had to be trained to run it.

He had been in discussion with Fighter Command about the "manning" and discovered that was the wrong word—the stations would be run mostly by women. It was estimated that over two thousand would be required when twenty stations came online. They would be WAAFs—Women's Auxiliary Air Force. Even planning where to house them and then busing them to the stations was turning into a headache.

Chadwick wanted to discuss his meeting with the navigational experts at Calshot, but Bostock passed a weary hand across his brow. "Allan, please give me the nub of it. I'm up to my eyeballs in problems."

"Essentially, we need to develop mechanical calculators to quickly determine intruder position and intercept track. I think, if I understand what you told me before, you'll also need a calculator to estimate intruder height, which—given range and aerial angle, and allowing for the curvature of the earth— may be the same calculator, which could do it all. It was mentioned to me that a company like National Tabulators had the expertise."

"Please send me a memorandum and I will pass it on."

Chadwick realized that Bostock had not read or had forgotten the report he wrote earlier on his visit to Calshot. "Sorry to be such a pest, Kenneth, but I have a new question for you."

"Yes, what is it, Allan?"

"Suppose an intruder changes course after its position, speed, height, and so on have been determined and plotted. Will the system be fast enough to issue a correction?"

"Short answer—at this stage of the game, probably not."

After lunch with Bostock and some of the scientists and engineers in a common dining room, Chadwick was driven back to Woodbridge. As he was climbing into his flying suit, he was approached by a squadron leader.

"Good afternoon, sir. I'm George Wilson, station master for my sins." It was an RAF tradition that the base commander was always referred to as the "Station Master."

Chadwick turned to meet the newcomer. He was an elderly officer who carried campaign ribbons from the war and sported a silver mustache. Chadwick introduced himself. "Just paying a quick visit to Bawdsey, sir. You'll probably see me again, as I'm very involved with those telecommunications chaps."

"Oh, I hope so. You've no idea how the sight of this magnificent machine lifted my spirits."

"Why is that?"

"Fighter Command planes drop in here all the time—Gladiators, Wapitis. There's a war coming, and those machines are dinosaurs. Now this—" he gestured toward the Spitfire, "this is the future."

They walked out to the plane. "Eight guns, eh? How are they harmonized?"

"Four hundred yards."

"Four hundred! In my day we thought a hundred yards was a bit much"

"Don't forget this machine is traveling much faster. You need clearance to break away."

"Good point. I'm not thinking of speeds like three hundred knots. Goodbye, Mr. Chadwick. Have a good trip back to Farnborough. This morning I was quite depressed. But now, meeting you, and seeing this magnificent fighter, I'm wonderfully cheered." Then, curiously, he muttered, "God Bless."

The trolley-acc was plugged in. Chadwick walked round the plane checking pitot covers and tire alignment and he shook the control surfaces. He climbed aboard. An airman helped with the straps, and he signaled a start. He pushed the Ki-gas pump, turned on the magnetos and cranked the engine. It started with a cracking roar and Chadwick waved away the chocks. After taxiing he turned into wind, set the brake, and quickly ran up the engine to test each magneto. All seemed well. He called the tower, set a little right rudder and a little nose down trim, and slowly pushed the throttle wide open.

The plane leaped across the ground like a gazelle and lofted into the air. Chadwick throttled back and slowly climbed to two thousand feet. He pumped up the undercarriage and locked the canopy shut. He intended to return to Farnborough at a low level, and a relatively low speed, two hundred and twenty knots. It was countryside he knew well, north of London. He looked for landmarks and patterns that were familiar, wondering if pattern recognition awareness had developed in prehistoric man so that he could make his way back to his cave after killing a mammoth. He called Farnborough on the radio when it was in sight, and landed carefully, a perfect three-pointer. He could well imagine some of the other test pilots watching through a window in their room.

Chadwick wrote a report on the visit for his RDR file. One problem he had discussed with Bostock over lunch nagged his mind—how to determine the numerical strength of an attacking force. The assignment of aircraft for RDR calibration and training was getting more complicated. He asked his sergeant to have a blackboard fastened to the wall of his office so that station names and assigned planes could be listed daily.

Chapter Thirty-Four

Within a few months Chadwick had logged over a hundred hours in his Spitfire flying to the squadrons providing planes for the RDR exercises. Pilots used to venture that they never really knew a plane until they had flown it over a hundred hours. Chadwick certainly felt that way about "Sally," as he had named his mount. He instinctively knew her little mannerisms when he adjusted the throttle or dropped the undercarriage, and in a dozen ways became intimate with the machine.

One day, he realized she was like a mistress, perhaps usurping Melanie, whom he rarely got to meet up with, due to the pressure of work. When he flew into airfields to talk to squadron commanders, he broached the possibility of assembling a flotilla of planes, perhaps as many as twenty-five, so that the Bawdsey experts could tackle the problem of assessing target strength. He finally arranged to meet a wing commander who controlled three bomber squadrons—Wing Commander Harris, who was based at RAF Church Fenton, near Leeds in Yorkshire. Chadwick arranged an appointment with him and flew north one grungy day with low cloud and haze.

He navigated his usual way by letting down over the sea. This time he picked up the River Humber and flew toward Goole. From there, he followed a railway line but realized after a few minutes that either he had missed Church Fenton or chosen the wrong rails to follow. He called the tower on H.F. but did not receive a reply. He turned round and flew a reciprocal heading until the river reappeared. When the great smudge of Leeds came into view, he flew northeast and, to his relief, spotted an airfield. On the signal square in front of the tower were the letters "CF." As he landed, Chadwick chided himself for being too complacent, realizing he could get into trouble one day.

To meet the wing commander, he had dressed in his best blue uniform under his flying suit. He made his number with the duty officer in the tower, cleaned up in the washroom, and prepared to meet Wing Commander Harris. An orderly took him to the office,

Chadwick saluted. Harris was a tall, aggressive man with a scarred face. Chadwick realized that he knew Harris. "Good morning, sir. Allan Chadwick. I believe we've met before."

"Really," grunted Harris, "Where?"

"In Iraq, sir, 314 Squadron."

"My God, yes, I remember you. You were flying with me when we were attacked by an eagle." Harris looked at Chadwick more closely, "Squadron Leader! What are you up to, Chadwick?"

"I'm working very closely with the people responsible for RDR. I organize targets which they need for development and calibration"

"Exactly what is RDR?"

"It's a radio system to detect intruders crossing into British air space. At present I can lay on six aircraft as dummy targets. What I came to see you about, sir, is a plan to fly up to two dozen aircraft in formation as a target, so that the boffins can come up with ways of predicting the number of planes in an attacking force."

"I'll be interested in a formation of two dozen bombers too, Chadwick. I have never seen that many bombers trying to formate on each other. Sounds like it would be a real Chinese fire drill. At present I command three squadrons of Blenheims, each with two flights of four aircraft. Sounds like we could put up twenty-four kites if they're all serviceable. Where would the intruding flight commence and finish?"

"I would have to discuss that with the boffins, but I would guess the simulated attack would cross the coast near Felixstowe so that the equipment at Bawdsey has it in range. Maybe someone in Bomber Command could choose the starting point. Assuming our potential aggressor is Germany, I guess their bombers would assemble over Bremen. It seems unlikely they would capture Belgium in a new war and, of course, France is protected by the Maginot Line. We won't be permitted to overfly Germany, but maybe an assembly point over the North Sea, west of Amsterdam would be suitable."

Chadwick paused. "By the way, it's assumed the Germans can tune to RAF H.F. frequencies, and so our communications are encoded. The signals people have this in hand and can tell your wireless operators how it's done. Perhaps if your crews haven't done much formation flying with all three squadrons, a few rehearsals would be in order."

"This is going to take a lot of organizing. You're the liaison lynchpin, I assume, so you can coordinate an exercise with the RDR people. How about planning this shindig to take place in about two weeks?"

"That sounds perfect sir. I'll get on it right away."

"Would you care to join us for lunch?"

"If you'll excuse me, sir, I'll take up your invitation another day. I want to get back to Farnborough as soon as possible. The weather was deteriorating when I landed."

"How did you get here?"

"I flew up in a Spitfire, sir."

"A Spitfire!" Harris exploded. "You Farnborough chaps certainly get the gravy. But this I must see." He walked with Chadwick to the tower and chatted as Chadwick donned his flying suit.

While Chadwick completed an external inspection, Harris climbed on the wing and peered into the cockpit. He clambered down and an aircraftsman helped Chadwick with the shoulder straps. "Contact." The Merlin started with its characteristic roar, and Chadwick waved away the chocks. Harris backed out of the slipstream and saluted as the Spitfire swung and headed down the field.

Chadwick endured a harrowing flight back to Farnborough. The weather was thickening as he flew down the coast at a thousand feet and ventured toward London where the Thames Estuary opened up. At Tilbury he turned left and followed the major roads along the south side of London to Reigate and Farnborough, a route he knew well from Bentley excursions. At Reigate he started to pump down the undercarriage and made a straight-in approach to the field with clouds pushing him down to under five hundred feet and rain slicing off the windshield. At the north side of the field an airman came out dressed in a rubber cape and waved him to the dispersal. He checked in with his sergeant and then enjoyed a beer with lunch. There was obviously no flying that afternoon.

Chapter Thirty-Five

After a delightful nap he called Melanie. The weekend was coming up and he had not seen her for over three weeks. He made his excuses and they arranged to meet at the same hotel near Euston where they had stayed when he visited Cricklewood. Chadwick wrote up a brief summary of his visit with Wing Commander Harris, ate an early dinner, and had an early night. The stress was getting to him.

The next day Chadwick took a train to London, signed in at the hotel and waited for Melanie. When she saw him, she gave him a hug and said, "Allan, you're looking tired."

"I've been rather busy."

Later, lying next to each other in bed, she said, "Allan, dear, do you love me?"

"Of course I do. What a silly question. Why on earth do you ask me that?"

"Maybe it's just lust, not love."

"Is there any difference? How can you tell?"

"A woman knows. I sometimes think you have another girlfriend."

"Melanie, how can you say that? We agreed when we started, no triangles."

Then a guilty thought crossed his mind. He had been referring to his Spitfire, "Sally," as his mistress. "I have to admit I've been spending a lot of time with a particular lady. However, she's aluminum and iron, not flesh and blood. Does that count as a triangle?"

"No, it can't do what I can do." And she proceeded to show him, and they forgot the whole inane conversation, at least for the while.

After a pleasant dinner, they popped into a cinema on Leicester Square. The main feature was *My Man Godfrey,* which they thoroughly enjoyed. The Gaumont British News showed Jesse Owens winning at the Berlin Olympics, to Hitler's annoyance, but then a happier Hitler saluting Mussolini. Allan whispered to Melanie, "That's an ominous sight."

They left halfway through a second-rate American crime picture about the FBI. At their hotel they wandered into the bar and ordered a liqueur each, which they sipped slowly. That put them in the mood later for some uninhibited lovemaking. After a late breakfast, they took a taxi to the Science Museum. On the fourth floor, Allan showed Melanie a famous Vickers Vimy, the very plane that had first crossed the North Atlantic non-stop, the same kind of plane he'd flown in Iraq. She said it looked very old-fashioned, and Allan had to agree.

They strolled into Kensington Gardens and watched the birds on the Serpentine. As they walked hand in hand, Melanie asked, "Allan, what is it that is making you so tired? Are you flying a lot?"

"I can't tell you much, darling. It's hush-hush. Basically, the RAF is getting ready for war, despite the efforts of your friends at Isbell's."

"But we are not at war. What's the panic?"

"You saw those two men in the newsreel, Hitler and Mussolini. They're unscrupulous and ambitious. We must get ready to defend ourselves. That's what I'm doing, helping us get ready. It's not the flying that's tiring, it's dealing with some of the people. Sometimes I have to get them to do things without fully explaining why."

They continued to Bayswater Road and managed to flag a taxi to take them back to their hotel, where they got their bags. At Paddington station they kissed fondly and said, "Au revoir." When Melanie settled in at Clair Court Hall, she had a long telephone conversation with Lord Lowestoft.

Back at Farnborough, Chadwick found a message in his pigeonhole from Doug Larson, his MI5 contact, requesting a meeting. But before he could arrange a meeting with Larson, Chadwick had to get back to Dr. Bostock and refine the requirements for a trial formation flight to develop a way to estimate intruder strength. He flew to RAF Woodbridge the next day and was sitting with the scientist by mid-morning. Bostock listened to his plan to have three Blenheim squadrons fly over the North Sea, simulating a raid launched from Germany. He suggested they discuss the plan with some other scientists and engineers after lunch.

Chadwick phoned the tower at Woodbridge and asked them to keep an eye on the weather for a return trip to Farnborough later. The meeting with a dozen of the RDR people started with a summary by Dr. Bostock of what he had learned from Chadwick in the morning. Almost immediately, objections were raised. An engineer suggested they start with a single plane fly-by, increasing incrementally to the full twenty-four. This would permit an appreciation of the signal changes caused by increasing numbers. Others pointed out that the tests would have to be repeated at varying heights. A physicist pulled a slide rule from his breast pocket and scribbled calculations on a pad. Chadwick did not respond to the contributions until Dr. Bostock asked for an opinion.

"A lot of the criticism makes sense," he acknowledged, "but there are limitations on the first trial that could be changed later on. Let's get something moving, see what the RDR results are and move on from there. First of all, the three squadrons will fly out of different RAF airfields, their home bases. They'll rendezvous at a point over the North Sea and start the trial. This is not a simple as it sounds, as there are almost no navigational aids except dead reckoning. My suggestion to deal with the problem of incremental changes of strength is to have one squadron—that is, eight aircraft—leave the formation after arriving at the coast and return home. Then the remaining two squadrons will fly back to the start and repeat the exercise. Then a second squadron would depart, and the remaining squadron of eight planes would repeat the exercise for the third time. I think this would take up most of the time available, that is, daylight."

More rancorous discussion followed but finally Bostock closed the meeting. On the way to his office he said, "You see what it's like, Allan, leading a bunch of prima donnas."

When Chadwick called the tower at Woodbridge, he was told a front was crossing the country from the west and Farnborough was already socked in. He asked the duty officer to get the Spitfire put in a hangar and to reserve him a room at the mess. When Kenneth Bostock discovered Chadwick was staying the night, he insisted that Allan have dinner with him and his wife, which turned out be a pleasant interlude. Kenneth played the piano after the meal and his wife, who was a trained singer, sang some operatic favorites.

While Bostock was briefly out of the room, his wife whispered, "I'll be delighted when this RDR stuff is finished. It will be the death of Kenneth."

Chadwick had a small bag of personal items in the Spitfire, but he could not be bothered to go to the hangar to get them. He went to bed and sneaked down to the hangar in the morning, and after brushing his teeth and a shave he felt like a new man. Sally had been refueled. The weather behind the front was gorgeous, with clear skies. He took off and headed to Church Fenton to brief Wing Commander Harris. He explained the plan to have the three squadrons separate after each run, and Harris gruffly acknowledged it sounded logical.

Chadwick climbed back in the plane and took off for Farnborough. He decided to fly directly there and skirt the western edge of London. He ran the Merlin at full power to climb to ten thousand feet, and then he leveled off and adjusted the throttle and mixture. The weather was unusually clear for the British Islands. After thirty minutes he spotted the great conurbation of the British capital slowly coming into view. He could see smoke from the millions of fireplaces streaming over Kent.

Suddenly the plane lost power. Chadwick sagged momentarily against the straps. He glanced at the inlet manifold pressure gauge—there was no boost. The engine had stopped. He switched the magnetos on and off, operated the fuel shutoff valve, and trimmed for a glide at an indicated airspeed of a hundred and twenty knots. He tried to start the engine, but nothing worked, so he left the magnetos off, the fuel line shut, and called Farnborough. He informed them he had suffered engine failure but could make the field on a glide.

The gyro instruments began to fail. The artificial horizon showed the plane entering a left-hand dive, which he ignored. He had plenty of height in hand and decided to pump down the undercarriage. A little extra drag would do no harm and it would be one less thing to worry about as he concentrated on the approach. He slid the canopy back and locked it. Glancing to his right, he could follow the Thames and just make out Pangbourne in the distance. He crossed Windsor Castle at fifteen hundred feet and side-slipped for an approach over the eastern fence. He dropped full flap and leveled off a few feet above the ground, kicked the rudder straight and landed with a loud thump. A tractor towed him in.

After signing the log and doffing his flying gear, Chadwick went to Squadron Leader Codrington's office to bring him up to date on the plans for a formation to simulate an intruder. Codrington suggested he write it up and send a copy to Bomber Command. He then went back to the flight line for an analysis of the engine failure.

"Magneto cross shaft is sheared," a flight sergeant told him. "There are also signs of a cylinder head crack. The engineering officer will decide if we should replace the engine."

That was the verdict. A replacement would have to be procured. The plane was grounded for at least three days. Chadwick wrote up the details of his visit to Bawdsey and Church Fenton and distributed copies to Codrington, Bostock, Harris, and the C.O. of Bomber Command. He decided tomorrow would be a good day to look up Doug Larson.

Chapter Thirty-Six

It was late afternoon before Larson could get away from the office. Chadwick traveled to Waterloo on the train and met Larson as arranged at a small pub called the Canterbury Tales near Lambeth Palace, just a short walk from the station. Once inside, Chadwick realized why Larson had chosen that particular pub—customers sat in enclosures with paneled sides. Larson ordered a pint of their best bitter, while Chadwick settled for a Guinness.

"Well, we have a lot to talk about, Allan, but first, how are things with RDR?"

"Heating up, Doug. I'm zipping all over the country organizing targets to train the operators."

"Is it going to be ready for '37?"

"I think a handful of stations will be fully operational. It's going to be an interesting exercise."

"Let's get back to that later. MI5 looked at the two students you were introduced to by Dr. Kegel. On the face of it, they seem to be what they claim. Both attended a soiree at the German Embassy last week. We got a copy of the program—English Folk Dancing. The man, Runge, is in fact spending some time with a woman he met when you attended the party at the Pomeroys—Miss Penelope Pomeroy."

"Interesting. A while ago I went for a plane ride with her. She has ambitions to become a commercial pilot."

"What? Women flying a commercial airliner? It'll never happen."

"Women are making the headlines, Doug—Amy Johnson, Amelia Earhart. Don't be too sure. We live in a remarkable age."

"Funny you should mention flying with her. The German student, Runge, has been up with her half a dozen times."

"Is that suspicious?"

"I'm not sure." In discussing Olaf Runge, Larson did not want to expose the extent of MI5 surveillance. Larson faced a similar dilemma when he wanted to quiz Chadwick about the "Isbell's Insiders." They were a group of great interest to MI5 but Larson did not feel it was wise to share too much of their knowledge of the group with Chadwick.

"Allan, we'd like you to stay connected with the Insiders. Just be neutral about their goals of preventing a war at any price. We have chaps in the agency who are almost chess grand masters. They always think five jumps ahead. They think the Insiders would be a useful insertion point for misleading intelligence if we need to. You've become friendly with Lady Fitzgibbon, yes?"

Chadwick hated anyone discussing the romantic side of his life. He actually blushed, before saying defensively, "She's widowed and I'm single, so why not?"

"Absolutely, old chap. I'm just interested in the linkage, that's all. It's an excellent way to stay connected." Larson knew that money was being funneled into the Fitzgibbon estate by the Insiders. This had been discovered by MI5 accountants who had access to bank records, but they had yet to find that money had been transferred to Chadwick's account in Farnborough.

"Tell me a bit more about RDR. We think this is strategic information of great value to a potential enemy. It's certainly a topic of opportunity for a little deception. So, you think the '37 exercises will test the system? How will it perform, do you think?"

"Probably not well. It's new, and the operators are only half-trained, but it can be mended."

Larson suggested they eat, so they ordered food, which was very tasty, and chatted about the Olympics, tennis, and the cricket season. Chadwick walked back to Waterloo and fired up his Bentley at Farnborough station by ten o'clock.

When Chadwick walked into the office at Farnborough in the morning, his sergeant said they had received a phone call requesting Squadron Leader Chadwick to visit the commanding officer at RAF Uxbridge as soon as possible. Uxbridge was the headquarters of Bomber Command. After he delivered the message, the sergeant said. "Excuse me for mentioning it, sir, but I spoke to the admin sergeant at Uxbridge. He rather implied that the report we sent them the day before yesterday was, well—you dropped a clanger, was the way he put it."

"Oh, dear. Thank you, sergeant. I'll drive over and see what I said to get under their skin."

Chadwick got his greatcoat, climbed into the Bentley, and left for Uxbridge, only a twenty-mile journey, but the roads were crowded and slow. He checked in at the orderly office of Bomber Command headquarters and was directed to the office of Group Captain Hearne. He saluted, and Hearne waved to a chair.

"Your report on the target practice for the RDR chaps caught the eye of the AOC—the Air Officer Commanding. He feels that commandeering a whole wing of three squadrons is somewhat of an empire-building enterprise."

"To my knowledge, I believe Farnborough was authorized to provide whatever the boffins needed to get RDR operational as soon as possible. I assumed this was cleared at the higher levels before I was told to take care of the details."

"Humff, yes. A little after the briefing for very senior officers at High Wycombe, it came to my attention. But there was no mention of the scale of this cooperation. We still have our training duties to perform."

"I don't think anyone understood the scale of the work six months ago, sir. I only discovered recently that teams will have to be trained in the near future to operate as many as twenty RDR stations in the next year. Each station will probably require a wing of bombers just like the exercise planned for next week."

"What? Twenty wings, you say? This is unheard of. I think we should see the AOC." Hearne signaled for a clerk and asked for an appointment with the commanding officer. He was back in two minutes,

"You may see Air Vice Marshal Stevenson in ten minutes, sir."

"Do you want to freshen up, Chadwick? There's a couple of minutes before we meet the boss."

"Thank you, good idea."

Hearne pointed down a corridor to the men's toilet.

An aide de camp ushered them into meet the commanding officer of Bomber Command. The commanding officer had a powerful face with vivid blue eyes under bushy eyebrows. His hair was streaked by grey. A cheroot smoked gently in an ashtray on his crowded desk.

"Now what's this new problem, Geoffrey?"

"This is Squadron Leader Chadwick, sir. He's just been filling me in on details of the cooperation we're involved with to develop RDR."

Stevenson turned to look at Chadwick. "Pleased to meet-cha." He glanced at the ribbons on Chadwick's tunic. "Served in Iraq, eh? What squadron?"

"The 314, sir."

"So, you got your time in on the old Vimys." He cogitated for a moment. "Sorry about the death of Squadron Leader Welch."

"Thank you, sir, I greatly admired him."

"Well, Geoffrey, fill me in."

Hearne proceeded to summarize his conversation with Allan Chadwick, emphasizing that the upshot was a great deal more flying by their latest bombers than had been anticipated. He mentioned Chadwick's role to lay on formations to act as targets while the boffins worked on the system.

"Had a word with the Air Secretary. Whitehall is giving utmost priority to getting this system up and running by next summer. The good news is that it will be turned over lock, stock, and barrel to the RAF before then, so we might see a little organization creep in. In the meanwhile, Squadron Leader Chadwick is coping with the civilian boffins. Are you happy with the arrangement, Chadwick?"

"Yes, sir, they're a bright bunch, and fun to work with."

"Good. Keep in touch with Group Captain Hearne. No surprises, eh?" He glanced at the clock on the wall. "Please join us for lunch, Squadron Leader. I'd be interested to hear about your time in Iraq."

As they left the headquarters building on the way to the officer's mess, the air vice marshal spotted Chadwick's Bentley. He stopped, put his hands on his hips, and laughed. "My God! Who does that monstrosity belong to?"

"It's mine sir."

"It's a Bentley, am I right?"

"Yes, sir, 1928."

"Friend of mine used to race these machines. Made a name for himself in the Le Mans Endurance Race. Knew him in the old Royal Flying Corp, Tom Barking. A devil with the ladies." Seeing the Bentley put the air vice marshal in a good humor, and he treated Allan Chadwick with deference over lunch.

After the meal, Chadwick started the Bentley for the benefit of several on-lookers, including the air vice marshal, and drove away to subdued cheers.

Walking back into the building, Stevenson turned to Hearne. "Good man, there. Keep an eye on him, Geoffrey."

Chapter Thirty-Seven

Chadwick drove back to Farnborough feeling very pleased that he had Bomber Command behind him. He was starting to believe that RDR targets with aircraft formations would be far better for simulating the real situation likely to be encountered in war than single aircraft. Maneuvering large formations was complicated. In a turn, planes on the outside had to travel further than planes on the inside and tended to get left behind. But when the exercises started in '37 it was clear that Bomber Command would have to provide formations, not single aircraft. Learning the techniques now was preparing for the future. Chadwick wanted the attacking planes to formulate their own procedures, rather than have them dictated.

Back in the office he wrote a letter to Wing Commander Harris, with copies to anyone he felt would be involved, especially Group Captain Hearne. His report laid out in general terms the conditions of the formation tracking, with a request to develop protocols and to rehearse them. At first, the trials would be carried out in daylight with good visibility. Wireless procedures must be decided to handle emergencies. A detailed log should be kept for comparisons with the Bawdsey results later.

Chadwick suggested the lead and flanking squadrons fly with vertical separation to be decided. Air speed should be chosen so that laggardly planes could catch up. Tactics for formation turns must be formalized, turns should be signaled with Very flares to maintain wireless silence. For the first trials to provide a target for the prototype RDR at Bawdsey, he suggested three squadrons assemble near 54°N and 4°E and turn near the English coast at Felixstowe, maintaining an altitude of between five and seven thousand feet. They would then turn left and fly a reciprocal course back to the starting point.

There they would turn left and again head for Felixstowe, but one flanking squadron would detach and return to base. The remaining two squadrons would turn again at the coast and fly a reciprocal course back to the start. The other flanking squadron would detach and return to base. The lead squadron would repeat the exercise and then return to base, giving the boffins at Bawdsey six opportunities to estimate the formation strength with either twenty-four, sixteen, or eight aircraft in formation. He emphasized that once the practical details had been worked out, this was probably the way most RDR stations would be calibrated, and operators trained.

Chadwick walked to the hangar in the morning to inspect Sally. She looked disconsolate, with no engine on the bulkhead and pipes and wires drooping down. A mechanic came over, saying, "Engine has already been taken to a maintenance unit. That's the new one over there." He gestured to a large packing crate near the wall.

"How long will it take to install it?"

"I think it'll be ready for a ground run-up in about two days, then it needs an air test, sir."

Chadwick went back to the office and waited for Harris to call him, which took a week. Chadwick took the time to thoroughly test the new engine installed in the Spitfire. When Harris finally got back to him, he reported they had run through two rehearsals of the exercise. Chadwick asked for a copy of the detailed instructions and emphasized it was Harris's call to pick the day, based on the weather forecast. He asked for a day's notice so that he could alert Bawdsey.

The formation exercise down the North Sea took place the next day. They assembled at the chosen point and started at nine, ack-emma. Chadwick called Dr. Bostock and suggested that any stations on the east coast that were partially running might try to detect the formation. He told the scientist he planned to fly to Woodbridge himself and witness the trial at

Bawdsey. He was in the air before eight and strolled into the control room at Bawdsey on the stroke of nine.

The assembled engineers and scientists were excited by a realistic trial. The telephone rang. The formation had started to head south. The lead aircraft had sent a coded message on H.F. wireless. Ten minutes later, the telephone rang again, and an excited voice told Bostock that operators of RDR at Flamborough Head had detected the formation. A minute or two later, Bawdsey began to receive reflections. At nine forty-five the station was receiving solid echoes. Bostock took a photograph of the cathode ray tube. The formation was tracked until it disappeared to the north.

At ten-twenty, the telephone rang with an announcement that the second run had commenced. Photographs of the trace on the cathode ray tube were examined carefully. At eleven forty-five, the third run began. But after ten minutes, the telephone rang. Something had gone wrong. The Flamborough Head station called to report the formation had turned west and was heading inland. Finally, Chadwick was called to the phone. Two planes had collided at the end of the second run as they turned for home. The lead formation returned to RAF Church Fenton.

Later in the afternoon, Chadwick was able to get in touch with Wing Commander Harris and found that one plane had managed to crash land at RAF Kirton-in-Lindsey, while the other had crashed into the sea. The Grimsby lifeboat was searching for the wreck and survivors. Later the lifeboat returned to port without having found anything, and a naval ship from Newcastle sailed to the coordinates of the exercise starting point. A careful search lasting two days revealed no sign of the crashed plane. The crew were officially listed as "missing, presumed dead."

The incident temporarily dampened the spirits of the people involved. Harris's wing planned a memorial service later. An investigation cleared him of any blame. The instructions for the exercise were considered clear, and the wing had performed two rehearsals. The verdict was "pilot error."

Chadwick flew to RAF Church Fenton the same afternoon the accident occurred and commiserated with Harris and the squadron pilots. Harris was philosophical; accidents happen, and the training must continue.

Dr. Bostock studied the results of the trial. At the longer ranges, the difference in signal due to the number of aircraft was subtle. He mentioned to Chadwick that this was expected at the frequency that Chain Home employed and would be a good deal easier to resolve at the higher frequency of the next RDR generation.

Chadwick flew to the memorial service for the crew missing after the crash of their aircraft in the RDR exercise. He landed at Duxford, the home base of the squadron that lost the men. The service was somber, but like many RAF fatalities, aircrew tended to take it in their stride as a fact of life for those who flew military planes.

After lunch with the squadron commander and Wing Commander Harris, he walked to the tower to check the weather and don flying gear. Sally had been refueled, as it was normal RAF practice when a plane landed, although the tanks had been three-quarters full.

The flight to Farnborough took only twenty minutes. Chadwick flew downwind and started to pump down the undercarriage. On the crosswind leg, as he started to lose height, and noticed the left undercarriage light was still red. Despite strenuous pumping, the light would not change to green. Chadwick applied power and circled the field as he raised the wheels and then lowered them again. There was no change. He called the tower and made a slow fly-past. They observed the plane with binoculars and reported the left oleo leg was half down, at an angle. They alerted the fire brigade and the ambulance and suggested a wheels-up landing.

Chadwick was furious with Sally. He knew a wheels-up landing would damage her badly, and probably she would be written off. He realized just how much he loved that plane. The thought of getting some beaten-up, slow plane for liaison flights filled him with horror. He tried another fly-past, passing the tower while at the same time rocking violently from side to side. The observers reported the gear was still stuck half down on the left side. He noticed a considerable crowd had gathered near the tower to watch the fun.

Chadwick thought furiously. He was determined not to lose Sally without a fight. He called the tower to inform them he would try some violent maneuvers at a higher altitude. The new engine pulled like a racehorse and he climbed quickly to five thousand feet. Then he throttled back and pulled the nose into a vertical climb. The speed fell off rapidly, finally entering a hammer-head stall. With one hand on the stick, he cranked the hydraulic pump on his right, pushing madly on the rudder bar to keep the plane going straight up.

Ultimately, the plane hung in the sky for a moment, and then snapped into a spin. Chadwick pushed the stick fully forward and applied opposite rudder. The motion was violent, pitching and yawing at the same time, but slowly the plane stopped spinning and he eased out of the dive. A glance at the instrument panel filled him with a mad joy—both lights were green.

"By God, Sally," he shouted, "You nearly got me that time, you vicious bitch. But I still love you."

He flew past the tower, and they confirmed both wheels were down. He made a tight curving approach to the field and touched on three points as he leveled the wings. Squadron Leader Codrington walked over as he climbed down from the cockpit. "Good show, Allan. Better have the riggers look at the undercarriage."

"I quite agree, sir."

Later that afternoon they put the plane on trestles and a technician pumped the gear. The wheels went up and down flawlessly. Chadwick watched for a few minutes, and the sergeant said, "Look at that, but we'll change the oleo leg anyway."

Chadwick asked him to find a piece of rope, which he tied to the wheel axle. Co-opting two beefy airmen, he got the technician to pump the gear down while the airmen strained from the tail end of the rope. Halfway down, the gear stuck and only jerked free and lowered when the airmen stopped pulling.

The sergeant looked at Chadwick with admiration. "By gum, sir, you put your finger on it. Only sticks when there is pressure to the rear, like the air pressure when you're flying"

Chadwick asked him to disassemble the hydraulics. A careful examination showed a microscopic ridge had developed on the piston. Later the chief test pilot cornered Chadwick and congratulated him on getting out of a difficult situation by using his brains. Chadwick joked with him, "Like you said, she's a lady. I wasn't going to abuse that beautiful body." He was enormously pleased that Chris Bligh had commented on his flying. Bligh was, after all, one of Farnborough's most famous pilots.

Chapter Thirty-Eight

After the service in the morning and the excitement of the landing, Chadwick's nerves were wound up to a fever pitch. He called Melanie from the mess. "Feel like dinner out, dear? I've had a rocky day."

Melanie was surprised to hear from Allan. He rarely called out of the blue. "Well, this is a surprise. What have you got in mind?"

"How about something sweet after dessert?"

"That sounds wonderful. Meet me at the Blue Bell, the one on the south side of the village, say in an hour."

"Just gives me time to change and Bentley over."

When Chadwick arrived, he saw Melanie's Vauxhall parked in a corner of the parking lot. Dusk was settling over the countryside. He parked next to her car and was soon sitting next to her in the cozy inn.

"What's the matter with you?" Melanie asked.

"Tell you in a sec. Must get a drink." Allan waved to a waiter and ordered a double Scotch.

"My, my, Allan, has war broken out?"

"I'm wound up like a clock spring, Melanie. It's been a hell of a day. Started off with a memorial for four chaps who went down in an exercise I was very involved with. Awfully sad, wives and girlfriends there blubbering. When I got back to Farnborough, Sally acted up. She would not put down the wheels properly. If I bellied in, the plane would have been destroyed. In the end I managed to get the wheels down in an aerobatic feat that came close to pulling her apart. I think you know what I need."

"I think I can unwind your clock spring, darling. Let's order." While they were waiting, Melanie said casually, "I had a chat with Freddy Rutledge a few days ago."

"Oh, yes. Lord Lowestoft. How is the old blighter?"

"Concerned as ever. He thinks the stuff you're working on—RDR is it? —is going to upset the balance of power. I don't completely understand his diplomatic language. I think he would like to talk to you again sometime."

"I can pop in, next time I'm in town. His girl makes a nice cup of tea, with scrumptious chocolate biscuits."

"Tonight, I suggest you leave your car here after dinner. We can drive to the Hall in my car. I'll bring you back later."

"All right, I'll just let the head waiter know that I'll pick it up later."

When they arrived at Clair Court, Melanie parked by the front steps. They dashed upstairs, and as soon as they closed her bedroom door behind them, they embraced in a tight clinch and started to pull each other's clothes off. Melanie sat on the bed as Allan advanced toward her. "Goodness me, Allan, don't trip or you will pole vault through the window, as the joke goes."

Allan laughed. "For a respectable widow, you have an amazing stock of dirty jokes."

"Blame the Women's Instit—" He interrupted her with a kiss.

Suddenly serious, she said, "I know you're stressed. That's what mistresses are for. Don't worry about me. Do what you want."

Two hours later, they reluctantly crept downstairs and Melanie dropped Allan at the Blue Bell. He promised to call as soon as he could. He drove his green machine back to Farnborough, feeling on top of the world. *How lucky I am,* he thought. *I still have two functioning mistresses and a Bentley.*

A few days later at the MI5 headquarters in London, Doug Larson received an invitation to meet the deputy head. The secretary knocked on a closed door and then ushered Larson into a meeting with four people. The deputy head made the introductions.

"Mr. Larson, this Wilberforce Viney. Mr. Viney has some thoughts about your interaction with the Air Force chap, Chadwick."

Viney picked up the conversation. "With reference to Mr. Chadwick, it seems somewhat coincidental that your friend from Egypt is now involved with RDR. In my profession I distrust coincidences."

Larson spoke up. "I knew him when he was stationed in Iraq and came to Egypt on two short occasions. When he was posted to Farnborough we stayed in touch and met in London. He has apparently been involved in setting up aircraft targets for the people building the prototype equipment. At the same time, he became involved with a group that call themselves the Isbell's Insiders—purely by chance when he met one of them at a party thrown for some visiting German students."

"Ah, that's what interests me, too," Viney exclaimed. "It all seems a bit pat, too smooth. The Isbell's crowd, of course, have caught our attention. Their motto is 'Peace at Any Price,' but whether they are a threat to the nation isn't clear. You see, Mr. Larson, not only do we have to prevent the details of RDR from being discovered by foreign powers, but the machinations of a foreign power to get them may lead us to their secret organization in the U.K., particularly the leader. The Chadwick affair may be a way in."

Larson digested this slowly. Viney continued. "Kegel, the cultural affairs attaché at the German Embassy, is almost certainly the head Abwehr agent responsible for nuts and bolts operations. From what Chadwick has told you, Mr. Larson, he was instrumental in getting Chadwick to that party. But he's not the man we're after. There is someone else who may have suggested the moves Kegel made, and who now will almost certainly make another move.

"Kegel is a pawn we could knock off the board anytime we want. But let's be patient. You see, Mr. Larson, the broad outline of RDR will certainly become known to interested powers. Those people at Bawdsey are throwing kilowatts of power into the ether, a child with a crystal set could discover it. Flights of RAF planes making seemingly random flights along the coast will catch the attention of any beach-goer. The way to protect RDR is more subtle. Perhaps we can call it deception—we must disguise its function and efficiency. The next time you have a tete-a-tete with Mr. Chadwick I should like to tag along and suggest a couple of questions he can answer. Thank you, Larson, that will be all for the moment."

Some animated discussion followed Larson's departure. The Deputy Head of MI5 silenced the meeting. "We're only looking at one end of the communications channel, but channels have two ends. Who is listening at the German end? Perhaps Six has something for us, Bertram?"

Bertram Massey was a member of MI6, the British agency responsible for secret service operations abroad. He lifted his head from his chest. He had not opened his mouth previously. If truth be told he was feeling tired. "I'll pass your request up the chain, sir. As I understand it, you're looking for an Abwehr person who is sufficiently socially connected that he can liaise with the head of strategic operations in Britain, correct?"

"Yes, that's close."

"There are several in the Abwehr of old military families, usually Prussian, who do not approve of the Nazi government, and in particular of Herr Hitler. But they are not anti-German. There may be an opening, I will raise it with M."

Larson left a message for Chadwick to meet him in London the next time he had a few hours to spare.

Chapter Thirty-Nine

Bomber Command, in the shape of Group Captain Hearne, took over responsibility for providing aircraft for RDR calibration and training. It was still Squadron Leader Chadwick's job to brief the aircrews on the maneuvers required and to coordinate aircraft scheduling with RDR operations. He was very busy for a few weeks, and then a spell of atrocious late autumnal weather shut down flying over the British Islands for a few days. Sally got a fifty-hour engine overhaul and Chadwick booked a room at a London hotel so he could visit Lord Lowestoft and Doug Larson and invite Melanie to spend a couple of nights with him.

Lord Lowestoft was very affable when he checked in at the Foreign Office. Chadwick sat in the now-familiar office, and the usual tea and biscuits were served.

"When I asked you to visit me, I had in mind a review of RDR progress, but I was just speaking to Viscount Addenbury and there is more serious news. The King refuses to give up Wallis Simpson and even wants to marry her. Of course, that is quite impossible. Baldwin is unmoving, and the King is adamant. He will not abandon Wallis. It's an impasse."

"I'm sorry to hear that. When will the situation become public?"

"Anytime. The papers have been discreet up to now, but I suspect that can't last."

"What will happen now?"

Lowestoft shook his head. "God knows. The government can't accept a twice-divorced American as Queen. The King may abdicate, in which case Bertie will become King—a sickly, stammering weakling."

"You're not fond of his brother?"

"Enough about the royal clowns. Tell me a little about RDR. I trust your opinion over the bureaucrats who talk to us here."

"This is classified Most Secret, sir. I'm not sure I should be talking to you."

"Nonsense, I have a security clearance into the stratosphere."

Chadwick continued, resignedly. "The aim is to have as many stations operational as possible by next summer, in time for the RAF exercises. Although a couple are up and running, I suspect half a dozen will be fully operational and perhaps a few more partially ready."

"These stations will report the position, speed, height and direction of intruders, right?"

"Yes, sir."

"And what happens after that that?"

"Fighters will be directed to intercept them."

"What kind of time margin do they have?"

"I am not sure. Probably fifteen minutes."

"Sounds tricky. I'll be very interested in the results of the summer exercise. I believe you've been to some of our Isbell's meetings. We are as patriotic as the next man. It will not be in Britain's interest to fight another war like the last one. I hope you agree with that."

Chadwick was silent.

"If the King abdicates, we lose a powerful voice for diplomacy, particularly in dealing with Germany. However, Baldwin will fall if there is an abdication, and the next P.M. may well be Lord Halifax or Neville Chamberlain. Both are sensible men."

They continued to talk until Lowestoft announced it was lunch time, and as usual, invited Chadwick to his club. He bid Lowestoft farewell after the meal and took a taxi to the hotel he had selected for the rendezvous with Melanie, a quiet place on Russell Square.

After signing the register and putting his things away in their room, he took a taxi to Whitehall to meet Doug Larson, who greeted him warmly. Larson introduced a thin, cadaverous man. "Allan, meet Will Viney, one of MI5's deep thinkers. Squadron Leader Chadwick, Will."

"Pleasure. Doug has given some insight into your work, but I have a couple of questions—not really for you, but for the scientists putting RDR together. I imagine you meet them frequently?"

"Yes, I know the boss quite well, Dr. Bostock."

"The first question is, how easy will it be for an enemy to jam the radio signal and render the operation useless?"

"That sounds like a very good question. I can't offer an opinion, but I will place it before the good doctor."

"Second question. The Germans tried using their early attempts at RDR to direct fighters in the invasion of Finland but concluded that control could never be fast enough to get a fighter onto an intruder in time to make an interception—or so MI6 tell us. Comments?"

"I will also put that to Dr. Bostock, although I have some ideas on that subject."

"Pray tell, Squadron Leader."

"I've watched practice sessions at the first RDR station. The technical stuff can be fixed. What I suspect will happen in the '37 exercise is much what the Germans apparently discovered, a huge administrative effort will be needed to get the vital information from the technical people to the fighter dispatcher, with only minutes to spare. But we have years to develop that. Tell me, Mr. Viney, what is the view in the intelligence agencies of when a war will break out?"

"A good many experts, from diplomats, generals, and economists to soothsayers ponder that question. I think the average is 1942."

"Assuming the enemy is Germany, which is rearming rapidly, what course will the war take?"

"Impossible to know. Clearly tanks, aircraft, submarines, and guns are far more advanced than in '18. Maybe the French Maginot Line and the Belgium forts will hold up, maybe not. The notorious von Schlieffen said plans rarely survive contact with enemy."

"To change the subject, I should mention I had a meeting and lunch with Lord Lowestoft this morning. He was very insistent on discussing RDR progress."

Viney chuckled. "Wonderful, the mice are sniffing at the cheese."

"Wonderful, Mr. Viney? Why is that?"

"Because, dear Squadron Leader, we cannot hide the presence of RDR, but we can obscure its performance to those who are eager to listen. The Isbell's crowd are a good entry point for such misinformation."

After some more discussion the meeting broke up. Larson invited Chadwick to go on a pub crawl that night, but Allan politely declined. Doug said, "I understand," with smirk.

When Allan got back to the hotel, Melanie was already ensconced in the bed, reading a popular magazine. "Allan my pet, it's awful outside. What better way to spend a rainy night than curled up with your true love?"

Chapter Forty

The news of the King's infatuation with Wallis Simpson hit the British press a week later. The Premiers of Commonwealth countries made it clear to the Prime Minister, Stanley Baldwin, that they would not accept a divorced woman as Queen, or even Queen Consort. The impassioned debate about what to do next split the country into bitterly divided parts.

Addenbury called a meeting of the Isbell's Insiders to gauge their feelings. Lady Fitzgibbon contacted Chadwick, who happened to be back at Farnborough the night of the meeting and arranged to meet Melanie at Isbell's. He drove over with plenty of time before the formal start of dinner. He was now accepted as a member of the group.

He stood in the great Tudor hall sipping a drink and slowly infiltrating into a small crowd listening to Viscount Addenbury. The Viscount was of the opinion that enough public support for the King would force Baldwin to resign and the King would marry Wallis. Most of the listeners were of the same opinion and murmured, "Hear, hear."

Lord Lowestoft said, "Wonder what Tom Carstairs thinks of all this."

Someone else added, "If it does come to an abdication, I suppose David would be forced to live abroad, and that wouldn't suit Tom."

Chadwick racked his brain, trying to place the reference to a Tom Carstairs, and then he remembered meeting him at a lunch with Lord Lowestoft several months before. When the dinner gong sounded, he stopped Lowestoft for a moment. "Sir, didn't I meet Tom Carstairs at your club a while ago?"

"Yes, you're right. Good memory. I wish mine was as good."

"How is he involved, sir?"

"Ah, well, Sir Thomas Carstairs was the senior aide de camp to David when he was Prince of Wales. Now that he's the King, Tom is in the middle of all the negotiations with the politicians, business leaders, and the Commonwealth. If it comes to an abdication, Tom will suddenly lose his eminent position. In fact, he may even be blamed for whatever goes wrong."

Allan spotted Melanie entering the hall. Before she became involved with the guests, he walked up to her and asked quietly, "Four Feathers later?"

"I'm ahead of you, dear. We're booked in for tonight."

While the waiters served the dessert, Viscount Addenbury stood up and tapped his glass for attention. "I think tonight's subject is of paramount importance for us all, so I shall not ask the ladies to retire. You've all seen the papers recently. They're full of what they call the Wallis Simpson Affair. Stanley Baldwin is being his usual obdurate self. No thought for the feelings of the King. Within days this crisis is going to boil over. Unless we can mobilize immense public support for the King, I believe he may be forced to abdicate. After all, the King is the King! Surely, he of all people is entitled to choose the companion he wants as he faces the immense task of governing the British Empire. Baldwin says Mrs. Simpson will never be accepted as Queen, but I can testify, Americans make wonderful wives."

There was a ripple of polite laughter. The Viscount was married to an American.

One of the press barons stood up. "I can assure everyone here that my papers are solidly behind the King. But there is an aspect that Viscount Addenbury has not referred to, the maintenance of peace in this trying time. By far the best leader we could have is David. He's kept in touch with important men in the German government and if anyone can smooth the way forward, it is King Edward the Eighth. It's what he was trained for. And while I have no animosity for his brother Bertie, he's just not the man his brother is."

He sat down amid prolonged clapping. Several men stood up and repeated similar sentiments.

As guests slowly filtered out, Chadwick lingered to allow Melanie to get well away. As he stood near the door shrugging on a heavy coat, two men approached and talked in knowing terms about the Bentley. Apparently, they had both owned similar models a few years previously but had given them up under pressure from their wives. One of them said plaintively, "She said it messed up her hair, had to change it for a saloon car." They all laughed.

It was only a ten-minute run to Reigate. Chadwick parked behind the inn and was soon in company with Melanie. They sat stark naked in bed, propped up on pillows, and for a couple of minutes talked about the pending abdication. But Melanie's wandering hand soon found something more substantial, and they immersed themselves in each other.

After an early breakfast, Chadwick drove pell-mell back to RAF Farnborough. He called Dr. Bostock, who had been unavailable for a week, and arranged to meet him at Bawdsey later in the day. The weather was cloudy but not forecast to get worse. Sally was in good spirits and the flight to RAF Woodbridge went smoothly.

When he was sitting with Dr. Bostock, he phrased his questions carefully. It seemed like a good idea not to mention MI5. Instead, he invented interest by senior RAF officers. "Kenneth, some high-ranking mucky-mucks asked me about RDR, and I felt I should get your opinion. I'm no expert, but can RDR be jammed?"

"Yes, it could be jammed, but it would be very difficult because of the pulsed nature of the beast. Also, as soon as jamming is detected, there are fairly simple countermeasures we could take."

"Thank you, that sounds encouraging. Secondly, what sort of organization is needed between the RDR stations and the RAF fighter dispatchers?"

"I was approached myself by fairly senior RAF types just recently. The organization you allude to will be strictly RAF. They've created a new group for it, Group Sixty. It will be under the command of Group Captain Seamus O'Brien."

"I'll try to meet him sometime."

"In my opinion they don't know what they're getting into. It will shake down after the '37 exercise."

After lunch with the technical people, Chadwick realized his ignorance of electronics, as they termed it, was a handicap. There were no books available on the subject but Dr. Bostock lent him a handbook on wireless telegraphy, published by the Royal Navy. It was a start.

Despite the forecast, the weather had deteriorated when he got back to RAF Woodbridge and the half-hour flight to Farnborough was at low level, following the rails. He knew he couldn't climb through the clouds, as he would never be able to safely descend again. Cloud cover at Farnborough was one hundred percent.

In view of the weather, he arranged to travel into London the next day to see Doug Larson and Will Viney. Chadwick relayed Dr. Bostock's answers to the questions of jamming and interception organization.

Then he mentioned why he had pushed to see them. He told them about the Isbell's Insiders meeting and the slightly strange remarks made about Sir Thomas Carstairs. Chadwick pressed his point that Carstairs should be investigated. As Aide de Camp to the Prince of Wales, and later enjoying an even higher role in the Palace, he was in an ideal position to funnel information to and from Germany.

Viney pondered the problem. "If we can get some important-sounding, unique, exclusive information just into Carstairs' ears, then if it emerges in the German Abwehr, in which we have contacts, that would be the smoking pistol, as Sherlock Holmes would say."

"I think Lord Lowestoft is an intimate friend of Carstairs and gives him a lot of stuff."

"Let's see what we can cook up," Viney said.

The news of the abdication of the King two weeks later hit the British public like a thunderclap. The King addressed his subjects over the BBC and announced his decision to step down, saying that he would be known in the future as the Duke of Windsor. Accompanied by Mrs. Simpson, he departed England to live in France. It was reported that he planned to marry when her divorce became final.

There was no news of Carstairs, and finally Chadwick called Lord Lowestoft and then went to see him at the Foreign Office. Chadwick confessed he was interested in getting the inside news of the ramifications of the abdication. Lowestoft told him that Carstairs had not moved to France with the Duke, and then seemed to feel he owed Chadwick some explanation.

"You know, the Duke does not receive as much renumeration from the Royal Purse as he did as the Prince of Wales. I suspect now he is limited to only two or three aides-de-camp. There is a rumor Carstairs is trying to join us here, at the F.O., maybe at the German Desk."

Chadwick declined an offer of lunch with Lowestoft, and instead grabbed a bite at a pub. He then he called on Larson and Viney at Whitehall. He mentioned the rumor that Carstairs may be attempting to join the Foreign Office.

"That's interesting," Viney said.

"Interesting!" exploded Chadwick, "Isn't that like putting the fox in charge of the henhouse?"

"You certainly seem to have gotten your teeth into the intelligence game, Squadron Leader. I should mention that with strategic intel we're playing the long game. Decisions have long-term effects. In this situation I'd like to kill two birds with one stone—namely unmask our traitor and at the same time improve the defense of the realm. For example, you tell me the '37 exercise will be a learning experience, and probably word of its failure will leak out. Hopefully the '38 exercises will go much better.

"But suppose our traitor passes the word that the British claimed success in '38 to boost morale and in reality, the exercise later was also a failure? We could add a nugget of misinformation, for example, that only thirteen percent of fighters dispatched reached altitude in time to intercept the bombers. This will confirm the German view, which they believe anyway. Thus, the Germans will underestimate our defenses and the traitor will have flagged us. I think you can see we must play our cards with subtlety, Squadron Leader."

"Thank you, sir. You live a complicated life, indeed. And please, call me Allan."

When he was back at Farnborough, Chadwick discussed the organization of the '37 exercise with Squadron Leader Codrington, suggesting that a visit to Fighter Command might be in order. Codrington agreed.

A few days later he drove over to Fighter Command HQ at Bentley Priory, near Harrow in northwest London. He sat down with Group Captain O'Brien, who was a brusque man without a trace of an Irish accent. Chadwick described his role in providing aircraft targets for the development of the system and training of RDR operators. He mentioned that he had got to know the technical leader, Dr. Bostock, quite well and in his estimation, Bostock was a very competent scientist. But he had not been charged with the creation of the operational apparatus that was needed to vector fighter planes onto the intruder. That creation, he believed, would now take place under the group captain and he would be happy to help in any way.

O'Brien stared at Chadwick as he made that offer. He was a political animal and he realized Chadwick at that moment knew more about what was needed than he did, and therefore was a rival. He decided to keep Chadwick well away from the activities of Sixty Group, but on the surface, he thanked the squadron leader, promised to visit Bawdsey, and wished him a polite good morning.

Chadwick drove back to Farnborough feeling a trifle dissatisfied. He had hoped O'Brien would ask for his suggestions about the design of the administrative system to report, plot, and dispatch defenders.

Chapter Forty-One

Within weeks the Prime Minister, Stanley Baldwin, resigned and the Isbell's Insiders went into action to ensure a new P.M. had ideas that were compatible with their own. After a good deal of lobbying and a newspaper campaign, Neville Chamberlain visited King George the Sixth to ask his permission to form a government. The Insiders were delighted, as Chamberlain had made no secret of his desire to avoid a war. British military leaders were philosophical; more time to the next war gave more time for rearmament.

One morning Chadwick said to his sergeant in the office, "I'm off to see Squadron Leader Codrington, if anyone is looking for me."

"It's Wing Commander Codrington now, sir."

"Thank you, sergeant, for the timely advice."

Chadwick walked into Codrington's office with a cheery, "Congratulations, sir, on your promotion."

"Thank you, Allan. What can I do for you?"

"I wanted to bring you up to date on RDR and my visit to Fighter Command."

"Good, sit down and make yourself comfortable. Would you like some tea?"

"No, thank you, sir. I think we'll be lucky to have five RDR stations fully operational for the summer exercise. Which brings up the point, who is organizing the exercise?"

"That will be done at Uxbridge. And I don't know yet who is in command. Obviously, the air vice marshal will keep a close interest in it."

"I was told by the chaps at Bawdsey that the stations will all fall under a new Group, Sixty. I went to Bentley Priory yesterday to see the new leader."

"Who is that, pray?"

"Group Captain O'Brien, sir."

Codrington gave a short laugh. "I know him well. He was my squadron commander ten years ago when we were flying Wapitis. How did you find him?"

"I explained what Farnborough had been doing to assist in the RDR development and more lately to train operators. He listened politely but didn't ask about my suggestions for the plotting and dispatching of defenders."

"That sounds like O'Brien. He's very ambitious for himself."

"I was hoping to express my concern over the delay in producing mechanical calculators to handle the RDR data. In view of the tight time frame to get a fighter on the target there's simply no time for human calculators. Dr. Bostock is very good, but he's completely tied up with the problems of the RDR transmitters, receivers, and aerials. He's not dealt much with way the information is processed."

"Um, let me think." Codrington was silent for a few minutes, then said, "You know what's going to happen next? O'Brien is going to suggest that Sixty Group take over our liaison responsibilities between Bomber Command and the RDR people. It even makes some sense."

Chadwick was silent, running over the ramifications of Codrington's remark. He was going to lose his job. Worse, he would lose Sally. He said slowly, "I suppose it does, sir. We've done our job and time has moved on."

"Yes, but they still need us. Farnborough is the center for all things new and exotic in the RAF. We must move on now to being the assessors, the judges. Who else can evaluate the summer exercises but us? I'll speak to our beloved leader here,

Group Captain Delaney-Jones, this very day and anticipate any move by O'Brien to jettison Farnborough."

A week later a directive came down to Fighter and Bomber Commands from the Air Council, the ultimate authority of the government controlling the Royal Air Force. They were commanded to perform a simulated attack by foreign, European-based air forces for a week in June consistent with good weather. The intention was to test the air defenses of Great Britain. The tests would be monitored by the Royal Aircraft Establishment, RAE, Farnborough, which would prepare a report of the efficiency of the methods to detect intruders and direct defending aircraft.

A committee was hurriedly put together by the relevant commands and RAE to plan the exercise, which was labeled "Exercise Torpedo." The planning was quite elaborate—RAE officers would be sent to the RDR stations to observe their performance. They would also travel to the centers of the Observer Corp, which would search for intruders after they had crossed the coast.

Only six RDR stations were operational, stretching from RAF Manston to RAF Thornaby, a distance of about 230 nautical miles. Bombers would cross the coast within range of those stations and have secret targets of major inland cities. Altitude was to be between two and fifteen thousand feet. The timing of the raids would only be divulged to RAE so that they could have aircraft airborne to observe any simulated attacks. All attacks would commence a minimum distance of seventy-five nautical miles east of the coast.

Wing Commander Codrington was put in charge of the RAE effort. He assigned ground observers to RDR stations and Observer Corp posts. Six Spitfires with pilots and support crew were temporarily based at airfields along the coast. All these personnel were required to keep a detailed log of their observations. Several meetings were held between Fighter and Bomber command and Sixty Group to iron out details. Exercise Torpedo was planned for June.

When a day was chosen for the start, RAE personnel went to their temporary bases and waited with great excitement for the action to begin. Chadwick was based at Woodbridge. He had a loose assignment. Although the telecommunications team at Bawdsey were not part of Sixty Group, they had agreed to keep an eye on developments and phone him at Woodbridge if a bomber group was detected. For two hours he sat in the flight office next to the dispersal area. Sally sat outside.

Squadron Leader Wilson stopped by. "Good morning, Allan. I know what's going on is secret, but rumors abound. Looks like you chose a nice day for it."

"George, I may be here all week. The exercise only runs from sun-up to sun-down. I'll drop in each day."

Then the phone rang, and Chadwick grabbed it. Dr. Bostock himself gave him a vector to an incoming flight estimated at twenty aircraft, height ten thousand feet. Chadwick walked over to Sally. An aircraftsman was standing by to help with straps and disconnect the starter battery. Once airborne, he climbed to twelve thousand feet and used full power to head for the bombers. The sun lay to the southeast.

After twenty minutes he calculated he should be on top of the incoming flight. Then he saw the glint of sun off a windshield and within minutes he counted fifteen Blenheim bombers apparently heading for London. He resisted the urge to make a mock attack and instead slowly overtook the leading aircraft and waved to the pilot. He got a vigorous waggling of wings in return. There was no sign of any defending fighters.

He headed for the coast and less than an hour after he took off, he was back on the ground at Woodbridge. Back in the flight office he waited by the phone. The officer's mess sent over a sandwich and a glass of lemonade. Squadron Leader Wilson dropped by again.

"Well, George, if this had been a real war, I could have nailed a couple, I think. But I have them on the gun camera."

"You might have got one, Allan, but in my experience, the other fellow wouldn't have been hanging around after that."

"Ah, words of wisdom, George."

With the sun low on the horizon, Chadwick made a quick, low-level flight back to Farnborough. As soon as he landed, he stopped by Codrington's office. "Greetings, sir, how goes Torpedo?"

"Hello, Allan, how was your day?"

"I caught a flight of Blenheims, streaking hell for leather for London."

"I think you're the only one. I haven't heard of any interceptions from the chaps up the coast. Tomorrow I'd like you to visit a couple of our fellows in the RDR and sector offices. I suggest you start at Manston, and then go up to Debden. Flight Lieutenant Stone is checking on Manston and Flight Lieutenant Pover is taking care of Debden. Perhaps if you spend the night at Woodbridge, you could sound out Dr. Bostock and then move north the next day. Please keep in touch with me."

Chadwick left early the next day and landed at RAF Manston before eight. He had been given a list of Bomber Command flights for the day and noticed a mid-morning flight was planned to fly up the Thames to London, a route that would put it well in the area scanned from Manston.

Chadwick and Stone stood out of the way in the busy receiver hut, where about a half dozen WAAFs operated the RDR controls, the calculator, and the telephone. They were supervised by an attractive flight officer who was obviously nervous in the presence of an older pilot with a campaign ribbon on his tunic. Chadwick asked her name.

"Flight Officer Spencer, sir."

"Don't worry about us, Spencer. We're from Farnborough, just seeing how this first exercise of RDR goes."

"I wish we had had more training, sir. This is rather nerve-racking."

Shortly after, the WAAF operating the receiver called her. "Good echo, miss, about thirty-seven miles."

Spencer strode over to the console and fiddled with the controls. They passed some readings to the calculator operator. The machine whirred and the operator spoke quickly on the telephone. Chadwick asked Flight Officer Spencer what they had found.

"Looks like a medium formation at seven thousand feet, give or take. I'll have position, range, speed, and direction when our companion RDR plots information from both stations."

Two minutes later the telephone operator gave her some numbers which she repeated to Chadwick. "Position fifty-one degrees, twenty-seven minutes north, naught-two degrees, thirty-five minutes east, range three-nine miles, one seven-five knots, two forty-one degrees."

Chadwick glanced at his watch—six minutes since the first reflections had been seen. He spoke to Flight Lieutenant Stone. "Call Sector Ops and find out when a squadron was scrambled, the vector they were given, and the type of fighter."

After a short delay Stone returned from talking to a WAAF holding a telephone. "Four Hurricanes just airborne now, sir. Vector north, making angels nine."

Chadwick looked at his watch again. Another twelve minutes had passed. The whole room was tense. Spencer looked at Chadwick and raised her eyebrows. "Four Hurricanes just scrambled. They should be at altitude in a couple of minutes."

He did a quick calculation in his head. The bombers would have moved about sixty miles since the first sighting. The fighters were too late. He spoke to Stone, "Dick, please pass the word when you get a sighting report from the fighters."

Minutes passed and then a WAAF handed a telephone to Stone. He nodded. "Yes, I've got that. Thanks." He handed the telephone back to the WAAF. "No sighting, sir, returning to base."

There was a long sigh from almost everyone in the room. Chadwick spoke to the disappointed WAAFs. "You see, ladies, that was a very tricky interception, because the dispatcher could not send them further west. It would have put them inside the coast, which is army anti-aircraft territory. The Observer Corp will track them from there. Possibly another intercepting squadron was alerted from further north, which means they could have been spotted earlier. Sorry 'bout that but keep up the good work."

After a quick lunch he flew to Debden. It was close enough that for the fifteen-minute flight, Chadwick did not raise the undercarriage but flew at one hundred and fifty knots. A higher speed would damage the undercarriage doors. He landed at Debden and was driven to the RDR buildings. The huge three-hundred-foot aerials dominated the landscape. Flight Lieutenant Pover was sitting in the sun on a deck chair. Behind him an open door led into the plotting room. Several WAAFs were busy inside.

"Very quiet here, sir." Chadwick knew from the Bomber Command list that a raid should develop in an hour, again aimed at London. He had noticed when he landed that a flight of Hurricanes was standing by. The pilots, like Pover, were lounging in deck chairs. There was a call from inside. "Faint echo just coming out of the noise. Looks like about ninety miles."

Chadwick and Pover both went inside to watch the WAAFs in action. Chadwick noted the time. Four minutes later, a telephone call from the sector controller confirmed a medium formation at angels twelve, range eighty -two miles, heading two six-naught degrees, speed one-fifty.

Pover crossed over to a telephone and asked to be told when a fighter flight was scrambled. Eight minutes later he nodded at Chadwick. "Two flights airborne, sir."

Chadwick glanced at his watch—fifteen minutes from the first detection. He felt this interception had a good chance of working. Thirty minutes later the flight officer took a call, listened, and then announced to the room, "Wonderful news! A formation of Wellesey bombers was intercepted ten miles off the coast."

The WAAF manning the 'scope suddenly looked intently at the screen. "There's another echo coming up, miss, same distance as the first one but moving faster."

After some manipulating of the controls and a session at the mechanical calculator, a WAAF called out the altitude, "Angels fifteen." All the information was passed onto Sector control.

Chadwick checked his watch and smiled to himself. Bomber Command had obviously given some thought to a sneaky plan. By coming in immediately after one raid, they apparently hoped to catch the fighters being refueled on the ground. He looked at his watch.

The flight officer took a telephone call. "Speed two hundred knots, two five naught degrees."

Pover asked a WAAF telephonist to confirm a scramble. Ten minutes later she announced a flight of Hurricanes had been scrambled from Woodbridge. Thirty minutes later Sector called. The bombers had got through, and the fighters were still gaining altitude when six Blenheim bombers flew over them, three thousand feet above.

Chadwick again silently applauded the Bomber Command planners. They had sent much faster planes on the second wave. He asked Pover to write up a report of the activities and then flew to Woodbridge, where he intended to spend the night.

Squadron Leader Wilson had learned of his plans and left a message inviting him to have dinner with himself and his wife, Barbara, at their house on the Woodbridge site. Chadwick walked to their house and was greeted enthusiastically by Wilson. His wife was a small, fussy woman who joined them for a glass of sherry before disappearing into the kitchen. Sitting in the neat and tidy front room, George asked, "When did you join up, Allan?"

"Actually, I think my service counts from when I left school and entered Cranwell."

Impressed, George said, "Oh, you're a Cranwell man! No wonder you're involved in this RDR stuff."

"It's more of a coincidence than you think. I was organizing a couple of bombers to act as targets for the developers of RDR and got to know them quite well. So, I had some appreciation of the problems."

"Your engineering education at Cranwell must enable you to fit right in."

"Yes and no. The stuff they're using to develop RDR is called electronics. It's so new that there are no books—only books on wireless, which is just one branch. These fellows are very bright and inventing it as they go along."

"Sounds dashed exciting."

They were interrupted by a call from the kitchen —"Dinner's ready."

An immaculate table was laid in the dining room. Barbara brought in a roast chicken, with tureens of potatoes, peas, sprouts, and a gravy dish. They all helped themselves. Chadwick found he was really enjoying the domestic atmosphere after the antiseptic rigidity of the officer's mess.

"Have you any children, Barbara?" he asked.

"Two daughters and a son," she replied.

"My son is doing well," George added. "He's a management trainee at Williams Deacons Bank."

"Our daughters are younger, after our son was born George was stationed in Egypt for a few years. I stayed in England," Barbara explained. "I don't know what they will do, probably get married after a couple of years. They're upstairs at the moment, doing homework."

After some custard and a cup of coffee, they moved into the living room. George waited and then said, "You know, Allan, there's one problem with a career in the Air Force you probably haven't thought about. You're still young."

"Yes?"

"You wind up with a pension but no house. The RAF has always provided accommodations, you see."

Allan confessed he had not given that topic any thought.

"And when you leave, you find the Building Societies will only discuss a short mortgage, which eats a hole in your pension."

"Somehow retirement seems a long way off."

"It comes quicker than you realize," George said. "This is probably my last posting, unless there's a war."

"Oh, don't say that," Barbara cried and playfully slapped his knee.

In the morning Chadwick had an early breakfast and landed at RAF Whitby by eight. He got a ride to the RDR station, which was on the coast a few miles east. Two RAE officers were already there, Flight Lieutenants Bottomley and Winters, who discussed the activity of the day before. Chadwick told them there was a bomber exercise planned for the next hour, with Coventry as the target.

Bottomley went to the receiver room, and Winters and Chadwick drove a short distance to Sector operations. Shortly after they arrived, the aerials picked up a formation about ninety-five miles east. The calculators went to work and within five minutes, the height, bearing, speed, and heading were relayed by a telephonist to Sector. An officer selected a squadron on standby and gave them an interception vector.

Five minutes later the airfield called to tell them six Gladiator fighters were airborne. The Gladiator was a biplane fighter that was obsolete by 1937, but until the arrival of modern monoplanes, Fighter Command had to use what it had. Factories were working as hard as funding allowed on the new monoplanes. Interestingly, a Spitfire cost twice as much to build as a Hurricane but had a better performance.

Chadwick had been calculating the RDR data and the interception vector given to the fighters. He decided they had no chance of catching the bombers. Suddenly, he was wildly inspired to get the driver to take him back to Whitby. He did a quick ground examination, jumped into Sally, ran an engine test, and roared off into the wind.

He pushed Sally to the limit. The sun, fairly low in the east, was a problem, but after fifteen minutes he ran into a flight of Hampden bombers flying west at almost two hundred knots. Using his extra height to gain speed, he swooped past the leader in a shallow dive, made a slow roll and climbed rapidly. Leveling off, he flew east for a few minutes and spotted the gaggle of Gladiators slowly struggling to gain height, miles behind the bombers they had hoped to intercept.

He slowed, formatted on the leader, shook his head, and pointed down. Then he pushed the throttle wide open and seconds later, the old planes were lost behind him. Chadwick felt tremendous *joie de vivre*. Flying a plane that outflew everything in the sky gave him a feeling of exhilaration and liberation. He reluctantly turned for the coast, dropped to a thousand feet, and joined the circuit for RAF Whitby.

On landing he made a quick trip to the RDR buildings, grabbed a hurried lunch, and said goodbye to Bottomley and Winters. He checked the weather and telephoned his sergeant at Farnborough. He planned to spend the night at RAF Thornaby.

The twenty-minute flight to RAF Thornaby was routine. On landing he noticed a Spitfire parked at the dispersal area and discovered it belonged to Squadron Leader Bligh, who was observing RDR operations for RAE. Chadwick made sure he was checked in at the mess for the night and arranged a trip to the RDR buildings, several miles away on the coast. The first person he saw when he walked in the RDR operations room was Chris Bligh.

Bligh gestured for them to go outside. When they were out of earshot of the WAAFs, he whispered, "Right cock-up this morning. Somehow, they got two targets mixed up, and the defenders flying from Thornaby were vectored twenty degrees off course. Never saw a thing, of course."

Bligh looked at his watch. "Better be getting back to Thornaby. Raid crossing the seventy-five-mile line in an hour. See you in the mess tonight, Allan."

Chadwick walked back into the RDR operations room. He introduced himself to the two RAE observers stationed there for Exercise Torpedo, Flight Lieutenants Lindley and Burrell. They gave Chadwick a few more details about the morning's disastrous interception. Then he introduced himself to the WAAF Section Officer. "I hear things didn't go too well earlier, Miss—?"

She blushed. "Clayborne-Rankin, Elizabeth, sir. I'm very sorry. We have very odd aerial performance here and at the partner station at Bridlington. The experts told us it's because of the nature of the ground. Produces funny lobes, whatever they are." She looked almost ready to cry.

"Elizabeth," Chadwick said firmly, "don't worry. That's exactly what Exercise Torpedo is for, to give us more realistic training and to discover weaknesses."

He walked over to Lindley and Burrell and said quietly, "I want one of you to go over to Sector. There should be some activity within the hour."

"I'll go," Lindley said.

"I want you to take particular notice of the time when you got the target information, and the time fighters were airborne."

Burrell lit a cigarette. "How is Torpedo going, sir? What do you hear?"

"It's early days. To be honest I've been involved with RDR for quite a few months, and I never expected this first test to go particularly smoothly."

"We live and learn, sir."

"That's the truth."

Just then the WAAF on the receiver called to the section officer. "Very weak signal, down in the noise, but I can just make it out. Range one hundred."

Section Officer Clayborne-Rankin crossed over for a look. "Good work, Mildred. Try to get a height reading. Susan, get these numbers into your machine."

The WAAFs were suddenly busy, and the telephonist began to pass data to the sector operations. Chadwick kept an eye on his watch. The door into the room opened and to Chadwick's amazement, Group Captain O'Brien walked into the room.

Chadwick saluted. "Good afternoon, sir."

O'Brien nodded. "What's going on here?" he demanded.

"They just picked up an echo, sir, extreme range. They're computing an interception heading now. I expect fighters will be scrambled within minutes."

"I wanted to see this from a bomber's point of view. I must assume the Huns will have the same thing for the next shooting match."

"A very astute thought, if I may say so, sir."

O'Brien looked at him closely. "Don't I know you?"

"Chadwick, sir. We met in your office at Bentley Priory a few weeks ago."

"Are you telling me they need a squadron leader to supervise this op?"

"I'm not supervising, sir. I'm observing on behalf of RAE. I arrived an hour ago to watch how this interception pans out. Section Officer Clayborne-Rankin is in charge." He nodded for her to come over. "This is Group Captain O'Brien, who's in charge of your Sixty Group."

The WAAF blushed again. O'Brien nodded but said nothing.

Burrell came over. "Excuse me—the fighters scrambled."

Chadwick looked at his watch. "Very good. Fifteen minutes from detection to scramble."

"At the range they were picked up, I think they'll intercept. What kind of fighters are aloft?"

"Hurricanes, sir."

They waited. O'Brien roamed around the room, occasionally poking at some equipment. The WAAF officer followed him and gave answers to grunted questions.

One of the telephonists spoke up. "The fighters have made contact, fifteen miles east of the coast."

"That's excellent, Group Captain. I think we can thank Section Officer Clayborne-Rankin's team for that good work." O'Brien brayed, "Good work, Section Officer. Thank you."

She shot Chadwick a look of gratitude.

In the mess at Thornaby, Chadwick asked Chris Bligh if he had managed to get into position to witness the interception that afternoon.

"It was a textbook interception, Allan. They were two thousand feet above the bombers and up sun. I was impressed."

"Well, obviously the system works some of the time. I'm going back to Woodbridge tomorrow. See you back at Farnborough."

Chadwick then noticed Section Officer Clayborne-Rankin standing in the anteroom. He walked over to her. "One of our RAE pilots saw your interception. He says it was textbook."

"Thank you, sir, and thank you also for the good word you put in to the group captain."

Chadwick looked at her. She was young and pert, and a lascivious urge crossed his mind, only to be suppressed by his affection for Melanie. He had never worked with WAAFs before. There were none in Iraq or at RAF Farnborough. He realized how vulnerable they were in a service dominated by men. His calculating mind predicted trouble ahead, despite regulations forbidding fraternization. "Can I get you a glass of sherry?"

"Thank you, yes, that would be delightful."

He brought her a glass and made small talk before making an excuse to join a group of RAE officers.

Chapter Forty-Two

The increased RAF activity over the North Sea aroused the interest of the German Luftwaffe, which resulted in them dispatching a Zeppelin into the region. It cruised at two thousand feet and was loaded with wireless equipment. RAF communications using H.F. were coded so that they gleaned very little, although clearly the huge towers were doing something.

Two days later, Dr. Kegel, the head of German tactical intelligence in the British Isles, received a message from Abwehr HQ in Hamburg. He was directed to have the positions of all the large towers marked on Ordnance Survey maps, obtainable at most booksellers. He decided that Stiller could deal with the south and southeast coasts and left a message for the young German to meet him at their favorite tea shop.

When they met, Stiller enquired after Inge Fischer, the young woman who had been sent to England at the same time as himself. "She's back in Hamburg, Stiller. I have no idea how she is being employed. However, I have an interesting job for you—the British are erecting large towers at frequent intervals along the coast. They're a hundred meters high, so they're easy to spot. Our superiors want English Ordnance Survey maps marked with the position of each one. I thought maybe a nice bicycling, camping holiday on the coast may be the way to go."

"I have a suggestion that may be much quicker. I've become very friendly with the daughter of the people whose party you took us to, the Pomeroys. She's learning to fly and trying to accumulate enough flying hours to get a commercial pilot's license. I've been on quite a few trips with her. I'm sure she would be happy to fly along the coast."

"Not a bad idea, but she must have no inkling of what you're interested in."

"I'll buy some of those Ordnance Survey maps and give it a try."

Penelope acquiesced readily to a trip along the coast in her Tiger Moth. The passenger sat in the front seat of the plane. Penelope was intrigued to watch Olaf, as she knew him, pay attention to something on his knees as they flew past the RDR towers. When they landed, she demanded to see the bundle he was ineffectually trying to hide.

"Why, Olaf, you're marking those towers on the maps. Why do that?" He said nothing. "Olaf, you're spying! How exciting."

Stiller mumbled, "A German friend just thought someone in the embassy would be interested." He seized Penelope round the waist and gave her a hearty kiss. "I love you and I love England, and I love Germany. I just want to avoid any trouble between our countries. The more we know about each other the better. Even your new Prime Minister said that."

"Did he? I don't care. I just love intrigue."

The Ordnance Survey maps, delivered to the Abwehr via the diplomatic bag, certainly caught the attention of Luftwaffe intelligence. They sent a new request to Kegel for some close-up photographs of the aerials, taken from the air so that the full height could be seen in detail.

Dr. Kegel passed this new request to Stiller. "Do you think your flying friend would cooperate to get some good photographs?" He passed a high-quality Leica to Stiller, saying "I suggest you fly past several aerials and shoot different levels on each, so that you don't seem to be hovering around one aerial. I have an idea, promise your friend a night in Brighton. There's an airfield there and snap the photos on the way. I'll give you funds for a weekend there."

Stiller had no difficulty persuading Penelope to spend a weekend in Brighton. He told her he had come into a little money due to the death of a relative. He booked two nights at the Grand Hotel and they had a very enjoyable stay. They both loved the Chinoiserie, and the Royal Pavilion built by the Prince Regent a century before.

Dr. Kegel was able to send a full roll of thirty-five millimeter film to Abwehr HQ. He got a message back that the technical experts were delighted, but they considered the British RDR to be primitive.

When Chadwick returned to Farnborough, he spent many hours with Codrington and the other RAE observers analyzing and collating the RDR Exercise Torpedo. After a week of intensive analysis, they prepared a short summary of the results, only two pages long, and included the observer's logs as appendices, which added another forty-eight pages. The summary indicated that great improvement in the system was essential. Of fifty-three simulated attacks, forty-one penetrated the coast without being intercepted. Of the twelve intercepted raids, seven were visual sightings only, and five were in a good position relative to the intruders to launch an attack.

Only one raid by Blenheim bombers was intercepted. This plane had a performance comparable to the newly developed Ju 88, which would be the mainstay of the Luftwaffe bomber fleet. In addition, only the Hurricanes achieved successful interceptions. Although the RDR equipment performed reliably, the range was marginal. All the successful interceptions were first detected at a one hundred nautical mile range or slightly greater.

There was confusion at Sector operations. Some raids were mis-labeled. There should have been a layer supervising the sector ops to coordinate raid identification and fighter readiness, one which could be viewed on an overall s plotting board, where decisions could be made on the fighters to be scrambled. The Observer Corp functioned well inland and gave between five and fifteen-minute warnings to Air Raid Precautions units in targeted cities, so that the alarm could be sounded.

The major recommendations were faster fighters, increased RDR range, and more supervision at the tactical plotting level. The new low-level RDR should be implemented as soon as possible. The report which Codrington issued was classified "Secret."

Chadwick put a copy in his RDR folder. He had been forced to neglect Melanie for a few weeks, and so he stopped by a jewelry shop in Farnborough and bought an expensive silver necklace. When he called the lady, her first reaction was, "Hello, stranger."

He apologized profusely and pleaded pressure of work. "I've even lost contact with Sally," he said plaintively. He suggested a weekend in London. He wanted to get a copy of the Torpedo summary to Larson and Viney, so why not combine business with pleasure? Melanie agreed and mentioned that Lord Lowestoft had been asking about him.

"He seems to keep an eye on you, dear. Why is that?"

Chadwick dodged the question by suggesting Friday and Saturday night at an expensive hotel on Park Lane, the Dorchester. Melanie complained that the subsidy from the estate might be stretched a little thin, and Chadwick replied this treat was on him as, after all, he was getting a squadron leader's pay now.

They settled the details of the rendezvous and then Chadwick first called Larson, who agreed to meet late morning on Friday over lunch. He then arranged to meet Lord Lowestoft in the afternoon. When he entrained to London, Chadwick took a copy of the Torpedo summary with him. It could not be sent via the British Post Office, as it carried the "Secret" designation.

At Whitehall he described Exercise Torpedo to Larson and Viney and gave them a copy of the summary, which he placed on Viney's desk. "As I understand it, the exercise can be considered a tactical failure," Viney said.

"Yes, but that was largely expected. We learned a lot, which can be used to make next year's exercise much better."

"Then we're in position to start the trail. Next year we'll spring the trap. Somehow, we must get a copy of this summary to the traitor we hope to nab. I've discussed our plot with very senior members of the Double-cross Committee. They believe revealing a few negative aspects of Torpedo will not seriously harm our position, and it baits the trap.

"Now, you think Lowestoft is a conduit to the traitor who has some vague connection with the Isbell's Insiders?"

"Yes."

"So how can you get a copy to Lowestoft without seeming to push it on him? Actually, there's something we learned a few months ago that may have a bearing. The Insiders, in the person of Lowestoft, have been transferring relatively small amounts of money to the Fitzgibbon estate. The estate itself is not in good financial condition. Yet the manager in Reading has then transferred identical amounts to your account at Lloyds Bank in Farnborough. That tidbit we only discovered recently. These sums are used to pay for your jaunts with Lady Fitzgibbon, I imagine."

Chadwick was shocked and embarrassed. He was silent for a moment. Viney sensed his embarrassment. "Allan, in this business we make no moral judgments. In fact, we often depend on people behaving with the basest instincts."

"My God," Chadwick managed to say thickly, "you fellows certainly know how to pry into things." He was silent again, and then asked, "Are you saying she was pushed onto me?" He was getting furious. "I can't believe that of Melanie."

Viney said smoothly, "It's very likely she has no idea where the money comes from. The manager looks after the books. I only mention it because Lowestoft may be tempted to try a little pressure on you to get a copy of the report. He might say it would not look too good if your service superiors knew you had money deposited indirectly from the Insiders."

"I've arranged to see Lowestoft this afternoon."

"Good. Play it calmly. You must give no hint that you know about the Insider's money transfer. If he tries a little blackmail—ugly word—then you must be shocked, but reluctantly give in. I would not recommend discussing this with Lady Fitzgibbon. The first thing she would do is confront Lowestoft, and he might be just smart enough to work back and sense that you must have got your information from someone like us, understood?"

"Yes, but you reel these things out like lines in a play. Why do you think you can manipulate people like puppets on strings, Will?"

Viney leaned toward Chadwick and said quietly but with great force, "Because I think I know how people will behave, and why. Men are motivated by lust for power, money, women—perhaps I should use a word popular in America, sex—because women aren't always involved. And finally, they are motivated by aberrant nationalism, which is often a manifestation of hatred for another tribe or race."

Larson felt things were getting a little heated and he interrupted to say, "I think it's time for lunch. Will you join us in the cafeteria, Allan?"

"Of course. Lead the way."

They went downstairs to a large, drab room in the basement. Staff stood in queues for a choice of one of three entrees on a tray. Chadwick chose a pork chop with onions and pile of mashed potato and peas. He sat down and tried a mouthful, wondering how chefs could make such attractive-looking food tasteless. They chatted over inconsequential matters and then went back to Viney's office for Chadwick's suitcase. He made his goodbyes, and after he left, Viney and Larson stood at the window and watched Chadwick stride toward the Foreign Office.

"A very nice chap, Allan," Viney said. "Clever, too, in his own way. And, I suppose, brave too, flinging those machines 'round the sky in all weathers. But naïve as a newborn baby."

"You're a terrible cynic, Will."

"Not at all. Since man dropped down from the trees thousands of years ago, he developed traits which I try to understand. If I was a don at Cambridge or Oxford, they would call me an anthropologist."

"You're still a cynic, Will."

Chapter Forty-Three

Chadwick arrived at the Foreign Office, and an orderly escorted him to Lord Lowestoft's office. The lord was affable. "Nice of you to find time to squeeze me in, Allan. I hear you've been very busy. I keep in touch with Lady Fitzgibbon from time to time, you know. Her family and mine go back generations."

"Oh, I've been involved in the RAF summer exercise. Then there was paperwork to do."

"I take it you're referring to Exercise Torpedo, the simulated air attack on Great Britain."

"Yes, I see you're familiar with recent RAF maneuvers."

"We like to keep abreast at the F.O., Allan, but we only get the gist of things. The report to us shared time with a description of naval trials off Singapore and some army trouble in Afghanistan. Presumably, RAE sees a much more detailed picture. What's your opinion?"

"Well, this is the first time we've tried to combine a number of early RDR systems into a cohesive whole. As you might expect, there were teething problems. But I believe the system can be improved. We'll know next year. By then, many more RDR stations will be operating, though that may not make the problem of coordinating them all any simpler."

"How much of the coast was involved in Exercise Torpedo?"

"Sorry, but as I've said before, sir, these are classified matters."

"Stuff and nonsense, Allan. We at the Foreign Office guide British policy at the highest levels. We'll ultimately receive highly classified, bureaucratized versions, but I'd like to hear your personal opinions."

"That's very flattering, sir. Thank you. To answer your question, the exercise covered about two hundred and fifty miles of the east coast."

"So, it was a reasonable simulation of a wartime attack. What type of bombers were employed?"

"Sir, I have to repeat, I am a trifle uncomfortable dealing with this information. The summary report was classified 'Secret'."

"Doubtless we'll get a copy in a few months' time! I'd like to see a copy as soon as possible. Could you get me one?"

"Of course, I have my own copy, but it's against regulations to make a facsimile of secret documents."

"Allan, we're both on the same side. We both work for the government. I'm simply cutting some red tape."

"Well, the report is fifty pages long, but the beginning is a two-page summary. I could make a copy of that, although it would put me in a very bad light if I was exposed."

"Allan, you're not in such a good light anyway. You've attended meetings of the Isbell's Insiders. Believe me, it's best to have me on your side. If there was any official investigation, which is very unlikely, they would look at your personal life and possible financial irregularities. I trust you are lily white clean, which I'm sure you are."

"Well, cutting some red tape is all right, if you'd be satisfied with the summary, which was classified 'Secret,' sir."

"Yes, that would be satisfactory, Allan"

"To be honest, I'm not sure how to get an extra copy. My superior, Wing Commander Codrington, is the nominal author of the report, and tightly controls circulation."

"Can you type, Allan?"

"One finger, yes."

"Just take a few minutes one evening to copy it. Leave off the security classification, and just mail it to me here. Mark the envelope 'Personal.' Here's my card. I'll mark my room number. By the way, what was your role in Torpedo? Did you intercept bombers?"

"No, sir. The Royal Aircraft Establishment was charged with monitoring and then reporting on the complete exercise. We had officers on the ground at RDR stations and pilots flying fast fighters to see things in the air."

"Wonderful. What did you fly, Allan?"

"A Spitfire, sir."

"Aren't those in short supply? There are no Spitfire-equipped squadrons yet, I think."

"These were early Mark 1s based at Farnborough for testing and assessment. They're lovely planes, light on the controls and very powerful."

Lord Lowestoft glanced at his pocket watch and smiled. "I'm afraid I have to cut our meeting a little short, Allan. I have a meeting to attend to that I can't miss. I see you're spending the weekend in town." He glanced at Chadwick's suitcase, standing near the door. "Goodbye, Allan, I look forward to your letter."

Chadwick took a taxi to the Dorchester, where he signed in for Mr. and Mrs. Chadwick. He followed a porter to their room and tipped him a shilling. His bag had been placed on one of two double beds. He opened it and took out the jewelry case, which he placed on the dresser. He sat in a comfortable chair and reviewed the day, which had left him with conflicting emotions. He had been more disturbed than he cared to admit by the knowledge Viney had exposed about his friendship with Melanie. It seemed that the money Melanie had insisted on using to support their trysts had come from the Insiders, and who knows where they got it from? He began to believe, against all his hopes and wishes, that their friendship had been manipulated, just as Viney manipulated people. But who was pulling the strings?

He wished he could talk frankly with Melanie, but Viney had warned him that their plot to conceal RDR and expose a traitor was far more important than his petty love affair. His frustration boiled over into irritation with Melanie. She had worn that revealing bustier on their first meeting. What was that but enticement? Allan felt manipulated again.

In the middle of these dark thoughts, he heard a knock and opened the door to a porter. Melanie was standing behind him. He took her bags and fumbled for another coin. When the door shut, she took him in her arms.

"Darling, it's been so long. Give me a big kiss."

Incredibly, Allan felt a singular lack of pleasure. "I have something for you, Melanie, look on the dresser."

"Oh, I love surprises— it's beautiful! Allan, dear, thank you, thank you." She tried to kiss him again, but Allan stood rigid, and she couldn't quite reach his face.

"I have something for you, too." She opened one of her bags and removed a flat cardboard box. Nestled in layers of tissue paper lay a white negligee. Melanie held it to her shoulders. "Do you like it dear? Of course, I'm wearing too much underneath at the moment."

Allan said woodenly, "It's very nice."

Melanie sensed Allan was not happy. "You seem very distant, love."

"It's been a tough few week, Melanie, and today I gave a briefing to some people which didn't go too well. Of course, I can't talk about it."

"How can I help?"

"I don't know. I feel completely different. Events of such huge moment are gathering pace, and I don't know how to stop them or get out of the way."

"My God, you poor man. Come on, you're paying good money for this fabulous hotel. Let's look around and have a drink at the bar." She led him to the door. "Got the key?"

After two leisurely drinks at the bar, they took a taxi into Soho and found a cozy French restaurant, La Coupole, which served a delicious shrimp scampi. Wandering the congested streets afterwards, they entered a club, the Windmill, which claimed to be private. But they became members for ten shillings, a device to circumvent the theatre censor. Young women danced topless and a cockney comedian, Maxie Miller, told off-color jokes, which were not very funny. The drinks were very expensive and as weak as the jokes. An hour was enough of the smoke and noise, and they headed back to the Dorchester.

Melanie did her best to be cheerful and considerate, but Allan was not feeling in the least bit romantic, and to his dismay, despite Melanie's new negligee, he was impotent. Melanie laughed. "What happened to my knight rampant? These things happen, Allan. You are obviously highly stressed right now. Do you know what the most effective aphrodisiac is? The human brain. Get a good night's sleep, dear."

Unfortunately, that didn't work. In the morning Allan was short-tempered at breakfast. Melanie said firmly, "Let's cancel our reservation for tonight and go home before we have a falling-out." Chadwick agreed and they parted ways.

Chadwick arrived back at RAF Farnborough in the mid-afternoon. The base was closed for the weekend, and so he decided to get the matter of making a copy of the Exercise Torpedo summary out of the way. He unlocked the door into the Flight Test section. In the room next to his office, he rummaged for some clean white paper and a sheet of carbon paper. He inserted the two sheets, with the carbon in between, in the clerk's typewriter.

He had been turning over in his mind the best way to lay a trail for the traitor. He decided to make three deliberate typing errors and to change the text slightly. Reading from his own copy of the summary, he laboriously typed the whole two pages using one finger. Separating the top sheets and finding some plain envelopes, he sealed in the sheets and addressed the envelope to Lord Lowestoft. He put the sheets made by the carbon into another envelope and added a hand-written note:

> This is a copy of the summary sent to L. There are three deliberate typing errors. Compared to the original, line 3, "g" substituted for "h," line 15, "a" substituted for "s," and line 31, "y "substituted for "t." In addition, in the section referring to successful interceptions, "one" Blenheim was changed to "two."

This envelope he addressed to W. Viney. He added a stamp to each and took them to his room at the mess. The next day, Sunday, he fired up the Bentley and drove into Oxford, where he dropped the two envelopes in a red pillar box and ate a modest lunch with two pints of bitter in a pub. He felt very unhappy with himself, not only for his irritation with Melanie, but also for posting the summary to Lowestoft, which, technically, was a treasonous act.

He sat on a bench by the river watching the rowing sculls until the cold sent him back to the Bentley. Early the next morning he waylaid Wing Commander Codrington and suggested he discuss the report with Bawdsey. Codrington agreed but pointed out that Bawdsey would not have received a copy of the report yet, Chadwick said he would make a verbal presentation.

Sally was already in the air when Chadwick's sergeant began to organize the office for the day. The clerk, a leading aircraftsman, arriving at his desk noticed that someone has been using his typewriter. "Probably the cleaner was messing with your stuff," was the sergeant's initial reaction.

And then the sharp-eyed clerk pulled some crumpled carbon paper out of the wastepaper basket. "Look at this, Sarge. This isn't mine. I haven't made copy in days."

The sergeant took the carbon and straightened out the flimsy blue paper on the clerk's desk. He could make out a few lines. "This looks like that secret summary the squadron leader was working on," he said to the clerk.

He sucked on a tooth, trying to figure out what to do next, and who to report this to. "Well, Squadron Leader Chadwick's gone for the day. So, let's ask the adj what he thinks."

.

Chapter Forty-Four

Chadwick flew to Woodbridge unaware he had left a ticking time bomb at Farnborough. Dr. Bostock sent a car for him, and Chadwick was soon sitting down with the senior staff of the telecommunications group. He produced the Exercise Torpedo notes and described the summary conclusions. He suggested the initial task of the Bawdsey scientists was to extend the range of the first reliable detection signal. Several engineers pointed out it was a question of differentiating the return signal from the noise, which was due mainly to interference from electrical devices, both near and far. The aerials could not be substantially altered now they were up, but the ground in front of them could be improved by laying down wire mesh. There was also atmospheric noise, a background that seemed to be everywhere.

Finally, a scientist pointed out there was a human element. Some operators were much better than others at picking the first, weak signal in the forest of noisy spikes on the oscilloscope. He called this phenomenon stochastic detection—some people had the ability to sense the echo was down there and guess its position on the 'scope display, frequently correctly.

Chadwick suggested they try a few improvements while he had the Spitfire there, reasoning that if they could spot a Spitfire, they could surely see the bigger echo from a bomber. He called his sergeant at Farnborough to let them know he was staying a few days to help with tests. The sergeant told him there had apparently been a break-in over the weekend, but nothing had been stolen. Chadwick paid little attention to the news.

The staff took Chadwick to the receiver room of the Bawdsey RDR. Bostock switched on the equipment, and a yellow line appeared on the scope. "We call this an 'A' display," he said. "The line represents time from when the wireless signal was transmitted. When a return echo is detected, the trace is deflected downwards, and thus appears as a kink in the line. The trace corresponds to the speed of the pulse in space. It travels a mile in five millionths of a second, so a plane twenty miles away would be seen as a pulse after two hundred millionths of a second, allowing for the pulse to travel out and the echo to travel back. Now I'll turn up the receiver gain."

The line became spikey and jumped around. "All those spikes are just random signals or 'noise,' as we call it, but they hide the echo we're looking for. You can see why some intuition is needed when looking for a weak echo. As a general rule, the further the range, the weaker the echo."

Chadwick suggested that he could fly Sally on a good heading corresponding to the main lobe of the receiver aerial and they could watch for the echo to diminish until it was no longer discernable. Various changes could be made in the equipment during the flights, he told them. However, there was no suitable H.F. wireless at Bawdsey for communication with Chadwick, so he suggested they telephone Woodbridge tower, which could relay a simple message such as "repeat exercise" or "finish exercise."

"Use the RAE call sign," he said. "No, we'll simplify to AE or Able Easy."

Chadwick took off on the suggested heading, flying at five thousand feet and two hundred knots. After fifteen minutes, he received a message from Woodbridge—"Able Easy, repeat exercise."

He pushed the transmit button on the throttle and said, "Able Easy Roger" and then turned onto a reciprocal course. At the coast he turned again. He made two circuits before landing at Woodbridge. A car was waiting to take him back to Bawdsey.

Over lunch Bostock confessed none of their experimental changes had significantly helped, but they had an idea to try in the afternoon. They had just received some new radio valves from America and an engineer and technician were putting together an experimental amplifier, which would go between the aerial and the receiver input terminal. They had also designed the tuned circuits to use a special low-loss wire, which would sharpen the receiver bandwidth and help reject unwanted frequencies.

After lunch Chadwick was driven back to Woodbridge to repeat the morning's exercises. When he returned to Bawdsey, he found that Dr. Bostock was cautiously optimistic. The range at which the echo disappeared into the noise had increased by about five miles. Bostock felt if the whole receiver "front end" was redesigned to use the valves and better tuning, the improvement would be significant. Engineers and technicians planned to work all night to build a new receiver.

Dr. Bostock again insisted that Chadwick stay for dinner with he and his wife. Allan had not brought any civilian clothes with him, and so apologized to Mrs. Bostock for wearing his uniform. She pointed to the ribbons, asking, "What's that for?"

"Actually, for a tour in Iraq. I flew Vimy bombers for nearly four years, mostly dull."

"And this one?"

"That's for a bit of a mess-up flying from Farnborough. We managed to drop a bomb on our own aircraft!" He laughed uproariously.

"You got a medal for bombing your own plane?"

"No, I exaggerate. The medal was actually for landing it, in more or less one piece."

"Doris, don't bother poor Allan," her husband interjected. "RAF pilots are notoriously modest. They don't like to talk about their daily brushes with death."

Their dinner together was very relaxed, and Kenneth excused himself to make a phone call when they had finished eating.

"He's calling the lab," his wife whispered. "He'll ruin his digestion. He'll probably be there most of the night."

The next day Chadwick repeated the exercise perfected on the previous day. He felt there must be an improvement because the orders to repeat came at longer intervals, suggesting the watchers at Bawdsey had kept his echo in sight for a greater range. When he joined the Bawdsey staff for lunch he got the distinct impression of exuberance, and Dr. Bostock said to him, "Big improvement, Allan. We tracked you for sixty-two miles, a fifty percent improvement. I'll suggest that Cossor adopt our design for the receivers they're building for the RDR stations now going up."

Chadwick flew back to Farnborough in the afternoon feeling very pleased. It seemed obvious that his visit had produced positive results and they had made inroads to one of the recommendations made after Exercise Torpedo. After joining the circuit, he was ordered to report to Wing Commander Codrington on landing. He left his flying suit in the crew room; his cheeks still showed the impression made by the oxygen mask as he walked into Codrington's office. Two unfamiliar men stood with Codrington.

"Allan, this is Squadron Leader Petrie and Flight Sergeant Lewis, from the RAF Police, Provost Marshal Branch."

Chadwick nodded to them.

"Squadron Leader, there's been some evidence of criminal activity, involving national security, which is the responsibility of the Provost Marshal Branch. I wonder if you would allow Flight Sergeant Lewis to take your fingerprints?"

"Of course."

Lewis approached Chadwick and took him to a desk carrying an ink pad. He held Chadwick's hands, one at a time, and pressed his fingertips on the pad and then inked a printed form. He passed Chadwick some cleanser and a soft rag. Chadwick cleaned his fingers while the two policemen took the form to a desk and sorted through a pile of paper.

"Things went well at Bawdsey, sir. Using my Spitfire as a target, they were able to improve the range of the detectable signal by fifty percent. This was due to improvements in the receiver equipment."

Squadron Leader Petrie asked Chadwick to step with him into an empty office next door. He closed the door. "Squadron Leader, a secret document was copied in this building over the weekend. We have identified the typewriter used, and your fingerprints are on the keys. Do you have an explanation?"

"May I ask why you believe a secret document was typed?"

"That's no secret. A discarded carbon paper was found in the wastebasket."

"Someone was careless, it seems."

There was a long silence. "Squadron Leader, this matter must be investigated further. I must ask you to remain confined to your quarters. No telephone calls allowed."

"I can assist you with the investigation, but you must make one phone call. I want you to call MI5, ask for Mr. Viney or Mr. Larson. I can get you a telephone number from my office."

"MI5! Squadron Leader, this is an RAF investigation of an apparent criminal breach of security, nothing to do with counter-intelligence."

"Petrie, you have unfortunately stumbled on a matter which may have very grave consequences if not handled right."

"You're acting very suspiciously, Squadron Leader Chadwick."

"I'm sorry, come to my office. I'll get you the number."

Chadwick felt a good deal more concerned than he cared to admit. If Viney and Larson did not fully back him up, he could see his air force career going down in flames. Squadron Leader Petrie did call Mr. Viney and explained who he was and added that he had confined an RAF officer, Squadron Leader Chadwick, to his quarters for copying a secret document. Viney sighed and suggested that Petrie stop by MI5 HQ in the morning and bring whatever evidence he had.

When Petrie called at Whitehall, the commissionaire had an orderly take him up to Viney's office on the first floor. Mr. Viney greeted him and introduced Doug Larson, without saying why he was there. Squadron Leader Petrie explained he had called Viney at Chadwick's suggestion, although he was not certain why MI5 should be involved.

"That was a very wise suggestion," Viney said, "and I hope we stop this matter going any further today. Please show me the evidence."

Petrie lifted a small item from his briefcase, consisting of two sheets of clean writing paper. Like a magician producing a rabbit from a top hat, he dramatically extracted the carbon paper from between the sheets and placed it on Viney's desk. "A clerk discovered this carbon paper in the waste basket. It was typed on a machine in his office and Chadwick's fingerprints are all over the keys," he finished triumphantly.

"Can you read the first line on the carbon paper, Squadron Leader?"

"Yes, it's fairly legible."

"Please compare it to the first line on this sheet." He handed Petrie the copy he had received the day before from Chadwick.

Petrie peered closely at the two documents and said in a puzzled voice,"They appear to be the same."

"Exactly, Squadron Leader. The copy was made for MI5."

"I don't fully understand. But where is the top sheet?"

"I'm afraid I can't tell you that, but your conscientious clerk has stumbled accidentally on a matter of grave national security. Today we must work out how to minimize any further leakage."

"I still don't understand."

"I can't tell you any more. Perhaps a little allegorical story will help. Imagine you're at a seaside resort and suddenly a huge shark starts to gobble up the bathers. A local fisherman fastens a large dead fish to his pole and attempts to catch the shark so he can kill it. Now, what is the importance of the large dead fish?"

"Well, in your allegory the fish is very important as bait to catch the shark."

"Exactly. You've said the right word." He placed his finger on Chadwick's message."Bait."

The light slowly dawned on Petrie.

"Squadron Leader, here we deal with threats to Great Britain's internal security, which range from deluded Marxists to spies from major powers. The small fry we leave for Scotland Yard, Special Branch. Unfortunately, you have stumbled across a very high-level operation—approved, in fact, by the Joint Intelligence Committee. You haven't by any chance, read this report?"

Petrie had not achieved the rank of squadron leader in the Provost Marshals Branch by being stupid."Oh, of course not. I don't need to know what's actually in a secret document in order to treat it as secret."

"There must be no written report on this matter. Quite a lot of people read circulated government documents. A hint in the wrong place could be disastrous. I can arrange for the head of MI5, Sir Cuthbert, to call your boss if that would help."

"Completely unnecessary, Mr. Viney. I shall mention back at Farnborough that Squadron Leader Chadwick was the unfortunate victim of a bureaucratic miss-up, fully exonerated."

"I think the clerk involved, and maybe his sergeant, might be posted to somewhere far away for year or two. The lower ranks tend to gossip, you know."

"I quite agree. It sounds like we must take every precaution. I'll get back to Farnborough and straighten things out."

"Just for your information, Squadron Leader, Chadwick was put in the position of setting this bait quite by chance, and in doing so, puts himself at considerable risk. In fact, I understand he was the officer who organized some of the secret maneuvers in the report, so we owe him a double debt of gratitude. He is a real patriot. You might care to mention that to the commanding officer, Group Captain Delaney-Jones while you're at Farnborough. I think we're finished."

"Yes, it's been a pleasure, Mr. Viney."

"Please leave the carbon paper here."

Viney rang for an orderly and had Petrie escorted to the entrance. When he was gone, Viney and Larson roared with laughter. "By God, Will, you certainly got Squadron Leader Petrie pissing in his pants," Doug Larson wheezed between guffaws.

Chapter Forty-Five

Petrie returned to Farnborough and had a long talk with Group Captain Delaney-Jones. When Petrie left, the group captain asked Chadwick to his office.

"Squadron Leader Chadwick, I've just had a talk with an officer from the Provost Mashal's Branch. It appears there was a bureaucratic misunderstanding which resulted in you being imprisoned in durance vile, for which I apologize."

"Think nothing of it, sir. The officer's mess isn't too bad."

"Chadwick, when you were first posted to Farnborough there was a rumor you had escaped from the Gestapo. Now I'm told by the police officer that that you're involved with the highest levels of British security—so much so, he was reluctant to even mention it. You seem to live a secret life, Chadwick, outside the service."

"Just rumors, sir. I assure you the Royal Air Force has my complete loyalty."

"I know you're very competent. Wing Commander Codrington often sings your praises. I've been informed that following the end of Exercise Torpedo, this institution, The Royal Aircraft Establishment, will be charged with coordinating the defense improvements that were recommended."

Chadwick next called on Wing Commander Codrington. "I hear from the boss that we're going to be heavily involved in next year's defense exercise and are responsible for coordinating the recommendations."

"Yes, we're going to need more people. Next year's exercise will involve the entire Bomber Command and virtually the entire Fighter Command. Sixty Group expect to have twenty RDR stations up to snuff, and the exercise will extend from Plymouth to Inverness. I'm going to take charge of Sixty Group and Fighter Command coordination assessment myself. I would like you to continue to work with Bawdsey and the incorporation of any improvements in the RDR stations as they are built. You may keep your Spitfire for liaison flights, but I'm afraid we'll need a great deal more office space. I'll have to squeeze you down to just your office. The sergeant and some additional clerks will work for me."

"That is perfectly understood, sir. I needed those men when I was dealing with quite a few bomber squadrons, but now I don't have that responsibility, so I don't need them."

The curious thing was that in the following weeks the sergeant and the clerk who had worked with Chadwick were both posted. The sergeant went to an RAF weather station in Iceland and the clerk was sent to a flying boat squadron at Rangoon, Burma.

Mr. Viney was informed by MI6 that it appeared the bait had been swallowed. Their contact at Abwehr HQ, a Prussian officer who disliked the Nazis more than he disliked the British, confirmed that details of Exercise Torpedo had filtered in for the attention of the Luftwaffe. A message went out: "Try to find out how many Blenheim squadrons were intercepted according to their source." The answers came back in a week—two Blenheim squadrons were intercepted. That definitely confirmed the conduit through Lord Lowestoft.

Viney attended a meeting of the Joint Intelligence Committee to inform them that the misinformation had without question come from their plant. The committee believed the link should be kept warm until the trap was sprung in the coming year. A subcommittee, the Double-cross Committee, was told to produce some trivial but accurate tidbits to feed into the link.

Viney pointed out they didn't know the identity of the person actually in communication with the Abwehr, but perhaps a few more carefully chosen bits of misinformation would help solve that problem. Viney was skeptical that the big fish they were after would respond to minor tidbits. He decided Chadwick was to be saved for the grand denouement next year. He would feed minor stuff through other agents who had penetrated the Isbell's Insiders clique.

Chadwick flew to Woodbridge to discuss his new responsibilities with Dr. Bostock. Bostock told him that the improvement in range during his last visit was a slight fluke. Later tests uncovered snags which had to be dealt with if the changes went into widescale production. The first problem that came to light was unexpected damage to the receiver. The receiver aerials were only a few yards from the transmitter, which put out pulses of several hundred kilowatts. Unless the receiver input was protected during the transmit period, the thin wire tuning coils burned out. This required very careful timing of the protective circuit, as the protection had to be removed as soon as possible after the transmit pulse was over, in order to receive echoes.

The second problem was that some of the new American valves were affected by sound and vibration. This could be cured by testing and preselection, but they had contacted RCA about tightening up production tolerances. As an early cure, the cooling fans were redesigned to reduce vibration.

Chadwick thoroughly enjoyed discussing these technical problems, as he felt he was gaining some elementary knowledge of electronics. He discussed one feature of the RDR detection which could be speeded up—height determination. The WAAF at the controls had to adjust several aerials to find a position of maximum signal. The switching took time, and Chadwick discovered the system used motor-driven switches. He suggested to Bostock that faster switches could have a useful impact on the total time taken to find the height of a target.

Bostock gave him an armful of blueprints of the existing system and Chadwick took them back to Farnborough. He borrowed a large drafting table from the design office and set it at an angle so that he could study the blueprints comfortably from his desk. One afternoon when he was thus occupied, there was a tap on his door and to his surprise, Penelope Pomeroy entered his office. She was dressed in a flying suit and carried a leather helmet in one hand.

"Hello, Penny. You're a surprise!"

"I hope you don't mind me popping in. I have the most marvelous news, and as I have just landed at Farnborough, here I am."

"You seem very excited. What is it?"

"I have a job with Marlow Air Freight and Forwarding. I am an assistant pilot. We just landed here to deliver some parts to the wind tunnel chaps. I told the captain I knew someone here, so he gave me permission to track you down. Isn't it marvelous? I can gain flying time and get paid as well!"

"Well, I'm certainly happy for you, but theoretically the RAF section of Farnborough is off-limits to civilians. But I'm sure nobody minds another pilot stooging around."

"So far, I've made ten trips to airfields in the British Islands and one trip to France. Do you fly much, here at Farnborough?"

"Oh, yes. I must make many trips to different RAF fields. I have a Spitfire for that."

"A Spitfire! How spiffing. Can you show me one another day when I'm here again?"

"I could probably arrange that."

She glanced round the office and her gaze fell on the blueprints tacked to the drafting table. "I recognize that." She pointed to a photograph of an aerial that Chadwick had pinned to the top of the table. "They're all over the coast. What are they for?"

"Well, they're supposed to be secret, so let's say they're wireless aerials to scare away the seagulls."

She peered closely at the blueprint. "RDR, that's what's on the box in the corner. Now I know something secret!" She gave a wave. "Got to fly. They've probably unloaded by now." And she walked out leaving Chadwick feeling slightly aggrieved that she had spotted "RDR" on the prints.

Chapter Forty-Six

For several days Chadwick examined the current design of the aerial switching arrangement and concluded the motor-driven switches could be replaced by electrical solenoids which would be faster and probably more reliable. He looked at the catalogs of several suppliers and flew to Woodbridge to discuss the plan with Dr. Bostock, who put him in touch with a mechanical engineer on his staff. They had a productive discussion and the engineer promised to keep in touch with him.

He flew back to Farnborough feeling satisfied he was making a worthwhile contribution. At the back of his mind was a lingering cloud—he had to mend fences with Melanie. He realized he'd been very upset by Viney's disclosure about the Isbell's Insiders funding of the Fitzgibbon estate and felt guilty, the price he had to pay for a surreptitious love affair. He had taken his bad temper out on Melanie, who was probably innocent of any involvement in the funding issue. He knew she left the details to the estate manager in Reading. Because of the on-going involvement of MI5, he could say almost nothing of the real reason for his ill temper. *After all*, he rationalized, *it was me who made the first approach, when I took the German woman, Julia, to her place in Pangbourne.*

After landing, he touched base with Codrington and then called Melanie from the officer's mess. "Hello, dear. I've called to apologize for the mess-up in London. It was my fault—mea culpa. I can only plead pressure of work."

"Well, we didn't descend to fisticuffs, so perhaps it can be mended."

"Dinner tonight at the Blue Bell?"

"Why not? Give me two hours."

A pleasant dinner in the old pub put them both in good spirits. Allan wound up in Melanie's bed and drove back to Farnborough in the small hours. With their love affair back on a firm foundation, Chadwick told Melanie he would pay for their romantic weekends.

"Ah," she said, "I see it now. Your manhood was threatened."

"It's as good an explanation as any," Allan conceded.

Chadwick was under a good less strain dealing with technical vagaries of RDR than his role previously. At times obscure technical problems arose with new RDR stations as they were installed further to the north and west. Sometimes the expertise of the original Bawdsey developers was needed to the untangle the technical problems and Chadwick flew them to nearby RAF stations in the Avro Anson. Slowly but surely, the Chain Home network grew, about one station a week became operational, then Sixty Group installed WAAF personnel, and training began with bombers simulating intruders.

At MI5, Mr. Viney had several meetings with the Double-cross Committee. Tom Carstairs had moved to the Foreign Office and Viney steered some choice intelligence cleared by the committee to Carstairs' attention, but none was reported by their contact in the Abwehr. Viney and Larson sat down one afternoon with Chadwick. They wanted to talk about meetings of the Isbell's Insiders.

"Allan, I don't think Tom Carstairs is our target anymore. We know a trail to Germany begins with Lowestoft, and he doesn't seem to have any contacts outside the Isbell's crowd, so there's a strong chance the person we're after is lurking in those meetings. We've infiltrated our man but he's very much on the periphery. You're considered a part of the inner core, nowadays. Any ideas?"

Chadwick shook his head. "I'm not an inside Insider. Lowestoft is on the inside and he's very friendly but, after all, Carstairs does not attend the meetings. I met him at Lowestoft's club. It could be anybody."

"We also have watchers at that club," Viney responded. "Nobody is ringing alarm bells."

Chadwick pondered what Viney had told him. "I know it sounds ridiculous, but is the Viscount, Addenbury, above suspicion?"

"No, I suppose not."

"We could try the same trick, a distinctive bit of misinformation."

Larson pointed out that to be any use in unraveling the trail, Lowestoft would have to be bypassed.

"Lady Addenbury," Chadwick said. "We must plant something via her. Perhaps they indulge in pillow talk. I know someone who has lunch with her fairly regularly, Melanie."

Viney mused. "Yes, but what do women talk about that would fit in?"

"Women talk about other women, and I think I know a subject that covers women and RDR."

Viney and Larson both expressed interest. "Go ahead."

"On the recent defense exercise, I found myself for the first time dealing with a lot of women. All the RDR operators are WAAFs, Women's Air Force. At one particular station, they messed up an interception. The flight officer in charge was nearly in tears. We've already acknowledged that the exercise went badly. Suppose Addenbury learns the WAAFs were hopeless?"

"Not a bad idea. Were they really that awful?"

"No, a later interception, witnessed by an RAE pilot in a Spitfire, went flawlessly. He called it textbook."

"I think you'd have to say the WAAF officer was actually in tears, though," Viney said, after some consideration. "I like it. At the German end it would confirm the misogynistic bias of most German military. Remember the phrase, Kinder, Küche, Kirche originated with the Huns." He glanced at Chadwick. "Children, Cooking, Church. Those were supposed to be women's interests. Are you a sufficiently good as a dissembler that you could plant the lie on Melanie, and she would plant it on the Viscountess and she would plant it on Addenbury?"

"I don't like to embroil Melanie, but she has no need to know the real intent of my grumbles about WAAFs. It's a cruel world, sometimes."

Viney had made up his mind. "Give it a try. It would be another link in the chain if it works."

Chadwick called Melanie when he got back to Farnborough and suggested a weekend in Bath, the old Roman spa town. They could catch a good train at Oxford and be there in time for a late lunch. Melanie agreed to make the reservations. Chadwick drove to Pangbourne in the Bentley, and they continued to the Oxford station in Melanie's Vauxhall. The train had them in Bath by just after one in the afternoon. The weather was clammy; the temperature about fifty degrees.

A taxi dropped them off at the Royal Crescent Hotel, located in a magnificent arc of Georgian houses. After a light lunch at the hotel, they made the *de rigueur* tour of the major tourist attraction, the Roman baths, for which the town was named. They had been restored after becoming derelict in the Middle Ages and natural warm water flowed into the stone pool. They read with surprise that the water flowing on that day had fallen as rain two thousand years earlier.

It was a little chilly for sightseeing in the town center, but they braved the cold for half an hour and warmed themselves up at a quaint teashop on Pulteney Bridge, sitting directly over the River Avon. After a quick tour of the Art Museum, they settled for dinner at a cozy restaurant on one of the small squares. As they toyed with an after-dinner liqueur, Allan decided they were sufficiently mellow for him to float the planned deception.

"I must apologize again for my ill temper in London, dear. I had just spent a rough week on some very important defense exercises, and I had flown to half a dozen bases to observe what was going on. They didn't go well."

"Well, I'm sure it wasn't your fault, dear."

"I felt very sorry for the people involved. They tried hard but the work was quite technical, and perhaps a little beyond them."

Melanie didn't seem especially interested, but he persevered. "Dragging these poor women into such a hot, high-pressure environment is a little unfair."

"Women?"

"Yes, most of the ground equipment is operated by WAAFs—Women's Auxiliary Air Force. It's unfair. There was one poor officer in charge, very attractive, couldn't have been older than twenty-two, who actually cried when the thing went wrong. I was very sorry for her."

"Did you feel like sweeping her into your arms and giving her a good consoling kiss?" Melanie said sarcastically.

"That would have been prejudicial to good military discipline, no matter what I felt. But if you take me back to the hotel, I might be able to work off that feeling with you instead."

Riding back in the taxi, Chadwick wondered how well he had planted the fib. It seemed to him he had made it sound inconsequential to Melanie, but important if it should fall on German ears. Due to parked cars, the taxi dropped them a few yards from the door of their hotel. The brief walk felt cold, and once inside Allan said, "Brrr, winter's coming." The hotel lobby was warm, and just off to one side a woman in an exquisite evening gown sat at a grand piano playing light Chopin compositions. Allan and Melanie sat on an overstuffed couch. The warmth, the music, and the comfortable seat made Chadwick feel languorous.

"How about a nightcap, Melanie?"

"Lovely. A Drambuie."

Allan signaled to a waitress and ordered two drinks. He stretched out. "This the life. I must stay here forever, and never go to work." Then a feeling of guilt crept over him, *"I've used innocent Melanie in a diabolical scheme. What a cad I am,"* he thought to himself.

Later, after they had finished their drinks, they took a lift to their floor. Inside the room Allan did exactly what he had proposed. He put his arms firmly around Melanie's waist and kissed her hard.

"My, my," she gasped when she pushed him away. "Am I a substitute for your gorgeous WAAF?"

"Perhaps," he admitted, "but if I tried to do this to her, I could be court martialed." He unbuttoned her jacket, massaged her lovely bosom, and kissed her through the thin silk slip.

"Come down a bit, my love. That will get me going up to your speed."

The morning dawned overcast, damp and chilly. They lingered in bed and finally went down for a typical English breakfast. They took a taxi from the hotel steps into the center of Bath and planned to tour the museum, but without leaving the taxi they could see it was closed.

"What do you do in Bath on a wet Sunday morning?" Allan asked the taxi driver.

"Pray," was his short answer. "The churches are open."

They went back to the hotel, drank some morning coffee in the solarium, and played a desultory rack of billiards at a deserted table.

There was a train to Oxford that left just after twelve. It was a stopping train and did not deposit them at Oxford General station of the Great Western Railway until after four. Melanie drove them to Pangbourne, and Allan stopped at Clair Court Hall for a cup of tea and a passionate kiss from Melanie before making a damp ride to Farnborough in the Bentley.

.

Chapter Forty-Seven

In the morning he found a message at the office to call Dr. Bostock. Bawdsey wanted him to fly an engineer and some technicians to Leuchars, in Scotland. Apparently, a new RDR station could not be brought up to scratch before being turned over to the operators from Sixty Group. Before organizing the trip Chadwick called Viney at MI5.

"I spent the weekend with M," he reported, "and fed her the story of the incompetent WAAFs."

"Topping," Viney said. "Let's wait and see if the bird sings."

Chadwick cleared his flight with Wing Commander Codrington and recruited a young pilot, Flying Officer Hicks, as the second pilot for an Anson flight to Scotland. He warned Hicks they might be there for few days, as the weather was turning nasty and the technical problem at the RDR station may take some time to correct. Four civilians boarded the plane at Woodbridge, and they took off for the two-hour flight to Leuchars. Chadwick left Hicks at the controls while he talked to Mr. Bragg, an engineer from Bostock's team.

"What exactly is the problem at Leuchars?" he asked.

"They can't achieve the specified minimum range of one hundred nautical miles," he was told. "We're bringing plenty of test gear," the engineer assured him. "We should be able to put our finger on the problem."

They flew up the east coast and were able to keep in contact with ground until north of Berwick, where a sea fog crept inland. The field at Leuchars was on the coast and Chadwick asked Hicks to call the tower on H.F. wireless and find out weather conditions. The report was not good—intermittent fog with a cloud base of two hundred feet and a visibility of five hundred feet when the fog cleared. But it was coming and going.

The height of the field was thirty-nine feet. Chadwick precisely set the altimeter and let down to one hundred and fifty feet over what he calculated was the sea. They turned west and carefully flew with one-third flap, hoping to spot the field. The flashing Pundit was operating full blast, they were told. They saw nothing for five minutes and then climbed and turned back over the sea. Without a landmark of some kind, they were in trouble, but they had enough fuel to keep trying for a while.

Then Chadwick had an idea. He called the tower to find out if the RDR station was operating and was given an affirmative. The RDR station did not have an H.F. wireless but was in touch with the tower by telephone. Chadwick told the air traffic officer in the tower to contact the RDR operators and ask them to provide course correction for the Anson which would bring them over the runway. He flew the Anson for ten minutes to the east and then turned west. He knew the RDR would lose him if he came too low, so he asked the tower to relay range and heading information as flew toward the coast at a thousand feet. Flying Officer Hicks was getting nervous and hesitantly suggested they head for an alternative landing at Edinburgh.

"We'll be all right. Just keep a good look-out for the runway lights," Chadwick told him.

The tower gave them several course corrections and, at a range of two miles, said contact had been lost. The grey fog swirled past the cockpit windows. Chadwick glanced at his watch. They were flying at roughly a mile a minute. He began a descent at three hundred and fifty feet a minute and warned Hicks to keep a sharp eye open.

Hicks suddenly shouted, "Left, left sir! I can just see the lights."

Chadwick lifted his gaze from the instruments and through the rain speckled windshield he just made out the lights too. He dropped the undercarriage, applied full flap and within seconds the wheels were screeching on the tarmac. He informed the tower they were down and at the end of the runway, he followed a vehicle which had been sent to guide them to the dispersal area.

After he shut down the engines and began to unbuckle, Hicks said, "That was the most amazing landing I've ever seen, sir."

Chadwick smiled, secretly glad he'd been able to pull it off without diverting to another field. "I think we've found another use for RDR—helping planes land instead of shooting them down."

When Hicks got back to Farnborough, his story of the landing at Leuchars entered Farnborough folklore. Meanwhile, the technical people took two days to bring the Leuchars RDR up to standard. One morning Chadwick took a taxi to the ferry across the River Tay, which dropped him in Dundee. The waterfront was busy and interesting. Many whalers had sailed from Dundee in the past, according to a story told in the maritime museum. Chadwick toured a marmalade factory and discovered the Spanish thought the British mad for buying sour oranges, but then found they made the best marmalade.

Mr. Bragg thought they would be able to leave the following afternoon, depending on whether or not the RDR commissioning team accepted the station performance. As it turned out, there were delays, but they left in the morning of the following day and flew to Woodbridge without incident. After lunch Chadwick and Hicks made the flight back to Farnborough.

Chadwick sat in his office composing a short note on the technical aspects of the trip, including the assist with a foggy landing, when he was again surprised by Penelope Pomeroy.

"We just brought in more stuff for your wind tunnel," she said, "and I remembered you promised to show me a Spitfire."

Chadwick sighed, but he hated to dampen her obvious enthusiasm. He rose to put the folder in a drawer.

"Is that your secret stuff?" she asked.

He didn't reply. "Come on, my Spitfire is in the hangar."

He led her to the plane, where he explained it was a Mark 1, still equipped with a wooden propeller. She asked a dozen questions about the flying performance and asked if she could sit in it. There was no parachute, so she was sitting low in the seat well and couldn't see over the instrument panel. Moving the control column back and forth, she suddenly put her finger on the gun trigger.

"Don't press that!" Chadwick shouted in alarm. "That's the trigger. The guns aren't loaded and besides, the trigger doesn't work on the ground. But you never know."

"How exciting!" she exclaimed.

He took her to the hangar door. "Have a good flight back to Marlow, Penny."

She turned and waved. "Toodle-loo."

For the next few weeks Chadwick was busy flying to the mostly new RDR stations. He frequently chatted with Wing Commander Codrington, who kept him up to date about the control layers being built into the RDR system. Literally hundreds of telephone lines were being strung directly between Sectors, Groups, and Fighter Command, some of them underground.

One morning Chadwick found a message in his pigeonhole in the mess announcing a Christmas Dance. There was little social life in the mess, compared to an operational squadron, because the majority of the staff lived off the base with their wives. He asked Melanie if she would like to go, and she decided it might be fun. She suggested booking a room again in Reigate, which was far enough from Farnborough to avoid any potential scandal.

Dr. Bostock told Chadwick that the first of the new low-level detectors had been installed at Bawdsey. The new network, when completed, would be called Chain Home Low. It was technically separate from Chain Home and would require additional operators. The Sixty Group had already provided some targets for evaluation.

Bostock invited him to Bawdsey to witness a low-level detection. Chadwick flew to Woodbridge and was soon in the receiver room at Bawdsey. It was getting quite crowded, with ten WAAFs operating the equipment or handling telephone headsets. Bostock said the new sets could detect planes down to five hundred feet altitude.

Chadwick told him about the incident at Leuchars when dense fog blanketed the field. He mentioned that, by flying at a thousand feet, they were tracked to within two miles of the coast which, luckily enough, got them within visual range of the runway lights.

Bostock was entranced. Helping planes land in poor visibility would be a tremendous new field for RDR technology. He promised Chadwick that when time allowed, he would make a preliminary design of an RDR to guide planes to a runway. He also mentioned that Chadwick had been very lucky, as the Leuchars station had tracked him to limits that were considerably better than could normally be expected.

The weeks passed more quickly than Chadwick could comprehend and before he knew it, the Christmas season was upon him. Melanie picked him up at the mess in her car and drove to the Four Feathers in Reigate. The place was crowded with Christmas guests. Melanie worried she might run into someone who knew her, so they decided to eat at a small restaurant away from the inn, after she had changed in their room.

The dance began at eight, and they arrived fashionably late at eight-thirty. It was held in the dining room of the officer's mess, which had been cleared of tables, and the room was already thick with smoke when they arrived. A small four-piece band had been hired to provide the music, which was mostly late Twenties and Thirties tunes with some modern American swing.

Waiters circulated with drinks, and Wing Commander Codrington had clearly been imbibing freely. He mumbled an introduction to his wife, Betty, and was obviously impressed when Allan introduced Melanie as Lady Fitzgibbon. He started a slurred conversation with Melanie, holding one hand so she couldn't escape. "Allan must tell you some fascinating tales. He leads an adventurous life, y'know."

Allan quickly intervened. "I don't talk shop. Melanie doesn't know much about flying."

"Well, it's not so much the flyin'—"

Allan realized, to his horror, that Codrington might mention the Gestapo or, worse, the episode of being "confined to quarters."

"Oh, this is our favorite number," he said, as the band began a new tune. "Excuse us." And he seized Melanie by the waist and stepped into the dance floor. After half an hour they had both had enough. Their eyes hurt from the cigarette smoke and the noise level almost matched a Merlin engine. Melanie was glad when Allan suggested they creep quietly away back to the Four Feathers and, and hopefully find a quiet corner in the bar for a nightcap. They were in love enough that they were happy just to be in each other's company.

"What was it the wing commander was going to say when you dragged me off?"

"I've no idea. A trivial flying story, no doubt."

She looked at him suspiciously. "Have you been getting into mischief?"

He felt like a small boy, upbraided by his mother. "Time for bed!" he said.

When they went back to their room, Allan kissed her. "Merry Christmas, dear Melanie." He then gave her a large, beautiful, chiffon silk bandanna.

The weather that winter was particularly bad, which delayed trials of new RDR stations. The head of Fighter Command had demanded three months of training for all the RDR stations before the start of the summer exercises. Chadwick drove to many of the stations on the south coast in the Bentley and was even forced to put up the canvas top. Even without participating bombers as targets, he had become so familiar with RDR procedures that he could assess the readiness of the WAAFs operating the equipment.

One afternoon he found a message from Mr. Viney waiting for him at his Farnborough office. Viney suggested a meeting in London as soon as he could spare the time. Chadwick called back immediately and entrained into Waterloo station the next day. Viney and Larson greeted him at MI5 Headquarters.

"Why don't you tell him, Doug?" Viney said

"We heard from our disgruntled Prussian in the Abwehr. Several officers on the British desk were making coarse, if not

In the months before the exercise, Chadwick flew to all the squadrons that would be involved. He stressed that as much instrument flying practice as possible should be accomplished before the exercise began. He also stressed that it would be impossible to accurately judge the distance to lights at night, and therefore caution was needed. The Air Council had directed that all bomber aircraft would be equipped with H.F. wireless telegraphy. Fighters would carry H.F. voice communications for contact with the RDR controllers, but fighters and bombers could not directly communicate with each other.

Chadwick found that pilots in both commands were woefully short of instrument flying experience and night-flying time. He was also concerned that night flying was dangerous for ground crews, as the dispersal areas in the dark were extremely hazardous—their ears were blasted by many engines, and they were working near whirling propellers. He found that the new control layers instituted by Fighter Command promised to cure many of the problems of the previous exercise.

Whenever he could, he snatched a few hours with Melanie, but they were few and far between. She knew that something very important was brewing that summer. He received several invitations to meetings of the Isbell's Insiders but missed them all, as he was often hundreds of miles away at some remote RAF base. He had one meeting with Doug Larson, who told him that Viney had organized surveillance of almost everybody that Addenbury had contact with, and they were optimistic the actual way in which information was conveyed to Germany would come to light. They had even sought help from MI6, which had expertise in the field of getting messages out.

Larson told him that German spies detected in Britain had started to use small wireless transmitters that could fit in a suitcase. American companies were pushing to develop valves for use in portable radios, for which they saw a huge market; they could be adapted for clandestine wireless transmitters and receivers. Larson showed Chadwick a miniaturized wireless set that was a credit to German engineering. It was captured due to a British quirk the Germans didn't anticipate—there was no standard domestic electrical outlet. Many companies made their own, and they weren't compatible with any other.

"The spy simply bared the wires and pushed them in the small holes," Larson explained. "He used matchsticks to jam them in. He even left the phosphorus heads on, which is why his bedroom caught fire. When the fire brigade spotted the wireless, they called the police. The spy skipped out just ahead of them and spent a rough two nights on the streets before we nabbed him. The post office is working on detectors which could pinpoint the location of secret transmitters, provided the transmission is long enough."

Chadwick was left speechless. He was amazed at the pace of technological change he had already experienced in his short career, both in the aviation field and intelligence.

Chapter Forty-Eight

For Exercise Periscope, Wing Commander Codrington organized the RAE monitoring in much the same way as the previous year. Officers would be based at RDR stations and at Sectors, Groups, and Strategic Control at RAF Uxbridge. Ten Spitfires would be flown by RAE pilots to monitor actual interceptions. Twenty RDR stations were considered operationally ready. Fighter Command planned to have thirty-two squadrons on operational standby—twenty-two Hurricane squadrons, eight Spitfire squadrons, and two Defiant squadrons. Bomber Command would have eighteen squadrons operational—eight Blenheim squadrons, six Hampden squadrons, two Wellington squadrons, and two Wellesey squadrons.

Periscope was the biggest maneuver laid on by the RAF since the closing stages of the Great War. In consultation with meteorologists, a week was chosen and announced to the participants a day before the exercise began. Chadwick flew to Woodbridge and spent the first day in the receiver room at Bawdsey, which had been converted to an RAF RDR station. The operators had a list of commercial flights which were not to be intercepted. Chadwick had a list of the Bomber Command flights for the day.

Two bomber flights were detected at Bawdsey, and fighters scrambled from Manston. The bombers did not turn inland and flew into the English Channel before passing out of range. Both flights were intercepted later by fighters from Biggin Hill. Chadwick learned that four fighters from Debden had almost run out of fuel, and landed at a civilian airfield, where an argument developed about who should pay for the fuel they needed before they could take off again. The pilots also discovered that high octane fuel was not available, and the engines had to be run at low power to avoid damage.

Chadwick took off the next day in Sally and watched the interception of a squadron of Wellingtons by twelve Hurricanes. The fighters were well-placed, three thousand feet above the intruders, but after the interception, the fighters milled about in a random way. Chadwick realized that battle formation, an art developed in the Great War, also needed to be reinvented for the much faster modern fighters.

The following night Bomber Command laid on four raids, crossing the coast between the Wash and the Scottish border, and aiming at Manchester and Glasgow. A squadron scrambled from Thornaby managed to intercept the navigation lights of a Hampden squadron, but they had been warned by the RDR controllers when they were two miles from the target.

The next morning Chadwick was informed that a member of the ground crew at Church Fenton had been killed when he had walked into a spinning propeller after the bombers landed following the night raid. When Chadwick spoke to Wing Commander Codrington, he learned that so far five aircraft had been damaged, mostly in landing accidents. Three air crew had been injured in the "cat fives," Codrington told him. The accident list included one category 1, minor damage; two category 3, serious damage; and two category 5, write-offs.

Later that same day, a flight of six Spitfires flying from Leuchars were caught by bad weather, which enveloped northern Scotland very quickly. The flight flew into a mountain, and the pilots of four Spits, demonstrating amazing reaction times, managed to just scrape over the summit. But two Spits flying slightly lower in the formation hit the rocky slopes and the pilots were killed. One of the planes which succeeded in landing had twigs and leaves entangled with the oil cooler intake and the propeller was slightly damaged.

On a brighter note, Codrington told Chadwick that Sixty Group and the strategic plotting table at Uxbridge were working well, with nearly eighty percent of intruder detections leading to interceptions. RAE pilots observing the interceptions reported that the majority had a height advantage.

Chadwick asked Codrington if he could witness the operations at Uxbridge and was given permission to return to Farnborough for a day. He flew back and landed in the dark, then jumped into his car and drove to Uxbridge, arriving just before midnight. The plotting room was a hive of activity. Two raids were on the table—the size, height, and other details were written on a large card stuck into wooden counters on the plotting tables. WAAFs wearing telephone headsets moved the counters with croupier's sticks. Lights at the positions of RAF airfields showed the state of readiness of fighter squadrons.

Suddenly a light at Biggin Hill changed from amber to green. A controller on the balcony spoke into his telephone, and the lights changed again to indicate a scramble. A WAAF put another counter on the table showing details for that squadron—six Hurricanes climbing at 2,200 feet per minute. The tension and controlled excitement in the room and on the balcony were palpable. The two counters grew inexorably closer, then a WAAF said something into her headset, and with a deft motion dropped a small red cup on the bomber counter—a successful interception, which at night meant the navigation lights of the bombers had been spotted by the Hurricane pilots.

Chadwick was fascinated. He realized he was seeing something historic. Never before had military commanders looked down on the battlefield, like Olympian Gods, and remotely ordered their warriors into battle.

He drove back to Farnborough and got a few hours' sleep before flying to Leuchars, a leg that would tax the Spitfire's range. To minimize delays at the other end Chadwick arranged to be tracked by the RDR stations near RAF Leuchars and was vectored to a good position to descend into the Tay Estuary and then head south to the airfield. As he walked into the crew room near dispersal, he was stopped by a wing commander, who introduced himself.

"Welcome, Squadron Leader. You're a rather surprising arrival. I was told by the tower you were in-bound, but we had considered the weather too clampers for flying."

Chadwick laughed. "I have a special relationship with the RDR stations. They vectored me to within a few miles of the airfield. My name's Chadwick, RAE. Just popped in, in connection with Periscope. Very sorry to hear you lost two chaps yesterday. Perhaps you can fill me in on the details when I get rid of this gear."

"You were vectored by RDR? Can we do that after an interception? Some of my chaps have difficulty finding the men's toilet."

"It's coming. Maybe the next generation of RDR. You see, once a squadron breaks formation after an interception, they're all over the sky. The RDR couldn't sort out all the echoes with the present equipment."

"Come to my office. I'll brief you on the exercise and the foul-up yesterday."

Chadwick learned that the interception had worked well, but bad weather reduced visibility while the planes were still over the North Sea. The flight formatted on the leader, who flew too far inland before doing a one-eighty and heading back for the coast. The formation broke up during the one-eighty turn. All pilots had been taught the safe minimum altitude when flying a heading to the east, but the two who had separated from the flight during the turn flew too low. Even so, in the opinion of the wing commander, the flight leader should have left more margin.

Chadwick sighed heavily. "We live and learn, and sometimes don't live, if we learn too slowly."

Chadwick checked the weather at Thornaby and found conditions were clear. The squadron pilots were surprised when they saw Chadwick lining up on the runway in what they considered atrocious conditions. But he had probably accumulated more hours on instruments than the combined total of all their "blind" flying and had no difficulty taking off and flying entirely on instruments until he broke into clear sky and brilliant sunshine at fifteen thousand feet. He could see the front lying over the Scottish border, and as he flew south, the weather cleared, and he landed at Thornaby. After dumping his flying gear, he got a ride to the RDR sector station and talked to the observing RAE officer.

"I've monitored sixteen intruder alarms since the exercise began," the officer told him. "Twelve were successfully intercepted under Group control. One of the missed ones was intercepted later when they flew into the Manston sector. One was missed because Group scrambled some Defiants that couldn't make the height in time. The remaining couple were at night, and the squadrons scrambled late. I have noticed it takes ten minutes longer to scramble a squadron at night."

Chadwick commented that things were a lot smoother than Exercise Torpedo the previous year. He went back to the mess and was comfortably reading a paper after dinner when he noticed Section Officer Clayborne-Rankin, a rather attractive WAAF he had met on a previous visit to Thornaby. He wondered whether or not to make an approach but decided squadron leaders were above that sort of thing. She saw him glance at her and was disappointed when he rose and left the lounge without saying anything.

In the morning Chadwick spent some time at the RDR receiver room and bid a polite "good morning" to Section Officer Clayborne-Rankin. He was expecting a bomber intrusion within an hour. It was detected over a hundred miles away and the WAAFs worked efficiently to get the information from the calculators and contact Sector. The bombers were intercepted by Hurricanes ten miles from the coast. Chadwick congratulated the WAAF officer and commented that obviously training had paid off. He called Wing Commander Codrington, who asked him to drop into RAF St. Eval. Four Spitfires had intercepted a plane from the Republic of Ireland, which they forced to land, Codrington told him.

The forecast called for scattered cloud and Chadwick made the flight from Thornaby in an hour. The flight took him over Cardiff and to the south coast of the Bristol Channel where the three runways at St. Eval stood out clearly. The Douglas DC2 they were flying had been picked up by RDR and a flight of Spitfires vectored onto it. They did not have H.F. wireless contact but flew alongside the DC2 and pointed down to the airfield. The pilot in the Irish plane nodded and started to descend.

And then suddenly the plane jerked upwards and almost stalled for a moment. Then it had again descended and landed as Spitfires flew parallel, banked steeply, and landed behind it. Aircraftsmen waved it to the dispersal area where four men alighted from the plane, wearing civilian clothing. They were escorted to the station commander's office, protesting volubly that forcing them to land was an act of air piracy and they should be released immediately.

The station commander called Group headquarters, and from there a message was passed to the Air Ministry. From there the call went to the Foreign Office, where someone eventually spoke to an Irish official who worked for the Prime Minister. The aircraft had been stolen by Irish officers, who left a message indicating that they planned to give the plane to Germany and join the Luftwaffe. The official asked that the plane be returned to Dublin with the four occupants. That was when the order went to Farnborough to escort the Irish plane back to Ireland, and the whole incident would be forgotten.

When Chadwick landed, he was informed that he must talk to Codrington before meeting the Irish. He was told to escort them to a point ten miles north of St. David's Head in Wales and to tell them they were expected at Dublin Airport, which was a short flight from there.

When he entered the room with the four Irishmen, he was verbally assaulted, all four talking at once. He managed to calm them down and explained he had been delegated to escort them back to Ireland in a fully armed Spitfire, and that this was at the request of the Irish Government. Chadwick discovered one of the four had argued for continuing despite the presence of the Spitfires, and for a moment wrestled the controls from the pilot. One of the Irishmen asked Chadwick how on earth they had been caught, as they had been careful to stay well away from the coast. Chadwick told him that RAF exercises were being conducted and they had been spotted by chance by RAF planes.

After tea and a plateful of cheese sandwiches, he walked with the Irish flyers to their plane. He pointed to Sally, saying, "I'll be right behind you."

They flew on the course he had given them, with Chadwick putting down a full flap and formatting about a hundred yards on their left. When the Irish coast was clearly visible on the horizon, he waggled his wings, gave them a cheery wave, lifted the flaps, rolled on left bank, and hauled strongly back on the control column, at the same time giving the mighty Merlin a burst of throttle. The DC2 disappeared in a second, and he laid on a course to Farnborough.

Codrington laughed when Chadwick told him that he had implied to the Irishmen that Sally was fully armed. In fact, she was not carrying ammunition and four guns had been removed, with lead blocks added to maintain the center of gravity.

Codrington suggested that Chadwick should spend the last day of the exercise at Bawdsey to get the opinions of the boffins about Periscope. Chadwick landed at Woodbridge and was soon in conversation with Dr. Bostock, who felt things had gone well. Chadwick mentioned landing at Leuchars with RDR support and the wish of the wing commander for that kind of assistance for his squadron pilots. Bostock said his team had been working on that and there was already a proposal to install a special receiver/transmitter in each aircraft in the future. When the plane received a signal that meant it had been swept by an RDR beam the transmitter sent back an automated code reply that appeared on the RDR receiver display. The original intention was to identify friend from foe on the RDR screens, thus it was to be called IFF, or Iffy. Once identified, a plane could be given a range and bearing to its home base, if requested.

Bostock confessed he was still amazed at how well the WAAF operators, with some practice, could accurately pick out weak signals in the electronic noise. "Due to the vagaries of wireless wave propagation, at extreme range only about one pulse in ten produces an echo strong enough to provide range information. And yet those girls can often find it. It's a bit like magic!"

When he returned to Farnborough, Chadwick was told by Codrington that the next job was to collect the reports of all the observers of the exercise and prepare a summary.

Chapter Forty-Nine

Chadwick joined seven other senior RAE officers working under Wing Commander Codrington to prepare a report on Exercise Periscope. They decided to list each identified intrusion according to the code assigned by the sector stations, and under each added the RDR report, RAE observer report, and the Fighter and Bomber Commands reports. This required considerable cross-referencing. There were seventy-two identified intrusions and seventy-five claimed by Bomber Command. Attention was paid to the formation strength, distance to the coast for the first interception, warning margin for the Observer Corp reports, and myriad details. When they were finished, the reports covered two hundred and fifty-five pages, forming an appendix which they knew would only be read by specialists.

Now they had to prepare the summary, for the eyes of the higher-ups. Chadwick was especially interested, as he knew the summary would form the basis for the misleading report to be dangled by MI5. Circulation of the summary was very limited; each copy was numbered and classified "Most Secret." For the deception to work, it was essential to ensure that the Germans would never see the true report. However, Chadwick kept a copy of the draft for his own files.

About a month after the conclusion of Periscope, Chadwick sat down with Viney, Larson, and a member of the Double-cross Committee to develop a misleading summary report as bait to catch the traitor and, perhaps more importantly, to disguise from Luftwaffe intelligence the true performance of RDR.

Viney waved to the man from the Double-cross Committee and said to Chadwick, "This is Mr. Sedgewick, representing a committee which coordinates all our deception plans. I've given him an outline of the RDR story so far, and today we'll compose the fake report on the performance of Exercise Periscope."

"Please go over the exact intention of this deception for me."

Viney spoke up. "There are two objectives. First, by tracing this report to the Abwehr, we hope to expose the source on the English side. Secondly, by down-playing the performance of RDR, we hope to induce a false complacency in the Luftwaffe intelligence, so that in a future war they will discount the effectiveness of British air defense. They received a version of last year's exercise which was essentially correct. Hopefully, this will lead them to believe this report, which will not be correct. Allan, could you please briefly summarize Periscope for us?"

"Periscope lasted a week, twenty-four hours a day. Bomber Command launched about seventy-two simulated raids on British cities. Twenty RDR stations which were fully manned reported to various control levels, culminating in a plot at RAF Uxbridge which executed defensive measures. Only modern, high-speed aircraft were used, such as Blenheims, Hampdens, and a few Wellingtons. These are representative of the aircraft the Luftwaffe would employ. Only Hurricane, Spitfire, and Defiant fighters were fielded by Fighter Command. Of the seventy-two raids detected, fifty-two were intercepted by fighters in time to launch an attack during daylight. Ten raids launched at night resulted in two interceptions, but of course, we don't have the equipment for a night-time attack on the bombers."

Sedgewick interrupted, "What will that take?"

Chadwick explained, "I believe we'll have to develop an RDR small enough to fit into a fighter to provide the pilot with range and bearing to a target—technically, a very difficult challenge."

"Do you have an appreciation of the overall feeling about the success of Periscope by RAF commanders, Squadron Leader?"

"I believe it's felt things went quite well for this stage of development and, of course, practice makes perfect. Next year's exercise will benefit from what we've learned this year."

Sedgewick pondered and then asked, "Let me try to review the objectives of this meeting as I understand them. Five has the tracing of the traitor in hand. It is expected this person will communicate the false Periscope report to the Abwehr, who will forward it to the Luftwaffe."

Viney answered, "In doing so he identifies himself to us."

Sedgewick countered, "And in that case, he secures immunity from any arrest, otherwise his handlers would question the report. True?"

"Yes, we've thought of that. He could still be a useful conduit for other deceptions in the future."

"Possibly, although too many deceptive reports would also raise a flag. Now, turning to our deception, what are the primary objectives?"

"We want Luftwaffe intelligence to believe that RDR will not play a significant role in our air defense."

Sedgewick continued, "Anything else?"

"No point in giving the Luftwaffe our aircraft strength by quoting the actual number of aircraft involved in the exercise."

"But surely the Luftwaffe has been monitoring such blatant RAF activity? Won't they have a good estimate of RAF strength?"

Viney conceded, "Good point. If we invoke about half the number actually involved that is probably within their accuracy tolerance."

"What percentage of successful interceptions do we claim then?"

Chadwick spoke up. "We must show some improvement over last year to be believable. I suggest fifteen percent of daytime raids were intercepted, and only one night-time interception. The major causes of interception failures were poor long-range detection at the receiver stations and long delays in getting fighters scrambled."

"Good. Squadron Leader, while you're here at MI5, please dictate a report we can type. Now, I understand last year's report was typed by you. Did you use standard RAF stationery?"

"No, I used plain white paper."

"Good, we can proceed. Please provide the good squadron leader with a quiet office and some paper, and then we need a typist who can mimic a beginner typing a report."

"I think I'll call this 'salient points of the report on Exercise Periscope,' so I won't claim it is a word-for-word copy of an official report, but rather my own summary."

"Excellent! I think you have a devious mind, Squadron Leader. To work!"

Two hours later they assembled again to discuss Chadwick's report. Sedgwick scanned it with a practiced eye. "Looks amateurish—several typographical errors, one clumsily-done erasure. Don't forget, Squadron Leader, you didn't type this on the same machine as the last one. Let's see—seventeen RDR stations operating over a week. Thirty-nine detections, typically at one hundred miles, including three at night. Six good interceptions, none at night. Errors at receiver level in detecting range and strength, scrambles took on average twenty-four minutes after first detection. Higher-ups are reasonably happy; it's an improvement over '37. Why did you report so many RDR stations as active, Squadron Leader?"

"The Germans can count as well as we can. Their Zeppelins have prowled our coast, so they must have logged all the aerials. I'm simply saying some aerials are not connected to receivers yet. Seems reasonable."

Sedgewick asked for comments, and Larson pointed out that Chadwick's well-being would be in jeopardy if the deception was discovered.

"Good point, which raises the issue—how are we going to cast our bait upon the waters?"

Viney said, "I'm satisfied. The details are not important, so long as Luftwaffe intelligence swallows the whole fish and discounts our ability to detect and intercept many raids. As for casting the bait, Squadron Leader Chadwick has a fan in the Isbell's crowd who asked for the last report. We assume the pattern will be repeated. It would be undesirable for Chadwick to push it initially."

"Good, this is our bait. There will be only one paper copy, which the squadron leader will keep."

Sedgewick picked up a small camera and carefully took a picture of the papers lying on the table, then he handed them to Chadwick. "Good fishing. A pleasure to have met you."

Chapter Fifty

Chadwick took a train back to Farnborough and called Melanie. "Sorry I've been ignoring you. Life's been pretty frantic. Fancy a weekend somewhere? Come to think about it, I have a few days leave due. How about a very long weekend?"

"Sounds wonderful! What do you have in mind?"

Allan had noticed an advertisement for a houseboat on the Norfolk Broads. "This just popped into my mind, but what do you say about renting a boat on the Broads?"

"Oh, that sounds different—let's do it."

In the morning Chadwick called the boatyard and reserved a small power boat for a week. He called Melanie to let her know the details and they agreed to drive to Wroxham in his Bentley, a distance of about two hundred and fifty miles, mainly over good roads. Then he arranged for Sally to be pulled out of the hangar and he flew to Woodbridge for a briefing with the boffins at Bawdsey. As much as anything, it was an excuse to get in some flying time. He was back at Farnborough before darkness.

Chadwick arranged to collect Melanie at Clair Court Hall in the early morning. "Wear a warm coat for the trip" was his common-sense advice, "something light for the boat." With a loud backfire the Bentley drew up to the steps of the Hall, and Melanie threw a suitcase on the back seat.

"I know the way to Uxbridge from here," Allan said. "You navigate from there. We want the Great North Road. The A10 gets us to Cambridge. There's an RAC roadmap in the door pocket."

The roads were crowded, but were mostly dual carriageway, two lanes in each direction. In small towns like Watford, Amersham, St.Albans, and Hertford, the road went through the

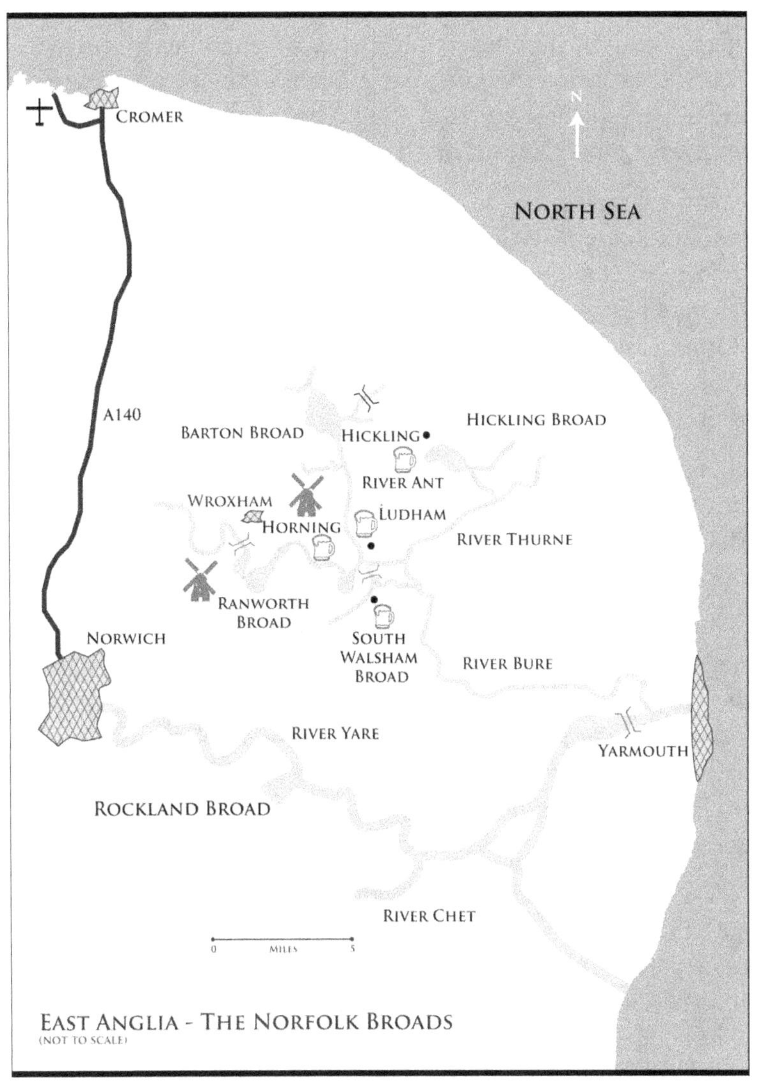

CROMER
NORTH SEA
N
A140
BARTON BROAD
HICKLING
HICKLING BROAD
RIVER ANT
WROXHAM
HORNING
LUDHAM
RIVER THURNE
RANWORTH
BROAD
NORWICH
SOUTH
WALSHAM
BROAD
RIVER BURE
RIVER YARE
YARMOUTH
ROCKLAND BROAD
RIVER CHET
0 MILES 5
EAST ANGLIA - THE NORFOLK BROADS
(NOT TO SCALE)

center of town with awkward turns and traffic lights, and heavy local traffic caused them to stop for long periods. The Bentley engine had no fan. It was designed for a flow of cool air through the radiator as the car moved. Chadwick anxiously watched the temperature gauge, which hovered near boiling. On the open road, the Bentley could overtake anything ahead with ease if there was room to pass. Allan cut it close on occasions and Melanie cringed as they pulled back into the left lane as a thundering lorry passed on their right, often with horn blaring.

At Royston, Melanie directed him to leave the A10 to avoid the anticipated dense traffic in Cambridge, and he navigated the car through some small villages on two-lane roads as far as the A11, which took them to Great Abingdon. There they stopped for morning coffee and a cream cake at a charming tea shop. Allan glanced at his watch. "It's eleven. I suggest lunch at one-ish. Let's see where we'll be by then."

The countryside became flatter, with watery areas, the fens, and they roared through Newmarket and Mildenhall, where Melanie pointed to her watch. "Next town, lunch and a drink," she shouted over the engine.

The A11 took them straight into Thetford, a picturesque village with thatched roofs and timbered gable ends. They parked the car and walked to the Bell Inn. On the way they passed a statue of Thomas Paine. A small plaque explained he was a native of Thetford and wrote dialogues on democracy which triggered the French and American revolutions. "Ah, a troublemaker," Allan observed.

Despite the small rooms, inside the inn was not stuffy but quite cool. Allan had to duck to avoid the thick, black beams. They had a quick lunch—Melanie chose fish, with a glass of Sauterne, and Allan chose Shepherd's Pie, with a local draft beer. Heading for Wroxham they found the landscape dotted with windmills. With directions from a bobby, they drove into the boatyard on the River Bure. The trip had taken over ten hours.

An air of decrepitude hung over the place. A large wooden shed was in need of paint, and smaller ramshackle huts littered the yard. Flimsy planks supported on poles driven into the riverbed formed docks, to which were tied a few wooden cabin cruisers averaging twenty-five feet in length. From a door in the big shed, a ramp sloped into the river; two rusty steel rails carried small trunnions with wooden beams across them.

Chadwick turned off the Bentley engine and it gave its characteristic backfire, which brought an elderly man in overalls out of one of the huts. Chadwick climbed down. "Good afternoon. Allan Chadwick. I made a reservation for a boat for a week."

"Aye, I recall. I'm Ezra Allerton, manager. Come into the office, please. There be a rental agreement to sign."

Allan followed him into one of the huts. Allerton shuffled some papers aside on a chaotic desk and triumphantly produced a pad of printed forms. "Put your name and address here, please. That will be one pound for the rental, and one pound deposit for damage, returned if the boat is unharmed. There is also a charge for the diesel fuel and paraffin already placed aboard, total three pounds, seven shillings and ninepence. She carries fifteen gallons of fuel and two gallons of paraffin."

Chadwick handed over the money, and once he had it, Mr. Allerton mellowed. "I'll introduce you and your lady to *Tinkerbelle*. Please follow me." Standing on the riverbank he pointed to a bluff-nosed boat. "There she is. Just step onto the plank one at a time. They kind of sway."

They all scrambled aboard. The cockpit at the stern had two benches running fore and aft, covered in cushions. The cabin carried a small protective roof over two feet of the cockpit. A companionway led below on the port side; on the starboard was a brass steering wheel and two levers.

Allerton pointed to the deck. "Engine is under there. You probably won't have to lift the hatch except to start it. This engine is very reliable, made in Norway. I'll give you a lesson on running it after I've shown the missus the downstairs."

They all trooped into the main cabin. Two couches about six feet long were ranged on either side. A collapsible table stood between them. "Back of the couch lifts up for sleeping. Sheets, blankets, and pillows are stored there." Forward of the benches was a bulkhead on the port side, and Allerton opened a door. "Toilet, with wash basin. Instructions on the wall. Towels inside."

On the starboard side was a small counter with cupboards underneath and shelves above. "Galley," said Allerton, turning to Melanie, "what you call the kitchen." There was a small sink in the counter, and over it was a brass tap and a brass handled pump. Allerton touched the tap. "Fresh water, twenty gallons. If you run out, any yard on the river can refill the tank." He touched the brass handle. "River water, used for washing up, cleaning the deck. Not recommended that you drink it." He opened a cupboard door. "Kettle, pans at the bottom, crockery above." He opened a small drawer. "Cutlery, tin opener. There, all the comforts of home."

Melanie looked around. "Where's the stove?"

"Ah, yes." Allerton opened another cupboard and produced a brass Primus stove. "Runs on paraffin, you need a little alcohol to get it started, here in this tin."

Allan said, "I know how to run that. We used them in the Boy Scouts."

Walking back through the cabin, Allerton pointed at a locker. "Open that and there's a quart tin and funnel for the paraffin. Use the tap there. There's a navigation lantern, red and green, to hang on deck should you travel at night. Also, a lantern for the cockpit." He pointed to the sides of the cabin, between the two portholes on each side was a paraffin lantern, with a glass chimney and a wick. "There's your cabin lights."

They climbed up the companionway steps. "If you can run that thing you just drove up in, you'll have no trouble with this engine," Allerton said, addressing Allan. He lifted up the front section of the hatch in the deck. Pointing, he said, "Fuel valve, on, off." He grasped a lever near the wheel. "Throttle, open a crack to start." Grasping the other lever, he said, "Gear, neutral and forward. No reverse." He put the lever in neutral and pointed to a valve on the single cylinder. "Decompression, open to start."

Then he took a piece of rope with a short wooden dowel on one end and wrapped it around the front of a massive flywheel. "Ready?" He gave a long, firm tug on the rope and the flywheel reluctantly made a few turns. He shut the decompression valve and the engine started with a low pitch rumble, running at about a hundred revolutions a minute. He opened the decompression valve and with a wheezing gasp, the engine stopped. Allerton shut the hatch. "Simple as pie. Any questions?"

"Where can we get some supplies?"

"Back in the village, grocery and off-license next to each other."

Allan said, "I think we'll stock up and leave in the morning."

"Anything you want is just fine with me. You're due back in a week. You can leave your lovely motor car in the big shed."

They left in the Bentley to buy some food and drink, and once out of earshot Melanie burst into shrieks of laughter. "Allan, what have we got into? Have we gone back to the Victorian age?"

At the grocery they bought a few staples—bread, cheese, tins of soup, tea, and a couple of oranges. The owner put them in an old wooden crate, which they placed on the back seat. The off-license was good for a dozen bottles of India Pale Ale. Allan drove down the Norwich road and found the only pub in in the village. Inside, they were told meals were not served, but if they sat at the bar something could be found for them to eat. They ordered the local ale and shortly after got plates of wonderful home-made pork sausage with peas and potatoes.

Back at the boat they carefully carried the food along the plank, made up the bunks and after a chaste kiss, both fell into a deep sleep. In the morning, Allan put the Bentley in the shed, started the diesel engine, untied the lines, and chugged slowly down the river. Mr. Allerton had left them a map of the river and adjacent broads—large shallow lakes. Pubs were prominently marked. The village of Horning was next, according to Mr. Allerton's map. As the rumbling diesel slowly pushed them down the river, an old windmill came into view.

"I wonder what these mills are for," Allan mused. A bend in the river brought them to a beautiful vista, Horning. Many cottages had thatched roofs, and an old church stood back from the riverbank.

Melanie insisted on tying up. "I have a little more shopping to do," she said.

"You go and shop to your heart's content, dear. I think the pub is open. I'll wait for you there."

Allan leaned on the bar and nibbled some potato crisps as he sipped on a cool draft beer. The landlord was polishing glasses. "What are the windmills for?" Allan asked him.

"Why, sir, them's mills pump water. If it wasn't for them, we's be swimming."

"Thank you, I never knew the land was so low,"

"Go look in the churchyard, sir. You'll see old bollards, in the old days, sea-going ships tied up here."

"Fascinating. Definitely worth another of your fine ales, please."

Melanie found him half an hour later. When she saw the empty glasses, she said, "Come on, you old soak. Time to push off, Captain."

Climbing onto *Tinkerbelle*, Melanie announced she would be the navigator, and glancing up from the map, she said, "Lunch on Ranworth Broad, I think, Allan. Watch out for the entrance on a bend."

The riverbank was covered by small bushes and tall grassy areas. Numerous butterflies flitted about, and small birds made swooping attacks on them. Inside the broad were several posts to hitch to. Allan tied up to one and stopped the engine.

"Well, that was a strenuous morning, we must have sailed all of six miles."

Melanie appeared in the cockpit with a plate of sandwiches and two bottles of IPA. They munched on the food and watched the wildlife on the shore nearby. Melanie suddenly pointed. "Look over there, on that tree, a beautiful blue bird with a long beak. What is it, Allan?"

"I've no idea, I know there are big birds and small birds, and black birds and brown birds and white birds. Apart from those categories, I'm stumped."

"We must buy a bird book, if we come across a book seller."

"Yes, dear," Allan mumbled as he dozed off.

An hour later Melanie woke him, and they decided to spend the night at Ant or Ludham, whichever looked the most hospitable. They passed under a fine old bridge as they sailed up the River Ant. Just after the bridge was a small dock with room for two or three boats and sign pointing to a path to Ludham, one mile.

"Just what we need," Melanie exclaimed. "Some exercise after being cooped up on the boat." Twenty minutes later they walked into the village using small bridges that crossed silent streams. "Ah, look there, a gift shop. I bet they sell bird books." Melanie darted into it.

Allan sat down on a bench outside and waited. She emerged carrying a book. "Just what we need," she said, waving it at him. "Birds of the British Islands."

They walked through the village, admired the old church, and had a light supper. The next morning Allan consulted their map and opted for a two-hour sail to Barton Broad along the River Ant. The map showed a prominent pub, the White Horse, that seemed to be worth investigation. The west side of the broad was home to several small villages—Neatishead, Barton Turf, and Irstead. They slowly motored up a narrow channel and tied up in the center of the village of Neatishead.

The pub had chairs and tables on the lawn with a good view of the river. Melanie pored over the bird book. "That was a Kingfisher that we saw yesterday," she announced.

The White Horse laid on a good dinner and Melanie got talking to one of the local residents, mentioning her interest in birds. His advice was to sail over to the east side of the broad, which was teeming with wildlife.

Melanie managed a passable scrambled egg for breakfast, after which they followed the local's advice and powered to the east side where Allan stopped the engine and they drifted with an almost imperceptible current. Melanie was delighted to identify half a dozen birds.

The next day they headed back to the River Burr, but Allan had been careless about stowing the mooring line on the foredeck, and the swell from a passing boat caused the line to fall over the side—where it inevitably wound itself around the propeller. The engine came to a sudden stop.

"What's the matter, Allan?"

"Dunno." Then he spotted the line stretching from the cleat on the foredeck over the left side of the boat, as tight as a violin string. "Uh-oh. I think I know what happened." Using a long pole with a hook on the end, which was conveniently clipped above the cockpit benches, he managed to push the boat toward the shore, which was covered with tall grass. When he was close, he tossed the anchor onto the land.

There was a metal step screwed to the transom of the boat which facilitated entering the water. Allan emptied his pockets and slipped beneath the surface. He could see the rudder and propeller in a blurry kind of way. Feeling with his fingers as his back bumped on the underside of the boat he was able to get hold of the rope, which was immovable. He came up for air, and holding onto the step, he asked Melanie for a sharp kitchen knife. Ducking under the water again, he cut the rope just ahead of the propeller, then with another breath he was able to unwind the short piece left from the prop.

He came up for air and passed the knife and the short piece of rope to Melanie, who was anxiously leaning over the back of the boat. "The rope is for the trash. I needed a swim anyway."

"I'll make some tea, darling." She soon had the Primus going and put together some teacups and biscuits on a small folding table in the cockpit. Allan sipped appreciatively.

"Just the thing. The water's not all that warm."

Later he looked at the end of the rope attached to the bow cleat and could see that it was unraveling. He poked around in the galley drawer and found some string. Looking at other mooring lines on the boat, he then copied a whipping at the end, which at least made it serviceable for the rest of the trip.

Allan started the engine. He was pleased to find the sudden stop had apparently not damaged it. They motored the short distance to South Walsham Broad, where the village dock looked inviting. They tied up for the night. Even though the village was tiny, it had a pub. Allan asked about meals and was told these were served if ordered ahead. He ordered a steak dinner for them both. They walked along the shore of the broad, with Melanie excitedly spotting birds, which were plentiful. She decided she needed a pair of binoculars. They had a drink at the pub and talked to a man who said he was the local historian. He shared with them the fact that South Walsham was mentioned in the Domesday Book.

The steak later was excellent, and they retired to the boat for a good night's sleep. In the morning, they cruised slowly along the shore for more bird spotting, and then returned to the River Burr and pushed up the River Thurne to Hickling Broad.

"You know, Allan, this boating is all very well, living rough and all that," Melanie said, as she served some lunch, "but the boat wasn't made for romance."

"You mean the bunks are too narrow, I think," Allan countered. He thought for a moment. "Tonight, we'll anchor in Hickling Broad. No strangers walking by the dock, and we can spread the cushions in the cockpit." When they arrived at the village of Hickling, at the north end of the broad, Melanie did a little food shopping and then they left to anchor in a bay to the south. As they guzzled delicious pork chops with fried onion, washed down with Pale Ale, Allan pointed out they could see no sign of civilization. They were completely alone.

As promised, he arranged all the boat cushions in the cockpit, and they made love as the sun sank lower. As it set, a bright new moon was visible. "All alone, this is my fantasy," teased Melanie. "I'm a woman in a harem, and the sheik wants to make love to me. He looks like Rudolph Valentino."

Allan laughed. "At an establishment I visited in Syria, they played out that fantasy with two ladies dressed in gauzy pantaloons."

"Well, what happened?"

"The sheik left them alone. The ladies had to amuse themselves."

"How could they?"

"I'll show you."

Melanie was quiet for a few moments, and then she began to shriek and shudder. "Oh, God, I can't take much more."

"You'll enjoy this better now," Allan whispered as he entered her.

They made love until it was completely dark, and Allan had to fetch some blankets. "Look at the stars," he said as they lay on the cockpit deck and gazed up. "How bright they are with no other lights nearby. Look over there. You can just see the Milky Way."

"That was fantastic. I'll always remember making love under the stars, Allan."

In the morning, eating a boiled egg with some fried bread, Allan said, "We'll have to be starting our way back. We should spend our seventh night back in Mr. Allerton's yard so we can be away early."

They made their way west, tied up again at Ranworth Broad and the next day arrived at Wroxham by ten. Mr. Allerton asked them if they had broken or lost anything, Allan confessed he had been forced to cut a couple of feet off a mooring line when it caught the propeller. Ezra laughed and said that could happen to anybody.

The familiar road signs of the Great North Road fell behind them as the Bentley gobbled up the miles.

"That was a wonderful holiday, Allan. You look much more relaxed. You know what I liked? For a week we didn't hear the news or read a paper."

Allan nodded. They pulled up to a small roadside restaurant for lunch. As they ate, they could hear a wireless playing in the background. Suddenly Allan stiffened. "Listen."

The announcer was saying that the Prime Minister, Neville Chamberlain, had flown to Germany to discuss German troop movements on the Czechoslovakian border.

"So, it's started," Allan said in a grave voice.

"What's started?" Melanie asked.

"The next war," Allan replied.

"That's silly," Melanie said. "It's just some fracas a long way away."

"The Great War began in Serbia. That's a long way off, too."

By seven-thirty they arrived at Clair Court Hall. Melanie walked through the front door and said, "First thing I'm going to do is have nice, hot bath."

"Sounds wonderful." Allan added, "Can I join you?"

Chapter Fifty-One

When he looked at the mail in his pigeonhole at the mess, Chadwick found a message from Lord Lowestoft tucked in between a postcard and two envelopes—*Meeting Isbells 8 pm Tuesday. Try to be there. Freddy.*

Chadwick arrived early and noticed no ladies had been invited to the meeting. He was soon talking to Lord Lowestoft and Viscount Addenbury.

"By Jove, Allan, you're looking quite tanned."

"Just spent a week on the water."

"Jolly good. Where did you sail?"

"The Broads. I was *not* fighting tempestuous seas." This remark was directed at Addenbury, who was a well-known yachtsman and had written a book about sailing in the Bay of Biscay.

"Very wise," Addenbury said. "A pub every night, that's the way to sail."

Everybody laughed politely. When they got a chance, Chadwick talked to Lowestoft alone. "I had quite a rough few weeks with Exercise Periscope, I needed a little relaxation."

"And how did Periscope go, Allan?"

"Not bad. Performance was little better than last year. There was a report, but it has been classified as Most Secret, and copies numbered for a very limited distribution."

"I am sure the Foreign Office will eventually get a copy, but with the Czech situation I was hoping to have more knowledge immediately."

"I knew you would like something, but I didn't get a copy myself. I prepared a summary of the major points, which I typed up, if you would like it."

"That's awfully prescient, old boy. In the present climate it's essential that the F.O. is fully up to date."

Chadwick passed over the fake report prepared by MI5. He realized that MI5 must prevent the true report from ever reaching the Foreign Office. Soon he sat down to listen to a rambling discourse by Addenbury on the need for Chamberlain to tread very carefully and not antagonize Hitler.

When he got back to Farnborough, Chadwick called Larson in the morning and passed on a prearranged code, "Package Delivered." He also mentioned his concern that the true report should never get to the Foreign Office. Two days later, Chamberlain flew back to Heston airport and became famous by waving a piece of paper, claiming it guaranteed "Peace in our time."

A day later Chadwick flew some boffins in the Anson to a new RDR station near RAF Lossiemouth in Scotland, which had been suffering from mysterious technical problems. The weather was so bad it was five days before he could return to Woodbridge, and then Farnborough. He found Larson had tried to contact him, so he called on the telephone.

Larson was excited. "Great happenings," he said. "Come into town. I'll give you an update."

Chadwick saw Larson and Viney the next day. Doug Larson was bubbling over with excitement. "Lowestoft and Addenbury fell for our fish—hook, line and sinker. Two days after you called me reporting the transfer, a watcher at the Addenbury establishment saw his valet travel into Knightsbridge and leave a package. A dead drop, as they say. First, he left a chalk symbol on a gatepost. Then he hid the package behind a telephone box. So, now we have the whole M.O.

"We opened the package before it was retrieved and photographed everything in it. It was addressed to Zimmer 121, which we know is Abwehr Hamburg HQ, so it was intended for the German Diplomatic Pouch. The report we typed was in it, along with a note saying it was supplied by agent Bismark, which is presumably Addenbury, or you."

"Wonderful bit of work. We exposed the M.O. and a couple of rank and file. We will keep an eye on the valet but do nothing overt yet."

Chapter Fifty-Two

About a month later the Luftwaffe Oberkommando held a meeting at the Reich Air Ministry on Leipziger Strasse in Berlin. It was for senior officers only, and Reichmarshall Göring would be in attendance. When the auditorium was full, an officer at the door called for attention. As Göring entered, the men rose to their feet and snapped a stiff-arm salute, shouting, "Heil Hitler."

"Ach, enough of that. We're all pilots here. Sit down."

Göring, in an immaculate white uniform, strode to the front and sat down in a wide chair specially placed there for his corpulent body. A colonel made the introductory remarks. "For two years, Luftwaffe intelligence has been following the development of a radio detection system by the British, which they term RDR. We obtained a confidential report on the performance during 1937 exercises. The performance was relatively poor, and in line with our own trials in the Baltic.

"We found that, although the equipment can detect aircraft over one hundred and fifty kilometers away, it is very difficult to get fighters in the air in time to intercept them. This year the British RAF organized a massive trial simulating attacks by bombers on the British Islands. Over thirty-nine mock attacks were made. Only fifteen per cent were intercepted by fighters. The bombers were detected at a range of about one hundred and sixty kilometers. From that point it took an average of twenty-five minutes to get fighters airborne. They would, of course, require another ten to fifteen minutes to reach the altitude of the attacking force.

"Doing the arithmetic, our current bombers, Heinkel 111 and Dornier 17, would travel about two hundred kilometers during the period from detection to fighters at an intercepting position. Clearly, interception would not be possible. When our most modern bomber is in full service, the Junkers 88, it would travel two hundred and fifty kilometers at the same time and would be about a hundred kilometers ahead of the fighters by the time they reached altitude.

"The purpose of this meeting is to discuss the tactical implication of the intelligence reports and also the strategic moves in terms of future bomber development. Any questions?"

"How reliable are the intelligence reports?"

The head of the Abwehr rose to his feet. "The '37 report was checked several ways and was deemed accurate. The '38 report was obtained from the same source. We have no reason to doubt its authenticity, but I have asked the head of the London desk to burrow for any other reports he could find on the '38 exercise."

The colonel rose again. "I have here a report from our technical people. Photographs of the RDR aerials were examined closely. They are using a very low frequency for this type of work and the results quoted in the report are probably the best that can be achieved with such technically inferior equipment. The chain of stations, which covers most of the east and south coasts of Britain, need an enormous manpower to operate on a continuous basis. So much so, the stations are mostly manned by women."

There was a general snigger from the audience at this announcement.

"And I have had intelligence that the women lack the ability to be trained to the same level one might expect of a male crew."

At this point the Reichmarshall lumbered to his feet. "The need for four-engined heavy bombers has been a debatable subject for some time in the Luftwaffe. Naturally, in considering such strategic matters, the manufacturing capacity of this country enters the equation. We could build two medium bombers for every heavy bomber produced. I think this intelligence analysis disposes of the issue. Our Heinkel, Junker, and Dornier medium bombers are quite sufficient for a war involving such ill-prepared foes as the British." The debate continued in the meeting, but everyone knew the matter was finished. The Reichmarshall had spoken.

In due course, the telex machine in the German embassy in London chattered away and an encrypted message for Dr. Kegel was delivered. He deciphered it in his office and then called the landlady, Doris Blackwood, to set up a meeting with Gerd Stiller. They met at the usual tea shop.

"HQ are very pleased with information and photographs we sent them of RDR. They apparently would like more, especially information about a recent RAF exercise to test RDR. I thought perhaps that flying friend of yours that helped take the photos may have some pilot's gossip?"

"I have no idea, sir. I can see her this weekend and ask. I've got her very much on our side."

Stiller called Penny Pomeroy at her home on Friday evening and arranged for a meeting at the Farnborough railway station the next day. He suggested a flight in her Tiger Moth if the weather was favorable.

That same Saturday morning, Allan Chadwick went to talk to a flight sergeant in the RAF hangar. He had reported sluggish gyro instruments when he last flew Sally. The instrument rigger had found a small leak in the vacuum system and repaired it. The sergeant suggested a flight test. Two airmen pushed the plane out of the hangar and connected the starter battery. Chadwick signed the duty log and took off. The weather was good for autumn, with ten-tenths cloud at six thousand feet.

Chapter Fifty-Three

When Stiller met Penny, he confessed that the photos they sent of the RDR aerials had been well received, and there had been a request for more about RDR. Penny replied she knew nothing about RDR but that she knew someone who was deeply involved.

"Who's that?" Stiller asked.

"Allan Chadwick. You remember meeting him at the party at my father's house a couple of years ago?"

"Yes, I think I remember him. RAF pilot?"

"Yes. Well, since I've been flying for Marlow Freight, I landed at Farnborough a few times and went to visit him in his office. The last time I was there I saw some blueprints which had RDR written on them. He put them in a drawer when he saw me looking."

"Interesting! Is it worth stopping by today on the way to Marlow? You might spot something else."

"It's a Saturday morning. Things may be closed down for the weekend. But I don't mind popping in."

As they drove into the RAF section of the base, they saw a Spitfire taking off. Penny drove her Austin Seven to the Flight Test hut and walked in. There was only one airman on duty, and he recognized her from previous visits. Pretty young women visiting senior officers always aroused the interest of the airmen.

"Squadron Leader Chadwick?" she asked.

"That's him, Miss," he said, nodding his head upwards. "Just took off."

"When I was here last, I left something of mine with him in his office. Can I just pop in?"

The airman nodded. Penny darted down the corridor. Chadwick's office wasn't locked. She quickly went to the drawer she had seen him store the blueprints in. There were several folders, all marked RDR, and dated. She grabbed the two most recent and pushed them inside her blouse. She pulled her coat closely around her and quickly returned to the orderly room.

"Couldn't find anything," she told the airman. "Say hello to the squadron leader when he gets back, please." And then she quickly left before the airman could ask her name.

Penny climbed into the Austin and started a drive to Marlow. She pulled out the folders and passed them to Stiller, who she still thought was called Olaf Runge. "Here, Olaf, look at these. I just grabbed them, willy nilly."

Stiller began to thumb through the documents. His heart began to race when he saw the details of the interceptions during Exercise Periscope. He realized that Penny Pomeroy had given him intelligence gold.

"How did you get these, Penny?" he asked.

"Oh, I just told the airman in the orderly office that I had left something with Allan on my last visit. So, he let me pop into his office for a minute, and then I grabbed what I could."

"So, they know you were there. I mean the airman knows, that one that you talked to?"

"Yes."

"That means if the papers are missed, they know where to look."

"I suppose so. I didn't think."

Stiller thought furiously about the situation he was in. The loss of the documents could be discovered any time. But information in the folders could be vital to the Abwehr.

"That little plane of yours. Could it fly to Europe, to Germany?"

She laughed. "Not from here. Too far. I could just make Holland or Germany from an airfield on the east coast, if there isn't much head wind."

"Penny, this may seem ridiculous, but we are in serious trouble if your theft is discovered. I think we should fly to Germany this afternoon."

"How could I explain that? It's impossible!"

"We could say we're eloping. I'll marry you if you want when we get the Germany."

"That's the strangest proposal I have ever hear of!"

"I mean it, seriously."

"I'll check the east coast airfields at the flying club. It would be a lark! And I might hold you to your promise."

Penny spent some time at the flying club library, and then reported back to "Olaf."

"There's a club based near Cromer. If we flew there this afternoon we could refuel and leave in the morning."

"Can't we get to Europe today?"

"Not a chance. You'd have me landing at a strange Dutch or German airfield in the dark."

While Penny and Gerd Stiller debated their next move, Allan Chadwick was making some violent movements of his own with Sally. He wanted to determine the maneuvering limits before the gyro instruments toppled. He wrenched the plane around in high "G" turns and bunted in pitch. When he was satisfied the instruments were performing normally, he rolled the plane upside down and flew inverted. This was guaranteed to topple the instruments. He was interested in the recovery time when he resumed normal flight. He trimmed the plane and looked through the canopy at the English countryside below. Some small pieces of dirt collected on the perspex. And then he spotted a small brass nut which had fallen onto the canopy. He reached down and slipped it in a pocket, something to show the instrument technician.

Then he rolled right side up and watched the instruments. They began to recover. He calculated they were back to normal in three minutes—except the gyro compass, which had to be reset to align with the standby magnetic compass.

He landed back at Farnborough ten minutes later, signed the log, and had a word with the flight sergeant to confirm the flight instruments were working normally.

He strode into the orderly office, and was told, "Young lady looking for you earlier."

"Who was it?"

"Didn't leave a name, sir."

The station was closed on Saturday afternoon. The officer's mess was quiet. Chadwick called Melanie for a chat but found that she was attending a meeting of the local conservative party later and then having dinner with some political friends to meet a potential candidate for the next general election. The conservative candidate was always elected in Pangbourne.

After lunch he drove into Farnborough to pick up a book he had seen reviewed and decided it would be an interesting read. On the way back to the mess, he filled the Bentley. Pilots instinctively filled fuel tanks whenever they could, in order to minimize condensation in the space above the petrol.

He had a quiet evening reading his new book and listening to music on the BBC. Just as he was deciding on bed, and perhaps a nightcap first, the mess orderly approached and said he had a telephone call. Surprised, Chadwick entered the telephone booth in the lobby and spoke into the handset. "Hello, Squadron Leader Chadwick here."

"Mr.—er—Squadron Leader, this is Honoria Pomeroy. I hope I didn't disturb."

"No, I was thinking of bed, but I wasn't in it. Nice of you to call."

"You might not think so when you hear what I have to say."

"Yes?"

"Two hours ago, I got a telephone call from Penny. She was at a hotel in Cromer, in Norfolk."

"Yes, I know it."

"She had flown there in her Tiger Moth. She was with her German friend, Olaf, and said they were eloping."

"These young people. What will they get up to next?" Allan offered.

"I'll tell you—they plan to get married in Germany! They're going to fly there tomorrow. Is that dangerous?"

"A little fool-hardy in such a small plane without adequate planning, I think."

"But that's not why I called. Some weeks ago, Olaf persuaded her to help take photographs of those big towers going up all over the coast. She flew by some on the way to Brighton while he snapped away. He told her some friends were very interested, and they wanted more on what they called RDR."

Chadwick's mind suddenly focused when he heard those letters.

"Penny told him you knew a lot about RDR, so to make a long story short, she stopped by your office and lifted a few documents."

"What! That system is very secret. She must be mad!"

"It gets worse. Olaf then persuaded her to elope. But when she thought about it later, at Cromer, she realized that it was only after he saw the documents. So now she's on the horns of a dilemma. Perhaps the documents are important. That's why she called me. I don't know what to do! I've agonized for a couple of hours, so I finally decided to call you. I feel this may be my fault. I've always encouraged her to think of the Germans as a very civilized, cultured country."

"Did she say where she was staying in Cromer, Mrs. Pomeroy?"

"No, some fleapit probably. She says they are refueled and will take off after sunrise. I am sorry to push this onto your lap, Mr. Chadwick, but I am at my wit's end."

"Leave it with me, Mrs. Pomeroy. You did the right thing. I will be in touch."

Chapter Fifty-Four

Chadwick looked at his watch, it was nearly eleven. He furiously turned over possibilities in his mind. Sally was locked up in the hangar and certainly not available. Even if he could fly, he would have to wait for daylight before landing, and that might be too late. Options raced through his mind as he walked quickly to his office. Fortunately, he had the keys with him. He let himself in and opened the drawer where he kept RDR documents, including his day-to-day folders. The two most recent folders were missing, and his heart sank as he recalled these contained Exercise Periscope details.

The enormity of what was happening slowly dawned on him. If those documents reached Germany and presumably the Abwehr, the carefully laid plot by MI5 to mislead the Luftwaffe lay in tatters. Then there was the question of the danger to himself. The Germans would not take kindly to being fooled. He quickly decided that he had to drive to Cromer and stop Penny.

His recent holiday had made him familiar with the roads to the northeast. Then he had another thought—Melanie had been his navigator. He called her number from his office phone. But before it rang, he put down the handset. A better thought was to call MI5.

He had Doug Larson's number and dialed it with trembling fingers. It rang and rang. *Damn,* he said to himself. *Saturday night, even the spies stand down.* He dialed Melanie's number and let it ring. It rang and rang too, and he was just about to hang up when the phone was lifted and a voice said, "Fitzgibbon residence."

He could have blessed her, whoever it was. "I would like to speak to Lady Fitzgibbon, please."

"She has retired. I can leave a message for the morning."

"No, it is essential that I speak to her. Please bring her to the telephone. This is Squadron Leader Chadwick."

"Well, I'll see what I can do."

After a few minutes, Melanie picked up the telephone. "Allan, is that you? What on earth is happening?"

"Yes, it's me. This is very difficult to explain in a short time, and time is of the essence. I have to drive back to Norfolk tonight. I would be very grateful if you would navigate because you know the way from our jaunt to the Broads. I have to be in Cromer by sunrise, which is a little over seven hours from now."

"Allan, it took us longer than that to drive to Wroxham, and Cromer is another twenty miles, and that was in broad daylight. It's impossible!"

"Impossible or not, it has to be done. It is a matter of supreme national security."

"Are you drunk?"

"Melanie, I know it sounds outlandish, but I'll explain on the drive. Will you do it?"

There was a pause, and then Melanie said, "All right. I'll be just as crazy as you are."

"I love you. Dress in some warm clothes, with overcoat and scarf. A thermos of black coffee may be a good idea. To save time, drive to the Blue Bell. I'll pick you up there in say, forty-five minutes. I love you."

Chadwick dashed back to his room, grabbed an overcoat and gloves, and then on an inspiration, some flying goggles. He jumped into the Bentley. The engine ground over for a moment and then fired with a throaty roar. He skidded onto the main road, gravel flying. The enormous ten-inch diameter Lucas headlights looked impressive, but they did not throw out a particularly bright beam.

He drove at the very limit of the safe stopping distance he could make out ahead. Despite the late hour, there was some traffic on the roads. He swerved to overtake, with reckless abandon.

Melanie climbed out of her Vauxhall when she saw the lights of Chadwick's Bentley sweep into the parking area. She was carrying a cloth bag. Chadwick skidded to halt and leaned across to open the left-hand door. "It's wonderful to see you, Melanie. Get in. We're off on a wild ride! Uxbridge first, I think. Do you remember the route after that?"

"Yes, Watford, Hertford, and then we meet the Great North Road and follow that for a good distance."

He looked at his watch, it was exactly midnight. He sped off through the dark streets of suburban London, paying no attention to the speed limit.

"What is all this about, Allan?"

"It's complicated, my dear. I really don't know how much to tell you. Sometimes it's dangerous to know too much. But I'm involved with some people who would kill if they were threatened."

Chadwick drove through the red light of a traffic signal and accelerated up a long hill.

"The way you're driving, I'm going to get killed anyway. So, you'd better give me the whole story."

"For the past couple of years, I've been very involved with the installation of a new defense system for Britain. It works by reflecting wireless signals off aircraft approaching the coast. It's called RDR. The RAF provides all the support so that fighters can be directed to intercept enemy planes. Naturally, the Germans are very interested in our progress. A while ago I was approached by someone who is sympathetic to Germany, or at least to the idea of avoiding a war at all costs, for such details of the RDR that I was aware of. A friend of mine in British intelligence told me that the details had ultimately leaked to the Germans. So, the idea was born to distort the results of the RDR tests last summer and leak misleading information to German intelligence. I helped to do that."

"How could you do that? I don't think you know many Germans."

"The leak is via the Isbell's Insiders."

"I don't believe it."

"The British security organization, MI5, has definite proof."

"Who is it, Allan?"

Chadwick shifted into third, and the whine of the gears drowned out his voice as he whispered, "Addenbury. But you must never reveal that. Knowing that could get you eliminated, as they say."

"I didn't catch what you said, Allan."

"Better that way."

Melanie had to concentrate on some navigation and gave Allan concise instructions for avoiding a work zone she remembered from the earlier trip. He was keeping up a steady sixty miles an hour, even though the area was built-up. In the small towns he slowed at traffic lights and then accelerated through the junction if there was no approaching traffic.

"Why are we driving to Cromer?"

"Some of my reports on RDR, which completely contradict the misleading ones fed to the Germans, were stolen earlier today by a young woman I know who's a pilot. She got them from my office, and her boyfriend, who appears to be a German agent, has persuaded her to fly to Germany in her Tiger Moth. I only found out when her mother called me less than two hours ago. She told me her daughter planned to fly to the continent from Cromer with the German agent and my reports as soon as it is light, about seven o'clock.

"I have had no time to make other arrangements except to drive to Cromer myself and stop her. If the Germans compare the two reports, side by side, the whole scheme is blown, and that could be very bad for our country if war breaks out."

Melanie was silent for a while, and then suddenly screamed, "Look out!" as a horse and cart delivering milk emerged out of the darkness.

Chadwick had the reaction times of a trained pilot and wrenched the wheel violently, missing the milk cart by inches. "The bastard had no lights," he complained. "What time is it?"

Melanie held her wristwatch under the single instrument light on the dash. "Nearly quarter past two. We should reach the Great North Road in about ten minutes."

Once on the dual carriageway, Chadwick accelerated to eighty when he could, but the road was cluttered with long-distance lorries, some of which did not like to be overtaken, and so eased right to narrow the lane when they spotted the Bentley's lights. Chadwick felt grit in his eyes. He realized that the lorry he was temporarily stuck behind has carrying ash, which was blowing onto the car.

"Melanie, please feel on the shelf under the dash and pass my goggles."

As his eyes cleared, Chadwick shifted into third and charged past the lorry with his right wheels on the grass verge. The goggles felt more familiar and comfortable on his face, and he kept them on for the rest of the trip.

Melanie rummaged in the bag she had brought, fishing out a biscuit, she handed it to Allan. "Here, eat this. Would you like some coffee?"

"Thanks, yes."

She poured some in the Bakelite cup and handed it to Allan. He took a quick gulp and handed it back to her. She drank the rest of the coffee in the cup and screwed it back on the flask. "What should we do about Cambridge? We should be there in an hour, and last time, if you remember, we bypassed it by heading over to the A11 at Royston. But that's about twenty miles on small roads."

"All right, we'll do the same thing."

After thirty minutes, Melanie said, "Allan, I'm not sure where we are. You're driving too fast for me to read the signs, which are pretty useless anyway. Better slow down. We're looking for a side road on the right leading to Thriplow."

Chadwick drove slowly until they came to a small road on the right. A stone marker by the side of the tarmac displayed "Melbourne," with an arrow. Melanie scanned the map carefully in the light from the dash lamp. "We've come too far. Dreadfully sorry, Allan."

"Can't be helped. What time is it?"

"Nearly four."

"We'll just stay on the Great North Road and deal with Cambridge when we get there."

Chadwick put his foot down. The road was fairly quiet, and he had no trouble overtaking the isolated vehicles ahead. The speed crept up—eighty, ninety. The great car seemed to sense the urgency. Chadwick's right foot was not down to the metal. There was still some reserve power in the thundering engine.

"Allan, you're scaring me," Melanie shouted over the tremendous noise.

"It's do or die time, dear."

"It's the die part I don't like."

"Cambridge will be quiet this time of night. What signs do we look for?"

Melanie stared at the vibrating map. "Newmarket. Then it's a straight shot to Norwich on the A11, which is dual carriageway, about seventy miles."

"Good. If the road is empty, we can do that in an hour, maybe less. Is there any coffee left?"

Melanie fumbled with the flask. She knew Allan had asked for coffee to keep her busy.

The outer villages near Cambridge flashed by, and soon they could see spires of the majestic buildings, lit by spotlights. Chadwick slowed to a conservative forty miles per hour and swept through the narrow streets flanking the impressive college walls. The city was well lit, which helped a great deal. Melanie spotted a road sign for Newmarket and soon they were leaving Cambridge behind them.

Chadwick eased up to sixty miles per hour, and after a few minutes Melanie shouted, "Take the right fork! We're back on A11."

The road was quiet, and Chadwick let the huge four-and-a-half liter engine have its head. The speed crept up to a hundred. Heat from the racing engine kept their feet and legs uncomfortably hot. In contrast, the cold air blasting over the back made their shoulders and necks bitterly cold. The headlights were useless, but the eastern sky was lightening, the outlying houses of Newmarket swept by, and Chadwick did not slow down as they rocketed through the center of Newmarket with its single traffic light that was on green, not that it made any difference.

In ten minutes, they approached Thetford, Chadwick's foot was on the floor. He decided they were just as dead in a crash at a hundred as they would be at sixty and flashed through the town, grateful for the streetlights. Melanie managed to read a sign which was lit by an overhead light, "Norwich, 32 miles."

"Allan," she screamed over the noise. "Norwich, thirty-two."

Allan nodded. His hands held the wheel in a vise-like grip, and he dared not take his eyes off the road for a second. The light was clearly getting better and, as the outskirts of Norwich swept into view, the sky was tinged with an orange hue in the east. He abruptly slowed down.

"I don't know where the airfield is in Cromer. Watch out for a policeman or someone we can ask."

Slowing down to thirty made it seem like the car had stopped. Norwich was a fairly large town. The suburbs seemed to stretch for miles. Then they reached the town center. In a square in front of a large church a few men were working to put up wooden stalls. Chadwick stopped the car and crossed over to a group.

"I want to get to Cromer," he said. "The airfield, actually."

The men looked in mild astonishment, "Take that road, zur, the A140," one of them said, pointing to a corner on the left. "Bain't no airfield that I know of."

Chadwick looked appealingly to others in the group. "I'm told there is a small airfield."

"Yers, Jeb, I've seed them little plane flying. There's a field on the way to East Runton."

"If 'e's right, zur, it be just west of Cromer."

"Very obliged. Thank you!"

Chadwick noticed that he could read the clock on the church tower—half past six. He climbed back into the car. The radiator had started to boil, and steam was spurting out of the cap with its Bentley wings.

Melanie pointed to it. "Isn't that bad?"

"No, it's because we stopped, and the engine is very hot. As soon as we move and air flows through the radiator, it will be fine." Gesturing to the church tower, he said, "Is the clock right?"

"Melanie looked at her watch. "Yes."

"Follow A140, the man said, and looked for signs to East Runton as we approach Cromer."

"It's only twenty miles. We'll be there before seven— if you break the speed limit," she added dryly.

Although the road was only two lanes wide, it was very quiet. It was Sunday morning, after all. They reached Cromer at ten to seven. A small road carrying a sign for East Runton appeared on the left. The sky was brilliant, and it looked like sunrise was minutes away.

Allan skidded the car onto the road to East Runton. It was little more than a sandy track with gravel. The country was very flat. Chadwick could see the North Sea on the right, dark as the sun rose behind low clouds. Melanie looked at the green field on her left and saw that it was bounded by a low, wooden fence. "Allan," she said, "I think this is the airfield on our left. Isn't that a hangar in the distance?"

Chadwick stopped the car, looking carefully to the left. "I think you're right. I'll drive a bit further and see if we can find a gate." He drove slowly. Pebbles showered into the mudguards. "Yes, I can just make out a windsock. Light wind from the northwest. There's a small hut too. That might be the flying club." He spotted a gate a hundred yards ahead and turned onto the field.

"Allan, I can see something moving."

"You've got good eyes, dear. I think you're right again. By God, it's yellow. It must be Penny in the damned Moth." He stopped the car.

"What are you going to do, dear?"

"I'm not sure. She's taxiing downwind to get a good run for the takeoff."

He put the car in gear and started to drive toward the plane. When he was a few hundred feet from the yellow plane, he said triumphantly, "It's definitely her. I can make out the last two letters of the registration—L. P. That's her." He accelerated toward the plane

Melanie shouted, "She's turning!"

"Yes, she has enough space to get off."

"What are you going to do?"

"Just watch."

The Bentley was rapidly gaining on the Tiger Moth. Chadwick could see the elevators. They were pointing slightly down. *She's keeping the skid on the ground,* he thought. Then he saw the elevators swing up, and the tail began to lift. *Christ, she's just about got flying speed.*

"Allan," Melanie screamed, "you're going to hit it."

"That's right!"

With a terrible crash, the front dumb irons of the Bentley plowed into the fragile tail of the Tiger Moth. The noise from the rending of wood, the roaring Bentley engine, and the high-pitched whine from the propeller was ear-shattering. Chadwick braked and watched the plane ahead. Events seemed to unfold in slow motion. The nose reared up, then the left wings slewed into the grass, and the spinning wooden propeller struck the ground. It shattered into pieces and a large shard hit the petrol tank in the upper wing. Fuel spurted over the cockpits. The wreckage came to a standstill.

Chapter Fifty-Five

The Bentley was stationary, thirty feet behind the shattered plane. Chadwick could see the occupants of both cockpits, slumped with their heads lolling. He dashed toward the plane, shouting, "Melanie, stay there, this thing is going to burn."

He climbed on the lower right wing and unclipped the small door panel. His expert fingers removed the pin of the safety harness and he grasped Penny by the shoulders. The smell of petrol was overwhelming. As he pulled her out of the cockpit, the plane went up with a horrendous "whoosh." A wave of incredibly hot gas washed over him as he dragged Penny to the ground and pulled her away from the burning pyre. The goggles saved his eyes from the inferno.

Melanie ran over to them. "Is she alright? Dead?"

He walked as close as he dared to the plane. The fabric and wood burned furiously, and already the steel tubular frame stood out like a skeleton. "There's nothing we can do about the chap in the front cockpit. At least he seemed to be unconscious. That's a blessing. Let's get Penny in the back seat and we'll run her into Cromer, then I'll come back."

Melanie climbed in next to Penny to support her, while Allan made a full turn and drove back along the churned grass left by the downed plane. The car seemed to be drivable, apart from some ugly scraping noise coming from the front wheels. He stopped to pick up some shattered wood with fabric still attached and some pieces of broken glass. After a careful look around, he drove back through the gate and in minutes drove down the seafront at Cromer. He stopped at a decent-looking hotel, the Sea View, and walked in through the glass doors. A man in a striped apron was sweeping the lobby.

"We're not open yet, sir,"

"There's been an accident," Chadwick stated in authoritative tones. "A lady has been hurt. She's not bleeding but she is rather upset. I would like to bring her in to rest. I'll probably book a room later."

"Of course, sir, bring her into the lounge."

Melanie had already started to get Penny out of the car, but the young woman could not support herself. Chadwick ran to the car and carried her into the hotel.

Chadwick spoke softly to Melanie. "There's been an accident and a man killed. I have to get the right authorities involved as soon as possible. Please stay with her and get something to eat as soon as you can. I'll call London from the desk."

He went to the man with the broom, saying. "I have to make an important telephone call."

"Well, sir, the telephone is really for the guests."

"I'll get the cost from the operator and leave the money on the counter. You can explain to the receptionist when she comes."

"Well, I suppose that would be all right, sir." Then he glimpsed the Bentley through the glass doors. "You go right ahead, sir."

Chadwick called Doug Larson's number at MI5.

"Import Export."

Chadwick hurriedly explained, "This is Squadron Leader Chadwick. It is vitally important that I get hold of Doug Larson or Will Viney as soon as possible. Ask them to call me at this number." He took the number off a cardboard disk on the phone. He asked the operator the cost of his call and left a ten-shilling note on the counter. Then he wondered if the incoming calls came through a switchboard. He told the cleaner that he was expecting a call back.

"The receptionist operates the switch," he was told by the man with the broom, who was still marveling at the Bentley.

"Come here, sir." He took Chadwick into a small room and plugged in a line. "Just lift that switch when it rings, sir."

The phone rang within five minutes, and Chadwick had to don a headset and talk into a microphone on his chest. "Chadwick here."

"Good morning, Allan, this is Doug. What's happening?"

Chadwick quickly brought him up to date, and when Larson learned that the pilfered documents were about Periscope, he became very serious. "Allan, Periscope and our little plot are the highest level of security. I will be out with Will and some Special Branch people on the next train to Norwich. Don't let anyone near the plane wreck. Tell the local bobbies it is 'Case Crimson.' That will get you a lot of respect."

"I'll meet you at the Sea View Hotel in Cromer, but for now I'll get back to the wreck and make sure nobody touches it."

He went over to talk to Melanie. "How is she?"

"Pretty faint. She should see a doctor."

"Help is on the way. Hold the fort here, dear. I'm going back to the field, but I should be back here within an hour."

As he went to the Bentley, a thought crossed his mind. He checked the fuel gauge, which was a rather unreliable instrument that worked on air pressure. It showed empty. He wasn't surprised. The fuel consumption would have been very high at the speed they'd been traveling.

At the field, a few on-lookers were gathered at a safe distance from the wreck. Just as he arrived, a uniformed policeman pedaled up on a bicycle. Chadwick intercepted him. "I was here earlier. I pulled a woman out of the wreck before it caught fire. She's at the Sea View Hotel."

The policeman said, "Doesn't seem much point in getting the fire brigade from Cromer, except they have to investigate all accidents like this, especially if someone is killed."

Chadwick asked him what rank the chief of police in Cromer held.

"He's an inspector, sir."

"Please call him as soon as you can and ask him to meet me here. My name's Chadwick. Tell him 'Case Crimson'."

"Case Crimson, sir?"

"Yes, perhaps the flying club is open, and you can call from there."

The policeman pedaled off. None of the on-lookers seemed tempted to approach the wreck, and Stiller's corpse in the front cockpit was a horrible enough sight to deter any sightseers.

Twenty minutes later, an MG sports car bounced across the grass and a heavily built man with an unshaven chin climbed out. "You Chadwick? I'm Inspector Mainwaring. I've heard of Case Crimson but never run into an actual example before. What's all this about then?"

"Sorry to get you up so early on a Sunday, but this is a sensitive matter. The man lying dead in that plane had stolen secret documents. Special Branch is on the way. No one must touch the plane until they're sure there's no evidence left. I rescued the pilot—she's recuperating at the Sea View Hotel. If you'll excuse me, I'll return to the hotel and leave you to organize a watch."

The inspector talked to the policeman who had returned on his bicycle and waved Chadwick away. Chadwick drove into Cromer and found the only petrol station in the town. He bought five gallons of petrol and realized he would have to get some money in the near future.

At the hotel Chadwick gobbled down an English breakfast. Melanie had already eaten, and Penny still seemed half-comatose. He dozed until awakened by a Midland accent.

"Allan, you're always sleeping."

Doug Larson was standing next to him with Will Viney and two serious-looking elderly men. He was introduced to them. One was a Detective Superintendent; the other was Chief Inspector Hamilton. Chadwick reiterated his story and Viney added more of the MI5 side. The chief inspector seemed highly intelligent and grasped the situation immediately.

"Let's have a look at this lady you rescued."

They walked over to Melanie and Penny. Chadwick introduced Melanie as his navigator for the mad dash from Farnborough. The chief inspector looked at Penny and quickly made a decision. "Get this woman over to a police doctor in Norwich."

Viney asked where Penelope lived, and Chadwick said she lived quite close to Farnborough.

"Good," Viney mused, "we want to keep her under cover. When she's fit to travel from Norwich, we'll transfer her to the military hospital at Aldershot near her home. MI5 has some pull there."

The chief inspector said that maybe a look at the crash site would be illuminating. Chadwick offered to guide them to the field. Outside the hotel, the chief inspector glanced at the Bentley.

"So, this is the car you made the mad ride in. How old is it?"

"It's ten years old, sir."

They stopped near the wreck. Inspector Mainwaring had placed a rope round the area and stationed two uniformed policemen. Hamilton looked at Stiller's body and then walked back to Chadwick and Viney, who were standing next to the Bentley.

"Mr. Viney does MI5 have a good idea who that chap is?" he asked, gesturing to the smoldering wreck.

"Yes, Olaf Runge. The German Embassy will be informed through the usual bureaucratic means that he died in an aircraft accident— let me think about that for a moment."

Larson moved to be near Chadwick. "Allan, you look a wreck yourself—singed hair, some smudges on your face. You've had a hard few hours. Why don't you go find Melanie and get some rest? We'll look after things at this end and make sure nothing damaging is left in the plane."

Hamilton patted the bonnet of the old Bentley. "Mr. Chadwick, it seems like the country owes you and your friend Melanie a good deal. But we especially owe this beast a medal for charging halfway across the country in pitch darkness to bring down a hostile plane, and possibly saving the British Empire!"

Chadwick smiled wryly. "So, Chief Inspector Hamilton, do you think my Bentley should be awarded a George Cross?"

Will Viney had stood quietly, thinking furiously, his mind rapidly considering gambits and counter-gambits. "Gentlemen, there are a few loose ends we must tie up." He paused, making sure he had the men's attention.

"One, did Runge contact Dr. Kegel from Cromer? If he did, then we must arrange Kegel's—er—elimination as soon as possible. Two, Miss Pomeroy must be interrogated when she is fit. Perhaps she can throw light on that last question. She must be kept in seclusion for a period. Three, Squadron Leader Chadwick and Lady Fitzgibbon were never here. Four, Mrs. Pomeroy must be informed her daughter suffered an accident but she is safe and well. Five, the theft at Farnborough must never be mentioned. Mrs. Pomeroy must be cautioned on that point.

"Six, Runge's death must be reported through the usual bureaucratic channels and the embassy informed as late as possible. Seven, because Chadwick was never here, the worthy constable must get the credit for rescuing Miss Pomeroy. Eight, the Bentley must be removed in a covered lorry and returned, in original condition, to Farnborough. Nine, Lady Fitzgibbon and Chadwick must be returned to the Farnborough area as soon as possible. We must arrange an air passage to Marlow, and from there a taxi. They can explain the Bentley broke down during an outing. And last, the accident investigation must conclude the Tiger Moth suffered engine failure at the moment of takeoff, crashed and burned."

Viney looked around, making sure he had been heard. "Have I forgotten anything?"

Epilogue

Dr. Gerhard Kegel never discovered the true cause of Stiller's death. He was evacuated with the rest of the diplomatic staff of the German Embassy on the third of September 1939. Stationed in Hamburg, he remained in charge of German agents in Britain and was involved when new agents were infiltrated into the country. Within a year of the start of the war, all German agents in Britain had been arrested and many executed unless they agreed to work for the British by passing misleading information produced by the "Double-cross Committee" back to Hamburg. Their greatest success was Operation Fortitude, which deceived the Germans into thinking Calais was to be the location of the D-Day landings. Even as the war was ending and Hamburg falling to the Allies, Kegel, unaware of their perfidy, in a final radio communication arranged for several of his (double) agents in Britain to be awarded the Iron Cross decoration for valor.

Doris Blackwood, the manager of the boarding house that catered to the Germans, was arrested early in the war and sentenced to ten years in Holloway Prison. She was released in 1946. She managed to regain possession of her boarding house and died an old spinster in 1979.

Inge Fischer, whose spy pseudonym was Julia Fassbender, returned to Germany in 1936. She remained with the Abwehr as an administrative officer until 1944, when she committed suicide by swallowing a cyanide pill. She never married.

Viscount Addenbury and his valet were not apprehended until early in 1941, although they were kept under surveillance. The government was reluctant to formally accuse Addenbury, as he was entitled to be tried in the House of Lords. He agreed to the confiscation of his estate, which was turned into an RAF base. His 18th century mansion was demolished to make way for a six-thousand-foot runway. Isbell's was sold to a developer after the war and knocked down. His valet was tried by a military court, found guilty, and sentenced to death. Viscount Addenbury was forced to watch his execution by hanging.

Lord Lowestoft was never informed of his role in the RDR deception. He was told Addenbury had implicated him as a source of information, but he protested he had no knowledge of Addenbury's connection with the German Abwehr and was quietly dismissed from the Foreign Office. The Isbell's Insiders never met again after the declaration of war in 1939.

Wilberforce Viney became a full-time member of the Double-cross Committee. He was a master in the complex game of confirming what the Germans wanted to believe anyway, despite other indications to the contrary. After the war, MI5 and MI6 were infiltrated by the Soviet KGB which slowly destroyed them from within.

Doug Larson continued to work in MI5 but became very involved with Scotland Yard's Special Branch when German agents were actually arrested. In 1943 he traveled to Ireland in pursuit of a suspect and was badly injured in a fight there with the Irish Republican Army.

Penelope Pomeroy recovered but retained no memory of the crash or the events immediately preceding it. She obtained a commercial pilot's license and when the war began, joined the Air Transport Auxiliary delivering new aircraft from the manufacturer to RAF bases. She was killed along with her flight engineer in 1943 when a Lancaster bomber she was ferrying from Woodford to Boscombe Down collided with a hill in the Pennines.

Honoria Pomeroy was horrified by the newsreels shown as Allied troops liberated German concentration camps in 1944-45. She felt totally betrayed by the German culture she had embraced earlier; she abandoned all her German language books and refused to meet any Germans. She died, embittered, in 1960.

Dr. Kenneth Bostock was sidelined after the war started by the massive intervention of industrial companies in radar development. In 1942 he was sent to the USA to assist with radar research using the newly invented cavity magnetron. After the war he was made a member of the Order of the British Empire and given a cash award for his leadership in the construction of Chain Home. He spent his remaining years as a Physics Professor at a red-brick university.

Wing Commander Codrington was passed over for promotion, and after the war he joined British Overseas Airways as an executive involved in converting the fleet to jets.

Allan Chadwick's Bentley was not seriously damaged by the collision with the Tiger Moth. The left headlamp was crushed and had to be replaced. The left mudguard was bent and pressed against the front wheel. It was easily repaired and repainted. It spent the war years in a small shed near Chadwick's parent's house. After France fell and the Battle of Britain took place, Chadwick flew a Spitfire with Fighter Command. In the winter of 1940, he was given command of a Wellington bomber squadron. He was posted Missing in Action when he failed to return from a bombing raid over Kiel in 1941.

Melanie Fitzgibbon became very depressed after the war began. Her son joined his father's old regiment and was wounded in Tunisia. When Chadwick was declared Missing in Action, she had trouble ascertaining his fate, as she was neither related nor married to him. Clair Court Hall was requisitioned by the government in 1940 and she was forced to live in the apartment over the stables

Glossary

Equivalent Ranks

RAF	WAAF	ARMY
Air Commodore	Air Commandant	Brigadier General
Group Captain	Group Officer	Colonel
Wing Commander	Wing Officer	Lieutenant Colonel
Squadron Leader	Squadron Officer	Major
Flight Lieutenant	Flight Officer	Captain
Flying Officer	Section Officer	Lieutenant
Pilot Officer	Asst Section Officer	Second Lieutenant
Warrant Officer	Warrant Officer	Sergeant Major
Flight Sergeant	Senior Section Leader	Staff Sergeant
Sergeant	Section Leader	Sergeant
Leading Aircraftsman	Corporal	Corporal
Aircraftsman	Aircraftswoman	Private

Common English, German and Technical Terms

Abwehr	German military intelligence organization
Ack-Emma	A World War I term for ante-meridian, A.M.
Adj	Slang term for the Adjutant of a unit, responsible for administration
Angels	Term used by controllers to designate a height in thousands of feet
Artificial Horizon	A flight instrument with a display that remains parallel to the actual horizon
ATA	Air Transport Auxiliary, a civilian organization that ferried new planes to airfields
Bank	Flying with wings not horizontal, as in a turn
Blighty	Slang term for Britain
Bobby	Slang term for a policeman

Boffin	Scientist
Broad	A shallow lake in the East Anglia region of Britain
Bumf	Slang for toilet paper, also term for official paperwork
Bunt	An aircraft maneuver that applies negative 'G'
Carbon Paper	A method of making duplicate copies on a typewriter using a coated paper
Chinoiserie	A decorative art style based on Chinese culture
Chocks	Triangular blocks of wood to wedge the wheels of aircraft
Crossley	A truck commonly used by British armed forces
Crystal Set	An early radio receiver with no electronics
de rigueur	Absolutely necessary
Domesday Book	The Norman invaders' list of inhabited places in England and Wales, circa 1086
Dumb iron	An extension of a car's chassis carrying mounts for the suspension springs
Ether	A hypothetical medium which supports the propagation of electromagnetic waves
Exponential	A hypothetical medium which supports the propagation of electromagnetic waves
G	The force of gravity
George Cross	The highest British award for gallantry by a civilian
Gestapo	Geheime Staats Polizei, a branch of the SS
Gong	Military slang for a medal
Green Machine	Chadwick's affectionate term for his Bentley
Halton	RAF school to train ground personnel
Hammer-Head	An aircraft maneuver in which the plane climbs vertically until stalling
H.F.	High Frequency, the radio band between 1.5 and 30 megacycles per second
Jude	German for "Jew"

K.C.M.G.	Knight Commander of the Order of St. Michael and St. George. A rank of chivalry bestowed by the Monarch.
Ki-gas	A method of starting internal combustion engines using a fuel mist pumped into the intake
Knot	Speed in nautical miles per hour, about 15% less than miles per hour
Kripo	German police responsible for criminal investigations
Luft Hansa	Name of the German State Airline before 1945
Luftwaffe	Aviation arm of the German War Department
Magneto	An electrical device to produce a high voltage for powering the spark plug
MI5	British Military Intelligence branch responsible for counterespionage within Britain
MI6	British Military Intelligence responsible for espionage abroad
Minox	A subminiature camera popular with spies for photographing documents.
M.O.	Modus Operandi, the method by which a crime is committed
NCO	Non-commissioned officer
Octane	A fuel rating denoting compressibility limit, a high rating allows a more powerful engine
Oscilloscope	An electronic instrument which displays electrical waveforms on a screen
Paraffin	British term for kerosene
Penny Dreadfuls	Cheaply printed publications featuring lurid stories
Perspex	A tough, clear plastic used to make cockpit canopies
Plenipotentiary	Fully authorized to negotiate
Pundit	A large flashing coded light at RAF airfields
Quid	Slang for a British pound (currency)

RAC	The Royal Automobile Club, an organization for motorists which provides assistance.
Radiogram	A polished piece of furniture containing a record player and a radio receiver
SA, Sturmabteilung	Paramilitary wing of the Nazi Party, known as "Brownshirts"
SD, Sicherheist Dienst	State Security Service, intelligence branch of the SS
Shandy	Beer mixed with a non-alcoholic beverage, especially lemonade
Slide rule	An analog calculator for multiplication and division using a sliding logarithmic scale
Sprog	A young, inexperienced person
SS, Schutz Staffel	Originally Hitler's bodyguard, became the all-powerful State Police
Stochastic	Guesswork
Synchromesh	A development of automobile transmission gear boxes, permitting "silent" changes
Todt Organization	German State organization responsible for civil engineering
Ton	Slang for driving a car or motorbike at 100 miles per hour
Topple	A maneuver that causes a gyro instrument to fail by exceeding the gimbal limit
Torch	Flashlight
Trolley-Acc	Battery in a cart used to start aero engines
Tube	Slang term for the London Underground Railway
Valve	A British term for an electron tube
Vauxhall	A British automobile in the medium-price bracket
Victoria Cross	Britain's highest military award for gallantry in combat
WAAF	Women's Auxiliary Air Force, the arm of the RAF for women

Acknowledgments

When the first draft was finished, Jody Freeman reviewed the plot and character development and made sage suggestions. My old friends Anne Flood and Lew Schatzer read an early draft and pointed out to me sections that could be clarified. Dr. Louise Hanson gave me the benefit of her wide interest in world history, and in particular her knowledge of German and German mannerisms. Bob Berg is a gunsmith and master machinist who kept me straight on all matters relating to guns during the preparation of the manuscript. Jack Doyle, a naval flight officer who flew F-4 Phantoms and F-14 Tomcats, checked the draft for accuracy and authenticity. Peg Daisley was my tireless editor, who reviewed and corrected each chapter as I wrote them. Jay Pizer designed the book and managed to produce legible maps that will be useful to all readers not familiar with the British Isles.

Finally, I must acknowledge that I could not have written this novel without having had my experiences in the Royal Air Force. The adventures I had, flying what were at the time some of the most advanced fighters in the world, formed one of the most exciting periods of my life. I hope this has spilled over into authentic realism in the flying sequences. The men I flew with and worked with had experiences that dwarfed my own. Many flew in WWII. Their stories, which I still remember vividly, helped me write this novel.

Flying Officer Forsyth at the controls of a Meteor Mark 8, Britain's frontline fighter at the time.

Eric B. Forsyth was born in England and served as an RAF fighter pilot. After Britain reduced her armed forces, he immigrated to Canada and obtained a commercial pilot's license, rated for single and multi-engine land and sea planes. Unfortunately, flying opportunities did not appear.

He enrolled in Toronto University Engineering Graduate School and was later hired to join the Scientific Staff of Brookhaven National Laboratory on Long Island, New York. He worked there for 35 years, eventually being appointed Chair of the Accelerator Development Department, which was responsible for the pre-construction planning and design of the Relativistic Heavy Ion Collider (RHIC), now the most powerful nuclear physics research tool in the United States.

Once established on Long Island, Eric enthusiastically took up sailing. His first sailboat was a 16-foot daysailer, but he soon advanced to ocean sailing. He currently sails a 42-foot cutter, *Fiona*, which he built himself from a bare fiberglass hull. His accomplishments with this boat, which include two circumnavigations of the globe and cruises to polar waters and through the Northwest Passage, resulted in the award of the prestigious Blue Water medal from the Cruising Club of America.

His sailing adventures are recounted in his book, *An Inexplicable Attraction: My Fifty Years of Ocean Sailing* which was included in Kirkus Review's 100 Best Memoirs of 2018. He published his first novel, *Wings over Iraq*, in 2020, inspired by stories he heard as a young man told by old-timers on his RAF squadron who had served in Iraq before WWII. His second novel, *Wings Over the Channel*, follows the turbulent time in Britain before the start of WWII when the British were desperately trying to develop a radar defense system.